ONWARD, DRAKE!

Edited by
Mark L. Van Name

ONWARD, DRAKE!

Baen Publishing Enterprises
P.O. Box 1403
Riverdale, NY 10471
www.baen.com

ISBN: 978-1-4767-8196-9

Cover art by Donato Giancola

First Baen printing, October 2015

Distributed by Simon & Schuster
1230 Avenue of the Americas
New York, NY 10020

Library of Congress Cataloging-in-Publication Data
    2015030701

Printed in the United States of America

10 9 8 7 6 5 4 3 2 1

TABLE OF CONTENTS

For Dave, of course.
Yes, you deserve it. Don't argue with me.

ONWARD, DRAKE!

Introduction:
It's About Time

Mark L. Van Name

A few weeks before this book appears, David Drake will have turned 70. A few weeks after this book hits store shelves, he will be a special guest of the World Fantasy Convention 2015 in Saratoga Springs, N.Y. These two occasions led me to propose this *Festschrift* to the immediately receptive Baen Publisher, Toni Weisskopf, but they served only as triggers. The true reason for this book's existence is simpler: it's about time we did it.

Dave is a friend of mine, a good friend, so you could argue that I'm biased, and I am, but that's irrelevant. Dave's accomplishments speak for themselves: dozens of books, over a hundred short stories, I don't even know how many essays—the man has been writing tirelessly and prolifically for almost fifty years. His first professional sale, the short story "Denkirch," appeared in 1967. Over the course of those decades, he's written horror, SF, and fantasy; dark tales and (often darkly) humorous ones; and he's still doing it. His pace has not slowed.

Dave has also influenced more writers than I can name. In this volume, fifteen of us pay him tribute in the way he would most appreciate: by writing. Both of his U.S. publishers add their voices.

Fittingly, Dave outworked us all: he contributed two original stories to this collection, one of them the first new *Hammer's Slammers* story in nearly a decade, and they are the two longest pieces here.

The work is what matters, Dave would tell us, and I agree with him, so read on for a wonderful collection of original stories and essays in celebration of David Drake.

The Great Wizard, Cabbage

David Drake

Caulis—Cabbage—sat in the corner of the shop as Berenice, the bronzesmith's widow, said, "I want you to magic them to death, Hesperus. I want you to melt the flesh off their bones! I want that faithless Tychos to scream for mercy, *scream*! And as for that slut Murmilla, well—"

Berenice went on at length as Cabbage listened, bug-eyed with astonishment. He'd heard angry women before—Ma had been pretty much furious all the twelve years of his life—but this was something special. He'd always thought the widow was one of the nicest people living here near the Viminal Gate, but it was hard to remember that now.

Personally Cabbage thought that Berenice was well shut of Tychos, a big fellow with strong arms and a black heart. Tychos knocked people around for no other reason than that they were in reach. As for Murmilla, well, she had a nasty tongue even when she was sober and that was no oftener than she could help.

Murmilla sure was pretty, though. And Tychos probably wasn't looking for somebody to talk to.

Berenice paused to take another breath.

"Peace, my good woman," Uncle Hesperus—the Wizard Hesperus—said. His voice was hoarse. He'd had a cold all the past week; they'd got rained on bad while they were hiking from Naples to Rome after Ma had died.

Even so, uncle made sure to pronounce the words clearly to show that he was educated. He'd explained that to Cabbage on the way to Rome: people could always tell real culture.

Hesperus raised his wand; maybe a little higher than he should have, because that showed where the moths had been at the armpit of his robe. Still, Berenice might not be able to see the holes from her angle, and anyway the light was bad. The shop was in a side-alley off Patrician Street. Even on a bright day things were pretty dim down here, and it had been looking like rain all this morning.

Hesperus stared at the wand and frowned. He told people that the wood was from a sacred oak in the Grove of Dodona. Cabbage thought that his uncle had trimmed it from a twig of the dead olive tree behind Ma's house, but he guessed that he was remembering wrong. Cabbage was used to being told he was wrong about things.

Maybe because uncle was thinking about Ma too, he took her skull off the shelf and held it in his other hand. "Mistress Berenice, I know that you are a god-fearing woman. Therefore you will understand when I tell you that it would offend against the plans of the immortal gods if mere humans took action against Tychos and Murmilla."

"What are you telling me?" Berenice said, though it'd seemed simple enough to Cabbage. He probably didn't understand. "Are you saying you aren't going to help me? Look, I been decent to you since you moved in, haven't I? I even told Priscus the bailiff to trust you the first month's rent because anyhow, he couldn't find a tenant for this hole."

"It's not me, good lady," Hesperus said, kind of waving the wand and Ma's skull in front of him like he hoped the widow would look at them instead of him. Cabbage didn't blame him. Boy, Berenice'd been mad before about Tychos and Murmilla, but she was looking now like she was about to catch fire. "It's the gods, you see—"

"I see a lot of hooie!" Berenice said. "You been taking it in trade from Murmilla, is that it? You men, you're all lying pigs!"

She reached out then like she was going to pinch uncle's nose. He jumped back and the wicker basket caught him behind the knees. He sat down on it.

The basket was where uncle kept his books of magic. Book, really, but it honest to Isis was a written book. Cabbage couldn't read anything, but uncle said this book was so magic that even he didn't know what language it was wrote in.

"I give up!" Berenice said as she stomped out of the shop. She'd have banged the door, but there wasn't one. Hesperus hung his older tunic in the doorway for a curtain at night. "There's no justice and nobody to protect a poor widow!"

Cabbage watched her go. A long line of curses dribbled back through the door after her.

Berenice was a widow all right, but she was about as rich as anybody on this end of Patrician Street. As for justice, Cabbage didn't know what that meant, but he was pretty sure that it was something he and uncle couldn't afford. They couldn't afford much of anything, if it came to that.

Hesperus stayed sitting for a bit, looking toward the doorway like he thought Berenice was going to come back in and *really* tear a strip off him this time. Cabbage kept where he was in the corner, because that seemed likely enough to him too.

After a little bit, he said, "You're really smart, Uncle Hesperus."

Hesperus got up carefully and put Ma's skull back on the shelf. "What *possible* reason would you have for saying that, boy?" he said in a tired voice.

"Well, because you know what the gods are planning for Tychos and Murmilla," Cabbage said. "I mean, if it was the emperor, that's different, he's important. But, they're just a couple dried peas for all they give themselves airs. I'll bet there's not another magician in Rome who would've known what the gods had up for them."

"Cabbage, child, you are very stupid," Hesperus said. He sounded more weary than he had three days ago. That was after they'd walked to Rome and finally found this shop to rent. "I, however, am even more stupid, because I refuse to take money for a charm of evil purpose. Even though the charm would be a sham, just like everything else in my life."

"I don't understand, uncle," Cabbage said, frowning.

"No, I don't suppose you do, boy," Hesperus said. "I don't understand myself, so why should you?"

He sighed and said, "Light the lamp, Cabbage. Perhaps someone needing a love charm will notice the doorway. I suppose a real love charm could do as much harm as the curse Berenice wanted, but the *intention* is good . . . and anyway, I don't need to worry about doing any real magic."

"There isn't much oil left, Uncle Hesperus," Cabbage said, fetching the ladder from the narrow sleeping loft over the back end of the shop.

"I'm sure there isn't much oil," Hesperus said without looking up. "And then there's the question of supper. But for now, light the lamp."

Cabbage set the ladder against the sidewall where he could lean out and lift the lamp off the hook it hung from. He climbed three rungs and had just got his hands on the lamp when the ladder's left stringer cracked. Everything came down. Cabbage pitched outward, the ladder bounced off the back wall where he'd kicked it, and the lamp dropped straight onto the stone floor.

The terracotta lamp shattered like you'd expect, as hard as the stone was. Cabbage slept on the floor since there wasn't room for two in the loft, and he knew how hard it was.

"Oops," Cabbage said, picking himself up. He'd landed on Hesperus, so he wasn't badly banged up. "I slipped."

"I noticed," said Hesperus, getting up also. The right

sleeve of his robe wasn't attached any more, but he
seemed to be in all-right shape himself.

He turned toward Cabbage. The light was so bad that
Cabbage couldn't tell much about his uncle's expression,
but it really didn't seem like he had one; just blank like a
chalk drawing.

"Cabbage," uncle said quietly. "I am considering
calling down lightnings from heaven to blast you to ash.
That would be undutiful to the shades of my late sister,
your mother, however. Instead, why don't you see if you
can get a lamp from Meiotes the Potter. A cracked one,
or maybe one missing the spout? I'll pay him as soon as a
few coppers come in."

"Yes, uncle," Cabbage said. "I'm glad you didn't blast
me to ash."

"I'm sure I will be glad some day too, Cabbage," Uncle
Hesperus said in that same dead voice. Cabbage scooted
out of the shop, just in case he changed his mind.

As Cabbage stepped into the alley, a big lizard which
must've been running down Patrician Street rounded the
corner. It gripped the brickwork with its two right legs
and sprang straight at Cabbage, hitting him in the chest.
He went over backwards.

"Save me!" the lizard croaked. "He's going to kill me!"

"Now, calm down," Cabbage said, because it seemed
like the right thing to say. He'd never talked to a lizard
before. This one didn't weigh a lot, but it must be as long
as Cabbage's five-foot height if you counted the tail it was
whipping around. "Come inside and I'll introduce you to
my uncle. He'll know what to do."

Cabbage got up carefully. The lizard wouldn't let go, but it wasn't digging its claws in. He cradled it under the back legs so that it wouldn't change its mind about what it ought to be doing with those claws.

"Uncle?" he said as he stepped down into the shop again. "This lizard says somebody's trying to kill him."

"What?" said Hesperus. "What in the names of all the gods have you done, Cabbage?"

"Her," said the lizard. "They're trying to kill *her*. My name's Zoe."

"Her name's Zoe," Cabbage repeated. He didn't think he'd done anything, but he thought he ought to say something when uncle asked him a question.

"Whose name is Zoe?" said Hesperus. "And where did you get that lizard? It's huge!"

"She's pretty big, isn't she?" Cabbage said. He'd never had anything to be proud about before. "She just came down the street. And told me her name was Zoe."

"Look, I don't mind mumming for Atlas," the lizard said. Her breath smelled of onions. "I draw the line at having my throat cut to make his spell work, though!"

Somebody stepped into the doorway behind Cabbage and blocked most of the light from the alley. Cabbage turned and saw a tall man wearing a shiny black cape and holding a twisty ivory cane. He looked into the shop. Cabbage couldn't see the stranger's eyes, but he thought he felt them flick over him.

"There!" the stranger said. "You have my familiar. Return him to me at once."

"Save me!" Zoe said, launching herself out of Cabbage's arm. Her hind claws slashed like so many needles, but mostly she kicked off from the rope that served him for a belt and that held fine.

The lizard scrambled right up the back wall, heading for the sleeping loft even without the ladder. The stranger pointed his ivory cane—and it had *quite* a point, more like a spear than a usual cane, and shouted, "*Anoch anoch katabreimo!*"

A blue spark popped from the tip of the ivory wand. The lizard froze and toppled back.

"Zoe!" Cabbage shouted. He tried to catch her as she fell, but his feet got tangled. At least he managed not to fall on top of her. He grabbed the lizard and stood up.

"You're a real magician!" Hesperus said.

"I am Gaius Julius Atlas!" said the stranger. "I am the greatest wizard of all time!"

He reached over Cabbage's shoulder with his left hand and took Zoe by the neck. Cabbage tried to hang on, but the stranger—Atlas—just kept pulling, and that wasn't going to help Zoe.

"I brought this familiar from the Western Isles through my great power," Atlas said. He sure had the business of sounding cultured down pat; Uncle Hesperus could take lessons from him. "It escaped a moment ago when I have particular need of it. You will have a silver piece for catching it for me."

"Uncle, you can't let him take Zoe!" Cabbage said.

Hesperus seized Cabbage by the shoulder with one hand and put the other over his mouth. "Hush, boy!" he hissed. "Of course Lord Atlas may take his own property!"

"She's not property, she's Zoe!" Cabbage said, but he

was crying so hard that nobody could've understood even if uncle's hand hadn't been muffling him.

Cabbage stopped struggling. It was just one of those things that was going to happen, like Ma dying. It wasn't right, it just *was*.

"Ah!" said Atlas. "I'll take that skull I see behind you until I can replace mine with something more suitable. I had the skull of an ancient Pharaoh, which the animal broke when it escaped."

"Not *Ma*?" Cabbage said through a gulp. It sure *sounded* like he meant Ma, though.

Hesperus pushed Cabbage to the side and stood as straight as the boy had ever seen him. "I'm sorry, Lord Atlas," he squeaked. Culture had gone off somewhere far away, but uncle was trying his best. "The skull in question is that of my dear sister Portia, the mother of my apprentice. I cannot sell her to you."

"You little *worm*," Atlas said. "I wasn't asking you to sell her, I was telling you that I'm taking her because I need her."

Uncle Hesperus closed his eyes, but he didn't move from where he stood in front of Ma. He said, "I'm sorry, your l-l-lord—"

"Or would you rather . . ." Atlas said, pointing his twisty ivory wand, "that I—"

"Not Ma!" Cabbage said and grabbed Atlas by the left wrist, the one holding Zoe. The magician shook his arm hard, but Cabbage didn't come loose. He didn't have much; Ma and Uncle Hesperus were everything he could think of, and it seemed he was about to lose both of them.

Atlas raised the wand high over his head and turned

to bring it down on Cabbage. His right heel stepped into the spill of oil from the broken lamp. Both of his feet flew up in the air.

Atlas sat down hard with a *clack!* and a funny grunt. He mumbled something, but Cabbage couldn't make out the words.

Cabbage let go of the wizard's sleeve and got up slowly. Atlas was just sitting there. He looked awful mad. Zoe was moving around again, scratching herself with those big hind claws.

Uncle Hesperus opened his eyes a little bit at a time. "Ah . . . ?" he said. "Can I help you up, Lord Atlas?"

Atlas toppled over on his right side. He'd sat on his ivory wand when he came down, and there wasn't but the handgrip at the blunt end showing outside his robe.

"Uh-oh," said Cabbage.

"Merciful Isis!" said Hesperus, backing against the wall.

"Good riddance to bad rubbish, *I* say," Zoe said. She raised her hind leg and sprayed liquid green feces on the magician's corpse.

"Oh, what will we do with the body?" Hesperus said, knotting his hands together.

"What do you have in the way of food here?" Zoe said, lifting her head on her long neck. Her tongue stuck out like she was tasting the air.

"Well, there's a little lettuce left," Cabbage said, lifting down the basket that served them for a pantry. "And a turnip, I guess, but it wasn't much good even when we found it in the street."

"Do you suppose we can hide him till the middle of the night and then sneak him out of town?" Hesperus said. "If he's found in a ditch in the morning, nobody will think about us. Mistress Berenice has a cart we could . . . but no, not after the way she left here."

He must be much talking to himself. He didn't seem to hear Zoe talking, and he didn't care what Cabbage thought. No reason he should, of course.

"Why don't we just go to the Watch station at the gate and tell them?" Cabbage said. "We didn't do anything wrong, did we?"

"No, Cabbage, we did not," uncle said. "But Atlas was obviously a wealthy man—this robe is silk—so our chance of convincing the Praetor that his death was accidental is not very good. About the same as the chance of the Emperor appointing me Chief Priest, in fact."

"Gosh!" Cabbage said.

"What is that animal doing?" Hesperus said, speaking louder than he had since Atlas came to their doorway.

Cabbage looked down. "I think she's eating," he said.

Zoe raised her head from the basket. "Rather, she has eaten," she said. "I hope you'll be able to do better in the future, but that will tide me over for the moment."

"The turnip was bad, uncle," Cabbage said. "And the lettuce wasn't much better."

"That's quite true, Cabbage," Hesperus said, "but they were also all we had. Well, perhaps they'll give us a meal in prison before we're thrown to the beasts. That's something to look forward to, isn't it?"

"I don't think I want to be thrown to the beasts," Cabbage said doubtfully. Then an earlier thought returned and he added, "Uncle? What will you want me to do when you're Chief Priest?"

"Cabbage," Hesperus said, looking at him like he was angry. "I know you're young; twelve, aren't you?"

"If you say so, uncle," Cabbage said. "I'm not very good with numbers."

"I think it's very possible that you'll grow up to be the stupidest man ever born," Hesperus said. "Somebody has to be, and I think you're in line for that status."

"Ma used to say that too," Cabbage said, nodding. "That's why she got to calling me Cabbage. I had another name once, but I don't remember it."

Hesperus jerked back like somebody had slapped him in the face. Cabbage looked around to see if somebody was standing behind him, but there wasn't. They'd have needed long arms, anyway.

"Yes, you do have another name," uncle said faintly. "Your father named you Bion. You're a lot like your father, from what I remember from my visits. He was very willing and goodhearted, but not . . . well, not a philosopher."

"Ma always said he was real dumb," Cabbage agreed. "I don't remember him myself."

Uncle cleared his throat. He turned his head a little to the side and said, "Would you like me to call you Bion, ah, Bion?"

Cabbage frowned. There seemed to be more to the question than he understood, but there usually was when people said things to him.

"Cabbage is fine," he said at last. "I wouldn't remember Bion, I guess. I'm used to Cabbage."

"It doesn't bother you to be called Cabbage?" Uncle said, looking at him again.

Cabbage smiled broadly. "I'm really dumb, Uncle Hesperus. Calling me Bion wouldn't make me smarter."

"You know," said Zoe, "there are philosophers with a poorer grasp of basic truth than you just showed, boy. For now, though, don't you think that you ought to get Atlas's body out of sight? Just in case somebody does come in here. I suggest the loft."

"Oh, right," said Cabbage. "But he won't fit in the loft unless we stretch him out."

"What do you mean, Cabbage?" said Hesperus. "Oh, yes, Lord Atlas. I suppose between us we can lift him into the loft until the midwatch. Though how we'll get him out of the city *then* I can't imagine."

The wand had pinned the middle of the wizard's right thigh up through his chest. Cabbage knelt and pulled on the visible end. It didn't move.

"Turn it boy, turn it," Zoe said. "No, no—the other way. This narwhal had a left-hand thread."

After a moment Hesperus bent to look closely at what Cabbage was doing. He had more than half the wand clear. There was some blood on the ivory. Cabbage tried to wipe it off on the robe.

"Oh, that's very clever," uncle said. "Turning it out, I mean."

"Zoe told me," Cabbage said. "You don't hear her, I guess. Uncle, what's a narwhal?"

"What?" said Hesperus. "What do you mean?"

"It's a small whale that lives around the ice in the far north," said Zoe. "Atlas claimed this was a unicorn horn, and I'm not sure he knew better. It's not a horn, it's a tooth, and there's no such thing as a unicorn."

"Thank you, Zoe," Cabbage said, because it was polite. The tooth came free. He leaned it against the wall and pulled Atlas's legs out to straighten them.

"Why are you talking to the lizard, Cabbage?" Hesperus said as he took Atlas's legs. They half-slid, half-lifted the body to the back where the loft was.

The ladder would've been helpful if it hadn't broken, but it would've been even better if Atlas hadn't killed himself. Though this way he'd stopped saying he was going to take Ma's skull.

"Well, she talks to me," Cabbage said, puzzled again at why uncle didn't see the obvious.

"I talk to him too," said Zoe, "but all he hears is grunts. You've got the same brain as Aristotle had. You just use yours for different purposes than he did."

Together Cabbage and his uncle shoved the wizard's body onto the shelf. There wasn't a bed curtain, but his black robe wouldn't show up unless somebody was really looking for him. Or the light got better, Cabbage supposed, but that would mean the four floors above them disappeared or the similar building across the alley did.

"What did Aristotle do?" Cabbage asked.

"What?" said uncle.

"Never mind, boy," Zoe said. "He couldn't have talked with me either."

Outside, probably on Patrician Street but loud enough to be heard in the shop, somebody said, "A tall man with a lizard and an ivory wand! Have you seen him?"

Cabbage didn't recognize the voice, but it was

Moschus the Beggar who said, "What's it worth to you, good—*urk!* He went in there! Just now!"

The first two men through the shop doorway looked each so big that Cabbage thought they ought to stick in the opening. They didn't, though, they moved as slick as gymnasts.

They wore swords, which was illegal in the city except for the Praetorian Guards; and they wore them openly, so they *were* Praetorians.

One of them said, "Master Tydeus, here's the lizard!" He drew his sword and added, "Mithras, look how big the sucker is!"

"Don't hurt Zoe!" Cabbage said. He picked up the lizard and fell on his butt. He'd slipped in the oil, just like Atlas had. He looked to see where the wand—the tooth—was, but it was leaning safely against the wall.

The man who came in behind the soldiers was thin and pretty; his hair was curled and he brought an odor of rose perfume with him into the shop. "Put that sword up, you idiot," he said. "The beast is necessary for the sacrifice."

Cabbage would have objected, but Zoe put a forepaw over his own mouth. "Don't!" she said. "Tydeus needs me, but he doesn't need you."

"You," said Tydeus, looking at Hesperus. His voice sounded like a snake was speaking. "You're the magician?"

"Ah, yes," uncle said. "Ah, yes, your lordship. Did your lordship want a love charm, possibly?"

"If you joke with me, you fool . . ." Tydeus said, never raising his voice, "then you will be carried to my master with two broken legs. Do you understand?"

"Ah," said uncle. "Yes."

"You were to meet us at the Viminal Gate, but instead the guards told me you had gone running down the street," Tydeus said. "You will not run again. Do you understand *that*?"

"Oh!" said uncle. "You were looking for—"

He stopped, covering his mouth with both hands. He lowered them and said, "Yes, Lord Tydeus. I understand perfectly, Lord Tydeus. What would you like me to do, Lord Tydeus?"

"The coach is waiting at the gate," Tydeus said. "Bring the tools you need, and get a move on. We're late already."

"That's his wand," said a soldier, picking up the narwhal tusk. "Say, it's bloody!"

"Bring the wand," Tydeus said. "I don't want or need to know the details of how this person prepares his equipment."

He looked down at Cabbage, still sitting on the floor. "This boy is your apprentice?" he said.

"My name's Cabbage!" said Cabbage, because uncle's mouth was opening and closing like a carp gulping air. "Zoe's mine!"

"Well, you bring the lizard, then," said Tydeus. "If she makes any trouble, we'll break *her* legs—and cut your throat for being useless."

"I'll be quiet," said Zoe. She clung to Cabbage's shoulder as he got up. "But tell him that you need to feed me apples from the fruit-seller at the gate. And there was some rather good-looking celery in the next barrow."

Cabbage followed Hesperus and the soldiers out of the shop. Tydeus was last, and behind them all in the sleeping loft was Gaius Julius Atlas. At least they didn't have to worry about him anymore.

Tydeus' vehicle was a mail coach with the leather curtains pulled down on the sides and back so that Cabbage and Hesperus couldn't look out. Neither could Zoe, but that didn't seem to bother her. She had pinned the last of the apples against the floor of the coach with a forepaw and was biting juicy chunks out of it.

Tydeus rode beside the driver on the front seat. The Praetorians who'd come to the shop with him were riding ahead on horses, and there were two more following behind the coach. It wouldn't have done Cabbage much good to wriggle out the back, even if there'd been someplace to go if he had.

The iron tires ringing on the stone roadway made a lot of noise. Uncle looked numb. He hadn't said a word since they got into the coach.

Zoe hadn't spoken either, but that was because she was so busy eating. Now she swallowed the apple core, seeds and all, and scratched herself behind the earhole. Cocking her head toward Cabbage she said, "I was thinking of another stick of celery, but I guess I'll wait for a while for that."

Cabbage looked at the remainder of the bunch Tydeus had angrily bought before they boarded the coach. There wasn't much left. He counted on his fingers: one, two, three stalks.

"Can I have one of your celeries, Zoe?" he asked. He wondered if uncle would want one, but Hesperus just sat with his head in his hands.

"Yes, boy," Zoe said with a wave of a forepaw. "We will replenish our store shortly."

Cabbage wasn't so sure of that. Tydeus had been right peeved when Cabbage insisted that they get food for Zoe before they went off. Zoe had said to say that her blood would dry up if she didn't have apples for the trip and Cabbage just passed that on.

Cabbage crunched the white end off the celery and chewed it thoroughly. He said, "How is it an apple keeps your blood from drying up, Zoe?"

"It doesn't, but Tydeus couldn't be sure of that," the lizard said. "Atlas kept me in a cage since we left Africa. I heard him tell the messenger that he was bringing the sacrifice whose bodily fluids would be spilled to raise the dragon, but there'd be an extra charge. Well! I had my own opinion about that."

Cabbage finished the celery. He really liked the leafy end, so he had left it for last.

Zoe spread the fingers of her right forepaw. The claws looked just as sharp as Cabbage remembered them being when the lizard kicked off from him.

"When the porter dropped the cage on the docks here in Rome," she said, "he sprung one of the hinges. It took me a little while to get the other one loose, but when I did, I took off running."

"Oh," said Cabbage, wondering if he could ask for another stalk of celery. "I guess it was lucky that Tydeus found you. Uncle Hesperus wouldn't be able to be able to feed you apples until somebody buys a love charm."

"Umm," said Zoe. "I think he'll do better than that with you and me helping him. But we'll deal with that later."

The coach slowed. Cabbage heard one of the Praetorians ahead of them shouting something. He looked out the front past Tydeus and the driver. The coach went through a gateway and started down a boulevard.

There were trees and clipped bushes, and well back from the road Cabbage could see buildings. They were fancy ones, too, not sheds and farmhouses.

They turned a little semicircle and pulled up. Someone outside unlaced the back curtain.

Tydeus looked over his shoulder and said, "All right, get out of the coach. And make sure that lizard doesn't get away. Don't you even have a leash for it?"

"I won't run away," Zoe said.

"She won't run," said Cabbage. Now that he had Zoe for a friend, he felt happier than he remembered being. Zoe didn't get mad at him the way Ma had, though he knew it was hard on her to have so stupid a son as Cabbage was.

He knew that, because Ma had said so at least once a day.

Cabbage let uncle get out first, then thought that maybe he should've gone ahead instead so that he could lend a hand. The guards watched with sneering expressions instead of helping.

"You get down and I'll climb into your arms," Zoe said. "It'll look better if you carry me."

Cabbage didn't see why that was, but he climbed out of the coach and held his arms up. Zoe stepped onto his shoulder instead, then walked behind his head to the other shoulder too and curled her tail in front of him. She didn't weigh very much, but she sure was long.

"Why, this is a palace!" Hesperus said as he looked around.

"Of course it's a palace," said Tydeus, who had come from the front of the coach. "We're at Tivoli. Did you think we were going to slip you into his camp when he's campaigning on the frontier?"

A group of men were waiting for them. One of them wore a toga, which Cabbage had only seen on statues before, and carried an ivory baton with gold knobs on the ends. He wasn't the biggest or tallest, but he was the one the rest kept their eyes on just like dogs do the leader of their pack. Leaving the rest behind, that one walked over. He was maybe the same age as uncle, but he was better dressed and a *lot* better fed.

"This is the magician?" he said to Tydeus. He didn't look happy. "My brother said he was a rich man already, which is why the price was so high."

"Here's his wand, sir," said a Praetorian, holding out the narwhal tooth.

"Don't give it to me!" the man said. He glared at uncle and added, "Take your wand, you fool."

"Yes, your lordship," uncle said. "At once, your lordship."

"Who are you?" Cabbage said. It made him mad to see the fellow being so nasty to Uncle Hesperus. Uncle always tried, and any food they got he split with Cabbage.

The man looked at Cabbage with no expression in his eyes. He swung the baton like a hammer and hit Cabbage on the forehead.

Cabbage fell down. He saw Tydeus raise his sandal to stamp with the heel, but Zoe twisted and snapped at him. The sandal was crimson suede, *very* pretty to look at, but from the way Zoe's teeth had gone through the apples, Cabbage figured Tydeus was lucky to have jumped back instead of stomping on Cabbage like he'd planned.

"He controls the lizard, sir," Tydeus said, edging a little farther away. "It's probably just as well to keep him around for now."

"His name's Laurentius," said Zoe. "He's one of the Praetorian Prefects. His brother's the governor of Numidia, and he's the one who hired Atlas."

Cabbage got up. He dabbed at his forehead; he already had a lump, but there wasn't any blood on his fingertips when he looked at them.

"Come along," the prefect said to uncle. "The emperor is dining outside tonight. I've had a marquee set up in sight of the dining alcove with the items you said you'd need. The staff here is so large that nobody asks why anything is being done."

"The emperor!" Cabbage said.

Tydeus reached under his cape and started to draw the long dagger whose sheath was sewn into the lining. His eyes were as sharp as a pair of needles trying to stick Cabbage to the ground.

The prefect touched Tydeus's wrist—just touched, but it was like he'd hit him with a club. Tydeus jerked his hand away from the dagger and closed the front of the cape again. Neither of them said anything, but they were both looking at Cabbage. There wasn't much to choose between the way they were looking at him, either.

"Boy, keep your mouth shut," the prefect said softly.

Cabbage nodded. His throat was too dry to have said anything even if he'd wanted to.

Cabbage and Zoe followed Hesperus as he walked between the two civilians. Two Praetorians led and two more were at the back.

Cabbage raised a hand to squeeze the lizard on his shoulder. Being with her made him feel better, though he couldn't say why. Well, he usually didn't know why he felt things or why things happened.

"If matters don't go our way . . ." Zoe said, "neither of us is going to survive the night. We'll just have to see that they *do* go our way."

Cabbage still didn't say anything, but he squeezed Zoe's bony hip again. Her skin was dry and sort of pebbled instead of being scaly. Her breath fluttered, like the way a dog pants.

There was sure lots of people at Tivoli. They must mostly be slaves, but they were all better dressed than most folks Cabbage had seen. Their clothes were clean and didn't have rips or patches. You could spend all day watching the crowds on Patrician Street and not see anybody as well tricked out as any of these.

Most of them looked at Cabbage, but he figured they were really looking at Zoe. Nobody ever noticed him.

They *did* notice Hesperus though. Walking—stumbling—along between Tydeus and the prefect, he looked like a turd with a couple gold bracelets. Uncle was trying to hold the left sleeve onto his robe, but he wasn't having much luck.

The prefect must've thought the same thing, because

he scowled and said, "Tydeus, give him your—no, you can't, you've got that cursed dagger . . ."

He snarled at a Praetorian, who unclasped his red cape and threw it over uncle's shoulders. "There," the prefect said. "I don't want people asking me why I'm walking through the palace with a rag-picker."

Tydeus snickered and said, "An unsuccessful rag-picker."

"I don't like them," Cabbage muttered to Zoe.

She snorted. "Nor should you," she said. "Nor Atlas either. But Atlas isn't a problem where he is now, and the day's still young."

They walked down a flight of steps to a valley between two terraces. There was a reflecting pool in the middle, and at the other end was a half-dome sheltering an outdoor dining alcove. Cabbage couldn't see much of the people reclining on the benches there, but there were a couple handsful of guards in armor on either side. They were big blond men with full beards, and they held their long swords in their hands.

Servants were carrying dishes to and from the alcove. There was just enough breeze from that direction that Cabbage caught a whiff of roast meat.

He still had two stalks of celery in his left hand. Part of him wanted to stuff them both in his mouth, but the rest of him knew that he might as well gobble a handful of grass for all the good celery would do for the rush of hunger that the smell of roast had given him.

Besides, they were really Zoe's celeries.

There was a line of canopies set back from the other side of the canal; that was where the food was getting its final sauces and garnishes. "Umm . . . ," said Zoe. "I could *murder* a stalk of that giant fennel. Well, perhaps another time."

The prefect and the rest of them were going to the single marquee of red silk on the opposite end of the canal from the dining alcove. Under it was a rectangular table holding a basin and something covered by a napkin. The guards stood at the corners of the marquee, facing out.

The prefect and Tydeus motioned Hesperus inside with them. Cabbage came too, but he didn't like this at all.

"All right," the prefect said. "It's time for you to earn your pay. Here is the basin, and here—"

He whipped the napkin off the other thing on the table. It was a marble bust.

"—is who you'll raise the dragon to devour."

Tydeus giggled. He said, "And maybe the dragon'll swallow a couple of those snooty German guards while it's at it, too. They could each have had a fortune if they'd just been willing to look the other way for a bit."

The bust was of the Emperor Marcus.

Uncle Hesperus seemed stunned. Tydeus and the prefect stared at him.

Cabbage looked at uncle too, for that matter. The choice was to look at the bearded marble head, and that made him sort of queasy. The emperor, the real man himself, must be eating down at the other end of the pool.

"I'll bet you never thought you'd be seeing the emperor in the flesh, did you, boy?" Zoe said. She was still on his shoulders, sticking her head out to the left side. Her body didn't bend the way a snake's did, but she was pretty flexible.

Cabbage shook his head. "I can't see him now," he said. "I guess he's there, though."

He kept his voice down, but the civilians could've heard him easy enough if they'd been interested. They weren't.

"If your uncle doesn't start calling out a spell and tapping the basin of water," Zoe said, "Laurentius is going burst a blood vessel. Or he'll tell Tydeus to open your uncle's throat, which seems to me to be more likely."

"Uncle, Zoe says you're supposed to touch the water while you're spelling," Cabbage said. "Like you do at home, right?"

Uncle, Tydeus and the prefect all looked at Cabbage. The other two were angry—angry at Cabbage now, not just at uncle—but uncle said, "Right!"

He tried to tap the water, the way he'd have done a sand picture when he was making a charm for a customer. The narwhal tooth was a lot longer than the olive wand he was used to—or maybe of sacred oak—so instead the point jabbed into the table on the other side of the basin. The prefect didn't look best pleased, and Tydeus reached under his cape again.

Hesperus was awake now, though. He used his left hand to slide the tusk back so he could short-grip it with his right. This time he rapped the basin. "Abracadabra!" he said.

Other than the water sloshing, nothing happened. "Zim zam whammie!" uncle said. He'd told Cabbage that he changed the words of the spell each time he did a charm, so if somebody came back when the first charm didn't work, uncle could do him a fresh one.

The charms did work sometimes, or anyway the girls who'd come—it was almost always girls—were happy about the result.

"When are you going to let the lizard's blood out?" the prefect said.

"How are you going to do it?" said Tydeus. "You don't have a knife!"

"Don't!" said Cabbage.

"I'm not going to use that t-technique," uncle said. His voice went up as he spoke, and he looked like a bunny between a pair of snakes. That was true enough.

For a moment, nobody moved. Then uncle tried to tap the water again and dropped the narwhal tooth on the table instead. "Eenie meenie keenie!" he squeaked like he was trying to talk to bats.

"Cabbage," Zoe said, "when I tell you, I want you to say '*Lampsoure othikalak steseon*,' and strike the water."

"This is ridiculous!" the prefect said. Moving faster than you'd guess for somebody so pudgy, he grabbed Zoe around the throat and swung her over the bust. "Tydeus!"

Cabbage jumped, catching Tydeus by the wrist as he brought the dagger out. With his left hand, Tydeus punched the boy in the head. Cabbage didn't fall, but everything went fuzzy. He didn't lose his grip on the knife wrist.

Zoe twisted her body up and sprayed green feces in the prefect's face. The prefect shouted and slammed her hard onto the ground.

Tydeus hit Cabbage again. Now the boy couldn't feel

anything. He was seeing things in shades of gray, and they were all very far away. Tydeus had his dagger out and bent over Zoe.

The prefect snatched up the narwhal tooth. He can't have been seeing clearly, though, because he stabbed Tydeus in the middle of the back.

Zoe squirmed under the table. "Now, Cabbage!" she said.

Cabbage said, *"Lampsoure othikalak steseon!"* He always tried to do what he was told, though he wasn't good at understanding what people told him. He still had the remaining celeries in his left hand, so he slapped the basin with them.

The guards around the marquee were looking inside now—well, all but one of them—but they didn't seem to know what to do any better than Cabbage did. Uncle was sitting on the ground where somebody'd knocked him. Cabbage hadn't seen that happen, but thinking back he kinda remembered elbowing somebody when he jumped to grab Tydeus.

Tydeus kicked and flailed twice; then he went limp. The prefect was trying to pull the tusk out, but he wasn't having any luck. He seemed to have stuck it all the way through Tydeus and on into the ground.

Cabbage didn't like the prefect much, but he always tried to be helpful. He started to say, "It has a left-hand twist, sir."

Before he could speak, he saw the water humping up in the pool, though. He still opened his mouth, but he just let his lower jaw hang. At first Cabbage thought something was coming out of the pool and it kinda was, but it was the water coming out—only shaped like a dragon. It had a big head and teeth, and it carried its heavy body on four flippers.

The dragon waddled toward the marquee. The pool behind it was empty, though a little water trickled through a pipe that entered midway for topping it off.

"Zoe?" Cabbage said. He hoped she knew what to do, because he sure didn't.

The prefect looked up. There were people screaming all around, but the prefect made more noise than most of them. He let go of the narwhal tooth and started running away. The other guards ran too; the one who'd kept looking outward had taken off as soon as the dragon climbed out.

Zoe turned her head, watching the prefect as he stumbled toward the buildings farther up the valley. The dragon was gaining.

"I think we'll just amble back the way we came," Zoe said. "You don't need to carry me now, but I think you'd better lead your uncle till he's a little more himself."

The dragon's head dipped. The prefect screamed again. The long jaws closed on him and flipped him up in the air. Before he hit the ground, the dragon lost its shape and sloshed back to water. The flood drained down the slope toward the pool again.

"He wanted to use *my* bodily fluids for a spell?" Zoe said. "Well, he got his wish."

"Come along, Uncle," Cabbage said, helping Hesperus to his feet. "We're leaving now."

"I'm afraid you'll have to walk back to Rome," Zoe said. She'd picked up the celeries that Cabbage had dropped and was crunching them. "It's over twenty miles."

"We're used to walking," said Cabbage as they started up the steps.

They had to go around a fellow who seemed to have fainted. He'd been carrying a wedge of bread. Cabbage plucked it away when a glance told him that despite all the people, nobody was interested in him and his companions.

"Those roasts sure smelled good," Cabbage said sadly. He tore the bread in half to share with his uncle.

"I was feeling glad to be home," Hesperus said as they turned in the mouth of their alley, "but then I remembered that, ah, I can't go to bed yet."

"Do you think that Sestius might have us use his wagon if we brought it right back?" Cabbage said.

Hesperus grunted.

"No, your uncle does *not* think that because a man lets you ride into town on his wagonload of crockery," said Zoe, "that it means he will help you dispose of a dead body. And your uncle is quite right to be doubtful."

It was pitch dark in the shop. "Nobody seems to have broken in while we were gone," Hesperus said.

"How can you tell, uncle?" said Cabbage. The wagon ride had saved them a long walk, but Cabbage had helped the potter unload at his stall. The pots were awfully heavy.

"Your uncle is being ironic," Zoe said. "He means there was nothing here to steal; which isn't true, of course, but he doesn't know that yet."

"I wish somebody would have taken Atlas away," uncle

said. "This morning I thought that things were as bad as they could get, but that was obviously tempting fate. Where are we going to get a handcart tonight?"

"I'll ask Mistress Berenice," said Cabbage.

"She'll never agree!" said Hesperus. "Don't you remember how angry she was this morning? Just this *morning!*"

They were both—all three, probably—really tired, and it seemed to have worn uncle's temper short. When he got snappish, he reminded Cabbage of Ma.

"Nobody but Mistress Berenice has a handcart in the neighborhood, uncle," Cabbage said reasonably. "We have to borrow hers unless we rent one, and we'd have to have money to do that."

"I know, I know!" Hesperus said. "And we don't have money!"

"Well, there's the gold coins Atlas weighted the hem of his robe with," Zoe said. "That leaves you with the problem of changing them into silver or bronze that you could actually spend around here, but it's certainly a start."

Cabbage walked to the sleeping loft and felt for the bottom of the magician's black robe. It hadn't been easy to see the body even by daylight—which was a good thing, what with Tydeus and the soldiers coming in like they did—but Cabbage remembered which direction the legs had been when they'd stuck him onto the shelf. Sure enough, there were round weights sewed into the hem.

"Uncle, do you have a knife or something?" Cabbage asked.

"What?" said Hesperus. Then in a breaking voice he

said, "You don't plan to butcher him? Oh, boy, have we fallen that low?"

"Never mind," said Cabbage. His thumbnails were thick and as sharp as a dog's claws. He got them into the seam and ripped it open with no trouble. He worked out two of the lumps and brought them to Hesperus.

"Zoe says these are gold," Cabbage said, handing over the coins. "I can't see when it's so dark."

"Cabbage, have you gone . . ." Hesperus said. He was probably going to say "crazy," but the light flickering toward their doorway made him and Cabbage both look up.

The clerk from the bronze-goods shop came in with a lantern. Right behind him was the widow Berenice herself.

The lumps Cabbage had just put into uncle's hand glinted. They were gold coins, all right. There were lots more coins—or anyway, round lumps—still in the hem, too.

Uncle jumped to his feet, looking around like he wanted a place to run to. There wasn't one.

Cabbage was pretty calm. No matter how mad Berenice was, Cabbage had just seen a magical dragon sploshing toward them. The dragon was worse.

"Mistress?" uncle said.

"Oh, Master Hesperus, I don't know how I could have doubted you!" Berenice said. "Can you ever forgive me?"

"I—*forgive* you?" uncle said.

"I hadn't left you for an hour when I heard that Tychos had strangled Murmilla this morning," Berenice said.

"And he was still so drunk that the Watch found him sleeping beside the body. I shudder to think of the things I called you!"

"Ah," said uncle.

Cabbage nodded. The things Berenice had been saying made him shudder too. She'd sounded like she meant them.

"I brought this—" she held out a brand-new lamp, brass but polished to shine like gold "—as a thank-you gift and an apology. I've been telling everyone how well you understand the will of the gods. I'm *so* glad you've come back. I was afraid that the neighborhood's ingratitude had caused you to forsake us."

"Ah," said uncle again. He looked as woozy as he had when Cabbage accidentally clouted him while he was wrestling with Tydeus.

"Ask her to change the gold coins," Zoe said. "Or at least one of them, so you can buy me something to eat."

"Mistress Berenice?" Cabbage said. "Can you change some gold for us? Zoe and me are pretty hungry, and I'll bet uncle is too."

"Gold?" said Berenice. She looked at the coins in uncle's hand and said, "Mother Isis! That is gold!"

"Ah, yes," Hesperus said. "It, ah . . . a recent commission. I shouldn't say more, you realize."

"Oh, I . . . ," said the widow, and now it was her tongue that stumbled over her thoughts. "I didn't know—that is, I'm so *glad* that you're doing well, Master Hesperus. So *very* well."

She pursed her lips and got an expression that Cabbage had seen her wear when she was counting up the day's takings. "Yes," she said after a moment. "I believe I can change one of those."

In a different tone, she then said, "I was wondering, Master Hesperus, if you had plans for dinner tonight yourself? I've been lonely since, well . . . *since*, you know."

Since Tychos left, and that was just the day before yesterday, Cabbage thought. But he probably didn't understand.

"Well, I would be pleased to dine with you, mistress," uncle said. His stomach growled, just to show how true that was.

"And I wonder, master . . . ?" Berenice said, edging a little closer. "My friend Glycera is worried about her husband. He's in the Alexandria trade, you see, and his ship should have been back weeks ago. Could you possibly help her? She's quite well off. For material things, you know."

Uncle looked doubtful. Zoe glanced up at Cabbage and said, "No problem at all. I'll need a piece of his clothing and a basin of water, that's all. But you'd better get paid in advance because the news may not be what the lady wants to hear."

"We can handle it, uncle," Cabbage said. "You can, I mean."

"Ah!" said Hesperus, but it was a cheerful "Ah," this time. "Yes, that can be arranged, I'm sure. Now, Cabbage, if you'll come with us to Mistress Berenice's shop, I'll give you enough money to feed yourself and, ah, my familiar while the mistress and I are engaged."

"I want radishes," said Zoe as she waddled out of the

shop at Cabbage's side. "And some proper lettuce, *hearts* of lettuce."

Ahead of them uncle was saying, "And may my apprentice borrow your hand-cart tonight, mistress? We have a delivery of sorts to make just outside the gate."

David Drake needs no introduction in this volume.

At my request, he supplied this afterword to his story.

The first series written by David Drake (hereinafter "me" or "I") involved a pair of 4th-century A.D. Romans, and Graeco-Roman history has provided settings for most of my SF and fantasy. In the spirit of explaining what "The Great Wizard, Cabbage" has to do with me, I could discuss the importance of Latin and classical history to my life both generally and specifically as part of my writing.

But I've said that elsewhere, so instead I'll comment on the fact that *Cabbage* is a lighter story than much of what I write; that in fact *Cabbage* is funny. (Okay, it's funny in an English sort of way, particularly if you're a guy with a juvenile sense of humor. Which is most guys, at least in my circle of friends.)

There's a lot of humor in all my fiction, but I think it's fair to say that the people who are most likely to appreciate that humor have been in some pretty bad places. Black humor is a welcome companion in environments which you know are likely to kill or maim you and your buddies. I have a writing career because that experience is more widespread than civilians tend to think, but it's not true of most people in the First World. (Thank goodness.)

I *have* written humorous stories, however. I collected these in *All the Way to the Gallows*. In doing so, I noticed to my surprise that almost all of my funny stories were set in somebody else's universe. I didn't (and don't) know why that should be, but I decided that for the fantasy Mark wants for this volume I would do a funny story. (He also wants me to do a Hammer story. I'm pretty sure that's not going to be funny.)

Two of my best stories (funny or otherwise) are "Airborne All the Way" and "A Very Offensive Weapon." *Weapon* was based on a full background by Roger Zelazny, and the story is novella length. That's much longer than I thought was suitable for this anthology.

All the background I had when I wrote *Airborne*, however, was a single card from the *Magic: the Gathering*™ pack. I therefore thought about *Airborne* and wondered how to get the same feel for the new story.

The first result of thinking about *Airborne* is that I switched the current story's viewpoint from the hedge-wizard to his apprentice. *Airborne*'s viewpoint character was the leader of a squad of goblins. She was brighter than the goblins under her command, but that wasn't a high bar: they were explicitly on an intellectual level with rocks. (They were brighter than *most* rocks.)

Something else I like about *Airborne* is that the goblins are all good-hearted. Sure, they're pawns (they're a balloon crew, so I can't call them footsoldiers) in a magical war, but they don't hate anybody. They're just trying to do the best job possible with their limited mental resources. That was an important aspect when I characterized both the apprentice and his master.

The biggest difference between the two stories is that *Airborne* is set in a game universe which I didn't describe or even understand (I'd never played *Magic*), whereas *Cabbage* is set in the Roman Empire of about 170 A.D. I know a fair amount about Rome and I wanted to get the setting right. It wasn't necessary for the story, but it was darned well necessary for *me*. (Reread the first paragraph of this essay.)

But you know? I'm not sure that this is such a big difference after all. For *Cabbage* I used a map and a topography of Rome, a large reference work on the Tivoli site, and the trusty volume of classical spells and curses which had been at hand through the years in which I wrote the Isles series . . . but I remember reading 19th-century ballooning memoirs for *Airborne*, and also studying coal gasification (because 19th-century sport ballooning generally used lighting gas instead of the extremely expensive process of generating hydrogen by pouring concentrated acid over iron filings).

In any case, herewith a light and I hope funny fantasy. Now to work out the details of a Hammer story.

Forward!

Incubator

Gene Wolfe

"You'll know it right away," Fil had said, smiling. He had a charming smile. "Our roof was designed by some lunatic, and it's all tile, sort of between a greenish yellow and a yellowish green." When she had said nothing Fil added, "Depends on how the sun strikes it. There's nothing like it for thousands of kilos—nothing else like it in the world, probably. I mean, who'd want a roof like that?"

She had remarked that she still did not understand why the locator would not take her straight there. "Don't know," Fil had said. He had golden hair, like someone in an old, old painting. "Something Father did, probably." Then he vanished, and a hundred vocal and keyed commands had not brought him back.

There it was, over there! That jumble of poisoned leaves! She guided L-87 with a gesture and told him to land with another.

It was all garden here, no paths at all that she could

see, no paved paths, no bridle paths, just lush green grass among straggling rose bushes. Were not roses supposed to bloom all summer? All winter, too, even here north of the line? These roses did not know the rules, or most did not. A few blue or green blossoms here and there. And foliage, though not as lush as she had expected.

She took a dozen steps before the thought struck, but once it did she knew that it was quite correct. These roses had not been chosen for their blossoms or even for their foliage. Chosen for something else. From fear, she refrained from naming it, even silently. No name, and no looking at those.

Left, then right, then straight on for twenty-odd steps and here was the inhabitation. She positioned in front of the lens, standing far enough back to give it a full view. Blond, she reminded herself. That was what Fil's yellow hair was called. Dark blue eyes? Was she imagining those? Could semihumans, even blond ones, really have two such eyes?

The voice of the door was not his. "Come right in. It's not locked."

A woe man's? An android's?

The door swung open before she touched it. The room beyond was large and many-shadowed, with a ceiling that had to be three stories high—no, five. It seemed to draw her up like sky, promising something she could not have named. A row of pillars to the left, mucus stretched from floor to ceiling.

"Father wanted you to come here."

She looked around. The shemale was almost near enough to touch, though not quite.

"I thought I'd better tell you. You'll want to think it was Fil."

She wanted to say they had known all along who it was, but that would have been snapping the truth. She replaced it with, "Is Fil your sibling?"

"A third." The shemale not quite close enough to touch smirked. "Same feather, diffcrent nest."

She thought she knew what was meant by *nest*, and was slightly offended.

"Now you say left third or right, and I say bottom third."

She stopped to look around at the shemale. "Then we'll skip it." The shemale had lion's-mane hair and enormous green eyes. Not at all like the near-brother Fil? Thinking that, she was secretly pleased.

House or hice? If she were permitted more than one, would she want one like this? She shuddered.

"Fil soft-pedals everything, but Father will tell you truth."

Was it time to resume walking? She decided against it. "What about you?"

"Oh, I won't tell you anything." The shemale paused thoughtfully. "Or at least, nothing you might believe."

"You just told me something."

"Doesn't count." The shemale's glowing teeth were not pointed, yet she knew somehow that they were terribly sharp—sharp as knives. What a horror it must be to have teeth like that!

"What does your father want?"

"You." The shemale moved off.

What if he cannot have me? "You mean he asked your semi-sibling to call me. What for?"

"He wasn't paid. He must do what Father says. So must I." This was said without looking back.

All right, two can play that game. A black leather divan waited between pillars. She crossed the room to it and sat down. There was a mirror in the shadowy distance, and she studied the images in that. Did she look tough enough? Clever enough? How tough was she? Really now? Though she did not move, the she in the mirror brushed back a lock of dusky hair.

A tall woman appeared at her left elbow. She looked around, half-expecting to see no such woman; but there was indeed a lofty figure wrapped in black there.

"May I sit with you?"

"I am sitting without permission," she remarked at length. "I will make no objection to your sitting, at present." She hesitated. "Are we inside or outside? I thought I knew but . . ."

"You have come to doubt yourself."

No. To be rid of doubt. She nodded.

"What you see could be a dream, an illusion. An hallucination—"

"Or a reality," she finished.

"Not so. No one can see reality. The mind processes a pattern of light reported by the optic nerves. The mind interprets that."

"What if I were to touch you?"

The tall woman—seeming even taller now that she was sitting—laughed. "Your touching me would have no effect. Everything is unreal and real. We may see the real part or the unreal part."

"Or both."

"Or neither. I look for oranges, I see apples which are figs."

"Really figs?"

"Is anything?"

"May I speak to Fil?"

The woman in black laughed. "Of course not."

"Why not? We communicated. That's why I came."

"He has left, gone deaf, is sleeping or insane. More if you like."

She nodded. "I understand. Unending fantasies and failures bar my way."

"Those you dispatch, you will leave behind you. When you have gone, they will rise and make haste so as to be ahead of you."

"Fil and I spoke shortly before I landed. Fil has golden hair and the voice of two poets."

"You thought him here."

"He said he was. I had no reason to doubt him. He promised to show me the Egg, so he must have been here."

"He was on a seaplane flying at a depth of five hundred fathoms."

"I take it the plane is bound for a volcano."

The tall woman in black said nothing.

"I have come to see the Egg."

"Or something else. Or nothing."

"Fil knows that—knows why I came. I told him."

"He is dead."

"You said he was on a seaplane."

The tall figure in black laughed. "Now I say that it crashed. Answer, clark!"

"Into the sea, you mean."

"It struck the side of a submerged mountain."

"I brought you something." Reaching into a pants leg, she produced a bauble.

The black-robed woman stared through tall eyes. "Is this valuable?"

"It is invaluable."

"Then come." The black-robed woman led the way to a crystal pillar standing among ferns. "I have no reason to spare you."

She went closer, to better see the Egg behind the crystal. It was copper-brown, with dots of rose, sallow, and ebony.

"In there? Is all the old humankind in there?"

The black-robed woman nodded, but by then she had seen the crevice, a crack no longer than her smallest nail. It grew by the width of an eyelash as she watched.

She stepped back, and fled.

Gene Wolfe attended Edgar Allen Poe Elementary School and has never quite left the ghoul-haunted woodlands of Weir. If you like this little story, you might look for *Innocents Abroad, Endangered Species, The Best of Gene Wolfe*, and other collections. He is old now, a widower who lives in Peoria, Illinois. But why should you care?

At my request, he supplied this afterword to his story.

Laugh if you like, but I feel a deep kinship with David Drake. As far as I know there are only three fantasy and science fiction writers who have actually gone to war and gotten shot at: David, Joe Haldeman (who was severely wounded), and me.

That's a shame. Combat makes you experience a different reality. It teaches you that the calm of ordinary American life is in fact the calm of an extraordinary time and place. Homicidal people, it seems, are not confined to certain defined hours and channels on TV. You yourself are a homicidal person and so are all your friends, if you're lucky. Explosions are not a mishap that occurred in an oil refinery in Oklahoma seven months ago. The most recent explosion was seven seconds ago and about five yards off, and here comes another one so stay down! Ditches are to live in, and women largely legendary. For all its virtues, science fiction must present a world that seems more or less plausible. The future will not be plausible. It never is.

Thus the story you have just read.

A Flat Affect

Eric Flint

On St. Anselm's feast day in the Year of the Hedgehog, King Bertrand of Wollend was seized by a sudden caprice. True, he was given to such things, but this was an enthusiasm beyond the norm.

"According to the texts," he announced to his privy council, "this year marks the millennium of the birth of Chefferax, greatest—by far!—of the generals of antiquity."

"Ah . . . which texts, Your Majesty?" asked Hubert Reese, the Chancellor of the Exchequer. His tone was deferential, but cautious. King Bertrand's whims were prone to make excessive charges upon the royal purse.

"I forget," the king said, waving his hand dismissively. "But I'm sure it's true. So let us have a season of revelry! A great pageant of ballads and poesy! Summon the minstrels and the troubadours and the bards!"

The mien of the chancellor grew dour. Minstrels were profligate in their demands; troubadours, worse; bards,

worst of all. Where honest workmen were satisfied with
unassuming wages and a modest bonus upon completion
of their task, poets insisted upon perquisites and
lagniappes at every turn—and lavish praise, to boot.

Hubert Reese would rather have applauded fishwives
in the street. But his was not the deciding view when it
came to these matters. For a moment, he thought to
appeal to his colleagues on the council, but the thought
was short-lived. They knew their monarch's moods as well
as he did; and, when all was said and done, enjoyed the
benefits of their positions in the council. Arguing with
King Bertrand when he was in the grip of one of his
fancies was not, as the lowlifes in trade would put it, a
good career move.

Several years back, the chancellor had heard a young
poet proclaim his desire—no, his pressing need!—to
speak truth to power. He grew no older. His bones
moldered somewhere in the bottom of the royal moat.

There was nothing for it. "As you wish, Your Majesty."
Reese glanced at his fellows on the council, but none
would meet his eye. "I'm sure we can have the services of
the Crown and Scepter Theater at a reasonable price," he
added.

King Bertrand's eyes widened and his mouth opened,
as if he were uncertain whether to be shocked or
outraged.

He settled for both.

"Preposterous!" he spluttered. "Are lays and ballads in
praise of history's finest *strategos* to be crabbed within the
confines of a glorified shack?"

He stretched forth a royal hand, splayed wide in full

decree. "I will not have it! An outdoor stadium must be built! Of solid wood and festooned with banners!"

The chancellor foresaw many hours in the future, when he himself would be crabbed over the kingdom's books, confined within the king's grandiosities and impractical disposition.

But he said nothing. Spoke neither truth to power nor caution to monarchy. Not even when the king piled on the final blow.

"And send for Garrick! We must have him! He's the finest *trouvère* on the continent!"

He was nothing of the sort, in the chancellor's opinion. The Garrick creature's lays were given to neither lofty judgments nor refined sensibilities. They were coarse and crude in sentiment; stark in execution; sung—if the word could be used—in a voice any crow would be proud to call its own.

But he made no protest. The king doted on the fellow. They'd been friends in their youth. No doubt a misspent youth on the part of the minstrel. The king's youth . . . Well, he was of royal blood.

The troubadour Garrick arrived three weeks later, by which time the new stadium was well underway. He was immediately ushered into the monarch's presence.

"Welcome, old friend! Welcome!" King Bertrand even rose from his throne to give the bard an embrace. "I can't tell you how much I've longed for your presence."

As he resumed his seat, the king waved dismissively. "Wollend's full of minnesingers now—but they're rank amateurs! The whole lot!"

"Each and every one?" asked Garrick. He was slender to the point of being skeletal, though his physique was still sinewy. Deep-set eyes looked out from either side of a hatchet-blade nose. "That seems unlikely, on the face of it."

Bertrand shrugged irritably. "Fussy as ever, I see. Fine, fine. Probably only the *moitié* are actual amateurs. But the rest might as well be."

The king began an exaggerated pantomime of a man playing a lute. "*Plunk-plink-plonk!* And the words are still worse! Sugary prattle piled atop treacle and vapor. Would you believe one of the louts compared Chefferax to a plum pudding? I had him soundly thrashed, I'll let you know!"

"Perhaps if you weren't so quick with the knout and bastinado," Garrick advised, "your minstrels would be more venturesome."

"Bah. Do them good to limp about on properly cudgeled feet while they nurse their lumps and bruises." The king now sprawled on the throne, his posture and countenance the very essence of disgruntlement. "You'll sing for me tomorrow, I trust."

"As you wish."

Garrick took the stage a little before noon of the following day. By then, word of his arrival had spread through the capital and the half-finished stands were full.

Initially, full of striplings drawn by the minstrel's fame. But they were soon cuffed and elbowed aside in the front rows by veterans of the royal army. Garrick was considered by them to be their poet. Others could listen;

but they were merely tolerated and could damn well take the back seats.

Chancellor Reese sat in the royal box to be left and just behind the king. He would have preferred not to attend at all, but rank hath its detriments as well as its privileges. Stoutly, he braced himself for the ordeal.

And ordeal it certainly was. Garrick's verses dealt with war and war alone. Of the finer and more delicate human endeavors, there was not a trace.

Nor was there a trace of martial refinement. In Garrick's lays, swords hacked meat and bone, scattering body parts with as much abandon as bodily fluids. Spears pierced brains; axes spilled entrails; entrails tripped advancing troops and cowards in retreat alike.

Blood was everywhere, along with any word that rhymed. Mud seemed a particular favorite of the bard.

Had his voice been muddy as well, it wouldn't have been so bad. Hubert could have let the words blend into meaningless mush. But, no. Garrick's voice was clear and sharp, if not in the least melodious.

Not in the least poignant or impassioned, either. The poet was as grizzled as the veterans who watched and listened. He favored a flat affect, his somewhat high-pitched voice spilling out the verses the way a rice merchant spills his grain. Each the same; each uninflected; each as flavorless as the sunrise on a winter day.

Blood. Brains. An arm here; a foot there; a loop of gut over yonder. Death, destruction and mayhem, ubiquitous. But the affect . . . flat. Always flat.

For their part, the veterans listened intently, their gnarly big-knuckled hands often cupped above a cane.

They applauded rarely, and then sparely. But throughout they nodded their appreciation and issued occasional grunts of approval.

When it was all over, many of them were heard to say: *So it was*.

The striplings crowded into the back rows were less favorable. Some made derisory comments concerning the sparse intonations; others deprecated the lean and scanty meter; still more deplored the unrefined subject matter. But they were soon sent to flight by irate veterans clambering their way up the stands.

Fortunately for the striplings, the veterans were doughty but arthritic. Their forward progress had little of the *élan* of their youth. Inexorable, surely; lightning-fast, not so much.

For his part, Garrick took no notice of the altercation. For the opinion of striplings, he cared not a whit. And while the same could not be said of the opinion of veterans, the troubadour was not given to gauging himself by the plaudits of others. In this as in his poesy, he favored a flat affect.

No ladies were seen to swoon.

King Bertrand heaped praise upon Garrick—praise and a considerable amount of gold, to the despair and disgust of Chancellor Reese. But within a short time after the poet's performance, the royal humor grew sour.

"I'm bored," the king complained. "It's always the same. The great Chefferax did this, the incomparable tactician did that, the matchless strategist did the other. I've heard it all. I'm bored, I say, bored."

Listening to the complaint, Garrick grew concerned. He well knew the king's temperament from long acquaintance. Nothing good was likely to come of this.

"Perhaps I could alter a key," he suggested.

"Bah. This key, that key, what does it matter? It's the *substance* of the great general's life that's the problem."

The poet definitely didn't like the way this was going. "What can one do? The past is fixed, inalterable."

"Is it?" demanded Bertrand. "In life, certainty. But we deal with poesy here, man! Which is to say, fable—which is itself but a stifling term for fancy. And I fancy something different. So."

Garrick greatly distrusted that "so." But he said nothing. There was still a chance—faint chance, but a chance—that the king's mood would pass.

Alas.

"So let's have a new epic!" Bertrand exclaimed. "A tale no longer bound by the cramped confines of time and space. Perhaps—yes! A great enemy from the future! Sent back in time to ravage the ancient world! Only Chefferax can save the day. With nothing more—I leave this entirely to your discretion and sensibility—than the aide of a deaf-mute from that same woeful future."

"How so is this *my* discretion?"

"Well, you'll have to devise the tale, of course. Who else could do it justice?"

Garrick gazed at the king from lowered brows. "I am quite busy," he pointed out. "As you should know—being the source of most of my commissions."

The king waved the matter away. "Yes, yes, I am aware

of all that. But you needn't take on the time-consuming and petty business of actually choosing the notes and rhymes. You need only limn the broad outlines of the story. I'll find some promising newcomer to do the scut work."

The minstrel's eyes were even more deep-set than usual. "We tried this once before. As you may recall, it went quite badly. The newcomer you found on that occasion refused to do the needed preparations. The end result was deplorable. The more so since you insisted on attaching my name to the shambles."

King Bertrand glared. But said nothing. Truth to tell, he was a bit intimidated by his nominal subordinate. They had been friends in their youth, and such histories often undermine the natural order of things.

"Well," he said. "Well."

Again, the king waved his hand, this time with more irritation than insouciance. "Oh, fine—fine. If you don't like the end result, you can extinguish your formal association with it. But I still insist that it be done!"

Garrick kept a rough silence. "For a suitable fee, naturally," the king added.

The chancellor's own brows were now lowered. Garrick's notion of "a suitable fee" was sure to be as profligate as that of any bard.

Unluckily for Hubert, Bertrand spotted his dour countenance. "Let's have no officious quibbling!" he commanded. "Always remember the great philosopher's dictum: *whatever is, is right.*"

In response, though he considered the statement preposterous, Garrick said nothing. He saw no point in disputing philosophy with a monarch. Especially one with an open purse.

Weeks passed, and Garrick eventually half-forgot the arrangement. But the day came when he was summoned once again before the throne.

"I've found him!" said Bertrand. The king seemed oddly gleeful, as if he were a child about to play a prank. "And would you believe, in his province he's considered a notorious malcontent! I'd have him chopped, but he's something of a droll fellow. Besides, he says he's given up his reprobate ways."

Garrick cared little of such matters. "Can he sing? Play the lute? Most of all, follow the dramatic logic in order to develop it properly?"

"Splendidly, to the first." The king waggled his hand. "Well enough, to the second—his fretwork could use some improvement. As for the third . . . well . . ."

The poet's brows came down. It might be said he glowered.

"Who's to say? Who's to say?" demanded Bertrand. Cheerfully: "Let's put him to the test!"

Garrick began to balk. To Chancellor Reese's great distress, the king increased his remuneration. In the end, the poet yielded. Not gracefully, perhaps, but neither with any disrespect to the royal person.

Always one to make his preparations ahead of time, Garrick had already detailed the ribs and sinews of the epic-to-be. Chords, meter, rhyme—those he left to the minstrel who would put it to song. His concern was that the tale be coherent; logical; the end flowing from the beginning in a graceful and sturdy arch; all triumphs and calamities in their proper place.

He met the king's chosen minnesinger—Fulchard, the fellow's name—in a nearby tavern.

"I am told you are a disruptor and a dissident." So he began, as he handed over his notes to the round and ruddy-faced fellow already seated at the table. "For my part, I care little about the public tranquility. More often than not, it's simply the peace of cows chewing their cud. Agitate all you will. But take care of my notes, and be true to the tale embedded therein."

Smiling cheerily, Fulchard took the notes. "Oh, that business is all behind me now. Mind you, I haven't recanted a single tenet or precept of my creed. Which may be summarized as: *whatever is, is wrong.*"

In response, though he considered the statement preposterous, Garrick said nothing. He saw no point in disputing philosophy with an anarchist. Especially one who might yet be of service.

More weeks passed. Eventually, Fulchard began private rehearsals in a rented loft, to which Garrick was invited. Partly out of civility and partly because he was curious, the poet often attended.

As the king had said, Fulchard's voice was accomplished; at times, even superb. His skills with the lute were . . . passable, but no better. Given the fellow's invariant courtesy and high spirits, however, Garrick lent him his advice. Even, from time to time, practiced with him directly.

As for the novice troubadour's ability to grasp the logic of a tale . . .

Here, the blessings were mixed.

On the one hand, Fulchard was no slacker. He studied the material assiduously; delved into ancient manuals and modern handbooks alike; questioned any and all who might shed light on anything of relevance. In this respect, Garrick was quite pleased.

On the other hand . . .

As might be expected of one with such a history, Fulchard was given to grandiose gestures and magniloquent turns of phrase. As time passed, his embellishments upon Garrick's taut narrative threatened to collapse the epic under its own weight.

"And then, you see—would he not attempt the feat?— the great Chefferax will lead his army across the Harichaca Desert! All of it! All hundreds upon hundreds of leagues! Guided only by the stars and his sure—"

"What would they drink?" queried Garrick, in a spare tone of voice. "There are no wells of record in the Harichaca and only two oases."

Fulchard was taken aback. He had not, admittedly, considered that problem. Poets rarely do. In this, Garrick was much the exception than the rule.

"Ah," he said.

"And how much time would this exploit take?" queried Garrick, his tone of voice becoming thinner still. "You may recall that my notes would have the general surprising his foes at Drumble Pass, early in summer. Yet you would have him emerging from the Harichaca halfway across the continent no sooner than mid-April."

"Ah," said Fulchard, beginning to look downcast. He had not considered the rigorous matters of calendar. Poets rarely do. In this also, Garrick was anomalous.

Garrick rose from the table where they'd been conversing. "Do as you will," he said. "My advice, however, is to hue more closely to the notes."

In the end, Fulchard chose to accept his mentor's counsel. Privately, Garrick was pleased. But he said nothing, either way. Praise and criticism both, he preferred leaving to others. Favoring, in this as in so many things, a flat affect.

King Bertrand was not so reticent.

"He's taking too long," he complained. "And I don't like his frills and hyperbole. Do something!"

"He's progressing," Garrick said mildly. "We must be patient. This is a grand epic, you know, not a sonnet."

"Bah." The king glared at Hubert Reese. "Why is the royal purse so lean these days, Chancellor?"

Reese looked much put upon. As well he might.

In the end, the epic was finished and Fulchard began its performance in the same open-air stadium that Bertrand had constructed for Garrick. But as time passed, the king grew fatigued and querulous. "It's too damn long," he complained to his favored poet. "You would have completed it by now. The veterans will grow disgruntled. Look! Not a one of them has yet stamped his feet on the stands in praise."

"Minstrels differ in their styles," Garrick said. "Lays and ballads do not lend themselves to simple measures and cuts.

The veterans seem well enough pleased. Several ladies have swooned. Best of all, the striplings are complaining."

"Bah."

Eventually, King Bertrand stopped coming altogether. A few veterans did likewise, but most remained. A few more ladies swooned.

When the epic was finished, there was considerable applause. Several more ladies swooned and one or two veterans even stamped their feet.

The striplings were dissatisfied, of course. But Fulchard gave them no more notice that would Garrick himself.

"So, what do you think?" he asked his mentor. There was a grin on his ruddy-cheeked face. "Perhaps whatever is, is not always wrong, eh?"

Garrick smiled. "It was adequate, certainly."

A year passed, and then another. A third, a fourth. Then, just before St. Anselm's feast day in the Year of the Marmot, King Bertrand collapsed on his throne. He was rushed to his bed, but never awoke. A fortnight later, he joined his illustrious predecessors.

The ceremony was held in the cemetery attached to St. Mansel's cathedral. The speeches of the dignitaries were long, ornate, full of plaudits and acclaim. Their oratory was fulsome and declamatory.

Chancellor Hubert Reese was particularly oleaginous, repaying the pecuniary largesse of the king he'd served with rhetoric that was more lavish still. There seemed no reason not to, words being the cheapest of coins.

Fulchard attended the service, but said nothing. As

was proper, given the modest position of bards in a well-managed realm.

Sadly, the same was not true of Garrick. By Bertrand's express command—he'd gone so far as to put it in writing, and affixed the royal seal—the final speech was to be given by the king's favorite poet.

The dignitaries braced themselves. The sun was long past the zenith and their bellies were now suffering from the excesses of their lungs. Lungs which did not begin to have the capacity of a man who'd been a troubadour for decades.

In the back row, Fulchard grinned. "After all this time," he murmured to himself, "you'd think the silly buggers would know better."

As he expected, Garrick was terse. He would expose in public his private philosophy, but in death as in life he maintained the same stance. Always, a flat affect.

"What is, is sometimes adequate," the poet stated. He gazed down for a moment upon the urn holding the royal ashes. "My liege and my friend Bertrand's life was quite adequate, I believe."

He stepped aside, his task complete. The dignitaries stared, dumbfounded. The veterans in the back pounded their canes on the ground with approval. Fulchard applauded vigorously.

No ladies were seen to swoon, however.

Eric Flint's writing career began with the novel *Mother of Demons*, published in 1997. With David Drake, he has collaborated on the six novels in the Belisarius series (*An Oblique Approach, In the Heart of Darkness, Destiny's Shield, Fortune's Stroke, The Tide of Victory*, and *The Dance of Time*), as well as a novel entitled *The Tyrant*. His alternate history novel *1632* was published in 2000, followed by many sequels, several of which made the *New York Times'* extended bestselling list. In addition to the novels in the *1632* series, of which there will be nineteen by July of 2015, he has edited eleven anthologies of short fiction set in that universe. He also publishes the *Grantville Gazette*, a bi-monthly electronic magazine devoted to the series which has now produced almost sixty issues.

Flint has also co-authored SF adventure novels with the South African writer Dave Freer: *Rats, Bats & Vats, The Rats, the Bats, and the Ugly*, and *Pyramid Scheme*. His comic fantasy novels *The Philosophical Strangler* and *Forward the Mage* came out in May of 2001 and March of 2002. He is also working on a major fantasy series with Mercedes Lackey and Dave Freer, the first four volumes of which are *The Shadow of the Lion, This Rough Magic, Much Fall of Blood*, and *Burdens of the Dead*.

Flint is also working on several other ongoing projects:

• With David Weber on a series of novels set in Weber's Honor Harrington universe. The first three of these, *Crown of Slaves, Torch of Freedom*, and *Cauldron of Ghosts*, have already appeared.

• A new alternate history series taking place in Jacksonian America, the first two volumes of which have already appeared: *1812: The Rivers of War* and *1824: The Arkansas War*.

• Further volumes in the Joe's World series, which began with *The Philosophical Strangler* and *Forward the Mage.*

• Two new SF adventure novels with Ryk Spoor, set in the universe they created in the Bemmie trilogy (*Boundary, Threshold,* and *Portal*).

• Two SF adventure volumes with K.D. Wentworth, *The Course of Empire* and *The Crucible of Empire.* He is now working on the third volume in the series, *The Span of Empire,* with David Carrico.

In addition to his own writing, Flint is the editor of several series reissuing the works of past SF authors. These include James H. Schmitz, Keith Laumer, Christopher Anvil, Murray Leinster, Randall Garrett, Tom Godwin, and Howard L. Myers. He was also the editor of the online science fiction and fantasy magazine, *Jim Baen's Universe.*

Flint graduated Phi Beta Kappa from the University of California at Los Angeles in 1968, and later received a Master's degree in history from the same university. Despite his academic credentials, Flint spent the next quarter of a century as an activist in the American trade union movement, working as a longshoreman, truck driver, autoworker, steel worker, oil worker, meatpacker, glassblower, and machinist. He has lived at various times in California, Michigan, West Virginia, Alabama, Ohio, and Illinois. He currently lives in northwest Indiana with his wife Lucille.

At my request, he supplied the following afterword:

Writing this little story brought back to mind the years I spent working on the Belisarius series with David. I began writing the first novel, *An Oblique Approach*, sometime in either late 1996 or early 1997; I forget which. David had produced the outline a year earlier, thereabouts. I finished the sixth and last novel in the series, *The Dance of Time*, in July of 2005. It was published in February of the following year.

Eight or nine years to write six novels—a total of about 850,000 words. Of course, the Belisarius series wasn't the only thing I was working on during that period. I wrote the first four novels one right after the other: *An Oblique Approach* was published in March of 1998; *In the Heart of Darkness*, in August of 1998; *Destiny's Shield*, in July of 1999; and *Fortune's Stroke* in June of 2000.

Four novels in a little over two years. That was a very fast pace, when you consider that I was still working a full-time job as a machinist. I didn't start writing as my exclusive occupation until September of 1999, by which time the first four books in the series were finished.

Thereafter the pace slowed, mostly because I was starting to work on other projects. My novel, *1632*, was published in February of 2000, followed shortly thereafter by the first of the many novels I would co-author with Dave Freer—*Rats, Bats & Vats*, which came out in September of the same year.

The fifth book in the Belisarius series, *The Tide of Victory*, came out in July of 2001—about the same roughly once-a-year pace the other four books had maintained. And then . . .

The series languished for several years. The final novel, *The Dance of Time*, wasn't published until February of 2006, almost five years later. During that same stretch, I wrote and published eleven other novels. Those were: *Pyramid Scheme, The Shadow of the Lion, Forward the Mage, The Tyrant*, 1633, *Crown of Slaves, The Course of Empire, This Rough Magic*, 1634: *The Galileo Affair, The Wizard of Karres*, and *The Rats, the Bats & the Ugly*. Except for *The Tyrant*, none of these novels have any connection to the Belisarius series.

To put it another way, it took about twice as long to produce the last novel in the series than it had to produce the first five.

There were two reasons for this odd situation. The first was that my career as an author really began taking off with the publication of 1632, and I had lots of other work at hand. The second and more important reason, however, was that by then Jim Baen had lost his interest in the Belisarius series and kept urging me to work on other projects.

Why did he lose interest? It's hard to say for sure. I think what happened was that Jim got soured by the lousy sell-through of the hardcover edition of the third book in the series, *Destiny's Shield*. And, truth be told, the sell-through was a bit dismal—not much better than forty percent. If you're unclear on the term, "sell-through" refers to the percentage of books shipped which are actually sold. The average for fiction publishing is somewhere around fifty percent, but Baen Books generally does better than that—probably close to sixty percent or so—and it was something that Jim took a great deal of pride in.

On the other hand . . .

Destiny's Shield was the first volume in the series that

Baen published in hardcover. The first two novels only came out in a mass-market paperback edition, until the reissue of the entire series in a trilogy omnibus many years later. Readers tend to get disgruntled when a publisher switches from paperback to hardcover editions in the middle of a series, and it was my opinion—and David Drake's—that that explained the problem.

Our assessment seemed to be substantiated by the sales and sell-through of the later volumes. In terms of sell-through, *Destiny's Shield* marked the nadir of the series. By now, as the years have passed, the sell-through has slowly crept up to the industry average of fifty percent. But the fourth book, *Fortune's Stroke,* had a sixty-three percent sell-through in hardcover—considerably above the average. The fifth book, *The Tide of Victory,* did still better, with a seventy-one percent sell-through in hardcover. The last novel, *The Dance of Time,* saw a drop in sell-through down to fifty-seven percent. But that's still respectable and not too surprising given the long hiatus before it finally appeared.

But Jim didn't seem to be paying attention any longer. For whatever reason, he'd lost his interest in the series. The final novel might never have been published at all, except than David and I finally insisted that it had to be written and Jim acquiesced.

For me, though, what I think of as "the Belisarius period" in my writing career will always be the two-and-a-half years when I wrote the first four novels. First, because that was all I worked on. To this day, despite now having forty-six novels in print, I have never again worked exclusively on one project for that long a stretch.

The other reason, however, is more important. That was the time when I went through what I think of as my apprenticeship as an author, and the man who was central to my development was David Drake. For all the many and obvious differences between us as writers, if you know where to look you can see the similar craftsmanship in the way we construct a story—the narrative architecture, if you will.

That's hardly surprising, since I learned that architecture from David. Those people who've seen David's original outlines for the Belisarius series generally think that the final outcome was radically different. That assessment is both right and wrong.

It's right, inasmuch as David's voice and mine are very different. But it's quite wrong, if you focus on the logic of the narrative rather than what you might call the colorations and embellishments.

Yes, my final product was at least twice as long as anything David would have written himself. He is generally a terse writer; I am not. He generally favors a flat affect; I do not.

But while those things are not trivial, they have little to do with a story's basic structure. That is to say, what is this story *about*? What is the central conflict; who are the key players and what are their motivations; and how does that conflict work itself out in the end according to the logic of those motivations. To put it more tersely, what is the narrative arch?

All that I learned from David. I added much to the Belisarius series in the way of colorations and embellishments—call them curlicues if you want, but show some respect; they're damn good ones—but the fundamental logic of the story didn't change a bit.

Trust me. I tried to change it, from time to time. And what I always found was that if I was embellishing the narrative logic, I had no trouble at all. But whenever I wandered away from the story arch, I ran into trouble. David was always very pleasant about it and never did more than advance mildly worded suggestions. As time passed, however, I learned to take those suggestions dead seriously.

That's how I learned to write. If you're wondering, yes, at one point I did plan to have Belisarius march his army across the Sahara, before the ridiculous notion collapsed under its own weight. Always a courteous fellow—to me, at any rate; I suspect there are a fair number of fools out there who've found themselves not suffered gladly—David never once said, "I told you so."

Even though he had, of course. Many, many times.

SUM

Cecelia Holland

"You think too much," Bardo said.

"No," I said, "I'm serious. How do you know you aren't dead?"

We were marching smartly in line along the canal street, Bardo and I in the lead, the four pikemen behind us in a single rank. Ahead the Daalseweg Bridge humped up the street. Beyond that was the tangle of lanes and alleys where we were going. Once we got into those narrow ways we would have to go in file. I smothered a little apprehension. I looked back over the four men behind Bardo, their pikes on their shoulders. Mauritz would be pleased; he loved straight lines.

"I'm moving," Bardo said. "I'm talking. So I'm alive. See?"

"You believe you are. But it could all be a delusion— a madness." We tramped up and over the bridge, and filed into the narrow alley. Although it was still afternoon the whole way was in shadow, cold, smelling of wet stone and rot. The crooked old buildings tilted anxiously over the cobbles. Bardo was a step behind me, and I said, "Maybe you're just shackled to a wall somewhere, raving."

"I would still be alive," Bardo said.

Midway down the street, on the right, as the informant had said, was a house painted blue and green. As we came up to it I held up my hand, and my command stopped with a stamp of their feet. At another gesture they turned in unison to face the house. I swallowed. I was an officer, I could handle this. I went to the door and knocked.

Nothing happened. I hammered my fist on the door, and when that brought no one I nodded to Bardo, who came straight at the door, shoulder first, and drove it in off its hinges. He had his uses.

I called in through the gap, "Stadtholder's orders! Come out at once!"

Silence. I took a step inside, into a ground-floor room, walls covered with painted plaster, a fine big fireplace, a cabinet full of blue and white pots, a Turkey carpet on the floor. I called out again, "Stadtholder's orders!"

The house felt empty. The air seemed dense, still, absorbing the sound: no ear out there to listen. With a wash of relief, I was suddenly sure there was nobody here.

I called to the others, and they came in after me; we would have to search the place. If there had been indeed Spanish spies here Mauritz would want to know and his busy mind would find everything interesting. I went on into the middle of the fine Turkey carpet, and then under me the floor gave way and there was a thunderous boom and I was falling.

❖ ❖ ❖

I woke in utter darkness, and could not move. I opened my eyes into nothing. Still dazed, I thought, *I am dead*.

But now, in the cold, under this terrific weight, I thought, *If I am thinking this I am probably alive*.

I was breathing, also; another good sign. Over my face, empty air. But my eyes didn't work.

I tried to move my head. Something massive above pressed it down, but on the other side the cheek lay on something rough and yielding. Dirt, maybe. Yes. A house had fallen on me. I remembered leading the squad in, pikes at the ready, expecting to find a cell of Spanish spies, and then the whole thing crashed down. An explosion. The house had been undermined, an ambush, and I had walked right into it. I wondered how long I had been unconscious.

Or dead.

A bomb of some kind. Mauritz would figure it all out, piece it together like a map. For an instant I was seeing this from outside: a problem of order.

Then the truth swept over me. I was trapped under the house.

I began to laugh, hopeless, and not happy. It was just funny, because I had come out here to study war with Prince Mauritz so I could taste some true experience of the world, away from my books and philosophy. Now here in my first important experience I was about to die.

This was so twisted. I could not let this happen. I clenched my fist, and my fingers scraped on the dirt. I had no strength. This was hopeless. I gave up and lay still, waiting to die.

I realized I was holding my breath, no reason of course to breathe anymore, if I were about to die. I let go, gulped in the cold air. My mind settled, but it would not be still. I had been working out a bit of Ovid, the day before, and now as the panic eased a little, the line from nowhere delivered itself to me.

Perfer et obdura, dolor hic tibi proderit olim. Be patient, stay strong, and someday this suffering will be useful.

That implied a someday, up ahead, when I would have uses. I gathered myself again to move. Called on the power of numbers: one—two—three—I strained my whole body, and a sharp pain tore up my left side. Gasping, I lay still, my heart pounding its double beat.

The pain faded. The heartbeat slowed. One-two. One-two. Perhaps I had gone on the wrong number. I loved Two. One was adrift, Three was dangerously rigid, but Two could move. I wiggled my two arms. The left was pinned tight but the right elbow bent, slid through loose dirt, and I could draw my hand along my side and across my chest and free.

Then to my amazement I could twist and lift the upper half of my body. My left arm slipped out from under the enormous weight that had held it, and I was halfway sitting up in the dark, propped on one arm, my head bent down against something solid, but empty space around me from the waist up.

I put up my hand to my head, and my fingers grazed a slanting wooden beam, thick as my thigh. A floor joist. Reaching around past my left shoulder I touched a blank wall of stone. Out in front of me was a jumble of broken wood and something slick and jagged that scratched me. Overhead, I drew my fingertips along wooden planks, side by side. On my right, the planks sloped down over my legs. That was what held my legs down, the far edge of that slab of wooden planks.

I was in the basement. I had dropped through a hole in the floor, and the house had fallen down over me. The beams of the floor above me had come down at a tilt against the stone foundation, one end on the basement wall and one on the ground. Under this hypotenuse I was sheltered. I groped around me in the dark, hoping to find some opening out of this tiny room.

Nothing. The tiny room was a death trap. My gorge rose, a numb rabbit-like mindlessness, and I slumped down again against the ground. A long, slow, horrible death in the dark. I thought, *I will kill myself first*.

I thought again of death, that margin, what would it be like, the shock of the event. Or perhaps not a shock? I had been reading something of Oresme's about impetus, and perhaps there was a spiritual impetus, so that after death the unwitting soul, existing only in its own memory, seemed to itself to go on as before. Perhaps that was what the afterlife would be, that last, fading, eternal moment.

So I could be already dead. In spite of that I was pushing myself up again, twisting, unwilling to lie still. There was something wrong with my leg, which was reassuring. If I were imagining myself, I would find myself perfect.

My good leg began to throb, and I pushed my foot down to escape the pain and my shoe came off. My foot, now smaller, could move sideways, and I pushed and twisted until it slipped under the edge of the planks and I could slide it free. Lying flat again, I pushed my whole body down under the sloping planks, and my left leg came loose also.

Carefully, using my hands, trying not to move the bad leg much, I eased myself up into the little space under the fallen floor.

Doing even that much wearied me, and it was cold and I was shivering. Around me the place stank of damp stone and mold. I huddled still, waiting for the stabbing pain in my leg to subside. But now again the black terror overcame me. It didn't matter what I had done, I would still die. Only twenty-two and already dead, having accomplished nothing. All my great plans, now foolish, stupid schoolboy dreams.

Obdura, I thought. *Listen to the master. Do not give up.*

I passed my hands over my little prison again. My body filled it from side to side, I could not raise my head all the way. The only way that seemed promising was in front of me, that rough wall of broken wood wedged in with something coarse, chunks of rock, and sharp edges. I felt along one of these protruding bits, felt a smooth curve. A piece of pottery. That broken wood was more of the floor I had fallen through. The rocks were the bricks of the fireplace. The coarse matter was the Turkey carpet.

I tore and clawed at the stuff in front of me. I got a brick loose, and then another, and then loose stuff began to cascade down around me. I huddled back, afraid of bringing down the rest of the house. But the triangle of my shelter was reassuring. Slowly the rattling faded. I groped over the wall of debris again. My fingertips hurt. I got my hands around part of the carpet, and pulled, and that shifted and more bits of stuff pattered down, and then I could not budge the carpet any more.

Some bits of stuff clung to my face, my beard. Little flecks of stone. There had been a china cupboard next to the fireplace.

I dug upward with both hands, above the carpet. I worked out another brick, a piece of wood with metal attached to it: the front of the cabinet. More pottery rained down around me. The air smelled of dirt and mold. I had more room now, and could stretch my legs out. I was moving forward, upward, through the pitch dark, crawling over rubble. I groped ahead of me, pulling loose bricks, wood. My fingertips slid along the edge of a metal pot and I wiggled that loose and threw it out behind me, where it clanged through the dark like a bell.

Another beam slanted down across my path, carrying another floor of planks laid edge to edge. The ends of the nails stuck through the beam like hooks. Carefully I felt along it. The expanse of wood stretched unbroken as far as I could reach.

This was the ceiling of the room, which had crashed down into the center of the house. Ahead of me, it seemed to be tilting steeply up, under it a clear space, as if everything had slid down when it fell. I began to crawl into this space, feeling my way with one hand, and dragging myself along on my belly.

I came on fallen plaster and broken wood and shoveled it back behind me with my hands. More carpet.

I pulled, tugged. The cloth too thin for carpet, surely. I gripped something under the cloth, yielding, cold, like a sausage, and yanked, and suddenly I knew I had hold of an arm.

I recoiled almost back entirely into the hole I had left. My hand tingled. I said, "Who's there?" and gulped. I wondered which of the other men it was, buried there in the dark, crushed in the house.

Or maybe he was alive. I inched my way back up my little tunnel, until I found the body again, but when I touched the arm it felt like a slab of meat. I knew he was dead.

Whoever he was. I panted in the dark, breathing the fumes of death. Finally I reached out and lightly, lightly ran my fingertips along the arm until I came to the hand at the end.

I knew the ring on the little finger. I had won that ring from him at dice, and lost it back again. This was Bardo's hand.

The uncontrollable black horror engulfed me again. I could not breathe; the house closed down around me. Not moving, not talking, so dead, by his own definition. Some truth in there somewhere, a mouse in the corn.

There was no other way to go but forward. Digging steadily on, through powdery plaster and wads of straw and hair, I uncovered Bardo's chest, and dragged myself across the dead man.

Pardon me, I imagined myself saying, belly to belly with the corpse. The ceiling pressed down over me, the space narrower with each move, my face down against Bardo's neck. We were never this close before, were we.

I was cold, and tired; I lay still a moment, gathering myself, resting on the body.

Bardo said, I am so you will be.

Not yet. Not yet. I moved, my back scraping against the unyielding planks above me. My cheek rasped against Bardo's. His beard in my teeth. My doublet snagged on the harsh surface against my back and tightened around my neck like a noose. I gasped for air. My face mashed against the side of Bardo's head. His cold clay chilled me, head to toe. Another sign I was alive: that cold.

Bardo said, He thinks he is, so he is, he thinks.

He had never been that clever. Dying had improved his wit.

I pushed on, my chin against his ear, and then I could move no farther. Wedged between Bardo and the collapsed house I could go neither forward nor back.

I lay still a while, feeling the cold seep into me, his death invading my body. My heart went thump-thump. One-two. I worked my right arm along beside the dead man, and reached up past my head, under another joist, and groped around. I touched rubble, and then empty space.

I gasped in relief. I forced all the air out of my lungs, to make myself flatter, and bit by bit, I eased my shoulder in under the beam. I turned my head sideways and wiggled it after, the beam grinding against my ear, I felt Bardo pass by along my chest, down my side. Well, I thought, hail and farewell, brother. Something sharp ripped my scalp. My elbow was free. Abruptly I could lift my head.

My hands flailed out through empty space. I dragged myself forward, over rubble, which slid under me away under me from a sloping wooden floor. Then I felt a breath of air against the back of my head, and I blinked, and I realized I could see.

I pushed myself up onto my knees. The light was faint, sifting in through a thousand holes in the broken roof above, but I could see before me a stretch of empty room: the attic. On one side there was more light. I crawled forward toward the light. And now even my leg felt better. I staggered upright on the sloping floor, holding onto the roof truss, and looked out through a gap onto the street.

The light was a hazy twilight: night coming. It had been midafternoon when we came; I had been buried for hours. The collapsed house half-filled the narrow street. By the edge of the rubble three pikemen were standing around talking: standing guard. Afraid to go in, likely, since it had blown up once.

I called out, and they turned. One ran off a few steps, looking over his shoulder, and the others gawked and pointed. I shouted again. Now they were running and shouting toward me, joyous, as if I were a marvel. As I was. I raised my arms, reborn, as my name meant. I am.

Cecelia Holland lives in California, where she writes, teaches and chases after her five grandchildren.

At my request, she supplied this afterword.

I wrote "SUM" to honor David Drake, the scholar-soldier, with the not-too-subtle Ovid nod, and also because I know he will get all the jokes.

David Drake

Tom Doherty

I met David Drake almost forty years ago at a science fiction convention. I don't remember which one, or quite when, but I do recall we had an interesting conversation which included a discussion of a Hammers story I had read in *Galaxy*. The year was probably 1976 or '77.

I had loved science fiction since I was a kid. Growing up in farm country, science fiction books were hard to come by, and I became a regular reader of *Astounding*, which became *Analog*, and of *Galaxy*. As publisher of Ace and Tempo, a young adult line that also published science fiction, I still often read them. When Jim Baen took over at *Galaxy*, the improvement he brought to the magazine's editorial content was impressive. We needed a strong editor to head our Ace SF program. I recruited Jim for the position. Shortly after he came aboard, he suggested we do a Hammer's Slammers collection. We didn't do short-story collections as first books by relatively unknown

authors, but by that time I had read two of those stories
and thought yes!—strong, different, we should do this.

We did, and it was a real success. In it, David began
the creation of a new form of military science fiction. We
bought that collection from David's agent, Kirby
McCauley, sometime in 1978 and published it in 1979,
just before I left to start Tor. Jim would come with me.
At Tor we would acquire the next book in the
Hammerverse, the first Hammer's Slammers novel, *Cross
the Stars*.

Tor would publish *Cross the Stars* in 1984, shortly
after it had spun off Baen Books. There were three
partners in Baen: Jim; a venture capitalist, Richard Gallen;
and myself. Jim would run Baen. One of my contributions
would be the contracts of any Tor author Jim had worked
with and who wanted to follow him to the new company.
I was delighted when David Drake decided he wanted to
write for both of us. By this time, I was not just his
publisher, I was his fan.

David had been there. He brought a realism to
military science fiction I hadn't seen before. I remember,
about the time we were publishing *Cross the Stars*, sitting
with him for dinner, and how during that dinner he made
it clear to me that he wouldn't have, couldn't have written
it if he hadn't been drafted out of Duke Law School and
sent to Vietnam. He arrived there just in time for the 1970
invasion of Cambodia and saw his part of the war from the
loader's hatch of a tank. He served with the 11th Armored
Cavalry, the Blackhorse. He believed then, and still
believed, that the Blackhorse was the best armored
regiment in Vietnam, but neither he, nor anybody he

knew there, thought they were doing any good, that the war could be won, or that the corrupt, brutal government in Saigon was worth saving, but they did their job, they were the Blackhorse. That experience was, he felt, the strongest influence on that book and, in fact, on all his writing for years to come.

We've known each other for a long time now and somewhere along the way he told me that he had come to believe that he wrote then, and continued to write, as a way to let out his anger in an acceptable fashion, that his writing calms him, probably because it's the one thing in life he knows he can control. I think it works. He may never be completely free of the anger and depression caused by that horribly useless and destructive war, but at least to me he seems more at peace with himself, less depressed than he was in the first twenty years or twenty-five years we worked together.

They have been great years. David is a great storyteller, and he brings to that storytelling not just the so real, so negative experience of a war that should never have been, but his erudition, his deep knowledge of his story and the classics. In *Cross the Stars* he drew on the *Odyssey*. In his latest series for us, his Books of the Elements, he shows us what the culture of first century Rome was like as reflected in the writing of those who lived it, such as Virgil, Ovid and Tacitus. For his longest Tor series, *Lord of the Isles*, he reread Horace, Virgil, Ovid, and the other Romans of the late Republic but the religion is Sumerian. For both he reread Polybius. You can see his translation of large parts of Ovid's *Metamorphoses* on his web site. I find David's use of earlier civilizations, so different yet still the base from which our own evolved, as source material fascinating, but mostly I read and publish David Drake for the great stories he tells. I hope to be doing both for many years to come.

◈ ◈ ◈

Tom Doherty is the President, Publisher, and Founder of Tor Books, LLC. He has been in publishing for fifty-two years. He started as a salesman for Pocket Books and rose to be Division Sales Manager. From there, he went to Simon and Schuster as National Sales Manager, then became publisher of Tempo Books. He was Publisher and General Manager of the Ace and Tempo divisions of Grossett & Dunlap before founding his own company, Tom Doherty Associates, LLC (publishers of Tor/Forge Books) in 1980.

Tor became a subsidiary of St. Martin's Press in 1987; both are now subsidiaries of Holtzbrinck Publishers. Tom Doherty continues as President and Publisher of Tom Doherty Associates, LLC, publishing under the Tor, Forge, Orb, Starscape and Aerie imprints. Many authors of the Tor and Forge lines have won honors as diverse as the World Fantasy, Hugo, Nebula, Edgar, Spur, Tiptree, Stoker and Western Heritage awards.

In 1993 Tom Doherty was the recipient of the Skylark, awarded by the New England Science Fiction Association for outstanding contributions to the field of science fiction.

For the last twenty-seven consecutive years, the *Locus*

poll, the largest reader survey in fantasy and science fiction, has voted Tor "Best Publisher" in these categories. Tom received a "Lifetime Achievement Award" at the 2005 World Fantasy Convention. In 2006, Tom received the Raymond Z. Gallun Award for outstanding contribution to the genre of science fiction. He received the 2007 Silver Bullet Award from the International Thriller Writers. Also in 2007, Tom received the Lauriet Award from the Western Writers of America for contribution to literacy; he was honored with a proclamation from Charles B. Rangel, the Chairman of the Committee on Ways and Means of the House of Representatives of the United States Congress, for outstanding leadership to enhance and provide literacy programs throughout the nation.

The Crate Warrior, the Doppelgänger, and the Idea Woman

Mur Lafferty

Steven had a sick pallor to his face at lunch as he trudged into the small backstage area we called the break room. There was a card table and if the room was full, well tough for you, go find somewhere else to eat your Subway. But if we weren't filming, Steven and I usually ate early, around 11 A.M., before anyone else could get in there.

Steven was tall, with super-pale skin that spoke of either Norse heritage, computer programming heritage, or windowless soundstage heritage. And we didn't talk about it much, but I'm pretty sure he was a mixture of one and three. His shock of blond hair was always messy, not in that adorable, just-woken-up way, but in a real-woken-up way, like half of it flat as if he'd slept on it, with the other half sporting a cowlick that spiraled out of his head as if Athena was trying to work her way out with a corkscrew.

I'd heard the word "lugubrious" used to describe two things before: a blobfish she had seen on a nature program, looking like it was sculpted from Play-Doh by an abandoned child, and a lumpy, sad (and ultimately murderous) man from a science fiction book by Douglas Adams. I loved the word, and it was what I always thought when I saw Steven. He doesn't know this, of course.

My sister once asked me, if I saw him in such a poor light, why did I hang out with him? Two reasons: we were both addicted to *Red Dragon Skies*, the hit online RPG, and he saved my life once. I don't feel I owe him friendship, but I definitely owe him not being an asshole. And so long as we talk about the game, the conversation can be spirited. Besides, he's a lot more fun (and outgoing) online.

His considerable frame collapsed into the folding chair. He looked at me from beneath too-long bangs. "Cassandra."

Uh-oh. He almost never called me by my full name. Had I done something to piss him off? I wracked my brain but came up with nothing. "What's up, Steven? Where's your lunch?"

"I didn't get anything. I just got done stacking the latest prop shipment backstage." He shocked me by beginning to cry.

I was at a loss for words. Steven and I weren't the touchy-feely type of friends, but I awkwardly patted his forearm. "Hey, what's going on, man?"

"I'm going to cause a multi-planar war," he sobbed, covering his face with his hands.

My spine went cold. "What did you do? Did you offend the director? Did you mispronounce her name?"

"Worse. So much worse," he said. "Her fiancé arrived today," he said, sniffling, still covering his face. It sounded as if we had a bad phone connection. "He must have gotten lost, and was wandering around backstage. It was dark, I was stacking boxes, and I didn't see him. I put down my last box, and—"

Panic made my head reel. "You killed the guest director's fiancé. With a box."

He wailed into his hands.

When we learned that fairies do exist, discovered by three scientists and their daughters who were walking through a field one day—I know, sounds like a joke, huh?—the world went crazy with excitement. Theirs did too, as I understand it. In the past six months, we have learned so much about the beings that live, as they call it, "just one plane over."

Fairies are a lot like us, only smaller, and with wings. We haven't seen them fly, but that doesn't mean they can't. I think they don't want us to get jealous. Steven thinks they only fly when they attack. Whatever, Steven.

Like some of our cultures in this world, fairies often marry for familial linkage, and sometimes to people they don't know. Which accounts for this poor sap wandering around backstage instead of being with his fiancé.

Fairies can live for thousands of years, and breed only rarely.

And fairies, like us, make movies.

When we discovered this, cultural anthropologists shit themselves, wanting to know how such media technology evolved alongside our own. Film students began studying every piece of fairy film they could get their hands on. And Hollywood, of course, wanted to know how to monetize it. My studio (ok, the studio I work for as a tiny food prop designer) was the first to successfully recruit one of the biggest fairy directors (or at least, as we understand it. They could have sent us the equivalent of a kid with a video camera for all we know) to direct a human film.

We couldn't pronounce her name, and she was horribly offended whenever we tried, so we called her "Ma'am" to her face and "HRH" for "Her Royal Highness" behind her back. The timing of everything was awkward, as she was expecting the arrival of her third husband-to-be amid all of the chaos. We were to treat him with the same respect as we treated her.

Steven apparently didn't get that memo, and decided to drop a box on the poor bastard.

I left Steven in the break room and went to where Steven had stacked the new prop shipment. All I saw was a green wing coming from underneath the box. It didn't quiver. It reminded me of the Wicked Witch of the East, and I shuddered.

I went back to the break room and closed the door behind me. "Yeah, that's one dead fairy. How could you not have seen him? They almost never shut up!"

"I was distracted, OK?" he said, dropping his hands. His pale face had bloomed two bright red blotches on his wet cheeks. "My grandma died last night." He plucked at his arm, which I just noticed had a black bandana wrapped around it.

"Is that a mourning armband?" I asked, eyes growing wide. "Is it suddenly 1944? What is wrong with you? People are going to think that's a tourniquet or something. People are more likely to assume you're a drug user instead of in mourning."

He wiped his nose with the heel of his hand. I considered yanking his black "armband" off and handing it to him, but then thought that might cross a weird line. I tossed him the napkin from my Subway bag. "We're getting off-topic. I'm sorry, I didn't know about your grandmother. But yeah, we have to deal with this now."

"How?" he asked, staring at the table. "The best case is I'll get fired. The worst is I'll get tried for murder in fairyland."

"Don't forget the multi-planar war," I reminded. I wondered if the government had a plan for attacking fairyland, and then realized they probably had plans for invading Canada somewhere; they certainly figured out a way to fight fairies about ten minutes after the news of the weird little people hit the cable networks.

I thought hard about what I knew about fairy culture. Murder was serious—there wasn't the same kind of trial as we have in this world, considering you would have killed someone maybe a thousand years old—

I groaned as a memory popped into my head. In the excitement, I had forgotten about who exactly this squashed fiancé was. He wasn't just a young bohunk to add to our director's stable of fairy man flesh, he was a prominent historian. Like one of the oldest fairies alive. The pairing was a huge political move, the antiquated hermit wedding a prominent mover in media and human diplomacy—he would learn about human history to add to his huge brain, and she could get plot ideas from him for movies. We were even going to film their meeting tonight at dinner.

I smacked the table, and Steven jumped. "Got it. Come on," I said.

We paused on the way out to remove the squashed fairy from under the crate. When I was a child, I had that cute squashed fairy book (since removed from the shelves for diplomatic reasons, as the author is considered a mass-murderer and snuff-film maker in fairyland). I can tell you that the mess underneath the crate was nothing like those pictures of mashed fairies. A lot more red glitter that I assumed was blood, and a lot less flesh. It wasn't gory, but it was definitely messy. I reached under and picked his green breeches and tunic—breeches and tunic, never thought I'd say those words outside the SCA as an adult—from the glittery mess and shook it out. Steven fetched a broom and we swept up the glitter and wing fragments and tossed them into the dumpster outside.

"This feels really wrong," he said, brushing glitter from his hands and wincing.

"You should have thought of that before you squashed the poor bastard," I said. "Let's go."

In the car I told him my plan. "See, they don't know each other, HRH has never met her fiancé. If we can find another fairy to take his place, we should be fine."

Steven stared at me so long I took my eyes off the road and glanced over. "What?"

"You're insane," he said. "You don't think she would

have researched him? You don't think she knows what he looks like?"

"Well, actually, no. He hasn't been in the public eye. I remember HRH saying the other day that she hoped he would be handsome. For all the cameras that are constantly around her, he's the opposite. We could present anyone to her and she would have to take us at face value."

"He's a brilliant historian," Steven said weakly, carried helplessly along with my scheme as he was. "He lived through, what, six wars, two of them civil wars? He can recite more 'begats' than the Bible has listed. In fact, HRH was telling me it was sad we needed the Bible, because she had a new husband that could keep all that and more in his head. This will not work, Cass."

I jammed on the brakes, causing our belts to lock up and my old Honda to shimmy down the road a bit and then groan to a stop on the side of the road. "Fine. The way I see it, our other options are turn yourself in, or run. Which one of those two would you like to do? If it's the second, I have to get gas."

He didn't answer me, but looked away, out the window at the gray day.

"All right, then," I said, and pulled into the parking lot we had screeched to a halt in front of.

"What's here?" he asked sullenly.

"Bar," I said.

"It's eleven thirty," he protested.

"It has a lot of third-shift patrons," I explained. "They need a drink in the mornings just like I am going to need one tonight."

We stepped inside, pausing to let our eyes adjust to

the dim light. A couple of hunched bodies sat at the bar, and a perky white couple sat uncomfortably in a booth. Tourists who picked the wrong lunch joint, I figured.

I spotted what I needed: the pool table.

Fairies loved movies, popcorn, and pool. They had a lot of sacred things, putting most of our world religions to shame, and it was hard to keep up with them all. Most pool halls had accepted the traveling fairies, and the seedier joints ended up attracting the seedier fairies. It was not official, but we all knew that more and more often the governments of the fae were exiling their undesirables here. You could call the whole human world Australia for the fairies. I wondered if that made us the native population, and squirmed under that line of thinking. One problem at a time.

"OK, so we need male, and probably green," I said, looking over the fairies. The problem with fairies was that even the least desirable of them were a hundred times more beautiful than any human you could find. Even Cillian Murphy, who I am still convinced is half-fae, but he won't admit it to the frequent queries by entertainment reporters.

The exiles of the fairy world flitted lightly around the pool table, sinking ball after ball. I had no idea why they liked it so much, considering I had never seen a fairy who was bad at pool. It was like me trying to do my niece's wooden dinosaur puzzle. Sure, dinosaurs are fun, but it got old fast. These pool sharks consisted of two female fairies and three male. Two of the male fairies had greenish coloring, with green wings, hair, and bright kelly green eyes that romance authors always liked to claim were pretty, but turned out to be pretty freaky when you saw them in real life.

The other three had blue, red, and a pinkish tint to their coloring, and all five of them perked up and watched, interested, as we approached. For most big cities, the novelty of fairies had worn off, and they didn't get so many interested humans watching them anymore. As long as they paid their bills and didn't bother anyone, they could stick around. But no bar fights. You didn't want to get into a bar fight with a fairy.

When they noticed us, I gave Steven a shove to his lower back. He looked at me, annoyed. "What? This is your idea, you talk to them!"

"But you're the one who killed the guy."

"I don't even know half your plan!"

I sighed audibly and stepped forward. "Greetings, friends," I said, using the typical greeting one used with fairies in a bar, or at least, what I hoped was typical. "We are working on a local movie and find ourselves in need of—" I paused, as inspiration hit me. "—a fairy to fill a role. One of you two green friends would be a good fit. Care to come talk to us?"

"Are you going to ask them why they're exiled?" Steven whispered to me as the fairies conferred among themselves, looking over their shoulders at us, and then back to the group.

"I wasn't planning on it," I said. My palms were sweaty.

"What if we get a murderer?" he asked.

"Steven, you're a murderer," I reminded him. "We can't be choosy."

He recoiled like I had slapped him, but I didn't take it back. I'd stick by him, I owed him that much, but I wouldn't sugarcoat why we were here.

The darker green fairy stepped forward. "What do you have in mind?" he asked, his voice light and golden, if a voice can be defined as golden.

"Steven, get us some drinks," I said, and motioned for the fairy to follow me to a booth.

By the time we were done telling the story, the fairy, who allowed us to call him Yuri, was frowning and staring at Steven, who squirmed under his gaze.

"I don't think you know what you're asking," he said, his voice downgrading from glorious gold into flat yellow.

"We know it's a big deal," I began, but he held up a long-fingered hand.

"Big deal doesn't describe it. You killed one of the greatest historians of our people. Even if I were to successfully pretend to be this woman's husband, there is no way I could replicate this fairy's knowledge. You can't just grab some fairy off the street and expect him to pretend to be a famous historian and husband for the next few decades." Yuri took a sip of his Zima (which had come back into popularity as soon as fairies showed a preference for it) and shook his head. "Do you even know who I am?"

I shook my head, as much as I would do to admit this was a horrendous idea, then took a sip of my beer. I glanced at Steven, who looked even more sickly under the pale lights of the bar. "Listen," I said, leaning forward, "I know you're an exile, yeah? That's why you hang out here.

They kicked you out of fairyland for whatever reason, we're not going to ask why, cause clearly we're not the best representatives of our race, either, but you're here and you can't go back, right?"

His face was stony. "And your point is?"

"If we pull this off, and you pretend to be this historian and marry the director, you get back into society. Not just your world, but married to a rich and powerful director! You'd be her third husband, and I'm not exactly sure what that means, but at least you wouldn't be carrying the husband duties by yourself. People would be impressed with you, invite you to places. Unlimited Zima!" I was getting desperate here, and he could tell.

He tented his fingers and regarded me. "You. You didn't kill this fairy. Your pheromones do not show any desire towards this human," he gestured to Steven, who looked offended, even though my opinion of him was never a secret. "Yet you are dedicated, determined, to help him. I want to know why."

It wasn't a story I liked to tell. I didn't like admitting weakness and Steven didn't like reliving the experience. But we were asking a lot from this fairy, and we had gone this far. "Steven saved my life once. We don't have a ton in common, but I owe him more than I can say. I'm by his side until he doesn't need me anymore."

"A life debt. I didn't know humans did that," Yuri said, regarding Steven again. "Do you know what happens if we are caught?"

I shrugged. "I'm hazy on the details, but Steven will go to fairyland for trial, or whatever you guys call a trial over there. As I'm actively trying to help him cover it up,

I expect I'll go with him. With you, is there something worse than exile? Will you come back here?"

"There is something worse than exile," Yuri said. "You people might call it a heavy box."

I winced. I didn't know they did executions. I thought about suggesting to Steven that he could get a job as a fairy executioner, but didn't think he would find it funny.

"What else can we do to convince you?" I asked. "We can't really ask around. We don't need every bar-hopping fairy exile to know that the director's historian husband is a fraud. You're our only hope."

He broke into a grin and pointed at me. "*Star Wars!* I've seen it. Wonderful film, but they should have listened to the wookie more."

I let that odd comment slide. "Well? Do you think you can pull off faking a historian? And would you want to?"

"I need something from both of you. I need to know you are willing to pay the price for something this big." He pointed at Steven's armband. "You, give me a secret from the person you mourn."

Fairies had different views of legal tender than we did. They loved to take things from human minds and souls, but only if offered freely. Some poor fools wanted to prove fairy tales wrong and had given fairies their names. The idiots were now living in fairyland with no sense of who they were, but as I understood it, were very well taken care of. High price to pay, though.

"How did you know he was in mourning?" I asked, distracted by Steven's armband again.

Yuri glanced at me, still pointing at Steven. "I have

studied human culture extensively. I know the mourning black sashes. You don't see them much anymore."

I gave a pointed look at Steven, but he didn't look at me. He stared at the table and traced a dirty word carved into the tabletop. "Gran was poor. She didn't have much."

"Love and memories require no money to create," Yuri said. "What secrets did she leave you?"

"Come on, Steven, did she tell you where something was buried, or tell you about a bastard cousin, or an aunt raised to be an uncle, or anything?" I prodded.

He shook his head, tears rising in his eyes.

"You are such a liar," I said. "We need that secret if we're going to get out of this."

"She only left me some recipes," he whispered. "I don't know what else to say."

"That," Yuri said, leaning forward hungrily. "The recipes. That's what I want."

"Really?" I asked. "Recipes?"

"They are his most precious memories," Yuri said, his voice low. "That is all I need. I can almost smell them, they involved . . . eggs?"

Steven nodded. "Deviled eggs. You . . ." He was obviously searching for the correct words.

"'You may have it with my blessing,'" I prompted.

He nodded and repeated my phrase, closing his eyes and letting the tears fall. Yuri did something odd with his hands in front of Steven's face, and my friend relaxed.

"Did you kill him?" I asked as he slumped against me.

"No, it is a trying process," Yuri said. "Now you."

"What do you want?" I asked.

"I want the story of how he saved your life."

❖ ❖ ❖

Saying Steven had saved me implied some active purpose on his part. He hadn't lifted a car off of me, or shot a mugger in the back. Steven had just been Steven, that bumbling, awkward guy, in the absolute right place at the right time.

It was before I had gotten a job at the studio and was washing dishes at a coffee house. A struggling indie one, not one of the ones named after Battlestar Galactica characters or large antlered animals. It was midnight and I was taking the trash out to the back alley, which we shared with a bar next door. I had taken the trash down the five cement steps—no railing, which was a work hazard our boss didn't care at all about—to the street level when I heard her.

"Hand over your phone," she said.

I turned, and saw the gun. The girl was in a black hoodie, her face concealed by the shadows. "You're really holding me at gunpoint for a secondhand phone?"

She brandished the gun, and I saw her hand was shaking. Still, deadly projectile was deadly shot from frightened hands. I reached into my pocket slowly, and the panicked mugger shouted at me to hold still.

"How will I get the phone out then?" I asked her slowly.

"Just give me your money and your phone and any jewelry!" she said, voice breaking. This chick was going to either shoot me or turn and run any second.

I thought about explaining to her that I was just getting out of a hipster phase and the only jewelry I wore was a My Little Pony pendant I had bought at Hot Topic, *but figured she didn't want to go into the issues of fashion. I tried to move slowly to get the items from my pocket, but the door opened then. Steven, who was bussing tables that night, had heard the shouts and come to check on me. He flinched when he saw the woman with the gun, and took a step forward to where I had dropped the trash bags on the steps. He tumbled down, pin-wheeling his arms and smacking the gun out of the woman's hand. It fired once, and I felt a searing heat along my arm as the bullet grazed me. Steven fell on top of her, breaking her ankle and spraining his wrist.*

The paramedics were delighted to have so many different injuries to deal with on a slow night, and we got patched up. The woman went to jail, and Steven was a hero, and I got a good scar.

I opened my eyes. Steven and I were in a booth in a bar, leaning on each other.

"What happened?" he said, lifting his head off my shoulder.

I looked around. I remembered fairies, and making a deal. I shook my head, as if expecting my brains to rattle around audibly. I felt gaps, but I couldn't remember why.

"There was a fairy. It took something from us," I said.

"How?" he asked. "They're not supposed to be allowed . . ."

"I know that, we must have said it was OK." I rubbed my face, and the details started trickling back to me. "Oh god. We found a replacement for the fairy you killed. Only he took stuff from us and took off."

"We just got rolled by a fairy?" he asked, sliding out of the booth.

I followed him. "This is not going to help my reputation."

"What now?" he asked.

"Go back to the studio, hope they haven't discovered the body yet, and if they have, hope it won't be tied to us, I guess. Or go on the lam," I said.

Do you remember what he took from you? I didn't ask. I knew he wouldn't.

We drove back in silence, Steven quivering in his seat, me thinking hard. Since we had struck out, and a fairy now knew of our crime, we had to face facts and pay the piper. I don't know if Steven had the same thought, but he so rarely had his own thoughts it was hard to attribute any to him.

When we walked into the studio, Marcellus accosted us at the door. He was a tall thin African-American man with deep black skin and an eye for continuity. He was a grip now, but they were girding him for an editor position considering he was so good at keeping things like facial wounds consistent over months of shooting.

"Where the hell have you two been? The director wants some sort of impromptu wedding, and demands that everyone be there!"

I glanced at Steven, my stomach dropping somewhere around my knees. "Impromptu wedding?"

He waved his hand irritably. "It's a fairy thing as I understand it. Her fiancé showed up. She liked him. She wants to marry him right away and start making little fairy babies or something. I just hope she does so after the film is done."

THE CRATE WARRIOR, THE DOPPELGÄNGER, AND THE IDEA WOMAN 101

"Really? What's he like?" I asked, willing my voice not to shake.

Marcellus frowned again, and held his hand around waist height. "This tall. Green. What else is there to know?" He turned and motioned for us to follow.

Steven relaxed a hair, and we walked to the sound stage where craft services had set up their tables to mimic a banquet. The whole cast and crew were seated around the table at whatever chairs they could find—including the throne from the movie we were shooting—with HRH at the head of the table, and Yuri beside her.

He wore the clothes of the dead fairy—had I given him those duds?—and gazed adoringly at his new wife. His eyes didn't even flicker our way as we pulled stools up to the opposite end of the table.

HRH, a tall fairy with red-tinged wings and flaming red hair, stood to address us. "My cast and crew, we may not be of the same race, but we share the same love of film. This unites our troubled peoples, and I am pleased to be here with you to celebrate the marriage with _____" here she made a sound that was apparently fairy language for Yuri's name, and we had better remember not to call him Yuri from now on, "my third husband. A celebrated historian, he now gets to live one of the most momentous weddings in history. Will you be writing this down, my darling?"

Yuri looked up to the woman he had known for twenty minutes and nodded, "Of course, my pet." He carried himself taller, now, and his voice was richer. He was green tinged and handsome and I thought we might actually get away with this. "May I address our audience?"

HRH looked surprised, apparently the groom didn't give speeches in fairyland. But she sat down and gestured for him to rise.

"Humans, I am honored to be among you and celebrating my marriage in such a glorious setting," he said, extending his arms to encompass our dark and cluttered sound stage. "This reminds me of a similar wedding I attended recently. But the story starts much earlier. Humans and fairies had not made formal contact then, of course, but some of you had seen us, and some of us had been caught or worse by you. This caused great stress between our people, at least from the fairy point of view. A young fairy once had his father caught between the pages of a book, and he vowed revenge on the human race. He dedicated himself to the martial arts and the fine arts of assassination, and began targeting humans."

He paused here for a sip of water, a smile teasing his green lips.

"Before he could kill his first, though, he was discovered and thrown into jail, and the key was thrown away. Literally. Fairies can live for a long time without food or water, but it can cause madness. Then Prince _____ and Princess _____ married, uniting two warring fairy kingdoms, and one of the provisions of the agreement was to release the prisoners who had committed crimes now forgotten. Fearing such confinement-induced-madness could harm fairy society, the criminals were exiled to the human world. When it comes to fighting humans, however, one fairy doesn't stand a chance. He must have a position of power before he could actually do any harm, so the exiles put no humans in harm's way. Resentful of his own people for jailing him, and still holding a grudge against the humans, our criminal tolerated his exile, and waited."

The table was silent. The humans looked at each other uncomfortably, while HRH looked plain annoyed. I swallowed past the sand that seemed to suddenly coat my throat.

"And?" HRH finally said, looking up at him. "How does our wedding compare with that one exactly?"

Yuri shook his head and smiled at her. "I'm sorry, dear, I have so many stories in my head sometimes I go on a tangent or seven. I'm sure I had a point when I started." He raised his glass and stated, "A toast to my lovely, powerful wife. May we have a very productive marriage!"

Everyone but me and Steven toasted the happy couple. Steven's hands clenched on his knees.

"Steven," I whispered out of the corner of my mouth.

"Cass?" he replied.

"We're going to need some more crates."

Mur Lafferty is the author of *The Shambling Guide to New York City* and *Ghost Train to New Orleans* (Orbit). She lives in Durham, North Carolina, where she podcasts her writing angst, plays video games, and pets her dogs. She is the winner of the John W. Campbell Award for Best New Writer and the Manly Wade Wellman Award. Although she acts tough, in private she collects LEGO figures of Unikitty.

At my request, she offered this afterword.

Lots of things about meeting Dave can make an impression on someone. His unflinching honesty, his welcoming nature, his loyalty to his friends, his living his life his own way. He's been generous to me and my family, inviting us to yearly parties, giving me one of my first interviews for my podcast, and blurbing my first book (which contained a complaint that his latest book was late to Tor because he was busy reading mine).

It's hard choosing one thing to pinpoint as the start of a Drake-inspired story.

Getting invited to a Drake party is a thrill, as it almost definitely means you get a tour of his amazing house with the dumbwaiter and secret door. My house has bookshelves stocked with books, and more books in stacks in other places, the car, under the couch, everywhere, but Dave has a dedicated library. And he'll let you wander in it and gawk at his book collection.

Strangely, and perhaps embarrassingly, Dave was the person who introduced me to history from the point of view from primary records: the point of view from someone who lived through historical events, instead of reading a historian's take on past events. Dave prefers these records, and nearly all of his historical accounts are eyewitness accounts. His interest in history and adherence to primary records stayed with me for some reason, and I wanted to write a story about a historian, and the grifter who takes his place.

Dave has never failed to be kind, welcoming, or available to me if I needed something from him, and it was an honor to be invited to this anthology.

Working with Dave, or, Inmates in Bellevue

S.M. Stirling

Dave Drake and I have known each other for decades now—dear God, it really is decades!

We've sometimes been lumped together as "military SF" writers, though both of us have grazed extensively in the varied paddocks of the science fiction and fantasy estate. It would be more accurate to call us *historically oriented* writers; human history is very colorful. More often than not the color is blood-red, war is the motor of history, and conflict makes a story. I started out intending a career in history and still love to study it, though closer acquaintance with academia made the life of a freelance writer look secure and welcoming by contrast. Dave approached the past through their languages and literatures, as a classicist.

Oddly enough, I can say I know and have collaborated

with two SF authors who have translated ancient literature, Dave Drake with Latin and Harry Turtledove with the Byzantine variety of Greek. As for myself . . . well, I can read a newspaper in French if it isn't too complex; I tried to do Proust in the original, and the result was not happy. My mother grew up speaking Spanish in Peru and told me she dreamed in it all her life, but alas she and my aunt used it as a secret code when they didn't want their children to understand them.

Dave and I both attended law school, an experience from which I benefited not at all save in the Nietzschean sense that all that does not kill you makes you stronger, and Dave, as I understand it, very little. Dave has said that he found driving a bus more satisfying than practicing law. My own take is that I would rather juggle live squid in a laundromat.

The project we worked together most closely on was *The General* for Baen Books, a series which amounted to a science fictional retelling of the life of the great Byzantine (or as he would have put it, Roman) general who conquered (or as he would have put it, reclaimed) much of the Mediterranean Basin for the Empire in the sixth century A.D. Only we had a better ending. It's fun to be God.

Belisarius fought in the service of his ruler, the equally great, if much less personally agreeable, Emperor Justinian—the patron whose servants produced the Hagia Sophia and the Justinian Code of laws.

Jim Baen was always an enthusiast for Belisarius, probably because he was held up as an exemplar of the flexible, ingenious strategist by Liddel Hart, the British military reformer and writer of the period between the World Wars. Jim also had a practice of pairing established and newer authors as collaborators; this often had very fruitful results, both in terms of the writing it produced and giving the junior author, which I very much was at the time, a valuable tutorial in the craft while earning a living, or at least "not starving."

At that point my main work had been an alternate history series featuring a lot of military conflict—alternate history's origins are partly an outgrowth of war-gaming and its emphasis on how historical conflicts might have turned out differently, and the consequences of that, as summed up in the old ditty:

> "For want of a nail the shoe was lost;
> For want of a shoe, the horse was lost;
> For want of a horse, the message was lost;
> For want of the message, the battle was lost;
> For want of the battle, the kingdom was lost;
> And all for the want of a horse-shoe nail."

The General gave me the opportunity to do a space-opera/planetary romance series together with a writer whose work I had read and admired for years, and I accepted eagerly.

At this point a brief (but hopefully interesting) historical digression is necessary.

Belisarius' life certainly provided an interesting template for fiction, since he operated during the wild-and-wooly transition between Classical Antiquity and the early Middle Ages. This period is often called the *Volkerwanderung*—the Migration Era, the period between the collapse of the western portion of the Roman

Empire and the emergence of the early stages of the familiar states of Europe and the first conquests of Islam in the Middle East and North Africa, and their aborted drive into Europe.

When the *limes*, the fortified frontier zones of the Roman Empire along the Rhine and Danube, collapsed in the early 400s, warrior peoples from beyond flooded into the temptingly rich and demilitarized provinces beyond, rather like hungry diners cracking the claw of a lobster to gorge upon the sweet flesh within. Most of the invaders were Germanic speakers; at that time those closely related languages predominated all the way from the North Sea to the Ukraine, including many areas that later became Slavic or Magyar-speaking.

Behind the Germanics, pushing them on and following them into the former Imperial territories, were nomadic steppe peoples from Central Asia, like the Huns of Attila fame (much like the later Avars, Bulgars, Pechenegs, Magyars, and Mongols). The Hunnic impact started a remarkable series of chain migrations, with groups picking up and moving and bouncing into each other like billiard balls all across the continent and beyond.

When the Huns arrived, migrating from Poland to Tunisia started to look good—which is precisely what the East Germanic tribe of the Vandals did, bouncing down as far as the southern Balkans before going north again, crossing the whole of Central Europe, crossing the Rhine, invading Gaul, then invading Spain, dragging along an Iranian-speaking group known as the Alans they'd picked up in the Danube Basin, and eventually moving into North Africa . . . of which more later!

In the Roman world, war had long been a matter for paid specialists, and the provincials were largely defenseless against groups among whom every free man was a warrior; there was very little between them and the drawn butter and waiting teeth.

Some of the "barbarian" invaders were relatively civilized, with monarchic political structures, a small literate class, and cultures already heavily influenced by Rome; many were already Christians, for example, though mostly of heretical varieties. The Goths and Burgundians came into this category.

Though the veneer of civilization could be rather thin—several generations after they invaded and settled in Italy, a group of the supposedly Christian Lombards slaughtered some Italian peasants who refused to take part in a feast on the meat of horses they'd just sacrificed to the old Gods. What made it into the chronicles, usually written by Churchmen, wasn't necessarily in full accord with the facts on the ground!

Other invaders were outright savages from the remoter parts of Europe, still collecting heads and practicing human sacrifice, folk to whom written words were baleful magic, and cities incomprehensible. They tended to smash things up rather than take them over.

Saxon pirates were raiding as far south as Spain from the third century on; by "Saxon" Romans more or less meant "German in a boat," and the raiders included elements from all over the northern Germanic world from the Rhine-mouth to Sweden. The whole phenomenon was strikingly reminiscent of the later, and better-known, Viking episode.

The Irish, at this time poetically inclined head-hunters who considered murder and theft the highest expression of human excellence and wrote epics about stealing the neighbor's cow, were doing a fair bit of raiding themselves. Being even more backward than the Saxons they did it in skin coracles rather than wooden rowboats, but that didn't stop them from getting as far as Gaul.

When the last Roman troops were withdrawn from Britannia, the Irish (known as the Scotii at the time) started settling in western Britain, especially the part later known as Scotland, after their tribal ethnonym. The Saxons, and their Anglian and Jutish kin did the same on the other side of the island, hence *England* and the language in which this essay was composed.

Meanwhile, East Rome—what we came to call the Byzantine Empire—was also feeling its oats and coming off the back foot.

Based on the richer and more anciently civilized lands of the Hellenistic world, and including what's now Turkey, Syria, Lebanon, Israel, Jordan, and Egypt, in the early 500s A.D. it had a series of strong Emperors who reformed the administration and the army; it had never been as dependent on barbarian mercenaries as the Western Empire, though the Balkans were repeatedly devastated by Goths, Huns, and similar "undesirables." Then in 527 A.D., Justinian the Great became sole emperor, with a battle-tried army, a full treasury, able generals and limitless ambitions. He was the last emperor to speak Latin as his mother tongue, and nobody had told him that the Dark Ages were about to set in, or that plague and Persian invasions were coming. He set out to reconquer the lost provinces of the West, and gave it the old college try.

Dave is a classicist and has been for a long time. I doubt there were many people in Vietnam in '69 stuffing shells into a 90mm in a tank *and* reading Horace in the original. He not only reads ancient literature, he's deeply familiar with the history—in particular, with the history as the people of the time saw it and saw their own ancestors and recorded in their chronicles. Naturally he'd read Procopius of Caesarea, the publically sycophantic and privately scathing (he thought Justinian was possessed by demons) historian of Justinian's reign and Belisarius' campaigns.

So we had the perfect template for a rousing adventure story: pirates, barbarian invaders, ambitious Emperors, bloody chaos everywhere. It would suck megalithically to have to *live* there, but that's another matter.

But the most flavorful setting for a story is useless without gripping characters.

Dave did the basic work of building the setting. He picked a scenario that's been a fertile one for many SF writers: a far future in which humans have settled many planets, founded a Galactic Empire (Federation, to be technical), and then fallen apart in civil wars and regressed technologically and socially. Assuming that faster-than-light travel ever becomes possible, it's depressingly plausible.

The planet Bellevue—a real madhouse—has recovered a little from the collapse of the old culture over a thousand years before. What civilization there is lingers around a vast inland sea, and the great river valleys to the east of it. The eastern sector, the Colony, is descended from immigrants from the Muslim world, mostly Sunni Arabs with a sprinkling of others and Swahili-speaking East Africans further to the south. The great middle oceanic basin was colonized by settlers from Latin America, who speak languages—Spanjol and Sponglish—derived from Spanish. To the northwest is the Base Area, where the Federation's military forces were centered; the ones on Bellevue happened to be mostly speakers of English, or as it came to be called, Old Namerique. After the collapse they came roaring down to conquer areas around the sea, each wave more backward and barbaric than the last, until only the heartland around the East Residence was left, where the Gubernio Civil (Civil Government) rules.

Enter Raj Ammanda da Luis Whitehall, from a noble but not wealthy background in backward, remote Descott County—the Appalachia of the Civil Government—whose prime export is fighting men. Not entirely by coincidence, the current governor, Barholm Clerett, comes from a Descotter family, though in his case it was his uncle who shot his way onto the Governor's Chair.

As an aside, this is an important part of the series' dynamic: the Gubernio Civil, like the Roman and East Roman/Byzantine Empires, has a monarchic form of government without much sense of dynastic legitimacy. Medieval European states *did* have a strong dynastic sense; even when there was a civil war, it was usually about controlling the monarch, not replacing him. That only happened when there was no clear legitimate heir, or a dynasty died out; nobody would obey you if you simply tried to seize the throne because you wanted it. But Rome started out as a Republic, and long remembered it. "Imperator," the term from which our "Emperor" derives, originally simply meant "worthy to command Romans," a title bestowed in the field by acclamation; "imperium" meant more or less "power" or "authority." The alternative term for imperial ruler, "Kaiser" or "Tsar" derives of course from Julius Caesar's name.

The first emperor, Augustus Caesar (formerly Octavian), was always careful to maintain the *forms* of the Republican government, even as he abolished the substance. His uncle Julius had been much less careful about that . . . which, together with his habit of sparing enemies and of going about without a bodyguard of barbarian mercenaries, was a major reason he ended up lying on the Senate steps bleeding to death from fifty-four stab wounds.

But in essence being emperor meant having the support of most of the army; the first sole rulers of Rome had simply been successful warlords in the civil conflicts which ended the Republican era. Being the previous emperor's son only mattered if the soldiers cared about it, which they sometimes did . . . and often didn't.

A monarchy where anyone with the necessary military force can seize the crown is indeed one where the head bearing said crown rests uneasy. Incompetent generals may ruin the state the monarch (the Governor, in Bellevue's case) rules; competent ones may overthrow and kill him.

Raj Whitehall is utterly loyal and has no desire to sit in the Governor's Chair . . . but his governor never quite believes that. From that, much of the plot derives. He's starved of troops and supplies as Governor Barholm sends him out to reconquer the barbarian military governments, but he succeeds anyway. Which makes his troops (and the army in general) respect and admire him . . . which makes the governor *even more* paranoid.

(The Caliphate on which the Muslim-dominated Colony is based had exactly the same problem and for very much the same reason: it was originally an elective office, not a hereditary monarchy. It became one by *coup d'état*, but the memory of the original arrangement never died.)

This gave us the central tension of the series: Raj loses by winning. Of course, if he loses, he *certainly* loses, and almost certainly dies. Heads I win . . .

In the case of Bellevue, more is at stake than pleasing the Governor or restoring the Gubernio Civil to a dominant position. This *is* science fiction, after all! Because under the Governor's Palace in East Residence are immense catacombs dating back to before the fall of the interstellar Federation, and among the ruins is a perfectly functional computer—a Sector Command model, waiting for the time and the man to restore civilization on Bellevue. Raj is the man . . . and to complicate matters, the Gubernio Civil has a religion which worships the memory of computers. This is known in the trade as a "Crystal Dragon Jesus" religion.

I won't go into the details of Raj's adventures—those who wish to find out can go read the series, now available in omnibus format and ebook. What may be interesting is the general method we used to write the series.

Writers differ in their methods. I generally don't do

detailed outlines; in fact, unless an editor (or collaborator) requires one, I generally don't write outlines at all. This might be called the *waaaaaah-splooosh!* school. You have a general idea of where you want to go, and then jump in and swim.

The upside of this is that it's less work. The downside is wasted effort—writing yourself into corners, ending up with meanders that have to be cut, and so forth.

Dave is a much more tightly organized writer than I am. He does *detailed* outlines. The books in the General series averaged about 150,000 to 200,000 words. Dave, as the senior author, did outlines that ran to 40,000 words each.

A forty-thousand-word outline is itself the length of a novella or short novel. Dave's outline covered *every scene* in the books. By way of comparison, back when I did a lot of collaborations, I sometimes received outlines of paragraph length for whole books. But not from Dave!

You might think that this was cramping or confining. On the contrary! I found it oddly liberating. The structure of the book, the bones, was right there. I could concentrate on the fun parts: thinking up cool features, and doing the little bits of business that flesh out characters and the incidents that make a scene vivid.

For example, the military technology of the more advanced parts of Bellevue is roughly equivalent to our 1870s or 1880s. The Civil Government's troops use a single-shot breechloader, and the Colony a repeating carbine with a tube magazine. Dave told me later that he had the trap-door Springfield and the Henry rifle in mind. Having grown up on tales of British derring-do (three of

my four grandparents were English, and my father
Canadian) I used the Martini-Henry rifle that Kipling
immortalized instead:

"When she kicks like a mule and throws wide
    in the ditch;
Don't call your Martini a cross-eyed old bitch.
Remember she's a lady, and treat her as sich
And she'll fight for the young British soldier!"

With the Winchester of Western fame for the Colonial
weapon.

This is more than a technical detail for military-history
nerds; it determines a lot of the action. Both weapons fire
at about the same rate in the long run, but as the man put
it in the long run we're all dead. The Martini fires a heavy,
powerful bullet to a considerable range, at a steady rate
of bang . . . bang . . . bang . . . as the lever is worked to
eject a round and another is thumbed into the breech.
The Winchester, the classic cowboy-frontiersman weapon
of the post-Civil War era, has a magazine—but every
round has to be thumbed into it. Hence it can fire rapidly
for a few moments: *bang-bang-bang* . . . and then *load-
load-load*. By happy non-coincidence this corresponds
roughly to an important difference between the Byzantine
and Persian/Sassanid cavalry of Belisarius' time—the
Byzantines used heavier bows and often shot while their
horses were standing, while the Persians used lighter bows
and galloped more.

Of course, there are distinctions—on Bellevue the
soldiers don't ride horses, which had never been
numerous in a star-faring, fusion-powered civilization, and
which failed to survive the collapse of civilization. Instead

they ride giant dogs, originally produced by genetic manipulation before the Fall as amusements and toys. Descott hillmen ride hounds. The pampered chocolate-box soldiers of the Capital garrison, of course, use poodles. There's a good argument that dogs, if big and sturdy enough, would make much better mounts for soldiers than horses. Horses are densely stupid, but not stupid enough to run onto a line of points. Dogs, like human beings, are social predators and creatures of the pack. They *will* do that.

Dave had determined that Raj Whitehall would be advised by Center, an ancient computer still operating in the catacombs under East Residence. I decided that Center would have a dry, pedantic personality and enjoy—or at least do a lot of—lecturing, with a slight tinge of having been driven to distraction by aeons in the cellars chewing over old data. And that Raj's initial awe of this divine being would eventually settle down to a wry resignation and even friendship of a sort. Dave had decided that Bellevue's native fauna were roughly similar to dinosaurs—and I had the fun of reliving my childhood fascination with the creatures by doing a lot of research and coming up with the most colorful types to pop up at inconvenient moments, all birdlike quickness and size and really, really big teeth. The nomad Skinners (more or less stand-ins for the Hun raiders and mercenaries of the sixth century) were in the outline; I decided that they'd be descendants of French Canadian settlers isolated in the outback by the Fall. Just because I could.

And so it went for four long books, war, love, companionship, tragedy, and history . . . and great fun it was to write. Dave was kind enough to say that the result was the book he'd have written if he'd had my knowledge base tacked on to his, and I've seldom had a finer compliment as a writer.

S.M. Stirling was born in France in 1953, to Canadian parents—although his mother was born in England and grew up in Peru. After that he lived in Europe, Canada, Africa, and the U.S. and visited several other continents. He graduated from law school in Canada but had his dorsal fin surgically removed, and published his first novel (*Snowbrother*) in 1984, going full-time as a writer in 1988, the year of his marriage to Janet Moore of Milford, Massachusetts, whom he met, wooed, and proposed to at successive World Fantasy Conventions. In 1995 he suddenly realized that he could live anywhere and they decamped from Toronto, that large, cold, gray city on Lake Ontario, and moved to Santa Fe, New Mexico. He became an American citizen in 2004. His latest book is *The Golden Princess* (September 2014); other titles are *The Change* (a shared world anthology) in June 2015 and *The Desert and the Blade* (September 2015), all from Roc/Penguin. His hobbies mostly involve reading—history, anthropology, archaeology, and travel, besides fiction—but he also cooks and bakes for fun and food. For twenty years he also pursued the martial arts, until hyperextension injuries convinced him he was in danger of becoming the most deadly cripple in human history. Currently he lives with Janet and the compulsory authorial cats.

Hell Hounds

Tony Daniel

I found Mom in one of the dog pens, partially eaten by the three pit bulls inside.

My first thought? *That figures.*

The pen gate was closed and latched behind her so that the dogs couldn't get out. These were troubled dogs—Mom didn't have any other kind—but not trip-hammer vicious, at least not to her.

Mom had names for her dogs, but I never learned more than a couple. After a while they become one horrible, unfriendly, barking, slathering mutt to me.

Each of the twenty-five dog pens in the barn contained two or three rescued dogs—sometimes more, since for more than twenty years Mom had continued to take in abandoned and mistreated dogs, and she had run out of places to put them.

How many were adopted out? None. Not one. In fact, every one of them was impossible to adopt. Most had been abused, neglected, and/or mistreated in some way by former owners—or, for the feral ones, other dogs. None of them were trustworthy. Not one.

Do I sound bitter? Hell, yes, I am!

Over the twenty years she'd had the barn, Mom had spent every scrap of money she possessed on feeding, medicating, and sheltering those dogs. I never expected to inherit anything from her—we were on the lower end of middle-class while I was growing up—but lately I'd been sending her chunks of *my* savings, and I knew every penny of it went for dog upkeep. I'd sworn never to do this, and I'd broken my promise. My only hope was that she spent some of the money for her own food, if only to ensure she could keep taking care of her dogs.

I figured Mom had been lying dead in the pen for about a week. From the looks of things, the pit-bull brothers in there had waited until their food ran out before starting in on her body. They weren't thirsty. Water came from a system of self-refilling troughs my father had constructed—so they didn't run low on that. But it was obvious from the general lethargy of all the dogs in the barn that none of those yammering mutts had been fed for days.

It was mostly the meat of Mom's arms and legs that the pit bulls had chewed off, although there was at least one bite taken out of her neck.

That was what I gleaned by observing from outside the pen. Now I had to get in, which I knew from experience was no easy task.

My father, who had constructed the whole barn complex single-handedly, and then promptly died of a stroke, had made the pens five feet across and fourteen feet deep, so the dogs actually had a fairly spacious living area. My mother fixed the pens up with doghouses (although the barn roof guarded against the weather) and she tossed in a layer of straw in winter. Every day for hours and hours, she fed them, medicated them—and shoveled mounds of dog shit from each pen while the pen inhabitants were exercising in the big fenced-in yard outside the barn.

And she refused most help. Plus, of course, she could never stop. One couldn't. It was a twenty-four-seven job, and this year she had turned seventy-five.

So frustrating. Always so damn frustrating, even to the last. Hell, I couldn't begin to grieve because I had to work through the physical problem of how to get past the goddamn pit bulls to get to Mom's body.

I'd already waded through her carpet of cats.

Oh yeah. There were cats, too.

The cats lived outside the barn. When you drove up, you encountered a mass of them in the parking area. They only reluctantly parted before you, like some feline Red Sea. There must have been a hundred cats or more out there. Mom fed them by emptying out a weekly fifty-pound bag of cat food on a couple of pieces of plywood elevated on saw horses.

The cats kept down the rodent problem around the barn, of course, but there were several hawks and vultures that had moved into the neighborhood. These would occasionally swoop down to catch a kitten or sickly cat, and carry it off to be eaten. Thus the number of cats did not grow exponentially—yet apparently there weren't enough birds of prey in Alabama to keep the lot of them from steadily increasing.

But now, how to get past three snarling dogs?

I knew a little of their history. These were sibling pit bulls Mom had taken in after they'd been dumped, probably by dog fighters, down in the Talladega River bottoms near the Highway 431 bridge. The only human beings who frequented the area were meth addicts, drug dealers, and my mother to feed the abandoned dogs that collected under the bridge.

The pups, which were about a year old at the time, had not only been beaten, scarred, and abused, but were skin-and-bones by the time Mom found them. They had grown up to be a trio of most unpleasant animals. I hadn't exchanged a word with them since they'd promised to rip out my throat on a previous trip to the barn.

I can talk to dogs. I can talk to cats, too, but I don't. Wild animals—okay, those I like. They don't tend to demand my mother's love and undivided attention.

I'm not as good as Mom was with animal languages. My strongest craft is water-witching, which is one reason I became a geologist. But I figured I'd have to give talking a try before I resorted to shooting the dogs in order to get to the body.

I knew Mom would hate it that I was even *thinking* of shooting them.

Then realization set in.

I don't have to worry about what Mom wants for her dogs ever again, I told myself. So fuck them.

Yeah, right. I wasn't going to shoot them.

I *would* protect myself, however. I looked around for

a stick and found a section of two-by-four about a yard long Mom had used to prop pen doors open. This would have to do. While I was searching for the wood, I let my spirit loosen up and spread out—at least, that's how I've always pictured it—until I could hear the pit bulls. They were arguing among themselves. Big surprise.

He'll take her away.

She's ours.

Smell him. He's her git. The son. He has claim.

Means nothing. We were sons, too.

He sees. He can look back into the before like she could.

He sees it was us that ate her.

He'll beat us.

I grasped my stick, turned to the pen.

"Did you kill her?" I asked them.

The dogs started as if stung. They hadn't realized I'd been listening.

No! We didn't!

We didn't kill her!

We just ate her!

"Then it is all right," I said. "I don't blame you."

We ate of her. This time it came across as more of a snivel.

Maybe there was the tiniest degree of self-realization there. Sadness.

Not going there, I thought. Mercy, yes, but not pity. Not for these dysfunctional pit bulls.

That way lay madness. My mother's madness.

"I won't hurt you because you chewed on her."

We tried not to.

"It's really okay."

But hungry.

Like before at the mud-water when we were dying.

She came.

We were so hungry.

I felt a wave of dog-shame roll over me. Shame in dogs usually led straight to aggression. Maybe it was because of their insecurity at no longer being wolves? Who the hell knew.

Don't talk to him! He has a stick.

We ate her legs.

He sees! He knows!

We ate her.

Get him!

Bite him!

I opened the pen's gate, stood there a moment, then showed them the board. After a moment, I dropped it to the pen floor.

"I'm not going to hit you," I said. "But I do need you to get out of there."

The pit bulls and I faced off for a few seconds. One was mottled brown. The other two were white. All three had skin lesions here and there from scratching. All three were heavily muscled. My mother dosed them daily with anti-itch steroids—which also served to pump them up. They looked like three doggy weightlifters.

If I had made another move, they probably would have attacked. I was ready for that. My hand was on the thirty-eight holstered in my rear waistband. I hadn't spent years wandering lonely oilfields without learning to carry protection.

Then the pit bulls appeared to arrive at a collective decision and bounded around me, out the pen door, down the center of the barn, and into the exercise yard. I followed them out and shut the yard gate, locking them outside.

Meanwhile, the commotion had set every dog in the barn to barking and howling. I kid you not, it always sounded like the dog apocalypse, complete with wailing and gnashing of teeth, when all seventy-seven of them got going together.

Pandemonium.

Apocalypse for the ears.

It had mercifully died down to a mild yip and bark chorus by the time I returned to the pen, knelt beside Mom's body, and examined it.

Not much to see. The pit bulls had left her face intact, but she'd settled partially facedown in the muck of the floor, and the skin there had turned black and moldy.

If it hadn't been a particularly cold November, there'd likely have been a cloud of flies. As it was, there were only a few maggots emerging from their burrows under her skin. The smell of death was intense, but not overwhelming to the point where I had to vomit. But I did need to stand up, lean on the pen fencing, and catch my breath.

Did I finally cry?

I should not have. I have no gift for divination, but it didn't take a portent-reader to see where her obsession with saving and hoarding animals was likely headed.

I'd expected something like this for a long time.

Yes, I cried.

Or rather, I let out a low whimper. This set the dogs

to howling again. I gazed through the chain-link pen fencing.

I hate you, each and every one, I thought.

But I didn't give voice to the sentiment. Of course, it wasn't their fault. She'd worked and worried herself to death.

It was telling that the person who had called me, worried about Mom, was Hailey Teague, the manager of the Tractor Supply where my mother bought her dog and cat food. No one else had missed her. I tried to visit once a month, but I'd skipped November because my work had piled up. Only once in a blue moon did she call me, my brother, or my sister. We had to call her. And any phone call was likely to be interrupted by one dog emergency or another.

"I'll call you back." This was Mom's refrain.

But she never did.

Anyway, my mother had missed two days of her usual dog food buys, and Hailey "just had a premonition" something was not right.

Hailey could have contacted Gretchen or Tom, my sister and brother. They lived closer. But Hailey and I had been in high school together. She was a year younger and even then was on her way to transforming into the maternal, checklist-obsessed adult she'd become. She'd known me best of Mom's children, so she'd called me.

I caught my breath and knelt again beside Mom's body. What was I going to do? If I called the sheriff or the county coroner, they'd see the dogs and haul them all away to the county gas chamber. My mother hated kill-shelters. I could imagine the sight of the barn dogs being snared about the neck by dogcatchers, and carted away, yelping and terrified, to their doom. If there was an afterlife, my mother would surely smite me from there, if it came to that.

On the other hand, Hailey Teague would call in the law if I reported that I hadn't found Mom. Then the sheriff would still investigate, find the dogs, and haul them away to grisly ends. I'd need to get the body out of here. There was a wheelbarrow. I could put her in there. I could take her out by the mailbox and say I'd found her there, obviously chewed up by wild animals, and—

Suddenly the task seemed overwhelming.

I needed help. Gretchen and Tom had their own concerns. Families. Health worries. Gretchen was halfway through chemo for breast cancer. I couldn't dump this on them. I was unmarried and unattached, at least for the moment. I had to deal with it.

Maybe Uncle Steven, I thought. Mom's brother. He lived on the other side of the county, in a cabin on the side of Cheaha Mountain.

Nah. He was seventy-nine. Not a good age to be slinging cadavers around.

I looked down at Mom's body. Then to the floor beneath her—

What was that?

Underneath the dirt of the pen floor. Something that had recently conducted magical power. I could feel it.

I scraped out a furrow of dirt. There. Underneath. A layer of blue-green mineral mixed with the brown soil. Also specks of pure black in the soil that sparkled like obsidian. I continued to scrape, followed the unusual mineral. It was forming a rough circle around my mother's body. I didn't complete the tracing, but knelt down, picked up a pinch of the substance and sniffed it. A burnt, chemical smell. Not organic. I dug up more of it with my fingers until a substantial section of the stuff was exposed.

Then I water-witched it. The sensation is a bit like taste, and a bit like getting a mild, but uncomfortable electrical shock. After years of practice, I could witch any rock or soil and *know* pretty much what it was made of, based on the water content, or lack thereof. This was part of my job searching for oil and natural gas. I was good at it.

The powder had a dryness I recognized from a thousand other witchings.

Some kind of salt. But not sodium chloride. The blue-green gave it away. A copper salt. There were many different copper salts, however.

It had burned. That was what the black specks were.

I left the pen, went to the edge of the exercise yard.

"What did you see?" I asked the pit bulls. "When she died, did you see fire?"

Yes. Flames. Shooting from the ground. Rising high.

We ran.

We were afraid.

We were too afraid to guard her.

"It's all right," I said. "Can you tell me what color the flames were?"

Contrary to what many think, dogs are not colorblind, but the range of the spectrum they see is limited. In addition to black and white, they can pick out blues, yellows, and violets.

Blue.

No, purple.
Blue!
Purple!
Blue!

A snarling, nipping fight erupted momentarily, but died down quickly. I walked away. I'd heard enough.

Blue to purple. Copper chloride. It was the copper salt residue that was left after the most powerful manifestations of magical power.

Particularly from the dark side of the craft.

Even now when walking through the woods of northern Alabama, you can stumble upon deep pits in the ground sinking down to blackness. These are pits that look dug, not like sink holes. More than a few hunters had slipped into such pits and fallen to their deaths.

In this region, these pits were usually known to the locals as "old copper mines," or "test pits." Sometimes they were known by their true name.

Devil holes.

So I'd found burnt copper salt under my mother's body. I went back and scraped away more dirt. The black-and-blue-tinged soil formed a large circle, about six feet in diameter. Mom's body was lying in the center of it.

Magic. Black magic.

Which meant someone—or some*thing*—had killed her.

I had to get out of here. I needed to leave and get my head straight.

Murder.

Someone had killed my mom.

I started to leave, but then the howls began.

Hungry! Hungry!

Feed us!

Eat my own shit, I did. Not good. Not good at all.

Dig, dig, dig, but there's no way out. Can smell the food.

So close, but we can't get it!

Hungry!

Feed us or we'll eat you!

We'll tear you limb from limb!

Let us out!

Please, let us out!

Please. She is gone!

She's gone!

The mother is gone.

Uncle Steven. He may not be much help lifting bodies, but he would be the one to ask about this.

He was a wizard, after all. Although we called him a "cunning man" in these parts.

"I left her there. I couldn't bring myself to move her," I said, shaking my head.

"I understand. What did you do then?" my uncle asked.

"Fed the dogs. She would have wanted me to."

"Ah, of course. They must have been very hungry."

"All except the ones who had chowed down on Mom."

Uncle Steven nodded solemnly. "Of course. Not them."

I paced around his cabin porch, setting off creaks and groans in the old wood planks.

"This is beyond me, Uncle Steven. I need your help."

Uncle Steven leaned back in the old rocker that sat on the front porch of his cabin—and had for as long as I could remember. Mom had told me once that her grandfather had made the chair with wood from one of the last groves of American chestnuts that survived the blight.

"And what do you expect me to do, Phillip?" my uncle asked. "If something was powerful enough to kill Maude, do you think I'd stand a chance against . . . whatever it is."

"But you're the most skilled cunning man I ever knew or ever heard of."

"I'm a shadow of those who used to be, Phil." Uncle Steven gazed out from the porch over the rolling hills below him. The cabin was built just below the state park boundary. It sat on a rocky promontory on the south side of Cheaha Mountain, which was the highest point in the state. The cabin had been constructed of old power poles. I never found out why, precisely. There was a creosote tang to the air around and within it that never went away. I remembered from my youth that it hung on Uncle Steven's clothing, as well.

I had once asked Mom about that. "Why does Uncle Steven smell like telephone poles?"

She'd laughed and shook her head. "He claims it is proof against a certain kind of haint. Something he says he ran into in Vietnam."

Those had been the halcyon days, if I'd only known it. A time when Mom paid more attention to me than to her dogs. Kids think that stuff will never end. Maybe adults do, too. And sometimes, after the kids are gone off to live their life, there's a void left, a place for mothering and caring that no longer has any object.

I'd always supposed this was Mom's reason for turning to the dogs. It was substitute for Gretchen and Tom. It was a substitute for *me*, the youngest, the one who would always be the baby. Baby brother to them. And to Mom?

Oh, my baby. My sweetie pie. Tell Mommy what's the matter.

You fucking left me for a pack of dogs! Now you're gone forever! That's what's the matter.

But maybe I flattered myself in thinking that she missed me at all. Maybe I was merely the final responsibility she had to discharge before she could get to her true love, saving animals.

I turned my attention back to Uncle Steven.

"There are stories of the old cunning men who could move whole mountains if they took a notion. Some could bring down stars."

"That sounds . . . farfetched," I said.

"Because you see with your eyes in one world, Phil. But you and I, we walk in another," Uncle Steven replied.

"And where the two worlds touch—that's what makes the ley lines," I said. "I've heard this lecture before. From you."

"I always said you have the makings of a ley scribe. Far better than I ever was."

"I'm a water-witch," I replied, almost resentfully. "That's good enough."

How dare he make me feel guilty for choosing the world of ordinary human activity over a life waving around a dowsing rod and spending my time casting spells with backward mountain magic?

"That's as far as I'll ever get with the craft. You want to spend your time mapping out a bunch of imaginary magical lines, go ahead. I'd rather spend my time productively."

I glanced at Uncle Steven quickly to see if I'd offended him. This *was* how he made his living. Farmers, construction contractors, real estate developers, even the occasional architect who'd heard of him, would employ Uncle Steven to check their land and orient prospective buildings for the best alignment with the spirit world. Sometimes they paid him to scribe a new ley line through an existing structure that had "a bad feel to it" or was reported to be haunted—usually a sign of a bad land-ley.

The ability to actually etch a new line of power into the land itself was very rare—and highly sought-after by those who could sense the old magic at work in the world, even if they didn't understand quite what it was they were experiencing.

My uncle, as always, seemed completely unperturbed by my dismissive swipe at his profession. He gazed at me for a moment with that ancient gaze of his—the gaze I remembered so well from my childhood—that said he was looking right through my defenses and into my soul. "You know, Phil, after I came back from Vietnam, I wanted nothing to do with the craft. I'd visited a screaming land. I'd seen too many disastrous, tangled leys and twisted spirits of the earth. My mind was bent in a way I thought I could never fix. I just wanted to hide from the bad effects knocking around in here." He tapped his knuckles against a temple. "But sometimes we don't get to make our own choices," he said. "Sometimes the talent chooses for us."

"I just want to figure out what to do about Mom."

"What do you mean 'do about' her?"

"I want to find out who or what killed her, and I want to destroy it," I said. The conviction came so suddenly into my voice, my mind, that it startled me. "I have been coming out here at least once a month for twenty years. I've brought her groceries, watched hours of God-awful *Law and Orders* and *NCIS*es with her—and I've taken care of *them*—and those pens—when she had to go to the doctor, or to visit that herb crafter she was friends with, or just get out for some reason." I was trembling. I wiped my eyes.

Cry later, I thought.

"Whoever did this took my family from me. I want them to pay."

Uncle Steven nodded. "Good. Know thyself. Even if the truth is ugly." He rocked for a moment in the chestnut rocking chair, then continued. "To trace the source of a power, follow the lines," he said. "There are dark places in the land where evilness and mayhem concentrate. It can be a mindless reservoir. It can also be a person. Or a devil."

"Jesus, Uncle Steven," I said. "A *devil*? You've got to be kidding."

"A spirit of the land that's gone bad, then," he replied. "Some are stronger than others." My uncle leaned forward. The rocking chair runners creaked against the porch. "It takes a scribe to draw a ley line. It takes a sandman to move earth, it takes a cunning man or a witch to set a spell on it and make a trigger."

"Are you saying some demonic power killed Mom? *Why*, for god's sake? She was just a crazy, old dog lady." I stared at Uncle Steven for a moment. "And why are you taking this with such an even-temper?"

"I'm not. But I've already made my peace with it."

I didn't know how he could have. I'd only been here a little over an hour. Then it hit me.

"You scried this, didn't you? You knew about it already."

Uncle Steven nodded. He smiled one of his bleak smiles—the slightly amused, slightly appalled look on his face that seemed to indicate he was gazing across possibilities, between the natural and the supernatural, and didn't necessarily like what he saw there. "You don't know much about your mother, do you?" he said. "About her task in life? I don't blame you, of course. She wanted it that way."

"I don't know what you're talking about, and I don't know if I even care at this point," I said. "And as far as evil beings go, maybe it was some devil that was tormenting her all these years, causing her to keep *seventy-seven* dogs! Maybe that's what finally killed her."

"You're closer than you realize," Uncle Steven said.

"Why don't you explain what you're talking about, Uncle Steven."

My uncle considered me for a moment. He had a stare that could strip paint. "I guess I'd better come with you."

"Come with me where?"

"To the scene of the crime," he said. "Let's go and avenge my sister."

He stood up slowly, careful not to leave the rocker rocking. To let it do so was a wide-open invitation to haints.

We took my car and returned to the dog barn. The structure sat in the middle of eighty acres of woodland. My mom had picked it for their "retirement." My dad had built the barn within an oak grove located about a quarter mile down the private drive he'd scraped out with the little Kubota tractor that he'd loved. He'd bought the Kubota before dog upkeep had eaten away all my parents' savings.

We got out, scattering the cat carpet before us as if we were walking through a field of flowers. Meowing, hungry flowers. For a moment, I thought Uncle Steven wasn't going to go in. He suddenly leaned over as if he'd been punched in the gut, turned around, and put his hands on the hood of my car. I thought at first he was gasping for air, but then I realized he was sobbing.

For the first time in my life, my uncle looked old to me. Worn. A flint that had been struck too often.

After a moment, he took a deep breath and straightened up.

"I'm all right," he said, responding to my tacit question. "Let's go in."

Mom had taught me how to recognize ley lines—in fact, I considered myself pretty good at it—but I'd only used the craft for dowsing for oil and gas, doodle-bugging for minerals, and water-witching. My family knew craft, although only Gretchen and I had major talents. Dad had zilch, and Tom could barely charm a lightning bug.

It didn't seem odd growing up with this thing that few knew about, and even fewer believed in. It wasn't a secret, but we didn't talk about it at school or church or the Quintard Mall food court in my home town of Anniston because . . . well, we just knew not to. It was a family matter.

Until the family broke apart. Death. Parenthood.

Dogs.

"So tell me," I said. "Mom's task."

"Her instinct was to protect you from it," Uncle Steven replied. "Maybe that was a good instinct."

The barn door was chain-link fence stapled to a wooden gate frame. It slapped closed behind us after we entered, drawn by its bungee cord closing mechanism. Dad had rigged this up, probably as a temporary measure for closing the barn door behind you after you came in, but it was still working twenty years later.

Uncle Steven sniffed the rank, doggy air, sneezed.

"Christ, it stinks in here!" he said.

"Stay a while and you'll be smelling it for days, no matter how many showers you take."

"I haven't been in this place for years. We always sit outside when I visit. Now I understand why."

We walked down the center aisle of the barn. The structure was large. It was about forty feet across and a hundred feet deep. It had no foundation. My father had built it of pole construction. He'd set the uprights using a special rig he'd made that fitted into the bed of his pickup truck—the red truck that Mom had never sold, that had sat outside on the edge of the parking area rusting for two decades.

Sometimes she used the truck as a pen for keeping dogs that had to be temporarily separated from the others, or that hadn't yet been assigned a pen. The pole-setting rig itself had long ago rotted away in the nearby woods, although its connecting bolts still lay on the ground under a layer of mulch and oak leaves if you knew where to look for them.

I slowed before we got to the pen where Mom's body lay. I let myself spread. I could tell Uncle Steven was doing the same. Maybe we could quiet the damn dogs, at least enough to allow us to think.

"Can you please calm down?" I told the barn at large.

Feed us! Feed us!

Hungry! Feed us, feed us!

"I already did."

Again! We're hungry.

"Dogs," said Uncle Steven, shaking his head. "The only things more predictable are cats and jaybirds."

The barking did die down a bit, though. We arrived at the pen where the body was.

My uncle hesitated, and then looked inside.

"Oh," he said softly. He stared at her for a moment. "We were the closest growing up. Played together all the time," he finally said. "Your mother could talk to anything, you know. Birds. Squirrels. Even trees, occasionally. The more lively ones like sweetgums, I mean." He moved into the pen entrance, stood there without fully entering. "One time we were down by Choccolocco Creek at that swing we had. I was messing around in an old boat we had found washed ashore on a sand bar, and she was up on the wooden platform Bobby built out of lumber from the old barn." Bobby was one of their six older brothers, dead for several years now. "The platform was supposed to be for swinging off of, but Maude liked to sit there and look at the creek."

I almost put a hand on his shoulder, but drew back. He didn't need comforting. All he really needed was to talk.

"I paddled under a tree limb, and a snake plopped right out of the branches and into the floor of the boat. It was a water moccasin. A big one."

My uncle shook his head. "I thought I was a goner. They are territorial, you know. One of the only snakes that'll attack you right out. I scrambled toward the back of the boat and that big old thing was coming *after* me. Fast. Then I heard her shout."

Steven shook his head, seemingly still amazed after all these decades.

"That cottonmouth stopped right in his tracks. Didn't move another muscle. I could hear it cursing up a storm, too. 'Let me go, damn it all! Let me bite! Damned trespasser. This is my creek!' That sort of stuff. Yep, it wanted to get *at* me, and it couldn't because something was holding it. That something was Maude's talent. She probably saved my life. I knew it then and I know it now."

He nodded. "That was the day I realized she was more than a craft-talker. She was a major talent. She was a maker like none that have been born for many years. She could spread herself out into the world. She could cause animals to *obey* her, not merely listen. Trees and flowers, too. Maybe even the land itself."

"Well, she must've lost it somewhere," I replied. "After she got the dogs, she sure as hell couldn't stop them from howling, shitting, and fighting all the time. It was all so . . . miserable."

We went into the pen. I showed Uncle Steven the burnt salts underneath the dirt covering the floor. We both avoided looking at the body as best we could.

He was silent for a time, and I knew he was reaching out, feeling his surroundings with his talent.

"It's like a bee's nest around here," he finally said. "I can barely follow the lines. It's like trying to watch a particular teaspoon of water in a river. *You'll* have to find the crack."

"What crack?" For a moment I thought he might be talking about drugs. But he meant craft. Magic. I looked down at Mom's body. She almost seemed to be smiling. Then a maggot squirmed out of the side of her eye. "Steven, what is this place?"

"No 'uncle,' huh? That's the first time you ever used my name without it." He knelt down next to my mother, his sister, and rolled her back over so that we couldn't see her face. "Enough of that," he said. "For now." He stood back up. "Those old cunning men I was telling you about?"

"The ones who could move mountains, change the course of rivers, and make sure the Tide wins the SEC every other year? Yeah."

"Not quite. I'm talking about the 1660s. The Barrons and Cooleys come over from Scotland. They get off the boat and disappear into the hills. And those hills were

HELL HOUNDS   141

haunted back then. Manitous, devils, giants—things I can't name because they haven't been seen in five hundred years. Evil that had taken form and stalked the land. They faced those evil things down. Some they destroyed, but the more powerful they could only bind."

"Are you telling me this barn is sitting on one of these bindings? Is that what the ley tangle is?"

"It's holding something old," said Uncle Steven. "Something's under this ground that must not walk in our world again."

"Did it get out?"

"Nah. We'd know if it got out," Uncle Steven said. "But I think it managed to stick a tendril, a small finger, into the regular world trying to claw its way back."

"And that's what killed Mom?"

"Yes."

"Did she even *know* she was sitting on one of these bindings?"

"How can you ask that, Phil?" Uncle Steven shook his head, evidently in amazement at my stupidity. "That's *why* she built the goddamn barn here. Maude was a tender. A keeper of one of the major bindings."

"And the craziness? Her sleeping like a bag lady on a cot in the loft? Her being a tender had something to do with that, too?"

Uncle Steven nodded. "Tenders are always kind of nuts. You get that way when you walk between the worlds every moment of every day."

"And the dogs?"

Uncle Steven considered. Blinked. "You know, I was a fool not to have seen it."

"What?"

"You heard them. That howl when they all get going together."

"Oh yeah."

"That's why they had to be wild or beaten up. Those kind of dogs know the scent of evil."

"They're . . . guard dogs?"

"We might as well come out and say it." Uncle Steven again smiled one of those snowy smiles that was one lip quirk away from a grimace. "They guard the gate to hell."

"And something is trying to get out. Something that got Mom?"

"*That* I'm not sure of. If it is, there will be a trail. A pathway, however small."

A pathway, however small? Yes, I had located such, I thought. The tiniest crack?

"That's what I'm good at," I said. "That's how I make a living. Finding what lies buried. But once I find it, what am I supposed to do?"

"Draw it out. You can't kill the old one, but you can hurt it. Let it know it can't come back into this world."

"Hurt it? How?"

"The usual way."

Even if you have the craft, unless you are a scribe, you can't immediately locate ley lines, lines of magical power. You have to turn your inner eye toward them. Or, in my case, I use my trusty dowsing rod.

I went back to my car to get it, wading through the cats. My rod was in the trunk. It was a tube of copper welded into a "Y" shape. The main tube, the pointing end, was about two feet long. All three end-pieces were plugged, and the rod was filled with cave water that had never seen the light of day. I'd collected it on a spelunking expedition in Tennessee.

I took it back to the pen and stood with it over Mom's body.

"How do I do this?" I asked Uncle Steven.

He considered for a moment. "Start with her," he finally said.

Once again I knelt beside Mom. So far, I hadn't touched her except by clothes to roll her over. Now I had to do far worse.

I reached down and, after a moment's hesitation, opened her mouth. My fingers touched soft rottenness inside.

I poked the end of the dowsing rod between her lips.

Then I grasped the handles of the rod with both hands, and let my mind flow.

The familiar sensation of travelling at immense speed. Travelling down, spreading into the liquid remains of her limbs, flowing through the places her body contacted the ground to enter the interstices of the earth.

Down. Spreading like water, forming a table of me, of awareness, that grew at a steady rate. Then my awareness bubbled up into the copper salt circle below the earth of the pen. I pushed harder. I explored the edges.

"It's like a hoop of iron," I heard myself muttering. "Keeps the power contained."

"There has to be a crack," said Uncle Steven. "Keep looking."

And then I found it, sensed it. There was the smallest trickle outward, the smallest leak of power.

A pinprick opening. Most water-witches couldn't have pushed their way through such a tiny gateway, but if there was one aspect of the craft that I'd practiced for years, it was dowsing—witching for water, organics, titanium, you name it. I was good at it. The line away from the circle was small, but very clear, unbroken, and solid. It led into a crazy knot of ley lines that met near the center of the barn. It took me a bit of unraveling, and I was able to find it, follow it—

Down, into the land, through the stone, flowing for a time with the water table. Then turning downward, plunging deeper still. Through the bedrock.

And then I was there. At the boundary of mantle and crust. Solid and liquid rock meeting, boiling with activity.

That's where I found it. Felt it. Touched evil with my mind.

Uncle Steven was right. It was an old one, ancient; it had crossed the Bering Strait when the land-bridge formed. It had come following the first humans, slithering behind them through the ice-filled valleys of the New World, tracking its prey.

The souls of men.

Growing every year like a tree adds a ring. Lurking in shadow so long the darkness seeped into its being. Emerging to eat first the men who lived in the caves, then those who worshipped on the mounds of mud, then those who built longhouses, and finally the ones who drove the others away, seized their land. Settlers.

But one day it attacked the wrong man. It even remembered the man's name, which was my own.

Caleb Montgomery.

But instead of sucking this man's soul, the old one found that it had fallen into a trap. The man, Montgomery, had been bait, drawing it into the midst of a net of ley lines.

Ley lines that were now pulled tight by the little men, the inconsequential nothings. How could this be? Yet it was.

It was encircled, bound by the power of the land itself, then cast into the bowels of the Earth.

The old one was not happy. It brooded for year upon year on one purpose.

Revenge.

Starting with those who bore the cursed name, Montgomery.

Like the tender. Oh, she believed she was clever, keeping her mind from me, always tightening the binding. But she dropped a stitch, left an opening. I could send fire.

I burned her, and feasted on her screams.

I knew it was talking to me. It had sensed me there. The fact that I was Phillip and not Caleb didn't mean a damn thing. I was Montgomery. It could smell this in the very craft that I used. The craft that had bound it.

You have widened the pathway by seeking me out, little human.

I felt its tendril-hands reach for me.

It won't do you any good, but you had better run!

Did I stand firm, find a way to dispel it, destroy it then and there?

I did not.

Instead, when it first reached for me, I broke like a bat out of hell for the surface.

I didn't know until too late that I was being followed.

The "tendril," the creature the old one sent after me, was only a tiny speck of its true being, a finger. Less than that. But very real. Very much composed of meat and bones—and teeth—held together by devil-craft.

It rose from the ground in the pen like a corpse breaking out of a grave, tossing my mother's body aside. It was huge, the size of five men, at least, and its head was mostly mouth, with a gnarled, teeth-filled maw dripping with steaming, corrosive drool. Its deep-socketed eyes were square-pupilled, like a goat. It scanned the perimeter of the dog pen, seeking prey.

What it saw was my Uncle Steven.

"Get back!" I yelled to him.

Uncle Steven gazed up at the beast as if enraptured. "In Pleiku," he said softly. Then he called out to the creature. "I've killed one of you."

"Yesssssss." Its voice sounded like a steam kettle that could articulate words. "But I will kiiiiill you now."

Uncle Steven stumbled back through the pen's gate. I was not far behind. The creature followed, taking its time, savoring our terror.

It opened its mouth.

And opened it.

And opened it.

When it was done, half its face was a lamprey-like circular maw. Big enough to fit around a man's torso. And probably strong enough to bite it clean in half.

From that mouth a long, spike-pointed tongue lashed out, faster than the eye could follow. Maybe my uncle felt a vibration in the ley lines. Maybe it was gut instinct. But Uncle Steven dodged out of the way. If he had not, the tongue would have pierced his heart. As it was, it lashed across one of his arms, ripping through his flannel shirt and tearing a gash along his upper arm deep enough to expose the red striations of muscle.

He reeled, sank to his knees, holding the wound.

"Uncle Steven," I shouted. "How? How did you kill it? The one in Vietnam?"

"C-four," he said. "Bullets. You still carry that Colt? Use it!"

Could bullets really hurt this thing?

There was only one way to find out. I reached behind me and pulled my Colt 1903 from its waistband holster. It had come down to me from my grandfather on my father's side.

The Colt fired .38-caliber bullets, and I had a full mag of eight hollow points.

The creature drew closer to Uncle Steven.

"You smell of night," the creature said. Talons sprang from its outstretched fingers. It rose over Uncle Steven, moving in for the kill. "No matter. You will burn in my gullet like any other."

Then, all around us, the dogs began a yowling session louder than any other I'd heard before.

The creature hesitated, looked around, perhaps trying to understand where so many dogs had come from. Their number was unbelievable, if not supernatural.

I fired a shot into its back.

For a moment it hung over Uncle Steven, talons at the ready. Then it slowly turned toward me. Its tongue shot out.

And knocked the Colt from my hand.

I'll eat your soul, well-witcher.

The pain was intense. But I was too busy scrambling backward to worry about whether anything was broken.

Evidently not. My fingers closed around the two-by-four lying on the floor of the pit bulls' pen, and I was able to grasp it.

The giant lamprey maw descended toward me even as I yanked the board up. The jaws clamped to rend, to kill—

But instead the two-by-four was jammed into its maw, keeping the mouth open. It recoiled back, shaking its head. The two-by-four refused to budge for a moment— thank God for pressure-treated wood—and the creature worried at its mouth with a talon, trying to extract it.

Behind the creature, Uncle Steven was on his feet. He was moving toward one of the dog pens.

The creature roared in frustration, but finally managed to wrap a talon behind the two-by-four and yank it out.

Then it turned its attention back to me, growing closer. A bit of its drool spattered onto my face and burned as if it were a fresh fire coal.

I had nothing. Nothing but words.

"At least tell me your name," I said, popping out the first thing that came to mind.

This caused it to hesitate once again.

Uncle Steven opened a dog pen. He moved to the next.

My name? It is older than the race of man. To speak it would drive you mad.

"I want to hear it anyway," I shouted. "Tell me your name."

You are clever. I am bound to answer this question. But it will do you no good.

Devils were bound to say their name when asked? I did not know that.

But somewhere, maybe from inside me, I heard old Caleb Montgomery chuckling. "But *I* knew, laddy," I thought I heard him say.

Very well. My name is—

That was when the first of the dogs hit the creature. They tore into the musculature of its legs with their teeth.

Meat! Meat! Meat! they shouted. *Bring down the meat!*

Uncle Steven opened another pen. And another.

Let us out! the ones still behind closed gates yelped. *Let us eat, too!*

Pit bulls, hounds, fiches, whippets, labs, mutts of all types—even a couple of fearless Pomeranians with pinprick teeth. The Pomeranians were sisters that my mother had stepped in front of an oncoming semi-truck to rescue and pulled off a busy four-lane.

The creature reached down, grabbed a dog—one of the lab-mixes—in its talons, and flung the poor beast across the barn. It hit the far wall and splattered against it. The creature bent to grasp another one.

And I dove for the Colt. For a moment, I fumbled for it in the dust and dog shit, but then I had it.

The creature saw what I was doing, moved toward me, dragging along dogs attached by their teeth to its legs.

The biting dogs clamped onto the creature slowed it just enough. As the creature leaned toward me, I emptied the rest of the Colt's magazine into its face.

On the seventh shot, its skull exploded.

I scrambled back and got out of the way as the creature fell in the center of the barn, throwing up a great cloud of disgusting dirt when it landed.

Across from me, Uncle Steven opened the last of the pens. Last but not least, he let the pit bull brothers in from the exercise yard.

The dogs chewed their way into the carcass with gusto. Large and small, they gulped down huge chunks of meat, and carried more away to continue gnawing in their doghouses, dens, and hidey holes.

Thank you! Thank you for letting us get to it! Bite it!

Meat! So good! Meat and more meat!

Give thanks! Give thanks to the master!

As one, the dogs turned to me. Ears up. Tails wagging—or at least stumps for those who'd lost theirs. They began to bark, to howl, to yap and yammer.

The din reverberated throughout the barn.

He is his mother's son!

Give thanks to the master!

He has taken down the meat!

Oh God, I thought. *Shut up.*

"I am not your master!" I shouted. But then I glanced at my uncle. He was holding his cut arm and obviously in some pain. But there on his face was that cunning man's smile. He was shaking his head as if he didn't believe my words. As if he'd scried the real truth.

He probably had.

"I am not my mother," I said with a low growl. "I am not your master, you goddamn dogs."

But, even then, I was starting to have my doubts.

Tony Daniel is an editor at Baen Books. He is also the author of ten science fiction novels, the latest of which is *Guardian of Night*, as well as an award-winning short-story collection, *The Robot's Twilight Companion*. Other Daniel novels include the ground-breaking *Metaplanetary* and *Superluminal*. He's the coauthor of two books with David Drake in the long-running General series, *The Heretic* and *The Savior*. He is also the author of original series Star Trek novels *Devil's Bargain* and *Savage Trade*. Daniel was a Hugo finalist for his short story "Life on the Moon," which also won the Asimov's Reader's Choice Award. Daniel's short stories have been much anthologized and have been collected in multiple year's-best compilations. In the 1990s, he founded and directed the Automatic Vaudeville dramatic group in New York City, with appearances doing audio drama on WBAI. He's also co-written the screenplays for several horror movies that have appeared on the SyFy and Chiller channel, including the Larry Fesenden-directed *Beneath*. During the early 2000s, Daniel was the writer and sometimes-director of numerous radio plays and audio dramas with actors such as Peter Gallagher, Oliver Platt, Stanley Tucci,

Gina Gershon, Luke Perry, Tim Robbins, Tim Curry, and
Kyra Sedgewick appearing in them for SCI-FI.COM's
Seeing Ear Theatre. He is currently writing and
producing a series of adaptations of the works of Baen
authors such as Eric Flint and Larry Correia for Baen
Books Audio Drama. Daniel took his B.A. at Birmingham-
Southern College, where he majored in philosophy. He
has a Master's in English from Washington University in
St. Louis. He attended the USC Film School graduate
program for one year before dropping out to write. Born
in Alabama, Daniel has lived in St. Louis, Los Angeles,
Seattle, Prague, New York City, Dallas, and Raleigh,
North Carolina, where he currently resides with his wife
Rika, and children Cokie and Hans.

At my request, he provided this afterword.

When I first came to work at the Baen office as an
editor, I learned that David Drake, whom I hadn't yet
encountered, had something of a reputation for being,
well, *prickly*. He was said to be particularly annoyed by
overly enthusiastic editors. When he found an editorial
change in his work that he felt was unwarranted, Dave let
his displeasure be known. Vociferously.

So when Toni Weisskopf, the publisher of Baen, asked
me if I wanted to coauthor a book with David Drake, I
answered with some trepidation in my heart (or maybe in
my gut)—but I also immediately answered, "Hell, yes."

I hadn't met him, but I had read him—and I liked his
work a great deal.

He was a damn good storyteller.

There was an old outline in the files for another book
in the General series, a series that had begun with S.M.

Stirling writing five books using Drake outlines, and then, when Stirling moved on to other projects, with Eric Flint writing two more books. Eric also moved on to other endeavors—most notably his very successful Ring of Fire alternate history series.

The detailed origin of the General series can be found elsewhere, but the short version is that Jim Baen came up with the idea, and had his best friend and trusted author, David Drake, write up outlines for a series. These outlines were not short, three-page deals. No, each outline was quite detailed, and filled with suggestive opportunities for subplots and characters. The outline I used was about fifteen thousand words long. In the end, I couldn't hold it to just one book, but had to make two out of it. These were the General series books *The Heretic* and *The Savior*.

I wrote *The Heretic* without meeting or consulting with David Drake once. All I knew was that he'd okayed me with Toni Weisskopf. When I turned in my draft of the book, I metaphorically held my breath.

Okay, I literally held my breath several times when I checked email to see if Dave had responded.

Dave got back within a few days. I'd expected weeks of anxious waiting.

"This is fine; I will put my name on it," was the upshot of his comments. There were a few notes, easy to incorporate, and that was it. I spoke with Toni Weisskopf about Dave's response.

"I guess he was good with the book," I said. "I hope he wasn't gritting his teeth when he approved it."

Toni laughed. "You don't understand. I've seen some of the responses Dave *can* give and *has* given. Dave liked it."

Months passed as the book was prepared for publication. During that time, I saw Dave from afar at a couple of conventions, once when he was going out to lunch with another author hero of mine, Gene Wolfe. But, even though I'd long overcome the writer's introversion that afflicted my early years, I felt shy. This was a guy whose ideas I'd lived with for months and months, and had tried to translate into as good a story as I could tell.

What if he didn't like me?

Then we were placed on the same panel at a convention and Dave and I finally met. It was pretty anticlimactic. During the course of the panel, he mentioned that *The Heretic* was coming out and that "I put my name on it. I didn't have to put my name on it. I have that written into the contract. So if I put my name on it, that means I approved of it. Very much." After the panel, Dave had to leave immediately for home, and I didn't get a chance to talk to him further.

When the book came out, we had a signing at a bookstore in Raleigh, North Carolina. Before the signing, we finally arranged to have dinner together. I brought my wife Rika; he brought his wife Jo.

It went well.

I had just read his novel *Redliners*, and we talked about that. I hadn't known it, but the novel was one of Dave's particular favorites among his books.

Since we live relatively near one another in North Carolina, I invited Dave to be on the podcast I host, the Baen Free Radio Hour, several times. Often we would get a meal afterward.

I didn't for a minute believe I *knew* David Drake. Still

don't. But I was becoming familiar with him. To my surprise, I didn't find him particularly prickly. What I did find was that he was a reservoir of great stories—and that he was a brilliant raconteur.

There were stories about his early years, his tour in Vietnam, his law school days, his decision to transition to writing full-time, and the early days of Baen Books, where most of Dave's books have been published. There were stories of his friendship with author Manley Wade Wellman, whose Silver John Appalachian fantasy stories I have admired since I'd read them as a teenager.

Did I know that he was Wellman's literary executor?

I did not.

Did I know he had written a novel as homage to Wellman and his influence?

Nope. But I really wanted to read it.

So I delved into the Baen archives and pulled *Old Nathan* from the shelf.

I loved it. It quickly became my favorite Drake book of all.

So when Mark Van Name asked me to write something for this collection, the first thing that popped into my head was to write an *Old Nathan* homage.

An homage is not a pastiche. Dave had not copied Manly Wade Wellman when writing *Old Nathan*, and I could not and would not attempt to copy Dave. An author should not presume that he *can* copy someone who is very good, in any case. So I got to thinking about the characters, and the part of the Appalachians that I know best: the area where I grew up in Northeast Alabama. Ideas started to trickle in. But not yet a story.

There is one thing about Dave's physical presence that always strikes me when I see him. He is a thin and wiry guy, and his face might as well have belonged to a Roman senator—if faces have past lives. It is aquiline. His stare is eagle-like.

He was profoundly affected by his time in Vietnam, for good and bad—for a while, *very* bad, as he's said before—and this has influenced his life philosophy. Dave himself is open and amenable, yet his life philosophy— which Dave has no trouble articulating, let me tell you—is quite austere. When Dave smiles, he smiles warmly enough, but it seems to me a hint of the stoic is always behind it, the indication that things could get worse and probably would at some point.

I knew I didn't want to write a character that was my conception of David Drake. That way lies madness. Yet, often actors will take an article of their character's costuming or a prop and build their character and his motivations around that synecdotal symbol.

When I sat down to write my story for this anthology, I did the same with that Drakean smile.

I started with the smile and a story began to materialize around it, like the Cheshire cat's body.

The rolling foothills of the Appalachians in Alabama. A favorite uncle of mine.

A dog-rescuing lady I happen to know quite well.

Oh, and one other thing I did that *was* in conscious imitation of David Drake's style, something found especially in his fantasy and horror stories.

I showed the monster.

There can be build-up, there can be suspense—

But, in the end, you show the monster and let somebody try to kill it.

They may not succeed, but let them at least *try*.

It's a story, goddamn it, not a psychological study or an exercise in world-building—although both of those usually need to be present within it.

But it's a story.

Don't mess around.

Tell it.

That is what I most like about Dave, and about Dave's work.

He does.

Technical Advantage

John Lambshead

The jungle grew more tangled and warped the closer they got to the base as if nature itself abhorred the presence of The Enemy. Trees grew at strange angles as if unsure which way was up and their branches intertangled and drooped like a crowd of drunks clutching at each other in vain attempt for mutual stability.

The Leader knew the dysfunction represented nothing more mysterious than the end product of decades of biological and chemical saturation, but emotional response always trumped intellectual comprehension so this place reeked of evil.

Others felt it too.

The Fighters were quiet, even the teenage girls pushing the supply bicycles had fallen silent, green and amber gloom draining their bird-shrill voices like an anechoic chamber. Neither the Leader's threats nor patriotic exhortations could shut them up for long but the jungle did the business.

Not that it mattered overmuch. The Enemy had long since ceased to use sound or chemical sniffers to detect Fighters, such devices too easily fooled by simple remedies like recorders or bags of human waste hung in the trees.

The girls gazed uneasily around, eyes flicking from side to side like animals being herded into an abattoir. One of them gave a little squeal, sounding dramatically loud. Her abandoned bike fell over with a clatter spilling garishly coloured cereal bars.

A green lizard shuffled onto the trail, head probing towards the startled girl. A serrated tongue slid from a slit in the closed jaws, flickering as if tasting the air. Thin orange fluid leaked between metallic green scales leaving a sour spoor in the leaf litter.

The reptile moved a step or two towards the girl with a stiff jerking gait like an old man with joints crippled by arthritis.

The Leader was upon the beast in three swift paces. He swung the heavy machete in his hand through a long overhead arc that ended at the reptile's neck. The crystal-sharp carbon blade sliced through bone and tissue as if it were nothing but straw.

The animal's head bounced among the detritus while its body twisted and rolled over, stumpy legs thrashing. Goblets of slimy blood flew through the air. Red pus stained the khaki blouse of the horrified girl.

"Take it off," The Leader said, studying her body through disinterested eyes.

She hurried to comply. The Gods only knew what foul mutated diseases oozed through the lizard's body fluids.

"Careful, don't let the muck touch your skin."

Underneath the girl wore a yellow singlet. The Leader examined her closely but there was no sign that the reptile's blood had passed through the coarse weave of the girl's battle blouse. The bare skin covering her pipe-thin arms was pale and clean.

The girl would die or she would live; he was indifferent. At this stage in the operation it didn't matter much one way or the other. One girl here or there was not important.

They followed the trail without further incident until they came to the river that marked the border between theoretically neutral McInleyland and Enemy-occupied Tashow. It was little more than a large stream this far into the dry season so was barely waist deep.

But they didn't ford.

Things lived in the water and the ones with teeth were the least dangerous. The microscopic stuff killed way more commonly and usually in ways that made being eaten alive seem tame. That wouldn't normally have stopped a Fighter patrol but today they had more pressing reasons not to risk the water.

The water reminded The Leader how desperately he wanted to bathe. His skin prickled and itched uncontrollably. He frowned and tried to ignore the sensation before it became unbearable.

The Leader turned and pushed through the two-meter-high grass lining the riverbank using his machete to chop through the more tangled clumps. He experienced the strangest illusion, as if he had been shrunk by some nefarious Enemy high technology to the size of an ant striking out across a meadow. He shook off the mood with an almost physical effort. It was not like him to let his imagination take hold like that. A lifetime of conflict had taught him to deal only with the here and now. Fighters who didn't grasp this simple truth tended not to have an extended future.

The grass thickened, slowing the column's progress to a crawl even though he rotated the point man at regular intervals, but fortunately they didn't have far to go. A hundred metres or so upstream a pioneer unit had arranged for a tree to fall across the river in a way that looked natural to an overhead observation 'koid.

The pioneers had cut a tunnel through the grass to the makeshift bridge to conceal their presence while they worked. The Leader had half-hoped it might still be there but the vegetation grew back so damned quickly. He simply didn't have time to copy the pioneers' caution. The trail left by *his* column would mark the bridge out to The Enemy as clearly as if he had put up signposts but by then it would have served its purpose. The issue would be decided, one way or another.

The Leader retook point to cross. He didn't bother to check for booby traps. If The Enemy had been clever enough to work out the secret of the tree trunk then they would've been clever enough to fit it with mines undetectable to the unassisted human eye.

This was The Leader's fourth run into Tashow, making him a veteran: a Fighter's first run was usually a death sentence. There were rumours of Fighters surviving five or even more runs but The Leader had never met such a superman. No matter how experienced, how cunning or how careful, a veteran sooner or later hit the lethal probability number. One day sheer random chance was bound to get you.

Personally, he suspected that rumours of multi-run heroes were concocted by Strategic Command to bolster morale. When a conscripted cohort was sent to The War their male relatives held funeral rites and the women tore their clothes in lamentation as if the soldiers were already dead. Bitter experience taught them not to anticipate returning heroes.

The jungle was thinner on the Tashow side. Enemy mekanoids sprayed the border strip with herbicides at the end of each monsoon but the trees grew back even through the dry season. There was always sufficient new growth and herbicide-blasted trunks to provide reasonable cover. Of course, that cut both ways. The Enemy mostly favoured technology over people so he didn't expect to encounter an Enemy ranger patrol. Nevertheless, The Leader scanned the jungle carefully. He always played the odds. Maybe that was why he had lasted this long; anything to delay that lethal probability number popping up.

The Enemy had no more respect for McInleyland's neutrality than The Fighters themselves, so nowhere was exactly safe, but the danger inevitably increased after entering Enemy controlled territory even if that control was more theoretical than real.

A splash and curse caused The Leader to swing around. He relaxed upon seeing a Fighter hauling himself back onto the makeshift bridge. Jumping to his feet, the dripping man scurried across carefully avoiding his Leader's scornful gaze.

The Leader made eye contact with the team Technician, who imperceptibly shook his head.

"You," The Leader said to the wet Fighter. He hadn't bothered to learn the man's name as he was a first-timer so probably wouldn't last long. "Take the rear and stop the girls straggling."

The Fighter sullenly obeyed, pushing his way roughly through the little mob of young women, all of whom had crossed successfully with their bicycles. He probably thought he was being punished but that wasn't true.

The Leader didn't punish minor infringements in the field. Stupidity or clumsiness normally earned its own reward. A Fighter who proved a liability was simply put where he could do no harm. In the field that was commonly a shallow grave but The Leader still had a use for this idiot.

The berry juice rubbed into his skin and hair irritated abominably which did absolutely nothing to improve his temper. He resisted the urge to scratch since drawing a single drop of blood might prove fatal. The Leader glowered at The Technician, the architect of this mad scheme. Perhaps it wasn't entirely fair to lay all the blame at The Technician's door but The Leader wasn't feeling fair. He was feeling tired, terrified and, to cap it all, his purple-juice-stained skin itched and he couldn't scratch.

"Move out," he said, leading by example.

They made good time and covered at least two kilometres in the next hour before the whine of Enemy 'koids above the tree canopy brought the column to a halt. There was no particular reason to stop moving—The Enemy stopped using primitive sensors such as motion detectors decades ago. It wasted too much ordnance on what was left of the wildlife.

Not that the Enemy didn't have the ordnance to waste but apparently using it to dismember wildlife upset certain Enemy political factions. Who could grasp the strange fancies of foreigners?

The Leader angrily waved a hand in a circle above his head and The Fighters spread out.

The *chuff, chuff* of canister discharges sounded over the motor whine. Orange cylinders about the size of a thermos flask bounced through the tree canopy dislodging leaves and causing howler-monkeys to flee, swinging from branch to branch on their elongated arms while uttering their characteristic *whoop, whoop* warning cry.

The canisters split open soundlessly as soon as they were in open air. Orange casings disintegrated into shards that fluttered on the 'koids' turbulent downblast like exotic butterflies.

Clouds of dragonflies burst out. Only these weren't insects any more than the canister shards; they were tiny 'koids that The Fighters dubbed killer bees.

One flew straight at The Leader. He showed no emotion but a close observer might have noticed whitened knuckles on the fingers gripping his machete; but there were no observers, close or otherwise. Everybody's attention was on the swarm.

The little machine paused for a quarter-second in front of his face, its electronic DNA analyser confused by berry juice but perhaps not quite confused enough. The leader stared back impassively. A psychologist would have been hard pressed to determine which was the man and which the machine if all he had to go on was the degree of emotion displayed.

The Leader waited through that long quarter second, watching rainbow colours generated in sunlight splintered by the flickering drive fields along the bee's body. A small part of his mind wondered curiously if it was now his turn to die but he didn't dwell on it. He would die anyway—today, tomorrow, here or somewhere else. He knew that like he knew the sun would come up in the morning.

Some circuit in the little machine's electronic brain clicked and it zoomed away over his head. The juice worked. This was not his time.

The bees converged quickly on the girls, who huddled together like sheep threatened by a pack of wolves. The little machines' detectors screamed in orgasmic electronic glee at the human DNA overload. They detonated a few centimetres short of the girls' bodies, attracted to the strongest source of DNA which was inevitably the largest area of bare skin—faces in this case.

Bees could be armed with all sorts of things. These had general-purpose grenades that exploded to generate a focused pulse of plasma designed to burn through body armour. That was a needless sophistication, as The Fighters had none. The effect of the plasma on unprotected human bodies was catastrophic.

The girls' heads exploded in bursts of steam generated by super-heated body fluids. Waves of bees attacked bits of ripped off body tissue, chopping the girl's corpses—or what remained of them—into smaller and smaller gobbets.

The attack was all over in seconds. Three of The

Fighters were also down, the one who'd fallen in the water among them.

Berry juice was water-soluble.

The other two dead Fighters must have been careless or just unlucky. Maybe they had been standing too close to the girls and got spattered in human DNA, maybe they hadn't applied the juice properly, maybe they had scratched their skin, or maybe they had just plain been unfortunate. Perhaps the gate on the DNA sensors of a couple of the bees had been set just that fraction wider, or the 'koids decision circuits had been just a little fuzzier. Maybe it all came down to a quantum probability decision over whether an electron tunnelled this way or that.

Who knows? Who cared? The dead were dead and the survivors had a job to do.

Killer bees were convenient in one way. They never left any wounded. The Leader wouldn't have permitted wounded Fighters to slow the column down but it was better not to have to kill your own people so early on in a run. It tended to affect morale.

The Technician dry heaved long after he had nothing left to bring up, his stomach contents scattered among the minced gore decorating the leaf litter. Ironic since he had devised the tactic of unprotected decoys.

Possibly The Technician hadn't entirely thought things through in his enthusiasm for his new idea. The Leader remembered that the man had referred to the tactic as "ablative armour." People who used military euphemisms for slaughter often found the reality disconcerting.

The girls were expendable, sacrificial goats in a

conflict that used up people like chickens at a battery farm. People were the one asset that never ran out.

They made better time without the girls and arrived at their destination after a couple of hours. The Leader paused to give his men a short rest. He had started with twenty Fighters and was now down to twelve. Twenty was barely enough for the task but he had been persuaded that a larger force would have stood out suspiciously from the various deception operations simultaneously undertaken along the border to keep The Enemy's attention off the real attack.

Oh well, twelve he had so twelve would have to do.

Their objective was a yellow effluent pipe that stuck out of a bank in a hollow above a small stream. Waste coated the bank in a sun-dried brown crust. Presumably the monsoon rains would wash away the muck but right now the hollow stank like a cess pit.

A mesh sealed the end of the pipe against animal intrusion. The Leader levered at it with the tip of his machete. The blade broke with a sharp crack, although the remaining stub proved efficacious. He swapped blades with a first-run who would have to make do. First-runs were also expendable. When it came to it, everyone was expendable. It was all a matter of degree and the expediency of the moment.

The diameter was just wide enough to allow a man to crawl up. No doubt the pipe had to be reasonably large to drain The Enemy base of storm water. Perhaps when it rained the runoff filled the pipe but for now little more than a foul smelling dribble ran along the bottom.

Those who had planned the run had assumed that

there would be various detectors inside capable of spotting the signatures of energy weapons, guns and other technology. The Enemy was nothing if not thorough, especially concerning the safety of his personnel, but no device yet made could distinguish a carbon blade from carbon effluent or the DNA in a human body from the DNA in human bodily waste.

The Enemy probably didn't really take seriously the threat posed to their perimeter security by the pipe. *They* wouldn't crawl up a sewage effluent system so they probably assumed no one else would.

The Leader had done worse things than crawl through shit. Shit didn't actively try to kill you.

He was beginning to revise this opinion by the time he reached the drainage grill. Some bastard had flushed and unpleasant solids coated his clothes and hair. He paused under the grille, blinking in the light while he listened.

After a few minutes of silence, he gently pushed the storm water grille to one side and levered himself out.

He was inside.

The base was shaped like a doughnut with a leisure garden in the middle. Paths wound between tall bushes covered in exotic blue-and-white-striped flowers. The Leader had been briefed to expect something of the sort but deep down he hadn't really believed the planners. The garden seemed so pointlessly self-indulgent.

The Enemy's horticultural excesses at least provided useful cover. He signalled for the rest of The Fighters to emerge.

They moved in single file along a path, boots crunching

in ornamental transparent gravel tinted in shades of red and blue. When intermingled, the chips created various shades of purple in patterns that changed with every footstep. The path led to a door secured only by a standard security code lock. The Leader typed out the six-digit code that he'd carefully memorised onto a screen which flipped to amber and sounded a soft chime.

Nothing else happened.

That wasn't according to the script. The door should have opened.

The Leader gripped his machete and cursed softly. What the hell should he do now? Desperate ideas flicked across his mind: find another door, try the code again on this one, or try to force an entrance. They certainly couldn't just retreat back down the effluent pipe: not after the enormous effort to get the team this far. His superiors would regard withdrawal as cowardice on a scale tantamount to treason and punish accordingly. Not just The Leader, but his whole family would pay the price.

He froze in a block of indecision.

Then there was a click and the door rotated slowly into the wall. A woman spoke in an exasperated voice before it had fully opened.

"That's yesterday's code. Why can't you people bother to read the bloody . . ."

The woman gaped when she saw The Fighters. She had a pistol in a holster under her left breast but she made no attempt to draw it. The Leader sliced the machete across her neck, neatly cutting through flawless skin so characteristic of The Enemy. A gush of arterial blood soaked her clean white uniform and added more stains to The Leader's battle dress.

He stepped over her body before it stopped twitching.

Inside, a radial corridor made of some artificial light-grey material curved around the doughnut. Hidden lighting cycled through restful pastel sky-colours: blue, yellow and pink. The Leader ignored the first few doors along the corridor, mentally counting until he came to the one specified by his orders.

He kicked it open and ran inside. Surprise was total.

The long control room was open-plan. Enemy operatives manned various rounded grey consoles or lounged about on strangely shaped sofas in primary colours. Holograms hung in the air and screens covered the walls.

The leader split the skull of the nearest Enemy and cut down a second with a backhanded swipe of his machete.

A third operative pulled out his pistol and pointed it at The Leader's chest but momentarily hesitated, apparently reluctant to shoot at close range. Ironic really, considering the power of the weapons controlled from this base and the number of people they'd killed.

The Leader had no such inhibitions. He chopped the hand that held the gun off at the wrist and pushed the operative aside for someone else to finish off. The Fighters were outnumbered and outgunned. Their only hope lay with speed and aggression, with shock action to panic The Enemy and stop them organising a defence.

Enemy operatives fired their pistols wildly, bright white plasma blasts ionising the air until it stank of ozone.

An Enemy officer in a powder blue uniform waved his arms. He shouted incoherently until a misaimed plasma bolt burst between his shoulder blades, hurling his corpse over a console.

Equipment exploded under the plasma bombardment. Power supplies arced and burst into flames adding to the confusion. The synthetic materials burnt bright yellow, emitting black powdery fumes that stung throats and eyes.

The Leader stopped to wipe tears away, an act that probably saved his life.

A man dressed in the green-and-brown-splodged uniform of an Enemy ranger patrol appeared from nowhere.

He gunned down two Fighters in half a second with quick accurate pistol shots. A third Fighter lunged over a control panel and thrust his dagger into the ranger's side. The man grunted and fell on one knee. Holding in his intestines with one hand, he pumped plasma bolts into the Fighter that had stabbed him, tearing the man apart in a cloud of superheated red steam.

The Leader hurled himself at the ranger's back. He struck hard at the base of the man's neck and kept hacking until the ranger stopped moving. Then he hit him a few more times, just to make sure. You didn't take any chances with a wolf like this. They didn't die easy.

The Technician appeared at The Leader's side, eyes very wide.

"He shouldn't have been here. Headquarter bases aren't staffed by rangers."

"Yeah," The Leader replied. "Shit happens."

Maybe the man was going on leave, or coming back from leave, or bringing something, or setting up a tryst with his girlfriend or with his boyfriend. Who the hell knew? Who bloody cared? The bastard was dead and he was alive and that was all that mattered.

The Leader checked around. All the Enemy operatives were down and his surviving Fighters were engaged finishing off the wounded.

"Smash up everything," he ordered, thrusting his machete into a screen.

Enemy tech was sophisticated but very fragile.

One of the first-run Fighters grabbed a discarded pistol in his enthusiasm for destruction and aimed it at a cabinet displaying flickering green and red lights. He pulled the trigger before anyone could stop him.

The personalised Enemy weapon exploded, blowing off the silly bastard's arm. He thrashed around a bit until The Leader cut his throat.

To be fair, the cabinet caught fire and burned with a fierce blue-white flame that set light to the ceiling so the idiot hadn't been a total waste of space.

The Leader gave the order for the Fighters to split up and comb the base for any survivors hiding out in other chambers. His intention was clear so he was astonished when a Fighter dragging an Enemy operative by the arm sought him out.

"Why is this one still alive?" he asked.

"You don't understand," the operative said, fear making him garble the words. "I helped you. I'm the one who leaked the plans to the base."

The Leader cocked his head to one side. He hadn't

given much thought to how the information in his briefing had been obtained.

"That's better," the operative said pompously, gaining confidence and pulling his arm free. "Your superiors said you'd have a suitable reward for me."

"Ah," The Leader replied, now understanding the situation and what his masters had intended.

He thrust the point of his machete into the operative's throat. Blood bubbled up and the man fell backwards gurgling.

"Was he telling the truth?" asked The Fighter.

The Leader shrugged, "Possibly but it doesn't matter. However you look at it he had outlived his usefulness. Who can trust a traitor?"

They left the base by the front exit. It was well ablaze and The Leader wanted to be gone before The Enemy reacted.

The Technician paused for a last look.

"It's a pity we couldn't carry any equipment back with us. The stuff in that base cost more than our army's entire annual budget," he said wistfully. "It gave them one hell of a technical advantage."

The Leader didn't bother to turn around. He was running through the route home in his mind.

Dr. John Lambshead is a retired senior research scientist in marine biodiversity at the Natural History Museum, London. He was also a Visiting Chair at Southampton University, Oceanography, and Regent's

Lecturer, University of California. He writes military history and designs computer and fantasy games. He is the author of swashbuckling fantasy *Lucy's Blade,* contemporary urban fantasy *Wolf in Shadow,* and coauthor, with nationally best-selling author David Drake, of science fiction adventures, *Into the Hinterlands* and *Into the Maelstrom.*

At my request, he supplied this afterword.

The great Sam Goldwyn, who knew a thing or two about show business, is quoted as saying: "Pictures are entertainment, messages should be delivered by Western Union," and in general that is good advice for most authors. The public buy your stories to be entertained, to wind down from the daily grind; if they wanted a political discussion they would read a newspaper or watch a documentary.

However, some storytellers transcend the normal limitations of the medium to say something profound about life and the human experience. This is the point where entertainment becomes art and the greatest art is classical, that is it has a timeless quality.

The *Iliad* is still read by soldiers, not because it explains Dark Age Greek warfare but because it defines all warfare. Whether men ride into battles in chariots or tanks is irrelevant compared to the experiences of men in battle. The weapons change but not the soldiers.

When David Drake first wrote the *Hammer's Slammers* stories they received a mixed response. One British reviewer—now an American I must add, your loss being our gain—is quoted as writing that "if Drake had really seen war he wouldn't write such queasy voyeurism."

But of course Drake had seen war, had seen it right at the sharp end as a conscript who served in the elite 11th Cavalry, the Blackhorse, in Vietnam.

Damien Walter writing in *The Guardian* in a much more nuanced look at military science fiction specifically singled out Drake's *Hammer's Slammers* and Haldeman's *Forever War* as making a contribution to discussion of the morality of war *because* of the authors' individual histories. Haldeman and Drake wrote classics because they had something profound to say based on their own personal experience.

Both authors' works sang to me but Drake's in particular had a personal resonance. To explain why, I have to digress a little.

My father was called up by The Duke of Cornwall's Light Infantry in 1939. A lorry came around to his house to pick him up. He remembered his mother leaning out of the top window to ask how long he would be away.

"Just for the duration of the emergency," was the answer.

My father fought in Tunisia as a platoon sergeant and his battalion was decimated. They formed the Cornish Company in a sibling regiment, the King's Shropshire Light Infantry who were then slaughtered twice in the hell of Anzio. They gave my father the Military Medal for leading the survivors of his company out of a trap when all the officers had danced the "Spandau Ballet." If you don't know what that means then Google "Hitler's buzz saw."

He was blown up in the end during the breakout by a mortar shell that might have been German, American or even British, it hardly mattered, and lay all night on a stretcher outside the hospital tent while it was being shelled.

He never talked about it, never wore his medals—his generation never did. Nobody talked about post-traumatic stress disorder. He was just demobbed after Japan surrendered, while training for Operation Olympic, married my mum and got on with it. My father had all sorts of problems which I never understood until I read *Hammer's Slammers* and a light came on.

David Drake's art taught me about my father, and of course I am my father's son. These things extend across the generations. I cannot begin explain how important that has been to me.

Which brings me to the present and my story. I write entertainment not art, but in this case I have disregarded Sam Goldwyn's sage advice and tried to send a message about warfare. Actually two messages.

The first is relatively trivial but it gives the story its title—the myth of technical advantage. A meme that won't go away is that wars are won by better technology. If that were true Vietnam would have been a walkover for the U.S.A. In 1940 and '41 German panzer divisions hammered British, French and Soviet armies with technically *inferior* tanks. They lost the war in '43 and '44 with *superior* tanks.

The second is more subtle and concerns what modern combat does to the survivors, who are released back into society with no more fuss than if they had been on a field trip to a national park.

The flat emotionless style I employ is the way soldiers learn to think in the combat zone. The stress is too acute and the situation too horrible to allow normal feelings.

People become types, Leaders, Fighters and, of course, The Enemy. Right and wrong doesn't even begin to come into it. It's simply us or them.

The combat veteran learns new and unpleasant reactions involving extreme violence to situations that a civilian would not think about twice. You can read of a tank veteran in The Filthy Fifth (the 5th Royal Tank Regiment) who shot up a road sign in Germany simply because it had been unbolted and leaned against its pole—they found the mutilated corpse of a teenaged Hitler Youth behind it.

Would the British tankers have cared if they had just killed a pregnant woman hiding in terror from the tank? Did they care that they had just killed a boy? At the time probably not, the dead boy still clutched a *panzerfaust*—literally a tank-fist—a lethal weapon that could burn through Allied armour like a blowtorch on ice cream to incinerate the whole crew.

But how did they feel about it ten years later?

Well, I'm not David Drake and I lack his skills. But I write this watching a bugler play the Last Post over the poppies in the grounds of the Bloody Tower. It is the eleventh day of the eleventh month of the year twenty-fourteen.

They shall grow not old, as we that are left grow old:
Age shall not weary them, nor the years condemn.
At the going down of the sun and in the morning,
We will remember them.

—Lawrence Binyon,
North Cornwall, 1914

Thank you, David.

Saracens

T.C. McCarthy

"The Polish King and the Italian monk," Alex said, "will take action. And people say the monk is a saint—sent from your precious God."

Florian shook his head. "I defeated a Saracen magician. In my dreams."

"They were just dreams and you were drunk. Again."

"I was not drunk!" Florian's fist slammed against the table with a loud boom, causing the plates to jump. "I was *not* drunk."

He looked out the window. The sky flickered with an orange glow that pulsed as one fire died and another began, their flames invisible behind the hills so that the clouds became a kind of mirror, reflecting the lights of watch fires and reminding everyone that the enemy was still there. They had been—for months. Days and weeks had blurred and melted, fusing into a sculpture of time that he refused to mentally examine for fear that it would shape into a form demonic. Time had always been cruel. It had bent Florian's back and hobbled his knees, making it painful to kneel, and withered his arms to the point where they carried no weight and made him long for the moment when Turkish sappers got close enough to blow them all up, ending everything, including growing old.

But what Florian had seen was real. The dreams could not have been just dreams, and a strength he hadn't felt in decades grew in his stomach and spread, sending warmth through his limbs to fight Vienna's autumn cold. And his visions had been clear; Florian saw them still, as if they'd been etched on the glass of this mind in smoky pictures so the message would be remembered forever: there was something for him to do and God had willed it.

Alex put his hands to his face, rubbing both eyes. "Father's house is gone. Crushed into the dirt of an empty field so the Turks will have no cover to approach the walls. But this won't work forever. Someday they will get close. Close enough to breach. And we will never bury our parents once Saracens take our heads."

"I am still a man of Christ," Florian said. "Though not a Priest. Father understood that and so should you."

"Was it that hard to resist her? And couldn't you have chosen someone with less influence than the wife of my General? You're so *old;* it disgusts me."

"Think whatever you want, Alex; I'm leaving. Dawn will be here soon."

Florian stood, bumping the wooden table and almost knocking it over; there wasn't much time. By now the Poles and Germans were massing for their attack and from his visions Florian knew that he had to move out before sunrise—to have any chance at infiltrating Turkish territory. He shuffled toward the barn door. The wooden panel groaned and creaked, making the horses stir, and Florian peered into the darkness of the alley, dimly lit by the glow of fires and a distant moon. Shadows filled the path surrounding the barn and to him it seemed as though sprits encircled the darkness, waiting for him to walk into the open where they could attack without warning. Florian made the sign of the cross; then he gripped his crucifix so the ends of it dug into his palm.

"Where are you going?" his brother asked.

"What difference does it make if I took the wife of an old General or a broom maker? It was a sin. But He has given me the way to redeem myself, by showing me the source of Turkish strength and how to destroy it. I'm moving south; I don't know where yet, but God gave me the way and promised safe passage."

Alex stood and moved closer. "God hasn't given you anything; He damned you for eternity. I could have been a General and you could have been a Bishop. Instead you had us stripped of title and land and this," Alex gestured to the barn in which they now sheltered, "this is our inheritance. If you go outside the walls, the Saracens will take you. And you *know* what they do to Priests."

"You said it: I'm not a Priest. Not anymore."

Florian stepped into the alley and began shuffling south, toward a small gate in the city wall, and wincing at the pain in his knees. He called out over his shoulder. "I'm old now, Alex. Old enough to know that this may be the last chance for us to do something important—something that matters. Whether you believe in God or not, I do."

Except for the reflection of distant flames, night flowed through the alley in a thick tide of black and Florian gripped his crucifix even harder. His brother followed. Florian didn't need to turn and look; he heard Alex's clicking boots and said a silent prayer of thanks because the dreams hadn't been specific enough to tell him whether he would face this alone, and to have a military man—an *ex*-military man—made him feel less desperate. It wasn't that he doubted the vision. It was more that Florian had less faith in himself, and worried that he might not have the courage to do God's will once he arrived, and having Alex made it easier to imagine that he wouldn't collapse in terror.

Florian turned onto a main city street. Stones paved the road and the fact that it was more level than the alley made the walk easier on his knees, allowing him time to look up at the houses on either side; curious people peered from windows, their pale faces poking from between half-open shutters. All of them watched the sky. As he and his brother neared Vienna's walls the reflection of Turkish fires became a bit brighter and when Florian first noticed the streaks he stopped.

Alex ran into him. "What's wrong?"

Florian pointed upward. "Those. Lines in the sky."

Paper-thin lines of purple light streaked overhead and spread across the city like a web, each streak disappearing into a home. They crackled. It was a soft noise, barely audible over the occasional boom of cannon fire, and the lines flickered in a way that reminded Florian of a kind of lightning. He kissed the crucifix, sensing the corruption and fear that almost dripped from the filaments.

"I see nothing," Alex said.

"God has given me sight. I can see a wizard's spell: one that fills the city with terror."

"Terror? Are you serious? Tens of thousands of Ottoman Saracens—who butchered and raped their way through Constantinople, then Greece, then the Balkans and Hungary—surround us; with such a blade over our heads I hardly see a need for a terror spell."

Florian shook his head. "You don't understand."

"Understand what? Your God? Parents in Hungary survived only to find their babies had been burned alive. It's better that such a God doesn't exist."

"Then why are you going with me?"

"Because. We're all dead tomorrow. So what does it matter? By going with you I won't have to watch Janissaries torture my wife and children, or watch them rape and then behead them all. At least I can die like a soldier."

"There are the Polish forces," said Florian, leading them southward toward the walls. "In my dreams, only the Germans attack—at dawn—and the end is murky. For all I know, the Poles later help win the field and the Saracens will never touch Vienna."

"You dream again. We are outnumbered, brother, even *with* Sobieski's Winged Hussars."

Soon the city's main wall loomed over them, casting a shadow among the shadows, a tall curtain of blackness broken only by a single watch fire near a small door. Three soldiers warmed their hands in the glow. To Florian's amazement the men said nothing when they approached; instead the guards nodded—as if expecting the brothers—and one stood and bowed deeply, his face an orange-pink in the warm glow of flames; he worked the mechanism opening the oak door, allowing the pair to duck into a small tunnel that dipped under the wall. The guard pushed past them with a torch. When they reached the other side, he grunted, lifted several beams from brackets that sealed the outer portal so it swung open, and then ushered Florian and Alex through. Florian flinched at the sound of the beams being dropped back into place behind them and then turned southward, squinting into the darkness and trying to match the scenery with his dreams.

Wide fields stretched out in front of them, their grass and weeds cloaked in darkness. At first Florian panicked. Nothing looked as it should have and with one hand he gripped Alex's shoulder when his legs began trembling, giving way at the thought that his brother had been right—that the whole thing had only been his imagination. Florian didn't recognize the trees. They swung in a soft wind, silhouetted against the Saracen flames, and the orange flickered in a pattern that reminded him of laughter, taunting with thoughts of failure. Florian lifted his crucifix and whispered a prayer.

"You're lost?" Alex asked.

Florian nodded, doing his best not to panic. The wind blew from the west and gently pushed his beard to the side at the same time it carried a murmuring hymn, sung with the deepest and most reverent voices, in a language Florian failed to recognize so that at first he thought it was a hallucination. Soon he recognized it: Polish. He was about to clap his hands with joy when a cry went up from the

Turkish camps to the south and a moment later war screams drowned the song, followed by cannon fire that illuminated far-off fields to the southwest with flashes of red and white. Florian began shuffling down a narrow path—away from the wall and toward the Saracen watch fires.

"You remembered the way?" asked Alex.

"No. But I still see the wizard's spell. The lines converge over Perchtoldsdorf, to the south. We must hurry to get there before dawn; the battle has begun and if we fail, the Germans and Poles will be slaughtered. For now, the Hussars' song helps to dispel all fear but they can't sing forever."

Alex moved down the path, following closely. "What is that song?"

"*Bogurodzica.*" Florian smiled at the thought and quickened his pace, already seeing the main road to Perchtoldsdorf ahead of them, a flat wide patch of darkness only a bit lighter than the shadows enveloping it. "It means *Mother of God.*"

The road disappeared into the night and both men moved as quickly as they could, careful not to trip over uneven stones; stars provided just enough light. Florian's legs trembled even more with the effort and he forced himself to ignore the pain, instead becoming lost in thought until tears clouded his vision. He recalled what his affair had cost. Memories of Alex's insults threatened to overwhelm him because they had been well deserved and Florian's betrayal *had* ruined everything. His parents had been so proud when he'd joined the priesthood. And a week ago, just before news of his affair with the woman broke, the Bishop had sent word that he was to report to

Rome—for an assignment within the Papal Office. *Rome*. Just thinking of the city turned regret to anger. Florian recalled the number of his fellow priests who had done worse, including having children and hidden wives, but who continued in their duties for the simple reason that their sins hadn't yet been discovered; their faults were still secret. *It wasn't fair.* Florian clenched both hands into fists, ignoring the pain in his joints, and then opened his mouth, preparing to shout at God.

Before he could scream something caught his attention: a series of shadows appeared out of the darkness, at the edges of the road—odd shapes, which transformed his anger into fear. He grabbed his brother's arm. The two crept forward and Florian wondered why they hadn't encountered any watch posts along the road until they got close enough to one of the shadows, its smell making everything clear. He grabbed his nose and dropped to his knees, crying.

On either side of the road pikes had been planted in the earth to hold impaled corpses, each arranged in deranged poses and in various stages of decomposition, their odor making Florian dry-heave over the paving stones. Florian grabbed Alex's hand to pull himself up, after which he waved his fist at the sky.

"*Why do you allow this?*"

"Quiet," Alex hissed. "You'll bring the Saracens!"

"There are no Saracens on this road. Look around. This place isn't guarded by men because it doesn't need to be; no man can travel here without God's protection."

"Protection! You hinted at it already; if God existed, he would never allow this."

Florian realized that now his brother was crying. He took his hand and squeezed it in a show of support before moving forward again, shuffling toward his dreams and the horrors that awaited them. "They are slaughtering everything, Alex—children and women. I can see it all now. The lines hum in the sky over us, energized with the blood of innocents and blocking this road with a curtain of terror. On either side of us, behind the corpses, I see them now."

"What?" asked Alex. "Again I see nothing. What's out there?"

Florian looked to his side. It was more than a glance—a period of long seconds in which he forced himself to relax his vision—and they formed out of the night, dark shadowy figures with red eyes. The creatures loped on all fours in the fields, laughing as they went and whispering something his ears failed to catch.

"Things not of this world. For now we have His protection but hurry; these creatures are hungry."

By the time they reached the village outskirts, piles of bodies replaced the pikes and Florian said silent prayers for the dead, whom he avoided looking at since all of them were missing heads. How could the Saracens be this blind? These were physical acts—not spiritual—meaning that men had to be the ones wielding the sword and ending the lives of even infants, and surely they couldn't all be evil; surely there had to be *good* Turks.

Florian paused to retch again and wondered: maybe Satan's influence extended far beyond what he'd imagined. And, if so, what chance did he, Florian the drunk, Florian the dishonorable, have against such power? But there were no answers to the question and he clung to his dream as if it were the only thing protecting them both. Florian moved forward again, leaning heavily against his brother's shoulder and filled with a sense of dread that forced a cold sweat to break on his chest, followed by an uncontrollable shivering that made his teeth chatter. Within a few minutes Alex stopped them both, tugging on Florian's robe.

"Why so many of those?" he asked.

His brother pointed to a group of homes. Each had been burnt to the ground and their stones gathered in tall piles that supported long poles, at least thirty feet tall and capped with a golden half-moon and star—the symbol of the Turks. An early-morning sky had begun to turn purple. It silhouetted the symbols against the heavens and Florian crossed himself before murmuring in Latin. "*And a great sign appeared in heaven: A woman clothed with the sun, and the moon under her feet.*"

"I never bothered with Latin, brother."

"It's from the Bible. It describes our mother, standing on the moon."

Alex sighed. "Then I suppose it's a relief that the moon is under her feet—that she has power over Saracens whose symbol she crushes?"

"Not necessarily," said Florian. "There's more to those passages. Elsewhere an angel blows a sixth trumpet, which brings a massive army *with breastplates of fire and of hyacinth and of brimstone, and the heads of the horses were as the heads of lions: and from their mouths proceeded fire, and smoke, and brimstone.* This army kills a third of the world before God wins."

"Fire, hyacinth, and brimstone—Janissary colors."

Florian nodded. "And the Turkish cannons. Some are crafted so the end is as the head of a lion, which spouts flame and smoke each time they fire."

"Superstitious *vomit*. It's coincidence."

Florian waved him quiet. The brightening sky illuminated Perchtoldsdorf in a kind of dim grey and he flinched, surprised when Alex produced a saber and wheel lock from underneath his cloak; the weapons underscored the danger into which the pair of them now headed, and which—until then—had been more of a dream than anything real. More clouds materialized out of thin air, lowering themselves to the point where they scraped against the town's roofs and provided a dim, reflected illumination that did little to dispel the gloom. Instead it provided just enough visibility to make Florian question his vision, squinting at every shadow to make sure nothing lay in ambush. And the violet lines almost disappeared. They quivered under the clouds like piano strings, vanishing for a moment within the grey only reappearing a few seconds later to guide them toward the town's center, which, when they saw it, forced both men into the doorway of an abandoned shop.

Saracens filled the town square. Florian counted at least thirty, all of them dressed in short white coats, and who spun so rapidly that what looked like long women's skirts rotated around them, floating upward to form weightless undulating disks of brilliant white. The sight hypnotized. At first Florian didn't even notice the music, a repetitive noise which seemed to come from under his feet rather than from the small group that played drums and stringed instruments at the side of the dancers near Perchtoldsdorf's town hall. Each Saracen spun to the music's rhythm and the dancers wore tall cylindrical hats, as grey as the clouds, and tilted their heads to the sides at the same time they grinned, a sight which disturbed him the most. At first Florian couldn't pinpoint what made the dancers look so strange; the light was too dim and their rapid movements blurred his eyes with confusion. Then, a few moments later he saw it; they had painted themselves—so the dancers' faces formed white skulls that glared at him over and over again, each time they spun, making him shiver with cold. He pointed to the center of the group and whispered.

"There. The lines descend from the sky and plunge underground, into that hole in the middle of the dancers where the paving stones have been ripped up. I want to get this over with before I lose all courage."

Alex shook his head. "This is truly Satan's doing; God help us."

"I thought you didn't believe in God."

"I," said Alex, making the sign of the cross, "may have been wrong. But He sent you on a fool's mission, Florian. How will we get to that hole? There's no way to get there except through the dancers."

Florian nodded. This had not been in his dream either. But the things he recalled were underground, in a windowless cavern lit with golden braziers so somehow he *must* make it to the hole. He grabbed his brother's cloak and pulled him into the square.

"What are you doing?" Alex hissed.

"The entrance is only twenty feet away and these men

are in a trance. In my dream, I made it underground. So it has to work."

"Yes, but what about me? Did I make it too? *Was I even in your dream?*"

Florian let go, trusting his brother would follow. The Saracens spun on every side and he felt the breeze of their coats as they whirled past, pushing the cold morning wind into his face along with the sensation of ice, pricking his face with millions of frozen grains. He pulled his cloak around him. Florian's bones ached. He had to act fast, which was always difficult at his age, and the Saracens moved in a coordinated dance, shifting to the side at the same time they twirled, forming a strange mobile obstacle course that he and Alex had to navigate without touching anyone; interfering with the dancers could break their trance. A pistol and sword would be useless, Florian knew. His brother would only kill a few before the dancers pounced, and both would then be put on display like the other corpses they'd seen: on a pike, overlooking the main road. It wasn't the kind of end he'd imagined.

Now that he was in their midst Florian heard a strange hum, a low single tone that emanated from each man's chest and resonated at a precise pitch so that it seemed to warble within his ears, dulling his senses and making him dizzy at the same time. He dropped to his knees. The paving stones spun underneath him and Florian had a vague sense that a Saracen was dancing closer, threatening to collide in seconds. And his hands felt as though they'd been glued in place; Florian did his best to crawl out of the way but it was no use and the Saracen grinned through a horrific painted skull, eager to land on the priest and awaken the rest of the dancers for a slaughter.

Without warning his brother's pistol cracked, sending one of the Saracens to the ground just before Alex pushed Florian into the hole, slamming into him from behind.

"Whatever it is you have to do, get it done!" his brother shouted. *"I'll try and hold them off out here!"*

Florian slid headlong down a flight of stone stairs, coated with an inch of ice that scraped against his face. He hit the bottom and curled into a ball. It only took a moment for the pain to recede, after which Florian opened his eyes to find he'd landed in a rough cavern where thousands of stalactites hung in a display of wet, fang-like rock, sparkling in the glow emitted from tall braziers. Tongues of flame licked against the cave's ceiling. They sent a flickering light throughout the cavern, which disappeared into the distance, reminding Florian of a fanged mouth that extended into an infinite throat.

In the middle of the cavern, a man stood with arms outstretched to either side and his head bent back at such an extreme angle that Florian thought his neck had broken. He wore a white robe. The firelight reflected against the fabric, sometimes making it look red or orange, mesmerizing in the way it constantly shifted in appearance, and it took a moment for Florian to notice that the robe moved on its own. The man stood still. But something underneath the folds of his clothing slid or crept, forming inhuman shapes that Florian couldn't identify but which made him step back, almost tripping against the stairs at the same time he grabbed his crucifix.

As if in response, the man's head shot forward. Florian

cried out when he saw that it was painted in the same skull pattern that the dancing Saracens used, and when the figure smiled at him, the skull's grin twisted into a gross caricature of man—somehow threatening Florian and all humanity in one simple expression. Another shot rang out from above. Florian flinched and then listened to the sound of his brother's sword, which clanged loudly against what he assumed were Saracen blades.

"He won't survive," the man said.

Florian noticed the purple filaments. They rose from every part of the man in a thin, almost continuous sheet of light that disappeared into the ceiling, and he imagined them rising from the street overhead, where they would split into an infinite number of lines to streak over the battlefield and into Vienna.

"Your spell is useless on me," Florian said. "I walk with Him."

"So you can see it; that's how you found me."

"*God* led me here. Not you."

The man shrieked, his face shaking before it twisted into an expression of rage. "I know you and your brother. We have special places prepared as soon as my Turks run a sword across his neck. His head will be displayed on a pike, but his soul will be ours forever."

"You're no wizard; you're not even a man." Florian's heart went cold with a suspicion of what he faced and it took all the courage he had to hold his crucifix steady. "*In nomine patris, et filii . . .*"

He nearly dropped his cross at what happened next. The man slowly lowered himself to the ground, contorting his limbs, twisting them around until he faced Florian on all fours with his head bent at an even more impossible angle, converting into a grotesque kind of four-legged spider; the popping of joints and bones sent shivers of imaginary pain. Florian wondered if he should turn and run; the dancing Saracens seemed a safer option.

"You *should* fear me," the man said.

"Give me your name," Florian said. *"Pater noster, qui est in Caelis . . ."*

"Behold. I am the god of flies. And now your brother joins us."

Alex fell down the stairs, his sword clattering on the stone and ice until he came to rest behind Florian, almost knocking him over at the same time a group of Saracens shouted on their way down, following. Florian didn't turn. He stayed focused on the creature and over the noise of his brother's battle there arose a buzzing, a droning that overwhelmed Florian's voice and brought with it a stench so horrible that he stopped his prayer, dropping to all fours. Flies filled the cavern. Florian had to swat them away from his face as he struggled back to his feet, and he raised his cross once more, an action that cleared the air around him to form a tunnel of air that linked him and the creature while the insects engulfed them both in a black cloud. The God of flies—*a prince of hell, one of the major demons*. Whatever it was that faced him was more powerful than he'd realized and his arms went numb with terror, his crucifix shaking with the effort to hold it up. And when Florian finished the Lord's Prayer the thing sat on the floor, mocking him with its grinning skull.

"Are you finished? The battle is turning against the Viennese and her allies. And your brother will soon fall."

Florian shook his head. "*Silence!*"

"Silence? Give up now and I will show you some mercy. The end will be painless."

She shall crush thy head, and thou shalt lie in wait for her heel. The thought popped into his head out of nowhere, so real that Florian thought he'd heard a voice again, a gentle song within the hum of flies so that he paused to look around, confused. He whispered the phrase to make sure he understood, and then gasped. As soon as he uttered the words the creature backed away and its face twisted to show a mouth full of teeth, filed to sharp points and from which bits of skin dangled, hinting that it had been feeding on Saracen victims. And where before the purple filaments had glowed with an unnatural light, strong enough to make even Florian doubt his chances, now they flickered—a few disappearing altogether.

Florian gripped his crucifix tightly and spoke so that his voice was clear over the noise of flies. "*Ave Maria, gratia plena, Dominus tecum . . .*"

"You're nothing more than a drunken whoremonger. Leave and I'll give you safe passage back to Vienna."

"*Sancta Maria, Mater Dei . . .*"

The thing continued to back away and Florian noticed that now the flies disappeared, dying in mid-air and dropping to the floor in piles. Alex cried out behind him. "Whatever you're doing, don't stop; the Saracens are faltering."

"We have your parents, priest," the thing said. "They'll suffer for everything you're doing—more than any other soul in our power. But if you stop now we will release them."

"*Silence!* You are a lie; return to hell and take the Turks with you."

He stepped forward. Florian sensed a shift in the cave's air, a lowering of the pressure that made it easier to breathe, and the smell of rot began to fade, transitioning into something that he recognized as a kind of flower—lavender. His knees no longer ached. Florian's back straightened and he heard a new strength in his voice, one that made him scared and brave at the same time because a force spoke through him, something unseen and without form but as real as the skin on his hands. The next words boomed throughout the cave, breaking a stalactite loose to smash on the floor.

"*Salve, Regina, Mater misericordiæ . . .*"

Alex shouted in pain. Without looking, Florian knew that a Saracen blade had found its mark and he stumbled over his prayer, wanting to turn and help but hesitating because he knew that to do so would give the thing a chance to regroup—an option Florian didn't have. But Alex still fought; the ringing of steel echoed against the rock walls and Florian sighed with relief.

"I'm all right," his brother said, breathless. "These bastards managed to stab me in the foot. *Keep going!*"

Florian took another step forward, forcing the creature deeper into the cavern. "*Ad te clamamus exsules filii Hevæ . . .*"

"*This is useless.*" The demon's voice became so quiet that Florian almost thought the words came from inside his head. "Long after you're gone, we will exist. Who cares if you push me away today? A hundred, two hundred, a thousand years from now we'll return in greater numbers.

Through Rome and all the way to Portugal. The world will be ours. We'll seduce the nations and gather for battle, in numbers as vast as the sand of the sea. Time is all we need, whoremonger. Just more time."

"*Et Jesum, benedictum fructum ventris tui . . .*"

"Who are *you* to do this!"

". . . *ora pro nobis peccatoribus, nunc, et in hora mortis nostrae. Amen.*"

But before the prayer ended, the creature fled. Florian watched the thing scurry into the tunnel so quickly that he almost missed it, a blur of shadow that made it look as though the demon flew close to the tunnel floor, skimming its way into blackness. He collapsed to his knees. Although his limbs felt light and the braziers flamed upward with a roar to banish any remaining shadows, the air became cold and crisp, bringing with it a sense of exhaustion that flooded over Florian to force his eyes shut. He prayed for his brother. He sensed that the danger wasn't over yet and knew that there was nothing he could do to assist but a moment later he heard it: the song. At first Florian thought he imagined the melody but as its words became clear, louder, it filtered into the cavern from overhead, soaking through the rock.

"The Poles!" Alex shouted. "They sing Mother of God still!"

Florian's eyes snapped open. The last few Saracens disengaged from Alex, flying up the stairs, and over the song came the screams of Turkish forces—the noise of a terror-filled retreat through the streets of Perchtoldsdorf above. "The Germans are holding their own. I told you it would be so; when he attacks, Sobieski will win the field and Vienna, and Rome, will be saved."

Alex dropped to the ground next to him. The man's hair had turned ash white and when Florian reached out to touch it, strands crumbled into dust, floating toward the floor and drifting away. His brother inhaled with a wheeze. But when he looked at Florian, he grinned and then laughed, hugging him in an embrace that threatened to crush his ribs so that Florian had to beat Alex away.

"I can't breathe."

"*He is real!*" Alex shouted. "And that was a demon?"

Florian brushed dust from his cloak. "Of course He is real. But you won't be so happy when you see what the experience has done to your hair; it's bone white now, burned and blowing away into nothing. It was a *greater* demon. And you saw it without the protection of God."

"Bah." Alex waved a hand at his brother, dropping his sword to the floor with a clang. "It doesn't matter. They *impaled* them, Florian. Alive. All I can see are the bodies of the innocent . . ."

Florian saw tears form as his brother's voice trailed off. He reached out again, resting a hand on Alex's shoulder. "This practice is the *Khazouk*. A favorite method of execution of the Turks."

"But their victims are alive when it happens? Even children?"

"Yes. But those murdered by Janissaries are in Heaven now and beyond pain; joy is all they know—especially the children. Let that give you peace."

Alex grabbed his sword. He used it as a cane, pushing down on it to shift weight onto his uninjured foot, and then reached down to grab his brother's arm, helping him to his feet. Florian shivered. He gathered his cloak and wrapped it around him more tightly as the pair shuffled toward the rough stairs, climbing them slowly. When they reached the street, Florian breathed deeply and sighed.

"I am sorry," he said.

"For what?"

Florian looked at the sky—making sure the filaments had vanished and relieved when he saw nothing. "For what I did to ruin our family. For everything."

"Nonsense."

Alex wrapped an arm around his brother's shoulder, walking them northward toward Vienna. For a long while they trudged in silence. A morning breeze made a low moaning sound as it coursed through the open windows of abandoned homes, reminding Florian of a the cries of ghosts, a kind of mourning song offered by the dead as their souls rose toward Heaven. Vienna seemed so far away. He barely saw the city walls through a light fog that drifted close to the ground, a mist that broke in places to show that the ramparts had filled with cheering people— Viennese who had come out to watch the fighting unfold. Once Florian and Alex cleared Perchtoldsdorf, cracks of gunfire became clear in the distance, and the sounds of Turkish screams over the rumble of German cavalry drifted toward them on the wind; it was just like the noise of an approaching thunderstorm.

"Forget your affair with the woman, Florian; you are forgiven. And what you returned to me is far more valuable than anything I lost," Alex said.

"What did I return to *you*?"

Alex grinned. He slid his sword into its sheath and sped up his limping gate. "Faith. Now hurry; the Poles might attack and mistake us for a pair of filthy Saracens."

T.C. McCarthy is an award-winning and critically acclaimed southern author whose short fiction has appeared in *Story Quarterly*, *Nature*, and in the anthologies *Operation Arcana* (edited by John Joseph Adams) and *War Stories* (edited by Jaym Gates and Andrew Liptak). His debut novel, *Germline*, and its sequels, *Exogene* and *Chimera*, are available worldwide. In addition to being an author, T.C. is a Ph.D. scientist, a Fulbright Fellow, and a Howard Hughes Biomedical Research Scholar. Visit him at http://www.tcmccarthy.com or watch him on YouTube (https://www.youtube.com/user/therealtcmccarthy/).

At my request, he provided this afterword.

This story, "Saracens," has nothing obvious to do with David Drake. But it's all about David Drake. The first time I met him, I had just won the Compton Crook Award and was invited to Mark Van Name's house for a party, where tons of cool people (mostly fans and aspiring writers) showed up. But there was no sign of Drake—until a few minutes *after* Mark asked me to give a speech about military science fiction.

That's when Dave showed up.

So I gave a little talk about how to write, all the while thinking *why the hell am I the one giving this speech when David Drake and Mark Van Name are here, IN THE*

SAME ROOM? I knew all about Hammer's Slammers; I'm a military gamer with tons of Hammer's Slammers figures, and my basement workshop looks like a future battlefield in miniature. And I knew all about Mark; his house looks like a museum of science fiction. So that had to be the worst "speech" I'd ever given and I still have no idea what I said.

Little would I know that I'd walk away from that night as friends with Dave and that despite not being able to see him on a frequent or regular basis he would always offer help, advice—whatever I wanted or needed. He isn't a normal human being; he's superhuman. Dave is a thoughtful, brilliant, intelligent, guy who has no problem saying exactly what he means and who was built without fear (as far as I can tell).

And that's why this story has nothing to do with Dave. The first ideas I had for this anthology were imitations of Hammer's Slammers, or something equally inane, so that it eventually hit me that my story had to be totally unrelated to him; there's nothing worthy I could write in tribute to someone like Drake. "Saracens" is the result of free association, a reflection and/or mixture of current events in the Middle East and faith, written as well as I could do it and given as an offering to one of the masters of SFF. And then as soon as I turned it in I realized: Mark had done it again. He'd asked me to give another "speech" on military SFF to David Drake.

Thanks, Mark! And cheers, Dave; anyone with half your career is a monumental success.

The One That Got Away

Eric S. Brown

"Captain!" Hank called as the stool he sat on, behind the store's main counter, creaked from the shifting of his weight. "You missed a spot."

Stephen Richmond grunted, trying to keep his expression calm. He stepped back from the glass door he'd been cleaning and examined it.

Curls of smoke, from the cigarette Hank puffed on, drifted upwards to the tar-stained ceiling above where he sat.

Finding the spot, Stephen scrubbed at it furiously. Hank was a good decade younger than he was but like most younger folks these days, he knew nothing about respect. The fact that Stephen was a veteran meant as little to him as their age difference did. Hank owned the store and that made him king within its walls. There was nothing Stephen could do but endure Hank's jabs if he wanted to keep his job. And he needed it. No one else would hire him.

"Guess that's enough cleaning for today," Hank said, pulling his bulk up off the stool. "It's time to lock up anyways."

Stephen nodded. The sun was setting outside and he was thankful to be heading home. He tucked his rag and bottle of cleaner away behind the counter then went to get his jacket from the back room.

Hank was waiting for him at the store's front door when he returned. As they stepped out onto the street and Hank turned back to lock up, he said, "Try to show up to work sober tomorrow for once, old man."

"Sure thing boss," Stephen lied.

He watched Hank carefully cram himself into the driver's seat of his Buick and drive away then headed for the ABC store across the street.

Three hours later and so drunk he barely managed to land on the bed he was aiming for as he collapsed, Stephen closed his eyes. . . . Rose was there waiting for him.

She leaped from her chair as he heard the words, "Captain, you'd better leave through the window."

Her hands reached out for the cylinder Sergeant Morzek lifted from his bag, her lips twisted in a feral snarl.

Stephen jumped up and threw himself at the window. His heart was on the edge of exploding inside his chest as the glass shattered and he tumbled through it to the yard.

Rose's father had disappeared from the chair he'd been sitting in and was suddenly at her side, grabbing her. Just as Stephen lost sight of them, smashing into the ground,

Morzek's cylinder detonated. Rose came flying over him in the midst of a blast of white fire that bulged the walls of the house.

Stephen awoke with a scream. It echoed off the walls of the tightly cramped apartment he called home. Sweat glistened on his skin as he threw his legs over the side of the bed and the soles of his feet made contact with the cold wood of the floor. He had swept up the pistol that rested on the nightstand into his hand, almost knocking over the lamp there. Bullets were useless against her kind but the gun made him feel safer.

Stephen's eyes darted about, scanning the shadows of the room. He never slept without a light on anymore but there were always shadows. They followed him and tore at what remained of the rational part of his brain.

Seeing he was alone, Stephen laid the pistol aside and tried to force himself to calm down. Years had passed since his days as a "ghoul," delivering the news that a loved one had fallen in combat to those who waited for them at home. He'd been offended when Morzek labeled him that but the term fit. His job was never easy but it was safer than being on the sharp end of things. Or so he thought until the day he'd driven Morzek to pay a visit to the Lonkowskis. Only the grace of God and a rather thick piece of drapery had saved his life that day. He could still hear the Lonkowskis' wails of pain as the white phosphorus burned away their flesh and kept burning down into their bones. Even so, it had taken them a long time to die.

The official report of the incident labeled Morzek insane. It was just another sad story of a man broken and driven mad by the horrors of war, made even more tragic by the family of a KIA soldier he'd taken to the grave with him.

The murder of the Lonkowskis at the hands of a decorated veteran caught the attention of the national news and though Captain Stephen Richmond hadn't been charged as an accomplice to what Morzek had done, it had ended his career. The army wanted nothing to do with him and he was discharged before the whole thing blew over and faded away from the public's attention. As far as the world was concerned, the whole mess was over with and something best left unspoken.

Stephen spent his days working for Hank at the corner grocery store, pushing shopping carts, cleaning, and carrying bags. It wasn't glamorous work but it put food on the table and allowed him to keep his rent paid. The rest of what he earned went to whatever kind of drink was cheapest on any given night: beer, wine, vodka, it didn't matter. As long as he had something to dull the edge of his memories and fear, he didn't care what he was drinking.

He had no friends and his family were all dead. One by one, they had passed on, leaving him behind. His wife had been the first to go. She had died peacefully in her sleep beside him. One morning, he simply woke up and rolled over to find her lifeless eyes staring at him. The doctors had no explanation as to what had caused her death. There had been no sign of sickness and the only signs of injury were two small marks on her neck.

His parents were the next to go. His sister, Helen, had phoned him on Christmas Eve to give him the news. With his limited finances and no car, Stephen hadn't been able to travel for the holidays and missed the get-together at her home in Charlotte. A terrible accident, she'd told him. Their car had struck a patch of ice and went spinning through a guardrail into the side of a mountain. Somehow the car's gas tank ruptured and there wasn't enough left of them to fill their coffins.

A year later, Helen, herself, had been brutally murdered in her home. Mrs. Kirkpatrick, Helen's boss at the law firm, had gone to check on her after Helen hadn't shown up for work two days in a row. It was unlike Helen to miss work. Helping those who couldn't stand up for themselves had been her life and she had thrived on the drama of the courtroom.

Mrs. Kirkpatrick had discovered Helen's door unlocked and let herself in to find Helen's rotting body dangling where it hung, inches above the floor. The leg of her kitchen table had been broken off and rammed, with impossible force, through her chest, pinning her body to the wall.

It was then that Stephen started to slip out of his denial. The memories of that day with Sergeant Morzek truly came flooding back into his mind. One had gotten away as the flames raged and the Lonkowski house burned. PFC Lonkowski's younger sister had been thrown from the house by her father at the last possible moment. Her gorgeous, red hair burned away to show the sizzling skin of her smoking scalp as he landed on the earth next to him. Her body was a mass of fire as she scrambled to her feet and raced away along the street. Stephen lay on the grass of the yard, watching her. He had seen that most of the flames dancing about her body were just ordinary fire, ignited by the heat of the blast, and not the Willie Pete that Morzek had detonated in the house's sitting room. No human being should have been able to stay on their feet through the pain that girl must have been in. She not only stayed on her feet though, she ran into the night with a speed that was utterly inhuman. The lines of her form blurred before she was simply gone. Morzek had known the Lonkowskis weren't what they seemed and in that moment, Stephen witnessed the proof of the story the sergeant had told before setting off the bomb he'd brought with him from Nam to end them.

His father had given him a gold-plated compass as Stephen shipped out to Vietnam. He'd carried it through the jungles, always having a piece of home with him. Pawning it to have the cash to attend Helen's funeral hurt but not as much as losing Helen. With her gone, he was left alone.

When he returned home, he saw her face every night in his dreams. Not Helen but Rose. He remembered how beautiful she was as she sat listening to Morzek admit to killing her brother in Nam. He remembered her snarl as Morzek lifted the fat gray cylinder of White Phosphorous from the bag he had carried into the Lonkowskis' home. Worst of all, he saw how she must look now. Charred flesh that would never heal.

She whispered to him in his nightmares. Promises of the retribution that was coming. Her dream self showed him the night she visited his wife, creeping into their bedroom to taste Lorraine's blood while she slept. Of how she stepped into the road in front of his parents' car. The startled look on his father's face as he swerved to avoid her. His mother, trapped by her seat belt, as she was cooked alive inside the wreckage. But always, she took special pleasure in showing him Helen. She had approached Helen as a client, supposedly the victim of a fire born of negligence in the rundown apartment building she claimed to have lived in. Helen's heart went out to Rose and they became her friends.

One evening, Rose showed up on her doorstep. Helen let her in, expecting pleasant company and good conversation, only to be told the story of what Morzek had done to the Lonkowski family and Stephen's part in their murder. His sister, of course, understood none it. Stephen hadn't shared the real events of that day with anyone, not even her. When Helen realized Rose's intent, she tried to flee. There was no escape though. Rose easily knocked Helen unconscious with an effortless slap to the side of her head. The nightmare always ended with Helen's eyes bursting open as Rose drove the table leg into and through Helen's heart. Helen's scream became a gargle as she choked on her own blood rising up inside her and Rose twisted the wood back and forth, securing Helen's body to the wall, several inches above the floor.

Stephen knew Rose's whispers were true. Sooner or later, she would be coming for him as well. He took what precautions he could and went on with the wreck that was his life, drinking away the fear and pain.

Glancing at the clock, he saw that it was well after midnight but far from dawn. Stephen got up out of bed, picked up the pistol again, and walked to the fridge and got a beer. He popped its top and downed the can in one long chug, tossing it aside.

"Captain Richmond," a voice that sounded like the heel of a boot grinding on gravel called from behind him.

Stephen whirled about to see Rose standing beside his bed. Her lips were parted in a snarl that showed her teeth, gleaming in the light of lamp.

"Rose," he murmured, barely able to speak at all. The pistol fell from his hand, clattering onto the floor at his feet.

"I'm alone now, Captain," Rose said as she moved with supernatural grace, closing in on him. Her cold fingers reached out to caress his cheek. "As are you," she purred.

He stood there, rooted in place by fear. Captain Stephen Richmond had always been a coward and tonight was no different.

Tears welled up in his eyes. They flowed down to wet the tips of Rose's fingers where they lingered against his skin. He recalled the words of Morzek from what seemed another lifetime ago. "Something had to be done," the sergeant had said and now, it was up to him to finish it.

His hand dug around in his pocket, producing a remote detonator switch.

"Goodbye Rose," he said as his thumb pressed down on the center of the switch, igniting the cylinders he had planted in the corners of his apartment.

"No!" Rose howled in the flash of a second before the light and heat from several pounds of erupting white phosphorus washed over them. Stephen's last thought was of Sergeant Morzek's savage grin somewhere up in Heaven.

Eric S. Brown is the author the Kaiju Apocalypse series (with Jason Cordova), the Bigfoot War series, and the "A Pack of Wolves" series. Some of his standalone books include *War of the Worlds Plus Blood Guts and Zombies*, *The Weaponer*, *World War of the Dead*, *Last Stand in a Dead Land*, and *Kaiju Armageddon* to name only a few. He lives in North Carolina with his wife and two children where he continues to write tales of blazing guns and monsters.

At my request, he offered this afterword.

Reading David Drake's work taught me how to write. I cut my teeth on the Hammer's Slammers series and moved on to devour the bulk of his library of work. The thing I think that separates me from most of the people contributing to this tribute volume is that it's Drake horror I love most of all. *Night and Demons* remains my favorite Drake book. Those early stories he did before he became one of the kings of Military SF really moved me. As a child, *Weird War Tales* from DC Comics was among my favorite titles and I sought it out every month. Drake's early stories were very much like those comics only taken to a higher, deeper level. When given the chance to contribute a tale to this anthology I knew that for me to honor Dave, I really had to tackle his darker work. By trade, I am a professional horror author myself and trust me, the stories in *Night and Demons* are among some of the best horror ever written. "Something Had to Be Done" is arguably not only one of the best horror stories of the twentieth century but also one of the best vampire tales as well. Dave doesn't do horror anymore. He's managed to escape the darker places where writers like myself still tread. Nonetheless, to deny the fact that Dave not only wrote horror but wrote some of the coolest horror of the twentieth century would be wrong. My story, "The One That Got Away," is a direct sequel to Dave's, picking up years later with Captain Richmond and a member of the Lonkowski family who escaped Sergeant Morzek's fateful visit.

Appreciating Dave

Toni Weisskopf

I count Dave Drake as one of my oldest friends in my professional life in science fiction (and I've known him for a long time, too—rimshot!). Of course, he was good friends with Jim Baen, and that's how I knew him first, at least as a person and not some disembodied author name.

I knew his reputation as a writer years before that, as many of my friends in Southern fandom thought highly of his work, especially the Hammer's Slammers stories (first published by Jim in *Galaxy* magazine). I knew of him from reading the *Whispers* anthologies and from stories of the early World Fantasy Conventions that I'd read about when exhausting the Huntsville, Alabama, public library SF selection.

Early on, my favorites of his were the Old Nathan stories (as I was also a big fan of Manly Wade Wellman's Silver John stories, long before I knew Drake's connection to Wellman), and the *Lacey and Friends* collection. I am not ashamed to admit I didn't quite have the life experience to appreciate the Hammer's Slammers when I first tried them in my late teens. Now I do. Kinda wish I didn't, but then many of us have benefitted by Dave dealing with experiences in his fiction that he'd rather not had to have gone through, too.

These days some of my favorites of his are the RCN series—a kinder, gentler Dave Drake, with stories inspired by Jim Baen's love of the buddy stories of Aubrey and Maturin by Patrick O'Brian. I quite enjoyed his *Lord of the Isles* fantasies, which have some of my favorite Drake characters, the brother and sister Cashel and Ilna. His most powerful work I maintain is *Redliners*, an incredibly moving work of military SF. And I find it amusing that one of Baen's better selling collections is his *All the Way to the Gallows*, a book of (darkly) humorous military SF stories.

I'm not sure if I should reveal this, but it is not only Dave's writerly skills that have contributed to the success of Baen Books (we've been publishing his work since our first year of shipping books), but also his editorial acumen. He has a keen eye for what makes for a good story, and has unselfishly been sharing that eye with young authors for years, not only the writers we have paired him with for collaborations but with many others as well.

Dave was one of the first to appreciate a tricky piece of editing I'd done, and it cheered me immeasurably when I was just a fledgling editor to have him tell me I'd done a good job. He commemorated that work in a dedication for *Northworld*, one I will treasure always: "For Toni Weisskopf, who, like the Black Prince, won her

spurs among scenes of butchery." It wasn't a real field of
battle, but there was a lot of red ink expended . . . Of
course, it was a book of Dave's so there may very well have
been actual *scenes* of butchery I edited, so it's really a
double entendre—which is very Dave, to me. At any rate,
I knew that if I had met Dave's high standards, then I had
really done well. That encouraged me to keep at this field.

And that is the kind of guy Dave is. He calls 'em like
he sees 'em. I respect him for that, and appreciate him for
that. It also makes it very challenging to work with him
sometimes—hard to live up to his very high standards. But
you never wonder where you stand with Dave. Of course,
he is also a thoroughgoing professional, which makes it
very easy to work with him. I know that I will probably
continue to make missteps with Dave—and that he will
let me know, and I will figure out how to improve and
grow as a professional. Damnit.

We share many of the same values, too, which means
most of the time the communication is easy. I like to think
we also share your basic doggy virtues: loyalty, honesty,
affection, and a certain determined refusal to quit. Of
course, I'm more your Old Yeller type—a bit sloppy, kind
of goofy, and will probably die mauled from taking on a
bear much bigger than I am. Dave's your basic
Doberman: sleek, elegant, well-mannered, usually quite
self-contained. He's going to die from that same bear, but
the bear will have his teeth marks on its neck.

More seriously, I admire Dave because he always
strives to be a gentleman. My late husband Hank
respected him, too, because he also had that goal, and
appreciated just how difficult that could be at times. And

because I know a deep well of contentment is not at Dave's core, I find him inspirational. Because he is a gentleman, he inspires me to try to be a better version of myself.

And then there are the dirty jokes. We share a love of those, too. And one of these days, I really am going to use on the back of a book the beefcake photo of Dave posing in cutoffs and no shirt he sent to the office a few years back. Because really, if you can't have fun with science fiction, where can you have fun?

Finally, I'd like to thank Mark Van Name for putting together this volume. It was his idea, and his project, and I have to say it's very nice to do one of these things while the person being honored is still alive to appreciate it—to say nothing of the salubrious effect to the world getting two new Dave Drake stories. Well done, Mark, and thank you, Dave, for having such enterprising friends!

Toni Weisskopf succeeded Jim Baen as publisher of Baen Books in 2006. With Josepha Sherman she compiled and annotated the definitive volume of subversive children's folklore, *Greasy Grimy Gopher Guts*, published by August House. Weisskopf is a graduate of Oberlin College, with a degree in anthropology. She is the mother of a delightful daughter, and lives in a hundred-year-old house in a balanced household of three cats and three dogs. Taking care of those consumes most of her spare time, but she is also interested in space science and is a participant in the Tennessee Valley Interstellar Workshop.

Swimming from Joe

Barry N. Malzberg

For David Drake and Spalding Grey

I

Much later Hammer could still remember the actress, distended, inflated, enormous, drifting above the killing fields like a balloon. In country he had dreamed of her in darkness and light, thinking of that Korean tour fifteen years earlier, Marilyn on that distant stage with five thousand troops screaming at her and he had awakened screaming himself, her image in swirls of paint and fire. This was after the campaign, after all of the fierce but failed conquests, after he had been taken to the rear lines in what he had thought was a body bag. "Joe, you never heard cheering like that in your life."

"Oh yes I have."

Oh yes he had.

II

What did they know of those fields back in the world? Marilyn drifted ever closer to him in the night, her mouth open with need, her thighs soaring before him and sometimes he would reach for her, emerge from that cocoon of space to attempt some kind of contact. It would never happen. Like the enemy itself she was there and she was absent, she was omnipresent and invisible, he could not touch her, she would not touch him, she was as remote as the Slammers, as close as the deadening, cooling fire.

III

He was not sure when he had first seen her. The campaign was arched in its annihilation of time. But years later Hammer had become convinced that he had not only seen but somehow caused her to react: that doomed actress, seven years past her suicide, hanging enormously over the fields, intimately in the tent, her body drifting slowly among the cloudbanks, the spurs of napalm and stink of the ordnance covering but never obliterating her. Oh, she was dead, she had to be dead, Hollywood had killed her as the War had killed the Slammers, dead men in living posture but to Hammer, not sure if he was awake or dreaming no cause, no person meant more to him than simply crawling to the next day. In her assumption of a circumstance larger than death she was somehow keeping him alive. We are born to die, he thought. All except her. She died to live. She was the engineer and circumstance of the helium that kept her high in the air, close in the tent.

IV

The Slammers had overtaken him. They had become the purest instruments of the killing field. Down among the dead men he was as live man now, somehow brought through circumstance to something beyond. In the early films Marilyn had been nothing but fear, fear and nervousness in small roles: stricken models, stricken secretaries, a stricken babysitter . . . she had been driven by fear from the outset and had been taken to places beyond her capacity. She was the perfect handmaiden to the Slammers for that reason: the Slammers could feel nothing, she felt everything. Everything and nothing: that was what In Country had become and Hammer did not know if he was poised beyond mortality or simply draped by it. The Slammers were the dead and the living in simultaneity, they were truly Schrodinger's Troops. "Oh come to me," he dreamed that he pleaded. "Show me your fear and I will show you mine and we will find salvation together."

V

This was before she had taken to suspension in the air,

clinging in the tent. This was before the First Sergeant had, broken, dispatched the anonymous kill order. He could theorize that it was in that abyss that Hammer himself might have engaged in stricken dialogues with Marilyn which however imaginary (like the Slammers too might have been) were no less testing or terrible. This war itself was imaginary, he was learning. Like Marilyn it hung suspended or came in sleep. Here it was another contrivance and its possibilities completely inseparable from its events.

VI

So there she was and there she would be, hovering near or far, close perspective and distant. He dreamed her in clouds and in the field latrine, dreamed her in postures grotesque and fanciful. "I never heard cheering like that." "I never knew anyone like you." "I never thought I would have but we had. Frightened: I am so frightened." She would say anything. Whether what she spoke was real or imagined was irrelevant, it was certainly real enough for him.

VII

So real, so evanescent. She had been dead all that time but just as the Slammers had bloomed under their commission, even as the dead men had learned to march, so had Marilyn grown in the squalor of her final posture.

If fear had made her ever more sensuous, then death had induced a gravitas to her fear which made it the War itself. I went to sleep and awakened here, she whispered. Who are you? Who are they? Why did all of their cheering fail to save me?

VIII

As with the Slammers, so it was for the Marilyn: the essential story, the central story had been taken. Nothing remained but fragments of that narrative dropped like shrapnel on the killing field, scattered and dispersed through the emptiness.

IX

"And so it was in that moment, in that single flash of cognition refracted from her enormous drifting suspended soul that I came to understand truly and for the first time who Hammer was, from where he had come and for what purpose. And why we had been assembled. And why Marilyn had killed herself."

Barry N. Malzberg, Pvt. E-2 USA, long retired, is the author of "Final War" (*Magazine of Fantasy & Science Fiction*, April 1968) and many other works of fiction over the succeeding near half-century. "Final War," a Nebula finalist in 1969, lost to Richard Wilson's "Mother To The World," which was in fact quite a good novelette. *Breakfast In The Ruins*, a collection of essays on science fiction, won the Locus Award in 2008 for Best Related Nonfiction Book and was a Hugo finalist.

At my request, he provided this afterword.

David spent years in country with the armored cavalry; he lived the ferocity and the fire. I spent six months at Fort Dix beginning in August 1960, eight weeks of them in Basic Training. This was still Eisenhower's sleepy and quietly resentful peacetime Army, nothing to compare with McNamara's Band but it was over a hundred degrees on the rifle range and bivouac and the forced marches, six miles with field equipment, left even well-conditioned kids gasping and First Sergeant Tommy Atkinson was coughing blood. The experiences were not to be equated and I do not equate them but David and I reached, nonetheless, similar conclusions about the Army and the Hastings of "Final War" would have found nothing unfamiliar about the Slammers. Down among the dead men. The primal, the universal alienation laid out by both writers in the flattest, deadest prose of repressed anger: PTSD prose, the lilies of the valley crushed in the noonday sun. Nothing about the actual experience of war is ideological or principled. Of course the three generations of chicken hawks who ran operations for half a century and are running them now would argue otherwise. *Dulce et decorum est.*

David wrote the Scott Meredith Agency twenty years ago in search of an ex-client Raymond Banks ("The Short Ones") to whom he wanted to send a long-contemplated

fan letter. His note came to the desk of the only employee
of the previous four decades who might have known who
Banks was (an obscure author of occasional science fiction
and mystery short stories) and I pointed him in the right
direction, unfortunately just a few months too late. David
and I fell into correspondence and it has not flagged in
two decades. We've shared a few panels at a few
convention meetings and the correspondence has
flourished like the Slammers (although in a different way).
He is one of my closest friends. He may be the closest
friend I have. That friendship is of course tied to the fields
of science fiction and/or that laughable occupation called
"professional authorship" but it has actually grown from
a commonality of misery and understanding. Hastings is
an honorary Slammer; the Slammers as rigid as
Bemelmans' line of Madelines surround Hastings in
eternal fire.

The Village of Yesteryear

Sarah Van Name

The North Carolina State Fair is a polarizing event. Some people get really into the whole thing: the food, the rides, the exhibits of farm animals and prize-winning hay. Some people hate it for the same reasons; they roll their eyes and say it's not worth the money. I've always been a part of the former camp. Frankly, I think people would be less dismissive if they knew what happened there when I was eleven. Or maybe it would scare them away. But it doesn't matter, because no one ever believes me—except Dave, because he was there.

That year, Dave and his wife, Jo, were late meeting my family at the pretzel stand near gate seven. I was licking the butter off my fingers when they showed up.

"You made it!" my dad declared. "Got lost?"

"Yes," Dave said thoughtfully. "But we saw the exhibit of gourds. They were good this year. I mean *really* shapely, excellent range of colors. But I apologize for

225

being late. I am ready now." Jo hoisted her purse onto her shoulder and shot my mom a beleaguered look. Every year, Dave got lost before meeting us and dragged Jo with him. Dave wrapped his thin arm around his wife, the grey strands of her hair catching on his sleeve.

"Well," my dad said to the group, "shall we?"

He reached out his hand to me. I thought I was old enough to walk without holding anyone's hand. But I still took it.

Wandering through the fair was, and is, a unique experience. The full tapestry of humanity moves in throngs, people big and small, old and barely born. For me, the best moment is when you turn a corner and the road dips down in front of you, so you can see far ahead, the backs of so many people's heads moving and swaying. There is no way to be efficient about the fair. You have to amble. And that's good, because it means you move slow enough to take it all in.

We passed the candy shack, the pig races, and the booth with the mermaid woman. The ostrich-burger stand and one of a thousand soft-serve vendors. A tent selling fried candy bars and donuts. Over the fence to our right, I saw the midway with the rickety rollercoasters and puke-and-twirls.

After the Wisconsin Cheese stand, we turned right and found the carousel. Every year, I thought it was the most magnificent thing I had ever seen. Two stories tall, it was different from everything around it. It had no neon lights or flashing letters. Instead, it was lined with white bulbs like in the dressing rooms of old movie stars. The animals were made of wood and painted in fading colors, and the gold trim was chipping off to reveal bare pine underneath.

On the first story, there were small round booths with circular gold bars in the middle. You could sit in them and spin the bar and the whole booth would turn, creating your own tiny vortex in the middle of the carousel. These were my favorite.

My dad looked down at me. "Sarah, you wanna go on the carousel?"

"Yes yes yes," I said, bouncing on my heels.

"Scott, how about you?" he asked my brother. Scott shook his head, eyeing the stand that sold cheesecake on a stick.

Dave studied the carousel and announced, "I will go. It looks like a fine ride."

My mom and dad were happy with this. After I had nauseated them with my super-fast spinning last year, they preferred to stand on the sidelines with a camera, and besides, Scott was now begging for cheesecake. Dave had known me since I was born; his wife had been my nanny. My mom handed me four tickets and told me to wave when we passed by.

We wound our way through the line and stepped onto the first platform.

"I think I will ride on this fish," Dave said, sizing up a scaled beast as big as any of the horses.

"No, Dave, we gotta go in the spinny thing," I told him. I tugged him a few more steps forward to lead him toward the booth before another kid claimed it.

"What do you do?" he asked as we climbed in. Beside us, two boys hopped on a goat and a unicorn.

"You go like this," I told him. I put my hands on the bar and strained, pulling and pushing. Starting up was always the hardest. Slowly, we began to turn.

"Ah! I see. Do you want help?"

"You can if you want, but I don't need it."

At that moment, the lights got brighter, the music got louder, and the carousel jolted to life. I started spinning in earnest. Dave and I waved at my family the first time around, but I only took my hands off the bar for an instant. I spun us faster and faster and faster. The force of the motion pressed Dave back against the seat, and I leaned in.

"Good God," Dave muttered.

"You okay?!" I yelled. He didn't respond. I spun us until the outside was a neon blur. The only things in the world were that gold bar and my small determined hands spinning, spinning, spinning.

And then, the bump and squeal that meant the carousel's motor had ground to a halt. The motion slowed, the music quieted, and I took my hands off the bar. I sat back in the booth, breathing hard and gloriously dizzy. When the carousel stopped, Dave stood up unsteadily. I followed suit. It felt like the floor was shifting underneath me. We stumbled off the carousel and onto the dirt, where Dave promptly vomited.

"Ugh, Dave!" I was disgusted. I didn't even feel sick to my stomach.

"Well, that was a surprise," he said, wiping the back of his mouth.

"Let's go see if Scott has any cheesecake left," I said, looking carefully at the ground to avoid the evidence of

Dave's illness as I stepped forward. "Come on." I reached my hand out behind me and expected Dave to take it, but he didn't. "Dave?"

"Huh," he said.

"Dave, come on."

"We may be in a bit of a pickle," he said. I turned and followed his gaze upward, and that's when I realized we were in quite the pickle indeed.

The world immediately around us was the same: the dirt, the carousel, the velvet ropes blocking off the line. There was the ticket booth and the sign that said "you must be this tall to ride," which I had passed when I was eight.

But there were no other children. The man collecting tickets was gone, as were all the other parents. As were my parents. The whole area was empty, bound in by some strange fence that I hadn't noticed before.

"Mom? Dad?" I yelled. The sounds hit the air with zero impact. The hustle and bustle of the fair was still there in the background, but it felt . . . different. I was starting to get frightened. I edged closer to Dave. "What's going on?" I asked him.

"Well," Dave said, "either everyone left while we were on the carousel, or something strange is happening."

I did not like the sound of that.

"Let's look for your parents first," he said, and so we did. He took my hand and together we walked the perimeter of the carousel. Not a soul in sight. I started crying as we went, because I was eleven and my parents were gone and I was stuck with their weird friend. You'd probably cry too. The tears blurred my vision, and I followed Dave until he stopped, having completed a full circle.

He squatted down next to me. "It appears that one of two things has happened," he told me, businesslike. I wiped my eyes and fumbled in my coat pocket for the pack of tissues my mom always put there before we left for the fair. It was there, crumpled and familiar. It smelled like our house. I blew my nose.

"One potential is that we have physically moved location," he said. "That's unlikely, I think, since our immediate surroundings are the same as they were before we got onto the ride.

"Or," he continued, "we have traveled in time. Given the circumstances, and the state of the world beyond that fence—not to mention the fence itself—I think this is the more likely scenario."

I looked up. And that's when it really hit me that we were not in 2002 any more.

I had been blinded by dizziness and tears, so I hadn't noticed that the fence surrounding us was shimmering. At a glance, it looked like the black metal bars that bound the outer perimeter of the fairground, but it wasn't metal, nor was it quite black. It glittered transparently and didn't have all the dimensions of a real object—it looked the same from every angle, didn't catch the light. Like a hologram. It ran in a circle around the carousel and met in an enormous sign that stretched over an open gate. It was backwards to me, so at first it was hard to read, but I looked letter by letter and made it out: *Village of Yesteryear*.

"We're in the Village of Yesteryear," Dave said, his eyes following the same progression as mine.

"But that's on the other side of the fair," I said, confused. My parents loved the Village. Craftspeople gathered there to sell pottery and leather goods and fancy Christmas ornaments. My mom always said it was important to remember the old traditions. I thought it was boring.

"I think," Dave said slowly, "it might have moved."

"What?"

"Well, let's consider this more carefully," he said. He was ramping up into the voice he used when he asked me why I hadn't started Latin yet, even though I'd told him many times that my school didn't offer Latin until seventh grade. "If we've moved into the future, it would be logical that something from our year—this carousel—is, in fact, from *yesteryear*. That our year *is* yesteryear. And the carousel is the village."

"I see," I said, like I always do to make him stop. Usually I don't see. But I was starting to understand. "So I spun us into the future?"

"It would seem so," he said.

"Cool." I was impressed. I had always known my spinning capabilities were prodigious, but I never knew they had this much power.

"So . . . hold on," I said. "How are we gonna get back?"

"I'm guessing the answer is out there," Dave said, pointing at the gates leading into the rest of the fair. He held out his bony hand, and I took it.

As soon as we walked out of the Village, everything changed. The whole world got louder. After the carousel had stopped, the only sounds were the faint shouts of buskers and rollercoaster riders. The area immediately around us had been almost silent.

But now we were in the thick of the fair, and the noises were very different. Buskers were still yelling, but they were unbearably loud, some shrieking English words and some emitting noises in languages or dialects I didn't recognize. The people on the rides were still crying out, but not all the screams sounded happy. Some didn't even sound human.

Music was coming from every direction, the same kind of tinny techno I was used to hearing from fair rides, but louder—and including sounds I'd never heard on the radio. In music class, we'd had a unit on uncommon instruments. I heard some of those: a didgeridoo, a theremin, a zither. It sounded like all of the world's instruments were playing in one frantic orchestra.

And then there were the colors. The fair was always a whirlwind, but these were tones I'd never seen before, something flickering between fuchsia and aquamarine, a brown that looked gold every other time I blinked. Maybe I'm embellishing it in my memory. I just remember, in the first few minutes out in that world, feeling like confetti in a kaleidoscope.

But the real kicker was, as you've probably guessed, the people. Or . . . well, I guess you *would* call them people. You just wouldn't call them human.

What I find remarkable now is how quickly I recognized them as aliens. We're collectively sophisticated enough, now, to think that real aliens probably aren't the tentacled creatures of our mid-twentieth-century imagination. We think we can't possibly know what sentience from another world might look like. As a child, I had internalized that gooey 1950s imagery. But I was a smart child, so I knew on some level that if I did ever encounter an alien, I probably wouldn't recognize it.

And yet when I saw that all the people were green, some bearing an extra arm and all with bizarrely shaped ears—my immediate reaction was to tighten my hold on Dave's hand and whisper, "They're aliens!"

"Well, at least part alien," he said, distantly. I now suspect he was focused on keeping us safe. We were getting quite a few stares as we walked through the crowd. Looking around, I started to realize that Dave was right: The people were human enough that there had to have been some crossbreeding. But there really wasn't anyone like us. Not everyone was quite the same shade of green, and some people had only two arms, but no one looked normal. No one seemed quite human.

"Dave, what are we gonna do?" I asked him.

"We are . . ." he started, and then stopped walking and nodded decisively. "It only makes sense that if we spun one way on the carousel to get here, we have to spin the other way to get back. We're not having any luck finding the answer out here. I had hoped for an information booth or some such, but alas. I don't want to worry your parents. So we're going to return to the carousel."

We turned around. The noise and the lights and the strange green people were all around us, pressing in on us, getting louder and brighter and weirder.

It was then I remembered that Dave was terrible with directions.

"Screwed" was one of those words my parents used

casually and often at the dinner table, but I was not yet permitted to say. Whenever I protested, they said my teachers would get angry if I said the word at school. I didn't want my teachers to be mad at me, so I kept it out of my daily vocabulary. But I knew what it meant. And now seemed like a perfect time to practice.

"We're screwed, aren't we?" I said.

"Goddamn fucking horseshit," he muttered.

I waited and looked around while he cursed for a few minutes.

Eventually, he decided we were going to ask for directions. This proved to be difficult at first. The fair was swarming with alien-people, greenish and excited, snaking in long lines out from the fried-food stands and Ferris wheels. We walked slowly, trying not to get too much farther off course.

Finally, I glimpsed a grumpy-looking guy standing near a booth that had no line in front of it. He was yelling occasionally, but no one was taking the bait. The booth's side advertised *ARCHIE'S ENORMOUS ANCIENT "COW." ONLY FOUR LEGS. HEALTHY DESPITE DEFORMITY. SEE IT TO BELIEVE IT*. Before the words were some numbers and a bizarre symbol that I assume meant money. We approached him.

"Y'all wanna see the cow?" he growled as we came up. Listening to him speak up close, it finally struck me what was weird about everyone's voices. They sounded the same, but *wetter*, like a damp lisp.

"We were hoping for directions to the Village of Yesteryear," Dave said. The guy—Archie, I assume— looked at us skeptically for a moment, then picked his nose.

"Gotta pay to see the cow first."

"Are you fucking kidding me?"

The guy shrugged. "Not gonna give free directions to some prejudiced asshole."

Dave furrowed his brow. "What do you mean?"

"Won't sleep with our kind. Keeping your line pure and all that bullshit. It's the twenty-sixth century, time to wake the fuck up."

"Oh!" Dave said. "No. Listen, I recognize this sounds foolish, but we're actually from the past."

Archie picked his nose again.

Dave gave up and reached into his pocket. "Fine. We'll see the cow if you give us directions. Is five dollars enough?"

The guy's eyes went wide. In fact, I think his eyelids contracted fully into his skull to reveal more eye, which was something I could not do, but I guess that's what evolution will get you. He snatched the five-dollar bill from Dave's hands.

"What the fuck, man, where did you get this?"

"From my pocket," Dave said slowly.

"This is . . . shit, I've never seen one of these except in a museum." The guy paused, looked down at the bill again, and reverently folded it before placing it in his pocket. "You say you came from the past? Where's the time machine?"

"We think it's the carousel in the Village of Yesteryear," I piped up. "That's why we want directions."

"Got it." His ear flaps rotated slowly. "Tell you what, you paid to see the cow, you see the cow. You go on in and wait. I'm gonna get the Engineer."

"What about the directions?" Dave demanded.

"The Engineer is gonna be able to help you. I, uh, I don't know the area that well."

"Can you give us a map or something?" I asked, trying to be helpful.

"Just chill with the cow and I'll be back real soon," the guy said and ushered us inside. He zipped the tent flap behind us.

"Well that was fucking useless," Dave muttered. Although I couldn't disagree, I said nothing. I was too busy adjusting my mind to the fact of the cow in front of us, which in fact was not a cow but a horse. It looked like a perfectly normal horse. It had four legs and a snout and a tail, which it flicked at us in a vaguely irate manner. I went forward to pet it, stepping over the thin rope barrier separating it from the walkway. I would hate it here too, cooped up in this strange little tent.

I petted the side of its face, like my friend had taught me at her pony-riding birthday party. "It's all right," I said softly. "You're not a cow." It blinked one enormous eye at me and pushed its head into my hand.

Dave began to pace back and forth across the thin strip of dirt.

"This is not a good situation," he said. I continued petting the horse. In my head, I named her Lyra after the protagonist of my favorite book. "We're leaving. We can find a map somewhere else."

"But the weird guy told us to stay," I said.

"Yes, well, you have to trust me more than him," Dave said shortly. He strode to the end of the tent and reached down to pull up the zipper.

It didn't budge.

Dave cursed and tried the entry flap. That zipper didn't move either.

"Sometimes mine gets stuck in a piece of fabric from my coat," I said.

"It's not that," Dave said. He crouched on the ground, attempting pull up the zipper with all his might. "It's more intentional. I'm guessing a magnetization system of some kind. Regardless, it's working. We're trapped."

I leaned against the horse. I was starting to feel a bit sick. I wanted my mom and dad, and said so.

"Well, I'd like to see them again too, but I can't promise anything," Dave said. Tears sprang to my eyes. He took another look at me and, for the first time, appeared to realize that I was a child. Dave had a son, and it always mystified me to consider what kind of father he would have been. He always treated me like a grown-up. Now, though, it seemed like he understood that I might be having more trouble than the average adult. He sighed.

"We might as well talk about something else until they come back," he said. "Have you started Latin yet?"

"No," I said.

"But you know the basics," he clarified.

"No," I said.

"Ah!" he exclaimed. "Well, you've heard of the *Metamorphoses*, at least."

"Yes," I said, giving up. I *had* actually heard of the *Metamorphoses* in a book somewhere. I didn't know what they were or how they related to Latin, but that didn't matter. Dave was going to tell me.

So I petted Lyra's snout, and she looked at me with

one big lovely eye, and Dave talked about the *Metamorphoses* for a long time. He used all kinds of words I didn't know and referred to people I had never heard of, Roman emperors and conquerors and poets. He talked about his own struggles with translations and the intricacies of the stories.

I smiled and said "uh huh" in what appeared to be the right places, because he nodded at me and continued every time. Something I both loved and hated about Dave is that he always assumed I was right there with him, on the same intellectual level. It was difficult because I usually didn't understand his speeches. But it was nice to have the benefit of the doubt.

Dave was right in the middle of a soliloquy on the poet-emperor relationship when I heard an odd click and the sound of a zipper. I jumped, startling Lyra, and turned toward the entrance. Dave stopped talking abruptly and followed suit.

The tent parted at the zipper and through stepped our friend from before. It was hard to tell on his alien face, but he seemed nervous. He held the flap open for a second person.

She was much more familiar. Much more human, I should say, because although I had never seen her before, she immediately made me feel as if I was back in a world I knew. She was young and dark-haired with only a slight green tinge to her skin. She had only two arms and the flaps on her ears were delicate, almost unnoticeable. She smiled at us widely as she stepped in.

"We need to leave now," Dave said. "We'll find our own way. Let us out."

"I am so sorry for the inconvenience," the young woman said. She had the same wet voice as Archie (who was now hanging back in front of the entrance, picking at a scab on his chin). Her voice wasn't clammy and gross, though—it was smooth and sugary, like the thin line of honey right before you stop pouring. She reached out a hand to Dave. "I'm the Engineer," she said. "It's an honor to meet travelers from so long ago." Dave kept his hands on his hips and said nothing. The woman lowered her palm.

"We're going now," Dave said.

"I was hoping you could help me," the woman said.

"We can't," Dave said, his voice rising.

It was as if she hadn't even heard him. "You see," she continued, "I discovered the carousel and built the Village of Yesteryear, and I'm very curious to hear more about life in your time. It would help me expand the village and make it much more realistic. After all, we have some photographs and the articles online, but the Internet was slow in 2002, and after the asteroid, well . . ." she shrugged. "It destroyed a lot of primary sources. Regardless, there's no comparison for firsthand witnesses. And I'm sure you must be curious about how the carousel works." She looked at me for the first time and smiled, a warm, sweet smile that reminded me of my favorite teachers.

"I am," I said. Dave shot me a furious glance and I immediately realized I'd made a mistake. But I *was* curious. I read all sorts of fantasy and time-travel books and I always wondered how the whole apparatuses worked. The authors never fully explained things.

"The carousel is linked to a very specific time: October 23, 2002, six o'clock through six-oh-three P.M. The idea is that as people ride the carousel here and now, the circular motion creates just enough of a link for them to *see* what the world was like in 2002, but not enough to actually interact with it, and not enough for the past world to see them. But it wasn't working.

"Or so we thought. Now I discover that it *was* working, but in a different way than we expected." She stepped over the rope and petted the other side of Lyra's snout. Lyra shuffled and turned toward me. "My question is, if you're here, where are all the other carousel riders? All my data indicates that the ride would have been quite full at that time."

"We were the only ones," I told her honestly.

"You don't have to lie to me," she said softly, leaning a little closer. "You can trust me."

"She is," Dave said, exasperated. "She spun that little booth so fast that it only took us."

The woman frowned and leaned back. "Possible," she muttered to herself, "but . . . no, it's so unlikely. Tell me where the others are."

"It's really just us," I said. I was starting to get afraid.

The Engineer looked down at me, opened her mouth, and then shut it again and smiled. "You're standing by that?" she said. I nodded.

She turned to Archie and jerked her head slightly to the right. That was the only warning. The next thing I knew, the green man had pulled out something like a gun from a flap on his side and shot Dave.

"No!" I screamed, but it wasn't as bad as I thought: He

was only bound. Two thin metal bands wrapped around him at the chest and shins. He fell to the ground struggling.

"Magnetic ropes," the guy said. "Good luck getting out of those. I've seen your movies. Knives ain't gonna do nothin'. Now, me, I could let you out right now—" He clicked the side of a metal disc on his belt, and the ropes loosened for a moment. Dave was starting to stretch out his arms when the guy clicked the disc and the ropes tightened again. "But I won't."

Dave started cursing at them in a long, steady stream. Terrified though I was, I had to admire the sheer variety of words he was throwing at our captors.

The Engineer turned to Dave and spoke over him, her voice loud and dripping. "I've done a lot of research to make this Village as accurate as possible. But until now, I couldn't know everything. I want all the details, and I need a variety of primary sources to get a full picture. Plus, there are the scientific possibilities. There are no full humans left, no matter what those purist groups claim. We could learn so much from you."

She crouched down to just below my height. She was truly beautiful, like an elf from the movies. Her ear flaps fluttered like feathers.

"We won't hurt him if you tell us where they are," she said to me. She reached out to my cheek as if I were the horse. I shied away.

"I don't know," I told her.

"Get away from her!" Dave yelled from his place on the floor.

She leaned in close and whispered in my ear, her

breath damp and cool like a winter swamp. "We *will* hurt him if you don't."

My mind went wild. "The Wisconsin Cheese Stand," I blurted. The woman's brow furrowed. "I mean, where the Wisconsin Cheese Stand was in 2002, I guess. I don't know what's there now. But that's where they were headed. We got separated from the group."

She stood up and turned away from me, moving toward Archie. She nodded her head pointedly and they stepped outside. I heard a small click after they fully zipped up the flap. Outside, their voices were audible but muffled. The Engineer was tense and excited, her sidekick less so.

"Sarah," Dave hissed, jerking me over with his head.

"We need to get out of here," I said to him.

"I fucking know," he whispered urgently. "Keep your voice down. Now listen. I would tell you to run for it on your own, but I'm not sure you would make it. I think that bitch is going to leave us in here while she looks up her goddamn antique maps to find out where the cheese stand used to be. We'll be alone with the idiot. I'm going to distract him so you can steal that disc from his belt."

"I can't do that," I said. I was starting to panic.

"Yes you can. Here—help me up—" He had managed to sit and was struggling to get upright. I pushed and shoved until he was steady on his feet. "Listen very carefully. This is our chance. While I'm talking, try to get closer to the asshole, and when I say Catullus, that's when you take it. Click the top button and the button on the side. If I'm right, the top should unlock the tent and the side should unlock me.

"Once I'm free, I'm going to attack. We won't have a lot of time before the Engineer gets back and finds us gone. So after I disable him, we're getting on the horse and leaving."

"But we don't have any idea where to go," I said.

"Yes." Dave exhaled. "That's still an issue. But it's the least of our problems. And we can cover a lot more ground on a horse than we could on foot."

"So we're just going to ride around until we find the carousel again?"

"Yes."

"Do you know how to ride a horse?"

"I know how to ride a motorcycle. It can't be that different."

"Dave."

"Sarah." He looked severely into my eyes. "You can do this. You need to do this. Believe me when I say I would not ask you unless it was absolutely necessary. He won't be looking at you; you just have to make a run for it, quietly."

"But what if I—"

Dave shushed me. "Go back to the horse," he said under his breath, and I hurried back to Lyra. She sniffed around my pockets, which still smelled like pretzels. Her hot breath was oddly comforting.

"You're gonna save us from the weird aliens. A cow couldn't do that," I whispered to her as the carnie and the Engineer walked back in. This time, she started directly toward me.

"Sweet girl," she said, "I just wanna make sure. You aren't lying to me, are you?"

I shook my head. I think if I had spoken, I would have started crying.

"It's not that I don't trust you. If you're telling the truth, I'll escort you to a room for the night. Unfortunately, I'm afraid you'll never get back to your own time. There are too many people who would pay to talk to you. Get some of your DNA . . . the possibilities are limitless. But if your companions really are at the old cheese stand, I'll treat you very well. Promise.

"But if you are lying," and she sank down right next to me and looked so hard at me that I had to look at the ground, "I will not be so kind."

"I promise," I said, voice quavering.

My parents had taught me never to lie. It was a cardinal sin in our household. But I stared at the dirt and tried to lie even to myself. I imagined a group of scared kids standing where they thought they would find Wisconsin Cheese, lying with every fiber of my being. Because Dave had told me to do it, and I had to trust him. I did trust him. When I looked back up, straight into her clear blue eyes, I knew the lie was strong, and I saw her believe me.

"Okay," she said, straightening. "I'll just go check on that. My friend here is gonna stay with you."

She turned and left the tent. This time, I was watching. As soon as she stepped out and closed the zipper, Archie tapped the top button on the device on his hip. I heard that metallic click again.

"Your name is Archie, is that right?" Dave asked. The Carnie did not reply. "Are you also curious about this kind of history?"

"The Engineer's my boss," Archie said begrudgingly. "Not my boss directly. But we were all told if anything weird happens around the Village, go get her."

I started edging away from Lyra.

"Ah!" Dave said. "So you don't take a personal interest."

"Couldn't care less about ancient human assholes," Archie responded.

"Understood. I'm just wondering how much of what we considered history survives today. How much you know about ancient Rome, for instance."

I tried to step lightly. I crept closer to the wall, making a wide arc from the horse to the carnie. I was maybe a third of the way there.

"Did your people investigate human history when you arrived?" Dave continued. "You would have easily discovered Rome if so."

Archie seemed unsure of himself. "Heard about it," he mumbled, scratching the back of his neck. I was past the halfway point, getting closer and closer, slowly.

"I would certainly hope so," Dave said.

"You callin' me stupid?" Archie said angrily, taking a step forward—and just slightly changing my path. I shuffled and quick-stepped and was three-quarters of the way there.

"Not at all," Dave responded. "But it would be a pity if you missed learning about Rome. It's fascinating. I'm most curious about how the literature survived. Did you ever learn any Catullus?"

I wasn't there, not quite, but I knew it was coming as soon as he said literature. I leapt forward and reached out my small hand as far as it would go, my eyes and my arm and my whole being aimed toward that little silver disc, and it worked: I grabbed it, and as I was falling to the ground, I pressed the buttons and heard two clicks.

Archie reacted fast, roaring in fury and reaching down for me. A slimy hand grabbed my waist. But Dave was just as fast. I heard human footsteps and the hand tore away from me as Dave crashed into the carnie. I saw Dave grab at that blunt object on Archie's side belt before I heard him yell, "Don't look!"

So I rolled into a ball and hid my head under my arms, and I listened to Dave beat the guy into submission. I heard groans and punches and then, after a few seconds of nothing, the sound of a zipper. I peeked and saw Dave had opened the tent flap. Before I knew it, he scooped me up and placed me on top of Lyra, who had become severely concerned. Dave jumped up behind me, yelled, "Go!" and slapped the horse on her rump, hard.

To this day, I don't know whether Dave killed the guy or just knocked him out. I have no idea how he was able to get onto the horse safely, with no saddle, having so little experience. I'm not sure how Lyra knew how to get out of the tent, trampling Archie's limp body before running straight through the flap, but of course she did.

At first, she ran frantically down the middle of the dirt roads, green people leaping out of her way with shouts of alarm. I just held on tight, pinned between Dave and the horse. The sky was dark now and it was cold, and the sharp wind brought tears to my eyes.

"Keep an eye out for the Village!" Dave yelled in my

ear, and I did, but we saw nothing familiar: strange food stands and whirling rides and freak shows, yes, but not that carousel. The horse got tired after a while and slowed down, trotting from street to street, pausing to nose at frightened passersby.

Suddenly, Dave turned his head back with a sharp twist. "Shit," he muttered.

"What?"

"Nothing."

I looked behind us anyway. Dave had heard something I'd missed. Far back—way up the hill, just within our eyesight—I saw an army of security guards, big green guys dressed in black. Right in front was the Engineer. And she looked pissed.

Lyra turned a corner and they vanished. But ahead of us, I caught a glimpse of a glowing fence.

"Dave!" I shouted, pointing. "Is that the Village?"

"I can only see the fence," he said, squinting.

"But it looks like the same one, right?"

"It does. Giddy-up, cow." He dug his heels into Lyra's side and she reluctantly trotted a little faster. I craned my neck to get the first glimpse of whatever was behind that fence. And sure enough, after long seconds of waiting, I saw the edge of the carousel.

Dave saw it too, and we both let out a yell of delight.

"Come on, Lyra, go faster," I urged.

"Time to leave her," Dave said. "We need to move fast." He jumped off the horse and held out his arms for me.

"Thanks, Lyra," I whispered. I kissed her warm, dirty mane and fell into Dave's arms.

We took off running immediately. Dave went in front, brutally shoving people out of his way, and I followed him, running in the path he created or sometimes dodging wide green legs to keep up. From the ground, I couldn't see what was ahead of us. I just followed Dave.

I was starting to flag when we made a sharp right turn, and just a few seconds later, we were there: the crowd thinned and we bolted through the open, arched gates of the Village of Yesteryear. I paused for a moment to catch my breath. Green people stared at me. There was no one on the carousel—it was roped off, with a sign saying "Show at 19:00"—but the Village wasn't empty anymore. Several people were resting on benches around the area or inspecting the ticket booth. And they had all turned to look at us.

"Come on," Dave urged, grabbing my hand. "They're not far."

We ran up onto the carousel, under the dirty velvet rope. Dave scuttled between animals.

"What are you doing?" I called out. Everyone was staring. I didn't like their eyes without Dave to protect me.

"Finding the starting switch," he yelled from the opposite side of the carousel. "Get in the spinny thing. The one we used before."

I frantically looked around. Two booths were within sight. I closed my eyes and tried to remember, and long moments passed before an image flashed into my head: two boys, climbing onto a goat and a unicorn. I dashed to the one to my right and climbed in, the shadow of the goat falling over the red velour seats.

At that moment, two things happened.

First, Dave came into view just a few yards away from me. He'd made almost a full circle before finding the switch. Now, in an instant, he pressed a button and pulled a lever and the carousel sprang to life.

Second, the Engineer and her squad of goons flooded into the Village. Her eyes met mine and her pupils dilated, eyelids sliding back into her head as she yelled, "Get them!"

I screamed in terror. To my left, Dave spun and stumbled through wooden animals to get to the booth. To my right, an enormous green *thing* was running at me.

The carousel started to turn.

The alien adjusted its course.

Dave fell into the seat next to me and gasped, "Spin! Clockwise, opposite from earlier!" So I put my hands on the bar, and he took the other side, and we started to turn it with all our strength.

The carousel moved faster, the music speeding up and lights growing bright. But the alien sped up, too, getting closer and closer, under the barrier now. We spun and spun, and the carousel moved faster, and the alien might have been closer now, but I couldn't tell because the world outside was spinning so fast, and my heart was in my hands on that golden bar moving over and over, spinning as fast as I could.

I didn't dare stop, even when my hands got numb with cold and my arms started to ache. I didn't know where we were, when we were, where the thing was that had been chasing us. I was so focused that I didn't even notice when the music stopped and the carousel started to slow. I only noticed when Dave took his hands off the bar and began to laugh.

Dave has, to this day, a mountain-sized laugh that fills every atom of air in the room. When I was little and my parents had him and Jo over for dinner, it used to start me awake at night. It was and is a deeply comforting sound, joyful and delighted, a sound that can't help but make you smile.

"What is it?" I said, letting my hands slow for a moment.

"We are back," he said with an air of finality.

I took my hands off the bar and sat back in my seat. The world was still spinning, the colors blurry, but already I could tell a difference. The sound was right, little kids giggling and shoes kicking up dust. As my dizziness abated, the carousel made its last slow twist, and there in the distance I saw my family.

I shrieked. "Dave, come on come on come on come on," I said, grabbing his hand and pulling him out of the booth. I was a little wobbly and I might have knocked over some smaller children, but I didn't stop until I had reached them, hugging every single one of them to make sure they were real.

"We're back," I whispered, sagging in relief into my mom's hip.

"Are you okay, Sarah?" my dad asked with some alarm. "That's usually one of your favorite rides."

I looked helplessly at him and then up at Dave.

"You tell," I said. "I want to get ice cream."

Dave chuckled.

"An odd thing happened," he began. "You see, I've

always known the asteroid would come, but I never thought it would have passengers . . ."

Sarah Van Name lives in Durham, North Carolina, where she works as a marketing writer and spends weekends perfecting her focaccia recipe. She has been published in *Mission at Tenth* and on *The Toast*. In her senior year at Duke University, her thesis of short stories and photography won her the Bascom Headen Palmer Literary Prize and the Louis Sudler Prize in the Creative and Performing Arts. At the age of four, she helped create the papier-mâché pig's head that now haunts Dave's back porch.

At my request, she offered this afterword.

I do not remember a time without Dave. His wife, Jo, was my nanny until I was four; I remember making banana muffins and finger-painting with her. Dave was there when I went to her house, and on our family beach vacations, and in my parents' living room when they had folks over for dinner. My childhood fear of the dark meant that I kept my bedroom door open even when they were hosting parties, so sound filtered in unimpeded. Everyone would be talking quietly, trying not to wake me and my brother, and then someone would make a joke and Dave would burst suddenly into laughter. As I mention in the story, that's the first thing I remember of Dave—not his writing, not his bizarre non sequiturs, but his laugh.

I know Dave as family, and he is good family. He and Jo host Thanksgiving, the Fourth of July, and a yearly pig-pickin' that is as much of a tradition for me as any holiday. He always remembers the last conversation he had with me, even if it's been months since we've talked. He is unfailingly, sometimes painfully honest. Though Dave is above all a character, as a child I knew him as just another familiar weirdo in a big, strange household.

This perspective is the one I was trying to communicate in "The Village of Yesteryear." The story I tell there is partially true. He really did go on the carousel with me, and I really did make him lose his lunch. But as I remember it, he never got mad. He just stood up, wiped his mouth, and said, "Well. I wasn't expecting that." And then we wandered on, him and Jo and the rest of my family, to see that year's largest blue-ribbon pumpkin.

The Trouble with Telepaths

Hank Davis

The trouble with telepaths is that they're all officers.

That'll do for starters.

At least, they're mostly not *serious* officers, or there'd be even more trouble. Most of the peepers are just second or first louies. A few make captain. They tend to be unstable, and don't really make good officers, and a lot of them wash out for mental reasons after a couple of years.

The highest ranking one I ever saw was a lieutenant colonel. That was a few years ago when I was a buck sergeant, but I doubt that he ever made full bird, since at the time he was talking about retiring. It was common knowledge that he wasn't much of a peeper, barely scoring above the minimum on the Rhines. His main thing was being an officer with all the usual officer stuff; maybe an officer with a little extra. Very little. Being good at poker might have been as useful to his career.

Not that anybody plays poker with a telepath. Even other telepaths don't.

Fortunately, I don't have a trace of telepathic ability. Back when I joined and was run through a day's worth of tests, I scored random noise on the Rhines. Pure chance on the nose. The score was so dead on, that one of the testers suspected I was cheating, trying to hide being a peeper, so he called in a card-carrying, officially certified peeper to buzz around in my skull and see if I had cheated. I hadn't, of course.

It was the first time I had been this close . . .

"You've never been this close to a telepath, Zinman," he said. It was a statement, not a question.

He was a captain, so . . .

"Yes, I'm very good at it," he said.

I had been wondering if . . .

"No, you can't feel me reading you. You'd have to be another telepath, and you still might not notice anything unusual."

I was getting a little worried . . .

"No need to worry, Zinman, what you're thinking doesn't count as insubordination."

I had heard that . . .

"You heard right. It's covered by the Revised Code of Military Justice. Like the song you just thought about says."

I'd thought of a line from an old song: *You can't go to jail for what you're thinking.* Or even if I'm thinking . . .

"Not that either. You might even be right that I wouldn't be giving you the creeps if I weren't commenting on things going through your mind. Ask me if I give a shit.

You know that telepaths aren't volunteers." Again, it was a statement, not a question. "We're drafted as valuable weapons. Or valuable something. But you can think the word 'peeper' with impunity. Just don't say it out loud where a telepath can hear you. Saying it is still insubordination." He stood up, said to the test administrator, "He didn't cheat. He's a complete post."

"Post" was what the peepers called non-telepaths. It came from the phrase "deaf as a post."

He turned to leave, muttering, "Damned waste of my time. Damned . . ."

And then I flickered.

The captain turned around and walked back to me. "What did you just do?" he said.

"It's—"

"Never mind, I see that you don't have any control over it. I just asked you to bring the subject to the surface of your mind. That really felt weird. Yes, I know, you think telepaths are weird. But for an instant, your mind wasn't there anymore, and the place where it had been felt funny. Like I had stepped out of daylight, into an enormous dark cave, with odd noises echoing. Just for an instant, then you were back, just a regular post again."

That's how he described it. To me, it was like something dark passed over my eyes and was gone again in a fraction of a second. Doctors who had examined me had no idea of the cause—no sign of brain abnormalities—but it didn't prevent me from doing anything. Even the U.S. Army didn't think it was anything serious.

The peeper turned to the tester and said, "So that's

the mini-seizures you were thinking about. Are you sure he belongs in the Army?"

"He's been examined—" the tester started to say, then the captain cut *him* off.

"I see. They're too short to worry about, and they have no after-effects. Not a problem unless they get longer or have side effects. No worse than an occasional sneeze." Then he did leave, muttering, "Good enough for government work," as he walked off.

The whole thing gave me a weird feeling. A damned peeper calling me a post, as if there was something wrong with *me*.

That was several years, two more stripes, and a couple of rockers ago, and I'd gotten used to peepers, and wasn't nervous anymore. There aren't a lot of them, they're not really around much, and since they're kicked up to officer rank automatically, they don't fraternize with the enlisted troops and NCOs. In fact they don't fraternize with *officers* any more than they can help.

So I was as used to peepers as a non-peeper (or post, if you insist) can get, and wasn't thinking about them the day that I got the odd assignment.

I should have guessed that something was up when I saw the First Sergeant standing nearby, watching the morning formation, obviously waiting for it to be over. Actually, I did figure that something was up—I just didn't figure that the something had anything to do with me.

As soon as the word "Dismissed" echoed across the field, the First Sergeant headed over to me.

"Good morning, Sergeant," she said.

"Good morning, Top. Something up?"

"Something's up, all right. Tell Malone to take your platoon today, then report to Lieutenant Minteer at the chopper pad at oh-eight hundred."

This was not a good start for the day. Minteer was a real prick, even if he wasn't a peeper. "Report to Minteer, okay. And do what, Top?"

"You'll have to ask him that," she said. "You now know as much as I do about it."

Her eyes could look warm, the way brown eyes are supposed to, usually if she'd heard a good joke (preferably a dirty one), but they were hard now. Something was going on, and she was annoyed that she didn't know much about it. At least she wasn't annoyed at me.

I told Malone to take charge of the platoon, then told PFC Moriko to follow me to the motor pool. "I need one each chauffeur, O.D. in color, Joe, and you just volunteered. So let's go get a limo." The mini-seizures might be hazardous if anyone actually drove cars anymore, but my own car, like any civilian car, did all the driving. I could have used one of the Army buggies with no risk, either. They looked ugly, their shock absorbers didn't do much absorbing, and their seats were minimally comfortable, but they drove themselves, too. However, the Army was still the Army, and my med profile required that I have a driver, human-type, with me in the car, even though he wouldn't be doing any driving.

"What's up, Sarge?" Moriko asked, once we were on the way to the chopper pad.

"Damned if I know," I said, "but Lieutenant Minteer is supposed to be there, so watch the language. 'Always perform your duties in a military manner,'" I said, mimicking Minteer's eastern accent.

Minteer was there, all right, along with a full bird private. I told Moriko to stay with the car until I knew what was going on, then walked over to Minteer. We exchanged salutes and good mornings, then the PFC told me, "The chopper should be here in five or less, Sarge."

Minteer scowled and said, "Did I hear you address this man as 'Sarge,' soldier? 'Sarge' is what sergeants get called in comic books. Do you think you're in a comic book, *Mister* Luigi?"

The PFC looked surprised, with a deer-in-the-headlights expression. He must not have run into Minteer before. "Uh, no sir. Sorry, sir."

Moriko was behind me where I couldn't see him, but I hoped he was managing not to smile. Looking inscrutable wasn't his strong suit.

Minteer wasn't through. "And the vehicle that's on its way here is a Field Drive Transport Vehicle, not a 'chopper.' You can call it a FDTV, if that's too big a mouth full for you, but it's not a 'chopper'. 'Chopper' is what helicopters were called because of the noise they made, and it's ridiculous to call an FDTV a 'chopper'. Have you ever seen a helicopter outside of a museum?"

Luigi said he hadn't, but fortunately for him, the chopper was now in sight, and approaching rapidly. From past experience, I knew that Minteer was just getting started.

The egg-shaped vehicle came to a stop, humming, then settled to the pad on its runners. The door on the side opened, and a captain stepped out and walked over to us. Then I noticed that his uniform had the stylized brain with an eye in the center of it that was the patch of the telepath corps. I noticed that before I got a good look at his face . . .

Flicker.

. . . and realized that I had seen him somewhere before, but couldn't remember where . . .

Flicker.

. . . but mostly I was wondering why I had just had two mini-whatsits less than a minute apart. That had never happened before.

He returned our salutes and said, "Good morning, gentlemen. Nothing like starting off the day with a chopper ride." Somehow, I was sure he did that on purpose. Peepers have an advantage when it comes to getting under someone's skin. Fortunately for Luigi, he was already showing a poker face, and kept it up. Minteer wasn't as successful at suppressing the sour look on his mug. "I'm glad you brought transportation, Sergeant Zinman. Let's go." He nodded to Minteer. "Thank you for meeting me here, Lieutenant," then headed for the car, without waiting for a salute or further pleasantries. Minteer looked like he'd just been handed a maggot sandwich.

"We need to go to building D-12," the captain said, then got into the back of the car. Moriko and I climbed into the front. Moriko said, "Sir, that building is off limits . . ."

"Not to me, Mr. Moriko. Let's go." He could have told the car where to go himself—its A.I. pays attention to rank—but kept up the polite fiction that Moriko was actually driving the vehicle.

We rolled along and I still had no idea why I was here.

I didn't know what went on in D-12, but it must be restricted, since there was a fence around it with concertina on top, and an armed guard at the only gate, and I had a feeling that if the captain had clearance to go inside, I'd have to wait outside. Then I realized that I'd been trying to remember where I'd seen the captain before, and hadn't looked at his name tag.

Of course, he read me.

"Sergeant Zinman, my name is Carpenter, and I'll answer your questions once we get inside the building," the mystery officer said.

I flickered twice while he was talking. I was more puzzled by that than anything about Carpenter's business. Usually, months would go by without one of the microseizures, but I'd had a string of them just now. Maybe I'd be getting a medical discharge soon.

Carpenter had Moriko park the car outside the fence. "Wait for me," he told him.

"Just wait for you, sir?" Moriko asked.

"Sergeant Zinman may be coming back later," he told him, then, "Come with me, Sergeant," to me.

Carpenter was expected, which didn't surprise me, but I was on the guest list too, which was surprising. Inside the building, we walked down hallways with the usual drably painted walls, and came to a door that slid open when Carpenter put his ID in the reader.

The room wasn't large, and just had a conference table with a few chairs around it and a flatscreen on one wall. No windows, just the one door.

Carpenter sat down and gestured toward a chair on the opposite side of the table. "Have a seat, Sergeant."

I did . . . after I had flickered a couple of more times. I wondered . . .

"No, Sergeant, I'm not making you do that. Or maybe my presence is making you do it, but I'm not deliberately using any influence on you."

The flickering seemed to have stopped, but it felt different than usual, repeating that way. It was like I was building up a vague image of something that I had never noticed with the separated single flickers.

"Sergeant, what do you think of the Russian civil war?"

That stopped me from thinking about the flickers. "What? Uh, what do you mean, sir?"

"Don't you think it odd that the country broke apart like that, fighting against each other, even using a couple of tactical nukes, for no obvious reason at all?"

Well, everyone seemed to think it was odd. And it had caught all the Kremlin-watchers by surprise. "Yes, sir, I think it was odd." I decided to paraphrase Will Rogers. "But all I know about it is what was in the news." I wondered if . . .

"No, Sergeant Zinman, I don't suspect you of having gotten hold of any classified information about it. There's no classified information of importance, anyway. Just a lot of after-the-fact guessing. Actually, it was a trial run. Worked very well, too, and it didn't spread to other nations."

"You mean the U.S. started it somehow, sir?" And why was he . . .

"I'm telling you this, Sergeant, because we need to know just what you are. We need to know that before we start the main event."

"Main event, sir? You mean you're going to do the same to China?" And what did he mean, "What you are?" Surely he could see . . .

"Yes, I can see in your mind that you don't know anything about all this. Incidentally, we *are* going to do the same to China, but not just China; and when I say "we", I don't mean this country. But first, I needed to see about your odd flickering. You're a piece in the game that doesn't fit, Sergeant. Actually, that's not right, because you don't seem to be part of the game. But we don't know exactly what you are, and we can't take any chances."

Now I remembered where I had seen him before. Last Saturday, I had been in civvies, about to leave the fort and go into town. I had noticed the base C.O. talking with a captain, and just then I had flickered. And the captain had suddenly ignored what the general was saying and stared intently at me. It had been Carpenter. I had gone on and forgotten about it.

"Yes, you caught my attention that day. I had to find out what that flickering meant. Suppose I told you that the U.S. and China are about to have a nuclear exchange?"

I didn't understand, but I was feeling scared. Telepaths do go psycho, more often than, well, us posts. But I didn't think he was insane.

"Interesting. I expected that to make you flicker. How about this?"

Carpenter wasn't there anymore. In his place was a Chinese officer, a member of their telepath corps from the patch on his uniform. It, too, had a stylized brain, but with a dragon coiled around it. I started to get up.

Sit down, someone said to me. It wasn't a voice, but it was in my head. I sat down, not that I had any choice.

The Chinese officer was gone. Now a Russian officer was sitting across the table. "You know that a telepath can't lie to another telepath?" he said.

I didn't say anything, but I thought about how often I'd heard that.

Now, there was a different Russian officer talking to me. "I'm going from a double agent to a quadruple agent, Sergeant Zinman. When a Russian officer who happens to be a telepath tells another Russian officer who also happens to be a telepath that there's a group of traitors who are going to launch a tactical nuke at Moskva, he is believed. When the same officer tells another high-ranking telepath officer that traitors have taken over the missiles in Moskva and are about to attack the missile emplacements in the rest of the country, he also is believed. It worked. And it will work on the United States and China, too."

Somehow, I wasn't scared now. I should have been, but . . .

"Yes, it is odd that you're suddenly so calm. And I really expected you to start flickering again. Maybe we should take you apart to see if there's something different about your brain, but there isn't time. I guess you'll have to commit suicide." He took a small laspistol out of his uniform—I hadn't seen any sign of it before—and put it on the table. "Don't touch it until I tell you to."

I tried to reach for it, and nothing happened. "You wanted to know what I was—" I began.

"I still am curious, but as I said, there isn't time to satisfy that curiosity right now."

"What are *you*?"

"The name wouldn't mean anything to you. Nor would the number of the star of the planet I come from. Your astronomers have cataloged it and given it a designation, but I see that you, Sergeant, have only the most elementary knowledge of astronomy. Our telepaths are much stronger and more talented than any of yours, and I *can* lie to another telepath and be believed. Pick up the pistol now."

Flicker. "You're invading us? Won't the radiation poison—?"

"We are just eliminating possible competition. Pick up the pistol. Besides, we have ways of neutralizing radiation. *Pick up the pistol!*"

Flicker. He was looking nervous, and his face seemed to waver. Maybe he was close to reverting to his natural appearance.

He told me to pick up the pistol again, and got another flicker response. He started to reach for the pistol, and stopped. I could see he was trying to reach for it, but couldn't make his hand move.

And the flicker started and kept on going. It was like a color filter had dropped over my eyes, but it had nothing to do with color. I was standing up, now, though I didn't remember getting to my feet. And there was something in front of me, barely visible out of the lower part of my vision. I was looking straight ahead and had the feeling that I shouldn't try to look down.

Carpenter—or whatever his (its?) real name was—was staring at the middle of my chest. His human face looked terrified, and I somehow knew it wasn't an illusion.

Then something started speaking.

It wasn't using any words I knew. Most of the sounds wouldn't turn into anything like words, though some of them came into my head as nonsense syllables: *Ia! Frthgr! Nghall! Ia!* It made no sense to me, but I wasn't the intended recipient of the message. And somehow I could see into Carpenter's brain and hear what he was hearing. Not in words, but something more basic. *We have plans for this planet. You shouldn't have interfered with the property of others older and stronger than you. I see into you. I see where your pathetic little empire is located. We'll have to turn our attention to you vermin so that you won't interfere with us again.*

Carpenter was exerting all his concentration, I could tell. It was like I was a telepath, but I knew the other— *thing*—was doing all that and I was just picking up the overflow. He managed to get to his feet, and took a step toward the door while trying to reach for something in his pocket. Then he sat back down and picked up the laspistol. *In ten minutes*, the voice that wasn't a voice told him.

Then, the flicker closed back up. *I* closed back up. Somehow, it was like I had doors in my front and something had opened them and come partly out. It had kept me from looking down at it. I got the impression that seeing what it looked like would not be a good idea. I had a glimpse of its appearance darkly reflected in the flat screen on the wall, and started to scream, but something made me look away and somehow I forgot what I had seen, and wondered why I thought I needed to scream. The last thing I sort of heard was *close portal*. Then, I was leaving the room, and walking down the hall. I had the feeling that I had just had a talk with Carpenter, but couldn't remember anything about it. Or why he wasn't with me now.

I had an odd thought, about being chosen to be a portal to something else—sounded weird, like some kind of screwball religion or cult—then I forgot some more and wondered why I was thinking of the word "portal." Like I was trying to remember a joke I had heard long ago.

I went out through the gate. The guard asked me if Captain Carpenter was still inside, and I said . . .

Flicker.

I don't know what I said, but it satisfied the guard. I got back in the car. "Back to the platoon, Joe," I said.

"Is the captain staying behind?" Moriko asked, as he told the car where to go.

Flicker.

"What captain, Joe?"

Joe looked confused. "Did I say something about a captain? I must have been thinking of something else."

"Didn't you ever hear that you're not paid to think, soldier?" I said, imitating Lieutenant Minteer's accent so that Joe would realize it was a joke. For some reason, I was thinking about telepaths and how much trouble they were.

I must have been thinking out loud, because Joe said, "Look on the bright side, Sarge. Suppose Lieutenant Minteer was a telepath. That would be scary."

"I can't think of anything that would be scarier," I said.

We drove on.

Hank Davis is senior editor emeritus at Baen Books. While a naïve youth in the early 1950s (yes, he's *old!*), he was led astray by SF comic books, and then by A.E. van Vogt's *Slan*, which he read in the Summer 1952 issue of *Fantastic Story Quarterly* while in the second grade, sealing his fate. He has had stories published mumble-mumble years ago in *Analog*, *If*, *F&SF*, and Damon Knight's *Orbit* anthology series. (There was also a story sold to *The Last Dangerous Visions*, but let's not go there.) A native of Kentucky, he currently lives in North Carolina to avoid a long commute to the Baen office.

At my request, he supplied this afterword.

While I'm sure there are occasional exceptions, friends usually have something in common. In the case of my friend David Drake, our common interests include the science fiction pulps of yesteryear, movie serials (the cinematic equivalent of pulps), the history of science fiction, including once-popular writers and stories whose reputation has unjustly gone into eclipse (there's some overlap with the SF pulps here), and various less eccentric areas of interest, such as the late, great singer Peggy Lee. We also have in common, for better or worse, being Vietnam veterans.

Obviously, a story for an anthology commemorating Dave's big seven-oh year should involve some of those interests, and my first thought was writing a movie-type serial (on paper, not on film) with insidious villains, rip-roaring action, slam-bang fistfights, and a cliffhanger at the end of every chapter—but then I had a rare attack of sanity and remembered that movie serials typically had twelve chapters, fifteen in some cases, and such a segmented epic would take up too much space in the book, particularly coming from a mere dilettante whose story is appearing alongside others by genuine pros who have produced substantial bodies of work. So I decided instead to give a nod to Dave's military service, not to mention his towering status as the Dean of Military Science Fiction (though it should be noted that he's far too versatile to write only military sf) and go with a modestly short piece set in a future version of the U.S. Army.

Two other interests that we share are the strange happenings chronicled by Charles Fort and the cosmic horror stories of H.P. Lovecraft, and I threw those into the pot, too. (Had to hold the lid down—those Great Old Ones don't take kindly to being boiled.) People often quote Fort's famous line, "I think we're property" (and if you haven't read "The Trouble with Telepaths" yet, stop reading this now, or the story will be spoiled), but there's another striking line farther down the page that's less familiar: "That something owns this earth—all others warned off." I don't know if Lovecraft was influenced by Fort—he did mention Fort in "The Whisperer in Darkness"—but his Cthulhu mythos fits in neatly with the Earth being something else's property. I hope the story that resulted isn't too unworthy of a genuine pro writer like David Drake.

Still, I didn't manage to work Miss Peggy Lee in. Maybe some other time . . . something about a cosmic fever, perhaps?

Happy birthday, Dave.

A Cog In Time

Sarah A. Hoyt

"Not that Drake," the man said. His voice reached me with the hint of amusement that betrays someone choking back laughter. "My family in this time actually sued that Drake and asked him to stop using our coat of arms."

I looked across the crowded room, crammed full of all the time-displaced people in Elizabethan England at the time, and noted a shock of white hair, nothing more.

It was enough to get my attention.

It is said that time traveling is a young man's game. It is wrong. There are plenty of us young women at it too, but the truth is that time traveling, at least from the perspective of the Time Guardian Corps, which I'd joined over a year ago, was an old person's game.

You got sent to a few god-forsaken epochs, you tried to keep the merchants, tourists, and Mormon genealogy researchers from preying on or bothering the natives too much, or even you just carried messages, emptied chamber pots, and wrote a few lines. And then in the fullness of time, you got promoted a grade or two, and eventually you retired to your time of origin with your pension. It was all unglamorous and strange, and not what I'd thought I was volunteering for.

Which was why this party was so well attended, till we were all belly-to-belly and cheek-to-cheek. I think the Guardian Corps knew it had to throw this kind of get-together every once in a while, or it would have mass desertions or mass suicides.

I looked across the well-lit room, with electrical light, praise be, and the tables set with delicacies that were probably not the product of the time-period abattoirs. In the middle of the room, enthroned on a table was the largest, darkest, most splendidly frosted chocolate cake I'd ever seen. It must have been my height and it was surely three times as wide as I was, tier upon tier of delicious chocolate, out of time and out of place and calling out to me.

Never let it be said that biology isn't destiny. I was a woman and I wanted chocolate. Though, so apparently did a lot of the other people, including not a few men. Maybe it wasn't all biology but having to live in a time when camphor was considered a spice.

I started moving toward the cake, part volitionally and part by letting the crowd move me there. Suddenly, after ducking between two people speaking in what sounded like Canterbury accents, one of whom said, "Well, Master Marlowe was not all that," and caused his friend to laugh, I found myself by the cake.

The white-haired man was there too, and turned to me to say, "So, will you have a slice of cake?"

I nodded, confused by the sudden friendliness, and I stood there, trying to hold a glass of some fizzy drink, my slice of cake, and the fork, all while the eddies and flows of the crowd pushed us aside and away. But they pushed us still together, and I looked at his tag, and saw it said only "Drake."

And suddenly I thought, not Drake. I'd heard his stories, after all. He was one of the few operatives allowed to go to the future. But he was also one of the few operatives allowed in ancient Rome, where they took more care to keep the rolls of the people than in Elizabethan England. He could pass. That alone was enough for word of him to have made it through the ranks to the newbies. I didn't know how much of the embroidery put on his exploits was fictional, but I knew that we'd studied one of his missions in school.

"I . . . have read about you," I said. And noting the marginal closing in his eyes, I added, "I heard what you said about not being related to Sir Francis Drake."

His eyes lit up and he animated to his topic, "That ass, Drake," he said. "That—"

Suddenly and without warning, reacting to something I couldn't see or hear, he grabbed my arm and dove to the floor, near the cake.

There were screams from the crowd and sounds that might be some weapon firing. I wasn't sure, not exactly, but the sounds were like someone sucking air through a horn. They might very well be weapons.

The problem of being in the Time Guardians, of course, is that there are other time organizations from varying epochs, all of which have different weapons.

Drake must have recognized the sound, though, because he looked up and towards the place the screams and the sounds were coming from, and then made a sound that might be cursing or some really specialized cat imitation. Problem with a man who had been everywhere, his cursing tended to be highly diverse, too.

He looked around us, then grabbed my hand, "Do you know your way to the Theater?"

"What?"

"The Theater," he said. "Burbage's place. Shakespeare—"

"Oh, of course," I said. "I work in a tavern—"

"Yes, yes, good. Can you lead me there?" He'd changed yet again. The jovial man who'd laughed before I'd met him, the near-social talker who had set out to tell me Francis Drake's stories—a perennial only less popular among us time-worker-bees to the Sir Walter Raleigh stories. I'd heard more stories about how Sir Walter Raleigh had impregnated someone in public than I cared to think about—was now the professional, alert, alarmed, somewhat worried and definitely competent.

"I— Yes?" The yes was qualified only by the fact that first I'd have to find my way within this complex that was literally out-of-time and to Elizabethan England again. After all, while London of the time was bewilderingly unplanned, I'd been living there for sixteen months, and it wasn't that difficult to figure out.

"Oh, good, then let's go." Keeping an eye on the area from which the disturbance had come, he grabbed my arm, and started pulling me towards an exit. We were walking hunched over, and I tried to straighten. He didn't even say anything, just the look in his eyes was enough. I swallowed hard and let him pull me.

Through the exit, which was near the restrooms, we came to a totally empty corridor, through which he led at a trot. We passed, in quick succession: a ballroom with couples dancing to swing music—they parted, startled either at our running or at our Elizabethan finery—through a bar which looked medieval and where people in homespun seemed to be discussing of all things crops, and then through something refined and high tech where a strip tease appeared to be in progress. We ended up in another hallway, near a restroom, and he looked at me, "Well?"

I oriented myself, feeling for the direction. "I think we've been going the exact opposite direction of the portal to Elizabethan England, sir."

He made a sound, "Why did you let me lead, then?" he asked. "I have no sense of direction. I once crossed three time periods in search of soap."

I laughed, startled at the idea, and he dropped out of annoyance, joining in the laughter, "Stop laughing at me, you wretch," he said. "Besides, you know, we couldn't go in the other direction. There were Varian separatists there, and they'd shoot anyone."

"Shouldn't we be saving the people at the party?" I asked.

He shrugged. "No. We are going to what the Varian's are going to attack. This is just to prevent our people responding. We're going to respond. And we're going to stop them there."

"Where?"

"The Theater."

Um . . . all right. Sometimes I thought that everyone coming to Elizabethan England was trying to do something to Shakespeare. The surprise was not that the man had signed himself differently a few times. The surprise was the man still knew his own name. Yeah, yeah, I know the theory. Node in time and all that. It was still annoying.

I took the lead, taking him down a narrow hallway. At the end of it we had to crawl sideways through an opening that wouldn't normally admit people, and then through a room that looked like storage. We climbed over what looked like cases of wine, then past a bookshelf. I thought he grabbed something, but wasn't sure what. On the other side, I found the public hallway and the portal to Elizabethan England.

It was guarded by men in a uniform I couldn't recognize.

I stopped short but he didn't. He took something from his pocket. There was no sound but the men fell. I'd never had to kill anyone in my profession, yet. Though of course, we trained for it. I ran after him into the portal, thinking that maybe he'd just tranquilized them, but not really wanting to look too closely as we passed.

On the other side of the portal, we were in a normal Elizabethan street, and I swallowed hard and said, "No, this way," as he'd determinedly taken off in the wrong direction.

We walked down a mud alley within sight of traitors' gates, where the body parts of the latest conspirators against her majesty were on display. I'd grown inured to the smell of rotting human, and barely spared them a look. It seemed less real, after all, that these people were dead who had been dead since before I was born. But fresh from the shooting to get through the portal, I realized they were human too, and had been alive when I'd come here.

Then I turned my mind from it, and towards the task of getting Drake to the Theater.

This was easier said than done, as apprentices seemed to be rioting again. Or maybe it was all a merry prank. A very merry prank, judging from the groups running around hitting people with clubs and terrorizing merchants. It was sometimes hard in these days to tell "merry making" from revolts. Not that the apprentices didn't have plenty of reason to revolt, since their contracts made them near slaves, but their idea of fun came too close to serious rebellion.

I'd got used enough to this, to lead Drake into an alleyway, and up another, keeping close to the walls, which actually reduced the chances of being drenched in piss or worse thrown from the window above, because most people put some swing in the arm.

It hit me that he walked as though he were used to this time. Of course, he'd been wearing Elizabethan hose and doublet, with a collar of ruffled lace, but I'd never heard of his being deployed to our time.

I had no idea what his rank was, but surely someone his age and with the experience he had to have was at least an administrator first class? What was one of those doing in the field and knowing Elizabethan England as well as I did, who had been emptying chamber pots and gutting fish at the Mermaid for the last several months?

He didn't even bat an eye when we approached the Theater and there was what looked like a crowd blocking our path. He made some sound about actors and writers only getting paid when they owned the place, then seemed to take his bearings and ducked through a gate I didn't know was there. Not a big surprise, since I didn't normally go into the Theater, not even when I had time. It wasn't entirely safe. It was so thronged with time travelers I was likely to get trampled down. I heard the Globe which had replaced it/would replace it in a few years would be/was even more crowded with time travelers.

There were some actors rehearsing on stage, while stagehands, or other actors—the two were hard to tell apart back in this time—set up the scenery for the afternoon performance.

No one batted an eye at us, possibly because we'd dressed for a party, and were therefore in the guise of important people, which meant people who could wander about the Theater at will, in case they took a wild desire to give money to the players or extend protection over them.

Drake, however, took a narrow door, and narrow stairs up, like a man who knows his way up the hallways and byways of this place. For someone who'd been lost before, he now was surefooted.

"You've been here before," I said.

"Every damn week, I swear. Irredentists, Redemptionists, Center Supremacists, Varians, Garians, and Florians, they all want to come here and do something to Shakespeare. The things vary, but—"

He stopped near a door, and I walked forward to open it. He pulled me aside, reached over and banged his fist on the door. A ray of light came through the door burning a hole in it and the rickety wooden wall opposite.

"Every damn week," he said, in a tone that mingled annoyance and tiredness.

By that time I'd recovered my wits, or at least what wits I had, I'd realized this was one of those bona fide adventures I hoped would happen, when I'd first joined the Time Guardian Corps. I wasn't armed, but we'd trained to be able to do things in these circumstances.

I backtracked to where there was a pile of wooden logs on the floor, probably fodder for some fireplace nearby, and grabbed a couple. Drake had turned to watch me. As I crawled along the bottom of the door, where they couldn't see me through the turned portion, and he realized what I intended to do, he said, "Good woman."

I threw the logs, obvious as coming from my side, and then ran, very quickly around the bend, chased by the smell of lasers and burning.

I stopped once I'd rounded the bend to make sure neither my long hair nor my long skirts were on fire, but there were no sounds of pursuit. There were sounds, of course, but not of pursuit.

When I got back step-by-step, knit through the wall, ready to rain destruction on the head of whomever tried to detain me with my wooden log, the battle was over.

There were three men dead in the room, and Drake was standing, looking around with an expression of intense disgust.

I looked around too. Two of the men had uniforms

that matched the ones of the guys who'd dragged the gate. But the third . . .

The third was Master Shakespeare, formerly of Stratford upon Avon. He lay on his face, immobile. I knelt to feel his neck, and there was no pulse. My heart sank within me.

Drake was barring and locking the door, and propping one of the tables in the room so no one could look through the open hole. He looked like a man on his last shred of patience, which was not the reaction I expected from someone who found a time-node had been eliminated.

"Shakespeare is dead," I told him, in case he hadn't noticed.

"Yes, of course he is," he said abstractedly. "Be a dear and stand by the door and tell me if you hear any sounds like someone is meaning to come knock on the door or something. I'm going to have to call for a time gate."

"What?" I said. Time gates could theoretically be opened to any room, anywhere. At any time. But there were so many rules and regulations against it, it wasn't even funny. For one, it could get someone from the past into the future, get a local killed, or do any of the things that the Time Guardians were founded to prevent.

"Only thing to do. You know that."

"But he's dead," I said, thinking that he probably thought he could still save the erstwhile Will. "I mean, really dead. He's pushing up—"

He looked at me like I was dim and said, "Honey, he's been dead for twenty years. When someone is a time-node, there are too many people wanting him dead to keep him alive. We have to be lucky all the time, they only have to be lucky once. Keep an ear out, will you?"

I wanted to protest, but he didn't sound like a man with time to spare, so I didn't. He took some communicator out of his pocket and did something to it. He talked into it in a language I didn't understand. I wondered if he was speaking in code, or in some long lost dead language I'd never had the need to learn. Something obscure like early-modern twenty-first-century English.

There was something like argument from the other side, and then suddenly a flare of light. Three men rushed out. As I watched, they propped Master Shakespeare up, took his head off, did something to it. I realized I was looking at electronics and links. The skin that had felt so real under my fingers was some synthetic skin so advanced that even I had never come across it.

Before my eyes, not only did Master Shakespeare become whole and seemingly alive again, even if he took no notice of any of us, but the people in uniforms I didn't recognize also patched up the door.

Then they left, through the same place.

I turned to Drake, "You're not," I said, "from my time."

He frowned at me. Master Shakespeare was shaking his head, coming awake. "I beg your pardon," he said.

We begged his in return, said we'd come to the wrong room, and left.

"You're not from my time," I said again, in the hallway.

"No," he said. "From before your time, when they needed people to guard the time stream, before the

Guardian Corps was established. But I've worked in your time."

"You mean . . ." I said. "As an operative?" There were more time travelers than locals in Elizabethan England, but it had never occurred to me that the same might apply to the twenty-fourth century. Then I thought even in our time we knew he'd worked in the thirtieth and . . .

"I have a Time Guardian Corps identity in your time." He looked around. "Shall we go back to the party?" he asked.

"But . . . people . . ."

"There were guards there, and from the fact we're not mobbed here, it was a small attack. And besides there's chocolate cake. Yes, it was a tragedy, but it was a tragedy for those who got killed. We were lucky." He gave me an evaluating look. "You'll survive many such attacks on your way where you're going."

I didn't ask if it he spoke from knowledge. I had a feeling this was a man who would tell me the absolute truth, and sometimes you don't need that. And sometimes you do.

"The Time Guardian Corps," I said. "Is it always this exciting for other people? I thought it was all about emptying chamber pots."

He gave a strangled laugh that made people on the stage which we were then crossing turn to look at us. "Cherish your time with the chamber pots," he said. "When things get interesting is when people die."

I was starting to understand that. But I was also starting to understand we were needed to keep history going. All that rot they tell you in school about protecting the past so we'll have a future? Probably not, but the point was to keep the past as it was so these innocent and oblivious people around us—those who weren't Mormon genealogists pursuing a clue—would have a future. Or at least their lives wouldn't be any worse than they should have been.

"Yeah, sucks," Drake said, as though reading my mind. "And it's not what I would have chosen. I got pulled into it by accident and because I knew history. But I don't care to have time dissolving against me because some bright boy killed Shakespeare again. Or even Hitler. So, I keep working in the field." He thought about it for a moment, as we walked down the street and towards the fixed gate that would take us back to the get together. "And sometimes are there decent moments. Maybe we'll stay in the party of the time of Swing and do some dancing."

"I can't dance."

"I can't either. Well, at least not that. But doing it wrong is a prerogative of those out of time, and no one knows there anyway."

We walked towards the gate. So, the job might suck, but sometimes there were interesting men and chocolate cake.

I realized I'd stopped when he turned to look at me. "I'll never find the way on my own, come on. What's wrong?"

"Nothing. I just realized I can do this job, after all."

Sarah A. Hoyt writes science fiction, fantasy, mystery

and historical fiction. At last count she had two dozen novels and over a hundred short stories published (in anthologies, magazines like *Asimov's* and *Analog*, and collections). Her novel, *Darkship Thieves*, won the Prometheus Award in 2011. Without David Drake's advice and encouragement, she would have published three books and maybe a dozen short stories. She's hard at work on the next two space operas and the next fantasy novel.

At my request, she provided this afterword.

I first approached this story all wrong, trying to make it David Drake fanfic, which I couldn't possibly write, even if I love reading him.

Then I decided to shamelessly Tuckerize him, starting with how we met at a Tor party (sorry, guys, we're not Time Guardians).

I decided to make it a time-travel story because that is one of the things that Dave and I share: a love of history. And in a way the reason I like his books, both fantasy and science fiction, is because he takes you on a form of time travel, and makes history (and reflected history, which is what Space Opera is in large measure) come alive for you.

In a way too, this reflects how our friendship started because Dave told me the truth about the job—no, no, writer. I swear we're not Time Guardians—and thereby in many ways convinced me to continue with it, though I'm not sure that's what he intended to do (or what anyone sane would do. But then Mr. Sanity hasn't been seen around my place for a long time.).

I threw in two of Dave's characteristics that amuse me: his very useful ability of telling the truth, which can also be uncomfortable as heck, and his inability to find any place.

Oh, and the viewpoint character isn't me. If it were, we'd both still be lost somewhere in the Time Guardian's complex. My sense of direction is about like his.

Fortunately most days we can find our desks and write.

All That's Left

Mark L. Van Name

Crane froze a step short of the doorway. The room screamed indifference and menace. He looked at his husband and shook his head.

Bobby—always Bobby, never Robert, even through the years of their youth when all their friends were sticking with the formal versions of their names, even though he himself always, always used his full first name—smiled and took his hand. "We talked about this, Joseph."

Crane shook his head again. "You don't understand." Bobby couldn't possibly understand. He hadn't been in the Army, hadn't walked into hundreds of institutionally bland rooms filled with institutionally calm superior officers who dispensed the fates of others as if they mattered no more than paper clips—which they didn't, in the end. Nothing really did.

Bobby held his hand tighter. "So you can help me understand later, you know I've tried and will try again, but right now we need to go inside." Bobby smiled again. "It'll be fine. I'll make sure of it."

Crane had always been a sucker for that smile, and for the sincerity behind it, even when Bobby was wrong. The Army wasn't in the business of making things fine.

But he had promised. He'd told Bobby he'd investigate the therapy, and so he would. At seventy-five years old and fifty-two years into his relationship with Bobby, he wasn't going to start breaking promises now.

He nodded.

They walked inside the room.

The drab of the moment was sand, the walls a desert of Army false calm. Centered on three of the walls were posters about the new therapy; the fourth, the one behind the desk in front of him, sported a framed medical school diploma.

The man behind the desk, Captain Johnson if his nameplate was accurate, stood and extended his hand. "Corporal Crane, it's good to meet you."

Crane trembled with the adrenaline that surged through him. He wanted to yank the young man over his desk and onto the floor, stomp on his throat, and ask him where the hell he got off treating him like they still had some kind of control over him. Instead, he kept his hand at his side. "I haven't been a corporal in over fifty years." He heard the tremor in his voice and hated himself for the weakness.

After a moment, Johnson withdrew his hand and sat. "My apologies," he said. "Many of the men of your generation I've met appreciate the recognition of their former rank."

Did you ever ask them? Crane thought. He turned to leave. He had no time for idiots.

Bobby sat in the chair on the right and pulled Crane into the other one. "Thank you for taking the time today," he said to Johnson. He let go of Crane's hand after Crane sat.

Johnson gave a slight smile and nodded, an officer moving past the unintended slight of a lesser man.

Crane more than ever wanted to hurt him.

Johnson tapped his tablet, read for a few seconds, and looked at Crane again. "So you have trouble both falling asleep and staying asleep?"

Bobby stared at Crane until he nodded.

"Night sweats?" Johnson said.

Crane nodded again. "Sometimes."

"Do you remember the dreams that wake you?" Johnson watched him carefully.

Crane stared for a moment at Bobby. Bobby had always wanted him to share his dreams—thought he wanted him to talk about those nightmares—but Crane knew better. No good would come from that. He faced Johnson again. "Sometimes."

Johnson waited, his eyes never leaving Crane's face.

"Often," Crane said.

Johnson nodded and smiled again. He pushed away his tablet and leaned back in his chair.

Crane felt the sales pitch coming and wanted to run out of there, go home, and climb the stairs to his studio, where it would be just him and his paintings and music playing from the speakers all around the room.

"Wouldn't it be nice to sleep through the night?"

Johnson said. "To fall asleep easily? To not have those memories from Viet Nam haunt you?" The man leaned forward, folded his arms on his desk, and gave Crane what was certainly a practiced look of sincerity. "Wouldn't it be great to put that war behind you—no, not behind you, but *out* of you, to finally let it go?"

It's never out of you, Crane thought, the anger rising in him again. *It can't be. It changes you, and you and it are never again separate. If you'd ever seen action, you'd know.*

When Crane didn't answer, Bobby touched his shoulder. "You have to admit that sleeping through the night would be a great change."

Crane tilted his head ever so slightly. That wasn't the point, but it was true enough on its own, and agreeing would stop this part of the discussion.

Johnson nodded in return, a vigorous, "good man" gesture. "We can make this happen," he said. "We can remove all of your traumatic memories from the war. You can be free of them."

"Have you ever been in a combat zone?" Crane said.

"My experience is not the topic here," Johnson said.

Crane leaned forward. "Have you?"

"No," Johnson said, "I have not."

"Then where do you get off talking about being free, putting the war behind you? What can you possibly know?"

"I've never broken my arm," Johnson said, "but I know how to fix someone else's broken arm. It's the same thing. We've been conducting trials for almost two years, and the results are uniform and conclusive: we can make the bad memories go away." Johnson leaned back again. "Removing those awful memories is a huge step in the healing process. Our post-treatment surveys and follow-ups consistently show total removal of trauma-related memories from time in combat."

Crane flashed on a ride in a jeep, he and three others stripped to the waist and baking in the mid-afternoon sun, the vehicle jarring their spines as it bounced in the ruts and holes in the dirt road, a gray-mottled early Sixties tan Mercury Comet rounding the curve ahead of them, guns emerging from the open passenger-side rear window, Benny, their driver, yelling and pointing, all of them lifting their rifles—

He shook his head.

"So I wouldn't remember what I did?"

"Not if it was related to any of the trauma you suffered," Johnson said. "All of that would be gone. You'd remember the normal stuff, the regular routines—just not the times in battle."

Crane again yearned to slam his fists into the man's face. He had no clue. Normal times? Normal was knowing you could die at any time. Normal was never having a clue when the next shot would come from out of nowhere. Normal was going to sleep and hoping you'd wake up. Or not hoping for that, on many days. What passed for normal *was* the trauma.

Johnson clearly took his silence for consideration. "So," the man said, "what do you think? Should we sign you up?"

Crane looked at Bobby. Bobby's stillness, one of his husband's greatest strengths, calmed him. He knew

Bobby wanted this, knew Bobby thought it would be best for him, but he wasn't ready for it, wasn't sure he ever would be.

"I don't know," he said at last.

"If you're concerned about the state of the treatment," Johnson said, "let me reassure you that we've had nothing but success erasing traumatic memories. We can show you the results of previous trials if you'd like to see the proof. And, though this procedure is still technically experimental, we're within six months of FDA approval. By signing up now, you'd not only be helping yourself, you'd also be helping make the therapy available for others."

Crane said nothing.

"How about this?" Johnson said. "Just agree to let us do the preliminary assessment, to make sure you're a good candidate for the treatment. You wouldn't have to commit to anything more than letting us run some tests."

Crane flushed hot and felt as if the walls might at any moment squeeze him into nothingness. He had to leave. He stood. "I'll consider it."

He almost ran out of the room and waited outside while Bobby no doubt smoothed Johnson's ego and made everything better. It's what Bobby did. Bobby fixed the damage Crane sometimes left behind, said the soothing words he could not bring himself to utter.

Bobby walked up to him, leaned in close, and said, "You know I love you, right?"

Crane nodded.

"And you also know," Bobby said, "that you can really be an asshole sometimes, right?"

Crane smiled. "Yeah."

Bobby squeezed his shoulder. "Just so we're clear on that."

As they left the building, Crane took his first full breath since they'd entered it, the hand of the Army no longer squeezing his throat. He couldn't wait to get home.

As soon as Bobby parked the car in their garage, Crane bolted into the house and climbed the two flights of stairs to the third floor, a single huge room that served as his studio. Light flooded into it from a dozen skylights and the floor-to-ceiling windows that occupied most of the walls of the space. With a single remote he could close the blinds on any or all of the windows, but he almost always left them open. They lived in the country on a forty-acre plot ringed with tall trees, so anyone who wanted to watch him would have to go to a great deal of trouble to do so. Not that he cared: as long as they stayed away and left him to his painting, he was happy.

Canvases filled the walls between windows and stood on easels all around the room. Scenes of villages, jungles, dirt roads, and small towns filled them, but none showed a single person. Sometimes, barely visible gray outlines shimmered where people might have stood, or fallen, or been shot. Some viewers barely noticed the absence of humans; others found it a heart-rending omission.

Crane could paint people. Before the war, he had. Afterward, in his mind's eye everyone in the moments he captured lived as he did: as a shadow, a presence always on the verge of extinction, a near vacancy moving through the world but never really part of it.

He flicked on the stereo. Jim Morrison and the Doors screamed from the speakers all around him. He assembled tubes of paint and brushes. Painting made the world go away. It didn't make sense of the world—nothing could do that—but it graced him with a calm that nothing else could match.

The memory of the Mercury Comet clung to his mind, so once again he painted the dusty dirt road and the old car and the guns, the roaring sun, the huts standing along both sides of the road, everything but the people. No two versions of this scene ever came out the same. He didn't care. He painted what he saw and felt in the moment, wondering as he often did whether each new canvas represented a different split-second snapshot of his memory, or if his mind created the moment anew in a spasm of active remembering.

When Bobby called him for dinner, he checked his watch and saw that he'd been working for almost three hours. He swallowed, noticing for the first time how dry his throat was. Three hours. He smiled. When he was working he knew who he was, he existed, he mattered, if only because the work deserved all he had. The rest of the time, well, he passed through those moments, another gray presence waiting only for the end so he could finally vanish.

Downstairs, Bobby had prepared the meal, as he often did. Crane took in the steak, the angel hair pasta with tomatoes, garlic, olive oil, and a dusting of Parmesan, the simple green salad, the glass of fresh iced tea—all of his favorites.

Bobby wanted something. Most of his husband's

dinners were vegetarian, as healthy as possible, one more way to fight off the additional weight that they both battled every day.

Crane kissed him, sat, and raised an eyebrow.

"Eat," Bobby said, "before the steak gets cold."

Not one to waste a good cut of meat—and when they ate red meat, it was always a good cut, Bobby made sure of that—Crane sliced off a small bite, smelled it, savored the richness of the beef, and chewed it happily. "Thank you," he said. "This is delicious."

Bobby smiled and took his own first bite. This small ritual—the person who didn't cook eats first and praises the chef, the other goes second—was one they'd followed for as long as Crane remembered, longer than that Captain Johnson had been alive. A simple practice, but a nice one, an exchange they both enjoyed.

Bobby waited until both of them had finished before he got around to what he wanted. "So," he said, "what do you think about the treatment?"

"We didn't learn anything today that we didn't already know," Crane said. "That man was useless."

Bobby nodded. "All true, but that's not an answer to my question."

Crane straightened in his chair. "I'm seventy-five. How much longer am I likely to have? Is it really worth trying something experimental now, at my age?"

"At *our* age," Bobby said. "I'm every bit as old as you are, and we're both in excellent shape—even allowing for the occasional indulgence in food sin like what we just consumed. We could easily live into our nineties, or longer. Which would be better: twenty more years of nightmares and poor sleep and night sweats, or those same years without all that pain?"

I earned that pain, Crane thought but did not say. *I deserve it. I did what I had to do, we all did, but I paid for it—I have to pay for it—and now it's in me. Now it is me. I can't escape myself.* All he said was, "It's not that simple."

Bobby reached for Crane's hand and held it. "I don't claim to understand what you endured. You know I never make that claim. But I've been your partner for all these years, your agent for most of them, and I've seen— and loved—all those hundreds and hundreds of paintings. I have some small inkling of what you must be carrying."

At that, Crane looked away.

Bobby gently grabbed his chin and turned his face until the two were staring into each other's eyes. When Crane started to break contact, Bobby held his chin tighter.

In the fading twilight, Bobby's skin, always so beautiful, so even in tone, as close to black as Crane had ever seen on a person, shined like glowing night. Crane could feel Bobby's love like a blanket, and a hug, and a punch, and he deserved only the last one.

"Will you at least think about it?" Bobby said. "Just the assessment." Bobby smiled, that crazy wide smile that had always melted Crane's heart.

Crane nodded. "Yes. I promise."

Bobby leaned across the table and kissed him. "Good. Now, I cooked, so you clean."

❖ ❖ ❖

Dirt sprayed over him as the sounds of the explosions slammed into Crane's ears. He huddled against the side of the foxhole, men on his right and left doing the same. The explosions hit all around him. You never knew when they would begin, or when they would cease and the base would return to what passed for normal.

A man flew over his head, crashed into the opposite dirt wall, and slid to Crane's feet. "Oh, god," the man said. "I made it." He stared at Crane. "Are we gonna be okay?" Before Crane could answer, the man looked down at his stomach. Crane's gaze followed the man's. The man's guts were spilling all over his legs and onto the dirt. "Oh, shit," the man said. "Help me."

Crane leaned forward and tried to shove the man's insides back into him, but his hands turned slick with blood, and more escaped than he could push inside. Crane pulled back and stared at the man. "I'm sorry," he said. "I can't. I can't."

As Crane watched, the man's head tilted to the left, and the man died.

Crane twisted and screamed wordlessly, his mouth open but no sound coming out, as he sat up in bed, eyes open, the dream gone but its tendrils still snaking through his mind. The room was cool, but sweat beaded his chest and face. He shook his head, forcing the nightmare from his memories.

Bobby turned on the light and propped himself on one elbow. He'd learned long ago that Crane didn't want contact until he was back in this world. "Joseph?" he said.

Crane forced himself to breathe slower. "I'm okay. Give me a minute." He threw back the covers, went to the bathroom, and closed the door. In the blue glow of the nightlight he barely recognized the old man staring at him in the mirror. How did that happen? A minute ago he was back there, and now he was here, and he was old. He was sure he would die there—part of him *had* died there— and now he was still alive, older and older every time he looked, but also always stuck there.

He splashed water on his face and chest, dried himself, and opened the bathroom door.

Thanks to the moonlight streaming through the skylights, Crane could see that Bobby had changed the sheets, put the damp white set in the clothes basket in the closet, and made the bed with a fresh light blue pair. Had he been in the bathroom that long?

Crane nodded toward the hamper. "Thank you."

Bobby patted the sheets beside him. "Come back to bed."

Crane checked the bedside clock, hoping he was close enough to morning that he could get up and paint.

It was barely after three, too early to start the day even for him.

He crawled into bed and pulled the fresh, cool sheets up to his waist.

"Better?" Bobby said.

Crane nodded. His mind knew—had known even then, back in that hole—that he could not have saved the man, that no one could, but his heart couldn't stop blaming himself. Still, this was one of the easy nightmares, because at least his rational self could accept his own innocence. He nodded again.

"I hate what that war did to you," Bobby said.

Crane nodded once more, but what he thought was, *You might as well hate the sun, for all the good it will do.*

"I know this therapy can't undo any of that," Bobby said. "Nothing can. But what if it would let you sleep through the night? What if you could stop having the nightmares? What if it took away the pain?"

What am I without them? Crane thought. *I can't be who I was before it. I can't even remember that guy. I am what the war left me.* All he said was, "I don't know."

Bobby leaned closer. "What *I* know is that you are a good man, Joseph Crane, and you deserve some peace."

Oh, no, Crane thought, *you don't know. You don't know anything at all. If you did, you wouldn't be here, which is one of the many reasons you never will know.*

"Don't think I don't see right through you, Joseph," Bobby said. "I don't care what you think: you *are* a good man."

Crane shook his head, all the answer he could make himself give.

Bobby put his arm across Crane's chest and snuggled closer.

Crane looked down and smiled, as he had a thousand times before, at the beautiful contrast of Bobby's black arm and his own pale chest. *The nightmares, the memories—they're what I deserve,* he thought. "What I don't deserve," he said, "is you."

"That's my choice," Bobby said. "You don't get to decide for me."

Crane nodded, turned, and kissed Bobby lightly. "Thank you."

Bobby smiled. "Let them do the assessment," he said.

"You can still back out, but at least find out if they might be able to help you. In the meantime, you can think about how great it would be to sleep through the night, night after night after night, every night, here with me."

Crane had to admit that the prospect of nights full of unbroken sleep was appealing. He stared at his husband, marveled again at his luck at having this beautiful man as his, and finally nodded. "Okay," he said. "I will. I'll call in the morning and set up the assessment."

Bobby kissed him again. "You won't regret it."

I don't know, Crane thought, *I've regretted everything about the Army, but maybe this will be an exception. I'll hope you're right.*

He closed his eyes and fell quickly back asleep.

Crane almost laughed when they showed him the test apparatus, a wrinkled metal helmet trailing dozens of wires as thin as fishing lines.

The tech, a twenty-something woman in hospital blues with no nametag and no apparent rank, must have read his reaction. "Yeah," she said, "we chuckle at it, too. It's like a prop from a Fifties sci-fi flick. But it does the job, and we don't have to poke any holes in your head."

"Holes in my head?" Crane said.

The tech winced. "I take it they haven't told you."

"No, they haven't."

"It's no big deal," she said, "really. For the final process, we have to insert a bunch of electrodes. We numb the insertion points, so you don't feel anything. We don't even need to shave your head, so no one will know anything happened."

"Uh huh," Crane said. "But for this assessment . . ."

"You sit in that chair," she indicated what looked like a fancy dentist's chair in the center of the room, "and wear the silly helmet. That's it."

Crane longed to leave, but he'd told Bobby he would try, so he didn't move.

"Speaking of which," the tech said, "if you would take a seat, we can get going."

Crane sat. At least the chair was comfortable.

The tech fitted the helmet on him, adjusted it a bit, and then ran a strap under his chin and fastened it to the other side of the helmet.

Johnson breezed through the door into the room. "And how are we today?"

It was as if the man was purpose-built to piss him off.

"I don't know how you are," Crane said, "but I'm thrilled to be here."

"That's great," Johnson said. "Just great."

Being impervious to irony might help you last in the Army, Crane thought. *You asshole.* He knew what Bobby would advise him to do and forced himself not to respond.

"Here's what's going to happen," Johnson said. "We're going to leave you alone in here and turn off the lights. Some of the instruments glow, so you won't be in complete darkness, but the lack of light should help you focus internally. We'll be monitoring you from a room on the other side of that mirror." He pointed to the big mirror on the wall to Crane's left. "We'll give you some instructions, you follow them, and we should be done in no time."

"What kind of instructions?" Crane said.

Johnson smiled. "Not very trusting, are you?"

No, Crane thought, *and if you'd ever seen action, you wouldn't be, either.*

When Crane didn't answer, Johnson continued as if he had. "Well, no worries. We're just going to ask you to think about different things. Okay?" Before Crane could say anything, Johnson said, "Great. Let's do it."

He and the tech left the room.

A few seconds later, the lights dimmed to off.

Crane sat, alone in the dark room, and fought to breathe slowly. He wanted to bolt, to throw off the helmet and get the hell out of here, but he'd told Bobby he'd do this, so he would.

The tech's voice played softly from speakers that seemed to be all around him. "It might help to close your eyes, but that's up to you. Please think of something you find comforting, safe, even happy."

Crane closed his eyes, and it did help a bit. He pictured Bobby holding him at night, the slow cadence of his husband's breathing, the comfort of their bed in their bedroom in their house in the woods, away from everyone.

"That's excellent," the tech said. "Thank you."

Crane nodded.

"Try not to move your head," the tech said. "We should have told you that earlier. Sorry."

"No problem," Crane said.

"Now," she said, "please think about some events—we'd like half a dozen, but we can get by with three or four—from the war that were unpleasant, memories that hit you in nightmares or that upset you or that you try not to think about."

Crane shook his head before he could control his reaction.

"I know it's no fun," the tech said, "but you don't need to think about them for long. Just try to summon images, hold them for a few seconds, and move on. And don't move your head."

"Okay," Crane said. He took a deep breath to steady himself. Recalling his time in country wasn't hard; *not* thinking about it was usually his challenge.

For a few seconds, nothing would come, but then they flooded over him so quickly that he had to fight to see each one vividly.

Riding in the jeep, the splotchy tan Comet coming the other way on the dirt road. Guns poking from its windows. Benny yelling. All of them raising their rifles and shooting shooting shooting. The Comet crashing into an old brown station wagon as their bullets slammed through metal and glass and flesh alike. Looking away as they passed it. He didn't want to see the people inside, had no desire to know what he'd done.

The soldier from last night's nightmare falling into the hole across from him. The man's expression of relief turning into terror and then into nothing, only slack-jawed death. Trying and failing to push back inside the man's guts. Blood, so much blood.

Staring at the village through Army binoculars steamed up from the humidity. Old men and women and children mingling in its square with the young men carrying rifles. Hearing the captain call in the air strike.

Watching as the first bombs hit and the village transformed into fire and dust. Holding his hands over his ears and looking away, glad they wouldn't have to walk into that firefight, ignoring everything else. Them or us always meant us, there was never any question.

Hearing the crack of the shot at the same time the captain's head exploded and the man fell two steps in front of him. Dropping, rolling, and firing into the jungle all around them, the whole squad doing the same, shooting and screaming and scrambling for cover and not knowing if they'd killed the enemy, never knowing for sure until they stopped, waited, and no one else fell.

Trying to fall asleep, more nights than he had counted, as shells exploded far enough away that no shrapnel should reach him but close enough that you could always hear the bursts. Wondering at first if he'd wake up and then, later, not caring if he did. The night the tent next to his vanished as friendly fire vaporized it, the force of the explosion knocking down his tent and burying him in dirt and rubble, his ears ringing and screaming with pain.

"Thank you," the tech's voice said. "We have all we need. Please wait for me to disconnect you."

Crane let out a breath he hadn't realized he'd been holding. His brow was wet with a sheen of sweat, his breathing ragged, his heart pounding. He focused on breathing slowly and calming himself.

The tech pushed open the door, turned on the lights, and came over to him. She quickly undid the helmet's strap and took the device off him. She looked at him as she worked. "I'm sorry," she said. "We can't calibrate without you focusing on the rough stuff."

Crane nodded. "So, would it work on me?"

The tech opened her mouth to answer but stopped before she said anything, because Johnson entered the room.

"She's not really qualified to answer that question," the man said. He stared at the tech, not Crane. "It takes a doctor, and not just any doctor but a trained specialist."

The tech hurried out of the room.

Crane hated Johnson more each time he dealt with him. He forced himself to say only, "Well?"

Johnson gave him the kind of smile that made Crane want to punch the man and then shower afterward. "You are an excellent candidate for the treatment. I'm confident we could locate and remove the major trauma-inducing memories, maybe even all of them." The man pulled a stapled set of papers from his clipboard. "All you'd have to do is fill these out, and we could schedule you." He stepped closer to Crane. "What do you say?"

Though he desperately wanted to smash Johnson and run from the room, Crane reminded himself of his discussion with Bobby, forced himself to walk slowly to the door, and, as he was leaving, said, "I'll think about it and get back to you."

Outside, he walked to a huge oak to the left of the research center and leaned against the lovely old tree. He felt the tree's bark against his back and ran his hands over it. He looked at his own skin and at the tree. Why did some things grow only more powerful and beautiful with age, while others, like him, decayed and became shells of their younger selves? He appreciated the little bits of control that age and practice had bought him, but how he'd become this white-haired old man was a mystery to him.

Standing in the shade, trying to forget the test and all the memories he'd summoned, he focused on the world around him. The morning light still played softly over the grass and the trees, the people walking on sidewalks, the cars on the road beyond the lawn. The building sat on the peak of a small hill that was covered in foliage except where a delivery road cut through the hill straight from the road across from him to a basement he hadn't noticed before. A green railing marked the edge of the cut-through.

A soldier in desert fatigues was leaning over the railing, looking down.

Crane pushed off the tree and jogged over there. "Soldier!" he said as he drew closer.

The soldier turned to face him, snapping to attention as she did. "Sir." She relaxed a bit as she saw that he was a civilian.

Crane noted now that she was a sergeant. "Sergeant Ortega, no one's called me that in a very long time. I worked for a living, and when I was in the Army, you would have outranked me."

She smiled. "I didn't mean it that way. It's reflex. You know, right?"

"I do." He leaned against the railing, sad at being slightly out of breath from jogging such a small distance. "Are you okay?"

"Why—" she flushed. "Oh, I get it. You thought I might jump. No worries; I'm not that type. I've just always found it useful to look down on things when I'm thinking. When I was a kid, I loved to climb trees and see the world from above."

Crane felt his own face turn red as he realized how wrong he'd been. "I'm sorry," he said. "I shouldn't have intruded."

She waved her hand. "Don't be. I don't mind someone caring, genuinely giving a damn, not like these doctors. They all seem to be more concerned about processing us than helping us, as if we were packaged meat." She laughed. "Which of course we are, to them."

He laughed with her. "Truer words . . ."

"What was yours?" she said. "Your war, I mean. You laugh like you understand."

"I do," he said. "Viet Nam. Way before your time."

She nodded. "Bad, though, right? My father did a tour there."

"Yeah," he said, "bad enough. Why'd you enlist? Didn't your father scare you off?"

"He tried to." She shrugged. "Not a lot of options, I guess. Plus, this is my country, you know, so serving it seemed like the right thing to do. What about you?"

"Drafted. I wouldn't have gone on my own, but when the letter came, I went. It was my duty."

"I get that," she said. She stared hard at him. "Did you have the treatment here?"

He shook his head. "No. I did the assessment, and they say I'm a great candidate for the therapy. My husband wants me to do it, but I just don't know. You?"

"Yeah," she said. "I did. Couple of months ago. After two tours in Iraq and more time here and there, I was tired of not sleeping, the dreams, the way I feel—you know."

"I do."

They stood in silence for a minute, and then another. She looked everywhere but at him. He felt like a voyeur, but she also struck him as the first person in this place he could relate to.

"Do you mind if I ask you something?" he said.

She still wouldn't meet his gaze. "Sure. Go ahead."

"Did it work? I mean, was it worth it? Doing the treatment?"

She finally looked at him, her eyes wide. "I tell my husband it was. I say the same thing to the doctors. And in some ways, it really was. I don't have the dreams anymore. I sleep through the night almost all the time. No matter how hard I try, I can't remember most of my time there. It's not blank, because you can see blankness; it's just not there."

"But?" he said.

She stepped closer to him and studied his face closely. "You saw action, right?"

He nodded.

"How do you feel about yourself?"

No one had ever asked him that. People had asked about what he'd seen and what he'd done, but maybe just to be polite, no one had ever asked that. His throat tightened as he said, "The truth?"

"What the hell else are we doing here?" she said. She looked like she wanted to hit him.

He looked to each side and wondered if he should leave now. He didn't owe this woman anything.

But he did, one soldier to another.

"Most days, most times, I'm numb. Good days, I feel good. If I let myself think about the war, though, and sometimes even when I don't realize I have, I hate myself."

She bobbed her head in agreement. "Yeah, exactly. These doctors, my husband, everyone who's never been there, they don't get it. But that's exactly right. That self-loathing, it's down there, all the time, ready to come out, catching you when you're unprepared for it."

"Yes," he said. "The PTSD and the anger, they stay with you, and a lot of people understand those things, or try to, but they can't get the rest. Not if they didn't live it, do what you had to do . . ."

"So you fight it, right?" she said. "The bad memories come, and you tell yourself you did what was necessary, to protect yourself, to take care of your squad, whatever. You fight it and most times you lose, but you have something to fight." She paused. "It's good to have something to fight."

He nodded his head as the memories he'd recalled during the assessment washed over him again. "Yeah. We never get to stop fighting."

"So that's the thing," she said, "the thing they don't tell you about the treatment. Maybe because they can't. Or they don't want to. I don't know."

"What?" he said.

"I still have that feeling," she said. "I still hate myself." She looked away for a moment, and when she stared again at him her eyes were wet. "But I don't know why! I don't know what I did. Did I do awful things? Normal things? I can't remember. Before the treatment, some days I felt like all I was, all I had, was that fight against what I did, that struggle to push the hatred back inside and carry on." She stepped back. "Now, the feeling is there, but I have no clue why." She shook her head. "Maybe it's better this way. I don't know. I do know that I always preferred an enemy I could see, even if it was my own memories." She forced a smile. "At least I sleep now."

"You are going to keep carrying on, though, right?" he said. "You wouldn't—"

She raised her hand in a "stop" motion. "Nah," she said. "I have kids. A husband. My duty. One foot in front of the other, right?"

He nodded.

They stood again in silence, each lost in thought.

"Thank you," Crane said. "Sincerely. I really appreciate you talking to me."

She waved her hand. "*De nada.*" After a few seconds, she said, "So, are you going to do it—the treatment? It does help in a lot of ways."

"I don't know," he said, even though he did. "I don't know."

She glanced at her watch. "I gotta go," she said. "I'm meeting my husband for lunch."

Crane nodded and left. After a few seconds, he stopped and turned. Ortega was marching down the hill, her posture erect, her stride purposeful, another soldier still fighting another war that should have been, for her, long over.

Bobby had lunch on the table when Crane reached

home. A fresh salad, maybe four ounces of lightly seared tuna, glasses of ice water. No treats this time.

As soon as Crane sat, Bobby said, "How did it go?"

"You haven't already talked to that asshole Johnson?"

"Of course I have," Bobby said. He smiled. "You said from the beginning that I could check, so I did. I know you're a good candidate for the therapy. I meant, though, what I asked: how did it go—for you?"

"It was no fun." He ate a bite of the tuna, which was, as always, perfect. If Bobby did something, he did it well. "But I've been through worse. Obviously."

"So are you going to consider it?" Bobby said. "The therapy could mean no more nights like last night."

Crane put down his fork, took a slow drink of water, and dried his lips. He forced himself to look right at Bobby. "I already have," he said. "I'm not going to do it."

Bobby leaned back in his chair, disappointment obvious on his face. "Why not?"

Crane stared at him. How could he explain about his talk with Ortega? How he really felt about himself? What he'd seen, much less what he'd done? He'd never found a way to make anyone who wasn't there understand. He shook his head. "I don't know how to explain it."

Bobby stood, anger replacing the disappointment. "That's not enough, Joseph," he said. "Not this time. I've accepted that for over fifty years, because there was nothing you could do to fix any of it, because I love you, because I realize I can never truly understand what you went through. But now you *can* fix it, and you won't, so you need to tell me why you won't."

I've painted the answer a thousand times, Crane

thought. *I've said it the ways I know best, the ways I can, over and over and over. The words would be just words, not real, not anywhere near the reality of it.* He said nothing.

Bobby shook his head. "Not enough," he said. "Not nearly enough." He grabbed his keys off the table by the door and left.

Crane walked to the window and watched as Bobby climbed into his car and drove off.

Bobby never looked back.

Crane stared at the emptiness that Bobby and his car had occupied. The tuna churned in his stomach. He felt sick. He stood and stared for five minutes, and then five more.

He cleared the table. Put a cover on the salad and stuck it in the refrigerator. Wrapped the pieces of tuna and put them in the cold, too. Loaded and started the dishwasher. Wiped down the table. Went through the kitchen and cleaned everything that wasn't perfect until it was just the way it was supposed to be.

Then he went upstairs to paint.

After mixing the paints and assembling the brushes, he set up a mirror, stared into it, and for the first time since he'd left for basic training, he painted a person.

Himself.

He started with an outline and worked it again and again, his strokes so much less sure than when he painted scenes. He laid down a base.

The world vanished, and he worked and worked and worked.

A little before six, he sat back and stared at the man in the canvas in front of him, then at the mirror, and back to the canvas. The face in the mirror was sad, the one on the canvas sadder. The eyes, though, were better on the canvas, as hollow as he felt inside, more hollow than his real eyes could possibly be. You could tell the man on the canvas had done horrible things; anyone could see it.

The painting wasn't as good as he had hoped it would be, but they never were. It was as good as he could make it.

He cleaned his brushes, tidied his workspace, washed his hands until they were free of paint, and went downstairs.

In the kitchen, he prepared a vegetarian meal, one Bobby would love. Kale and spinach stir-fry. Pasta from spaghetti squash. He freshened the salad from lunch.

Seven o'clock came, and dinner was ready. They never ate later than seven when they were at home.

No Bobby.

Crane sat at the table and stared at the cooling food. He leaned back in his chair, closed his eyes, and hoped Bobby would return. He ran through what he wanted to say to Bobby, what he wanted to show him. No, not what he wanted, but what he would do. He promised himself that if Bobby came home, he would do his best.

Seven thirty passed. No Bobby.

Crane closed his eyes, sat, and waited.

Just after eight, he heard the car pull up. He opened his eyes and watched the doorway until Bobby appeared in it.

"We're not done," Bobby said. His face and voice broadcast anger.

Crane stood, went to Bobby, and put his right index finger on his husband's lips. "Please," he said, "come with me." He removed his finger and looked into Bobby's eyes. "Please."

Bobby tilted his head in question but followed Crane to the stairs and up to his studio.

Crane turned on the lights. One of the overhead spots bathed the portrait in a soft glow.

Bobby stared back and forth between the painting and Crane, the man and the man in the canvas. "You've never . . ." he said. "What is this?"

Crane led him closer. "What do you see?" he said. He motioned to the canvas. "There."

Bobby stared at the painting. "You," he said. "It's beautiful, it's perfect, and it's you."

Crane shook his head. Bobby still couldn't see it. He had hoped the painting would be enough, but it wasn't. He took a deep breath, stared at the painting, and forced himself to talk. "I see a man who did things he can never tell anyone, not even you. I see a different man than the one who went to Viet Nam. I see a dead man waiting for his body to die. I see a man who deserves to die for all that he did, who could have died as easily as all the men he saw perish in horrible ways."

He stopped talking, unable to continue.

He blinked away tears.

No, he had promised himself that if Bobby came home, he would do all he could. He could do more.

"I see a man," he said, "I hate every day for what he did."

He looked now at Bobby. Bobby's eyes were wet, too.

"At least, though, I know what he did." His throat tightened, and now tears ran down his face. "I know every single thing he did—everything *I* did. When I hate him—when I hate myself—I know why, and I know that I deserve that hatred, and I don't deserve the love you give me. I try, though, every day, to deserve that love. I fight the memories. I fight the hatred. Some days, all that's left of me is that fight to stay alive and not surrender to that hatred."

He wiped his face.

"If I do the treatment, I won't be able to remember what I did, and though that might help me sleep, it would leave me with only the hatred—and no idea why I had it. I couldn't bear that."

He took a deep breath. He'd done all he could.

"Honestly," he said, "that is the very best I can do. If it's not enough—"

Bobby put his hand over Crane's mouth.

"It's enough," Bobby said. "It's more than enough. Thank you." Bobby pulled him into a hug so strong that Crane felt he could lean into it and let go of everything and still remain upright. "I love you."

After a minute, Bobby pulled back and stared again at the painting. "It's wonderful," he said.

Crane looked at it and shook his head. "I don't want to sell it. I don't want it on someone's wall."

"Sell it?" Bobby said. "No way. That's all mine. I'm going to frame it myself and hang it in my office here. You can hate that man as much as you need to, and I'll love him as much as I want to, and we'll see who wins." He smiled. "Deal?"

Crane nodded. He didn't believe for a second that Bobby understood, but he'd done all he could to explain, and that had to be enough.

He also had to admit to feeling the tiniest sense of relief. He didn't expect it to last, but in that moment he savored it.

"Deal."

Mark L. Van Name is a writer, technologist, and spoken word performer. He has published five novels (*One Jump Ahead, Slanted Jack, Overthrowing Heaven, Children No More*, and *No Going Back*), as well as an omnibus collection of his first two books (*Jump Gate Twist*); edited or co-edited three previous anthologies (*Intersections: The Sycamore Hill Anthology, Transhuman*, and *The Wild Side*), and written many short stories. Those stories have appeared in a wide variety of books and magazines, including *Asimov's Science Fiction Magazine*, many original anthologies, and *The Year's Best Science Fiction*.

As a technologist, he is the co-founder and co-chairman of a fact-based marketing and learning and development firm, Principled Technologies, Inc., that is based in the Research Triangle area of North Carolina. He has worked with computer technology for his entire professional career and has published over a thousand articles in the computer trade press, as well as a broad assortment of essays and reviews.

As a spoken word artist, he has created and performed four shows—*Science Magic Sex; Wake Up Horny, Wake Up Angry; Mr. Poor Choices*; and *Mr. Poor Choices II: I Don't Understand*.

My afterword, "Waiting for the asteroid."

If you hang around Dave for any significant amount of time, you're bound to hear him say that if he's lucky, the asteroid will hit. He's joking, and he's not joking.

I have never served in the military, and I have never been in combat, so I am not at all sure I have any right to have written this story.

I did, though, spend three years, from age ten to thirteen, in a paramilitary youth group. I went through its basic training and rose through its ranks, and along the way I did a lot of very bad things. I can rationalize them and explain why they were necessary, and perhaps they were, but I know what I did. I know everything I did.

Though Dave and I have never discussed whatever awful things he had to do in Viet Nam—and everyone in every war has to do awful things—I am completely confident that he also knows what he did, that he, too, knows everything he did.

From my years in that youth group, and from a longer and somewhat overlapping period of being a victim of child abuse, I suffer from PTSD.

Dave also suffers from PTSD.

We thus have more in common than most people can ever understand. We understand, though, and we have for decades.

Unlike Dave, I'm not waiting for the asteroid. I know that one day it or something else will claim us all, that, as

Dave likes to point out, in the end the heat death of the universe will consume everything and nothing will matter, but for as long as I'm alive, I will fight for meaning. Dave will say he is different, but I will always maintain that he, too, is engaged in his own version of that fight for meaning.

I also believe, though he and I have never directly discussed it, that each of us fights another battle every day, a battle that we entered via different paths but that pits us against the same enemy, a battle that most people thankfully will never need to fight.

This story is about that battle.

The Losing Side

Larry Correia

Despite the narrative to the contrary, my father was a good man. During the revolution the royalists called him the Butcher of Bangoran. General Vaerst was our spokesman, our inspiration, and their scapegoat. At the end of the war, the royalists dragged him out of the palace, stripped him naked, beat him, and then executed him with a ceremonial sword on the steps. They left his body to rot there for a week as an example.

I don't know who the royalists' god is, but my father was their devil.

In reality, he was just another husband and a father, no different than the tens of thousands of others who died during the revolution. He was a man who loved his planet, but who'd been pushed too far and took a stand against tyranny. It turned out that he was really good at it. I don't think Dad ever thought his words would start a revolution.

The last time I saw him was the night before my company shipped out for West Moravia. At that point we'd been fighting for two years. Dad was worn out, but the people were sick of those slaving royalist bastards and had risen up, so we were winning, and that kept him going. As we sat in his command bunker, listening to the shelling of Vakaga City above us, eating a last meal of ration bars, we talked about everything. About friends and family lost, but about how it would be worth it so that my children—his grandchildren—could grow up with freedom for the first time in our planet's history.

That was when he got the report that the royalists had somehow borrowed enough money to hire off-world mercenaries. At the time, I didn't understand why Dad looked so stricken.

"What's wrong?" I'd asked. "We're winning. We've got them on the ropes. Once we take the west, they'll fold."

He had gotten up and begun pacing. You have to understand, my father only paced when things were really bad. "I told the council we needed to lock them in, get them on contract, but those cheap do-nothings wouldn't listen to me. Now it's too late. We should have hired them when we had the chance."

"But what difference are some mercenaries going to make?"

"They're Hammer's Slammers, son. They'll make all the difference."

The explosion from the 20cm main tank gun obliterated half the apartment complex around us.

"Back up!" I shouted at the driver, but Cainho knew

his shit, and we were already heading into the subterranean parking level before the Slammers' tank could get off another shot. The flash from the blast had momentarily fuzzed out our tank's scanners, but we'd gotten a peek, that's all that mattered. The spotted target's position would be relayed to everyone else, and hopefully something they threw at it wouldn't just bounce off that monster.

"Shogun Six, this is Phantom One. Heavy in the open," I called in as our Lynx sped through the empty garage. I brought up the map, and tapped out a path for Cainho to follow. "We're moving to Isen Street."

"Roger, Phantom. Engaging the heavy. Proceed to Isen."

Not that I wouldn't have kept going anyway. If my little scout tank waited long enough to get orders confirmed we were dead. If one of our scout tanks was doing anything other than running or hiding, it was dead. We'd learned that the hard way.

As we bounced up the ramp and out into the street, the sensor package showed clear both ways, but half a second later I got a warning ping. Movement on the left, just a flash of iridium armor through holes punched in a concrete wall. *Combat car.* "Pig at nine." Its gunners hadn't seen us yet, or we'd be eating cyan bolts. I tagged a new path through the wreckage of what looked to have been a tractor dealership. The Lynx was the fastest armored vehicle on the battlefield, and in Cainho's skilled hands, it was a nimble little beast. He got us behind another wall and the flaming remains of some piece of industrial equipment and we hid.

"Shogun Six, this is Phantom One. Just spotted a pig at the end of Isen."

"Got it, Phantom. Tagged."

We waited. I could only pray that the nearby building fires were screwing up their thermal.

I could hear our gunner above me. Blanchard was breathing heavy as he tracked the combat car. Our 60mm autocannon hadn't had much luck penetrating even their smaller vehicles, especially not from the front. On the other hand their tribarrels would rip right through any part of our Lynx like it was made out of paper. *Come on . . .*

It was hot. Beneath my armor, I was drenched with sweat. My sinuses were filled with the stink of carbon and blood. I was so tired it took a moment to remember where the rotting blood stink had come from. That's right. It was the same reason there was a hole in the driver's compartment I could see a beam of daylight through, and why we'd just picked up a replacement driver. In the heat of the moment I'd already called Cainho by the wrong name a couple of times, but Haarde was dead . . . *What . . . Two days? Three?* They'd bled together. I couldn't remember.

"Keep moving, asshole," Cainho begged. "Nothing to see here."

Like their big tanks, the Slammers' combat cars were hover vehicles. I imagine they had to be really loud inside, floating on top of all those powerful fans. Our Lynx ran on rubberized tracks and had a small thorium reactor, so it was actually a pretty quiet ride. The combat cars had more human eyes manning guns all the way around, but their sensor suites didn't seem as good as the heavies, and not nearly as good as ours.

The one thing my home planet was good at was tech, much of it designed by my family's company. Moravia was great at designing sensor suites, which meant we got fantastic recordings of us getting our asses handed to us by the mercs with the heavier armor and bigger guns.

The combat car flashed past the holes and sped down the street in the opposite direction.

We could all hear the rumbling thunder of artillery through our thin armor. They were dropping shells on the tank. Red dots rained down my display, but one by one they flashed out of existence as the tank picked the shells out of the sky with its 2cm air defense system. Cyan bolts flew upward and explosions ripped across the air.

Something get through. Something.

The last red dot disappeared.

"Blood and martyrs," Blanchard snarled from the turret. The gunner's targeting displays had told him the same story. "Can't anything hurt these fuckers?"

"I heard a guy in the 6th rushed one with a satchel charge and tossed it under the fans," Cainho said as he maneuvered the Lynx around wrecked cars and rubble. "Blew it all to hell."

"Wishful thinking. They've got a point defense system for infantry too," I told my crew. "If that story's true, it's only because that tank was broken. A combat car, maybe."

The symbol of the tank disappeared from my map. The AI could no longer tell with certainty where it had gone. It could make logical predictions, but the mercenaries had figured that out first day, and were being annoyingly unpredictable. They were clever like that.

"Shit," Blanchard said. A missing tank meant they were going to make us go looking for it again.

"Phantoms." They didn't bother with our full call sign, because Phantom Two through Six were gone, all lost over the last twenty furious hours. It turns out when a soft little scout got hit with a Hellbore there wasn't much left. *"This is Shogun Six. We need eyes on that tank."*

"Keep your pants on, asshole." That wasn't for the command channel. That frustrated muttering was for my personal gratification. Shogun Six was twenty klicks from this slaughter. The AI might not know where that tank had gone, but my gut knew. It was waiting to pop us. The sensors on their big tanks were ridiculously good. I needed to look at the terrain models of this disintegrating city and figure out how to approach without getting our asses vaporized.

"Third Armored is approaching the east end of the park. They need to know where that heavy is."

The interior of the Lynx was tight. My compartment was worse. A lot of scout tank commanders liked to get their heads out of the cupola, thinking that made them more aware of their surroundings, and their visor would keep them up with the computer's feeds, but that was a trick. That was them lying to themselves. The sensor suite provided *too much* information, and most commanders found it overwhelming being bombarded by that much info for long. I'd been so plugged in and fried by the last few days of fighting, that I had the opposite problem. I was scared to unplug.

"There. You see the path, Cainho?"

"Got it, Vaerst." The new driver was excellent. He should be. Like me, he'd been fighting royalists since half the army had said enough with this tyrannical bullshit and the first shots were fired at Bangoran. He'd been an experienced tank commander himself up until a few days ago, when he'd had to bail out after his vehicle had been set ablaze by a tribarrel. The rest of his crew hadn't made it out. "You know, third is only running some cobbled together surplus."

In other words, they were as doomed as everyone else they'd thrown against these merciless bastards.

"Third is driving Pumas. Our 60mm barely scratches the paint. We have to get real lucky to do any damage, but those have 120mm guns. A good shot might punch one of those land whales," Blanchard said hopefully.

"Yeah . . . Well, let's find them a target."

Who were we kidding? The Slammer tanks were 170-ton iridium wrecking balls with guns that could shoot down satellites. Dad hadn't been kidding. They were running the most advanced armored vehicles in history. Even their light combat cars weighed nearly twice what our Lynx did.

The kingdom's hardware was obsolete garbage in comparison. Our software was good. Our systems were good. Our soldiers were tough. But hell, I might as well say we had truth and justice on our side too, since it turned out that all meant jack and shit when the bolts began to fly.

While Cainho moved us to the next hiding place, I expanded out the map until I could see the entire

Moravian coast. That was one of the dangers of being too plugged in, too aware. *Curiosity.*

We were getting crushed.

"The Slammers are really that good?"

"They're the best," Dad said. "Alois Hammer has put together one of the most successful fighting outfits in human history. No bullshit, no politics, no ass kissing. They don't play games, they don't have to make anybody happy. They agree to a mission, sign a contract, then they fill it. They're very good at that. Maybe the best there's ever been. And sadly for us, they've landed in the west."

"They can't be that good." Oh, how naïve I'd been back then. I'd seen some combat by that point, so I thought I knew a thing or two about war. My brothers were fighting for liberty, for our families, and for each other. I couldn't comprehend someone fighting just for money. "Only honorless scum would fight for anyone as evil as King Soboth!"

But Dad was wise, and he just shook his head sadly. "It isn't about good or evil to them. Hammer doesn't give a damn about Soboth beyond the fact the man is willing to mortgage a planet to save his crown. They only care about completing the mission and getting paid. Most of their trigger pullers won't even bother to read the briefings to learn what each side believes in, just which color uniform they're supposed to shoot. They've done it on plenty of other worlds, and they'll do it again somewhere else when they're done here."

"Not if we beat them."

Dad just laughed.

I watched the displays in horror as 3rd Armored was ripped to pieces.

The old Pumas crashed through the trees of Grand Park, big guns booming. The Slammers' tanks were moving across the grass, far too fast, and every time one of those 20cm Hellbores went off in a blinding flash, another one of our tanks turned into an expanding ball of plasma. The combat cars were darting about, using the terrain, popping over rises to rip off bursts from their tribarrels. They were concentrating on our infantry. Rockets and small arms fire were lancing out from the surrounding buildings' windows, but the tribarrels responded and ripped those facades into concrete dust.

"Shogun Six, this is Phantom. Targets are marked."

But there was no response, just dead air. I pulled back the screens. Shogun was gone, icon blinking red. The artillery battery was overrun. I didn't even know where those attackers had come from. No time to think about it. We were on our own.

A warning pinged, but Cainho's instincts had kicked in even before the AI had decided we were in danger and our Lynx was already scooting backward down the hill. A combat car was flying across the lake in a huge spray. Water exploded into steam as molten bolts lashed out and tore apart the rocks we'd been hiding behind. Flaming gravel clanged against our armor. That's about all it was good for.

There was nobody left to spot for. That fucking combat car had been chasing us all morning, and it was used to us running away. It would be expecting more of the same. As Cainho reversed us through the manicured flowerbeds, crushing carved topiary beneath our treads, I flagged a new course for him. "Come around the bottom of the hill." Using the terrain, we could stay low until the last second. "Blanchard, shoot that pig in the ass."

The Lynx hit the bottom and turned on a dime. The combat car would be climbing the hill. The AI told me that it was unlikely the pig would silhouette itself on that hill, even for a second, but I knew the AI was wrong. We'd been an annoyance. They wanted us dead, and they would figure if they risked climbing, they could get a few shots at us while we scurried for cover.

We swung around the bushes and every warning ping we had went off at once. Sure enough, the combat car was above us, tilting across the blasted rocks. By the time I shouted, "Fire!" Blanchard had already launched the first burst right into their fighting compartment. The rounds that hit the iridium armor left orange glowing dents, but the ones that entered fragmented inside and caused the vehicle to puke fire. Blanchard kept the triggers mashed, raking 60mm AP into that pig. A severed arm sailed through the air. An empty helmet bounced down the hill.

The combat car began to skew sideways. One of the tribarrels was cranking our way, but the edge of its skirts ground on the rocks, and the blast of air pressure suddenly drove one side of the pig into the dirt. The tribarrel fired wildly. Cyan flashes ripped burning holes into the grass towards us. "Pull back," I ordered. Cainho calmly reversed as Blanchard kept shooting. The helmet crunched beneath our treads. The gunner was so focused on killing that pig that his last few rounds hit nothing but the earthen berm we were now hiding behind.

We'd only been in the open for a moment, but already other things were vectoring in to kill us. The compartment was filled with powder smoke. Fans were blowing and the respirator in my helmet had kicked in. I tagged another route, keeping our head down, using the streambed and drainage culverts, and before I was even done, Cainho had us tearing across the park, quickly accelerating to sixty KPH. Considering the state of the ground, it was stupidly fast, but if we slowed down, we were dead.

There was an explosion from the top of the hill. Something had cooked off. We'd killed a Slammer's combat car. We'd actually done it. I had nobody to call that in to, and by the time I checked the screens, the twenty Puma tanks of 3rd Armored were all dead.

I had never seen my father like this. Even though we'd fought hard, built an army, hell, built a whole government, overthrown a king, and beat the wretched royalists, it was like he already knew we'd been defeated.

"Our only hope is to wear them down. Attrition. The people are on our side. The king will get what he paid for, but not a peso more. Hit and run, bleed them as they bleed us. To Alois Hammer this planet is just an entry on a profit and loss statement, but it is our fucking home."

He didn't sound convinced.

"I'm sorry, Captain Vaerst. Your father is dead."

I'd been plugged into the Lynx's systems continually

for so many days that actual face-to-face human communication took a while to sink in. I stared at the major for a really long time, not understanding the words coming out of his mouth. There were no symbols, flashes, lines of movement and terrain paths, AI estimates, pings for threats, or stress load outs. All I could communicate now were tanks, how to keep mine alive, and how to make theirs dead, fast. It was like I was stuck in high gear and couldn't downshift.

"He was murdered by royalists during peace talks at the palace." The major rested one gentle hand on my armored shoulder, taking my dimwitted exhaustion for shock. He patted me. "There, there." And it raised a cloud of dust. "We can take you off the line until we know what's going to happen in the capitol."

That was meant to be comforting, but I didn't . . . couldn't *get* comfort. For the last three weeks I'd fought in my tank, slept in my tank, shit through a chute in the bottom of my tank, drank from a tube in my tank, and ate ration bars that were occasionally dropped through the open cupola of my tank whenever we stopped to resupply. So I just stared at the major, unblinking, until he took his hand away.

"Or not . . . That's fine, Captain. The battalion is falling back toward the river today. Carry on." He unconsciously wiped the dirt on his hand on his fatigue pants as he walked away.

I went back to my tank.

Cainho was asleep in the shade between the treads. Blanchard was painting another marking on the Lynx's battered turret. The sixteen red vehicles were royalists.

The four black ones were Slammers. According to the screens—and the screens were my whole world now—nobody else had pulled off anything close to that. Sadly, *every* Slammers vehicle could paint a board like this . . . If they even bothered to count us.

But I didn't care. I just wanted to sleep.

"You know what they're saying about our little Lynx around camp? *Too cute to die, too deadly to live*. We're one tank, but they're calling us Task Force Phantom, all by ourselves . . . Good girl," Blanchard said, touching the turret with more actual love and kindness than the major had just shown me. "Word is they saw a Heavy in the forest fifteen minutes ago, Cap."

I wasn't plugged in. I'd missed that ping. *Weird*.

"Before this is over, I really want to paint a heavy kill on here," Blanchard said wistfully as he put away the stencil and spray can. We'd replaced the 60mm autocannon with a 3cm power gun we'd looted off a Palace Guard wreck a week ago. It was a hell of a lot of gun for such a little tank. The main differences were that we killed things better now, but the compartment always smelled like melting plastic instead of burning carbon. I kind of missed the carbon smoke. "Did I tell you they blew up my town, Cap?"

Blanchard had taken that hard. "Yeah, man. I know." He didn't need to tell me. I'd been there with him when it had happened.

"Whole damned town . . . Sniper fires from a window, they blow up the whole town. You don't need to blow up a whole town. That's overreaction. That's just plain rude. I really want to paint a black heavy on here."

"Let's go find one for you then." I thumped Cainho's leg with my boot.

He snorted and woke right up. "Any news?" our driver asked immediately.

"Something about the capitol . . . My dad . . ." Neither of those things was near this camp or this forest, so it was out of my hands. I popped a couple of Stay Awake pills. "I don't know . . . . Let's go."

Once I got my helmet on the AI booted up, I could see clearly again. Fox company was in the north of Glad Wood, and they'd tagged a heavy. It only took a few seconds of running probabilities to see the mercs intended to seize the bridges at Constantine. I flagged it, but our chain of command had fallen apart, and our orders were a mismatched bunch of panicked gibberish. They sounded like squawking chickens over the net. They were sure upset about something.

It didn't matter. We'd just do what we always did. Harass the shit out of the other side, murder them when given the opportunity, and then run away to do it again later.

I checked the grids, the tank stats—the chameleon projector needed to be replaced soon—the tactical maps, expanding out further and further until I could see the whole war. It wasn't until I watched the news footage of the mob beating and kicking my father, and then clumsily hacking at him with a golden sword that it finally registered.

This was what it felt like to lose a war.

My father knew that night why we wouldn't win.

I didn't understand until later. When my little tank was broken and full of holes, and I was bleeding, wading through the mud, dragging my burned gunner away, and that giant fucking monster tank came over the rise, riding on a dozen tornadoes, and it aimed that giant space gun right down at us, and blinded us with a spotlight, like some wrathful ancient war god . . . and as we stood there blind, battered by the wind, being weighed and measured and found wanting, then I knew too.

I spent the next few years in prison, mulling over the reasons we lost.

My father wasn't a real general. He was a businessman who got rich designing and exporting sensor packages for military vehicles, who could give a rousing speech, and who had the balls to stand up against a tyrannical lunatic. But he never wanted to make war.

Alois Hammer was born to make war.

I was a soldier. Everyone here knows my service record, but I was nobody. I knew heroes. Real heroes. I saw our best and brightest fight for what they believed in . . . and I watched them die.

Because Hammer's Slammers exist only to make war.

We were fathers and mothers, brothers and sisters, students, teachers, workers, merchants, and slaves . . . turned soldiers. And once the war was over they all went back to being whatever we were before.

Hammer's Slammers were soldiers. Then, now, forever. Period.

So here we are, years later, and another Vaerst is standing before this council. You're beating the war drum again, calling for another rebellion, and you need

*yourselves a general, and who better to be your figurehead
than a war hero?*

*I will heed your call. I will accept this commission, and
I will help the people throw off the yoke of tyranny . . . On
one condition.*

We hire Hammer's Slammers.

This time I want to be on the winning side.

Larry Correia is the *New York Times* bestselling author
of the *Monster Hunter International* series, the *Grimnoir
Chronicles* trilogy, the *Dead Six* military thrillers (co-
written with Mike Kupari), and the epic fantasy *Son of
the Black Sword*, from Baen Books. Larry is a retired
accountant and firearms instructor who lives in northern
Utah.

At my request, he provided this afterword.

The first time I read something by David Drake was
around 1985. I was ten years old. The reason I bought it
from the grocery store with my own money was because
there was an awesome space tank on the cover. Hammer's
Slammers rocked my little world. I loved it.

I've been reading David Drake's work ever since. His
style was a huge influence on me. If I had to pick one
favorite, it would *The Sharp End,* and *The Voyage* would
come in second.

When Mark asked me if I'd like to participate in this
anthology, the first thing I did was go through all my old
boxes of books I've accumulated over my life looking for
that first paperback. I'm ninety-nine percent sure it was

At Any Price, but I couldn't find it, and that's been bugging me for a while because I hate losing books. I've got it on my Kindle, but that's just not the same as a book a little kid bought with his limited chore money and whatever coins he could fish out of the couch cushions.

Thank you, David, for writing such great stories and inspiring the rest of us.

Save What You Can

David Drake

Raney didn't think she'd been able to sleep more than fifteen minutes or so on the run from the spaceport, but when the truck rocked to a halt she heard someone outside shout, "End of the line, troopers! Out! Out!"

"This is Mormont?" she said to the trooper beside her. If it was, she'd slept most of six hours.

"I guess," he said. "Unless they changed their bloody minds again on the road. Which is likely enough."

Raney slung her sub-machine gun, then put on her commo helmet. She wasn't netted in to the First Platoon channel; that was the first order of business after she reported.

"Say?" she said to the trooper shuffling to the open tailgate ahead of her. They'd loaded at night, and she only knew a few people in First Platoon. "Who's the CO?"

They'd been crammed in so tight that you had to negotiate to get room to curl up to sleep, but that was all the talking Raney had done during the ride. They were all slugged out from Transit; they'd offloaded from the ship and packed straight onto the trucks without the usual couple days' stand-down to acclimate.

"That's Sergeant Krotcha," the trooper said, "but they said we're with a section of combat cars and the El-Tee of them's in command of the team. Say, are you a recruit?"

"Not exactly," said Raney, feeling her lips grin a little. She was thirty standard years old, twelve years a veteran of the Slammers. "I'm a sergeant/gunner from Third, but my jeep's deadlined. My driver's with the vehicle, waiting for the rest of Support Section to land. Major Pritchard stuck me in First because Third had already pulled out and they need all the bodies they have up on the border."

"You watch," said the other trooper, holding the tailgate latch with one hand as he stepped from the truck's bumper to the ground. His 2cm weapon banged between the tailgate and his body armor. "We'll be here freezing our butts for a month without our hold baggage, and nothing will happen."

"That's okay with me," Raney said, swinging down in turn. She thought of asking the fellow's name, but there'd be time later so it didn't matter.

Or there wouldn't be time, that could happen too. Then it mattered even less.

Their convoy was four civilian trucks—the one Raney had been aboard had *Glover Shirtwaists* painted on the side—with a combat car ahead and another behind. They'd halted in an irregular plaza surrounded by one- and two-story fieldstone houses with slate roofs. It had stopped snowing, but at least a decimeter lay on the roofs and pavement.

Sky, land and buildings were different dirty shades of gray, and it was as cold as a witch's tit. Raney saw no sign of civilians.

The last truck was a stakebed carrying the infantry skimmers snugged down with cargo ties. They were being offloaded now, but Raney figured she'd better report before she picked up the skimmer they'd assigned her at the spaceport.

She'd only had time to glance at her skimmer, but that was long enough to see that it was a clapped-out junker. If she had to do any serious travel on it, she was well and truly screwed.

Krotcha was a heavy-set man, not old—forty, maybe—but bald except for a black fringe circling above his ears. Raney knew him slightly. He was talking to somebody on his commo helmet when Raney walked over to him.

"Top, Major Pritchard attached me to you just as you were pulling out," Raney said. "I'm—"

"You're Raney," Krotcha said. His gaze was disturbingly sharp. "You got a tribarrel in Third, don't you?"

"Yeah, but the jeep's deadlined for parts until the *Sundquist* lands," Raney said. "Maybe tomorrow—"

"And maybe next month," Krotcha said, shrugging. "Well, I'm glad to have you, Raney. I'd be a long sight gladder to have your gun too, but in a ratfuck like this I guess you take what you can get."

A younger man in clean khakis and new body armor joined them. He'd gotten down from the lead combat car, *Camptown*. Krotcha looked toward him and said, "El-Tee, this is Sergeant Raney from Third. I'm putting her in

Wetsam's squad. Raney, this is Lieutenant Taggert from Charlie Troop, he's in charge."

"Sir," said Raney. "I'm still on the Third Platoon net. There wasn't time—"

Krotcha leaned forward to read the serial number from her helmet, then spoke it into the AI of his own unit. A machine voice in her ear said, "Accepted." A moment later the same voice said, "Command net, accepted."

Raney nodded thanks. Top was treating her as a sergeant rather than just an extra trooper, though she wouldn't have any command responsibilities unless something went badly wrong. She didn't know the people in the platoon well enough to be giving orders, but she'd do what she could if it all hit the fan.

"There isn't time to breathe," Taggert muttered. He suddenly looked very young; Raney wondered if this was his first command. "The Bessies mobilized as soon as they learned the Commonwealth had hired us. It looks like they hope to take the spaceport before the Slammers have landed, all but us on the *Garrett*."

"We'll have backup soonest, sir," Sergeant Krotcha said. "The other ships can't be more than a day out, and then it's just a couple hours before there's a company of panzers barreling down the road to us."

He sounded reassuring, upbeat even, when he spoke to the green lieutenant. You'd scarcely imagine that he was the same man who'd muttered to Raney, another veteran, that the rest of Hammer's Regiment might not land for a month.

"I'll get my ride and find Wetsam," Raney said, turning away. The combat cars were in air-defense mode, their tribarrels slanted up toward the north. They would sweep incoming shells from the sky before the combat team—and the nearby portion of Mormont—was in any danger.

Three locals in gray uniforms had come out of a building facing the plaza and were walking toward the command group. Two of them carried long-barreled coil guns; the middle-aged man in the middle had only a pistol.

Raney used the locator of her helmet as she walked toward the stakebed. It was taking time to unload the skimmers; the catches of the tie-downs had frozen. She wasn't surprised to find Sergeant Wetsam in the crowd at the back of the truck.

"Sarge, Top assigned me to you," Raney said to the trooper highlighted by her face-shield. "I'm Raney."

Wetsam—short, sturdy and thirty; a male equivalent of Raney herself—gave her a wry smile. "Lucky you," he said. "Did he tell you were he'd put us?"

"I don't know squat," said Raney. "Pretty much like usual."

The skimmer being driven off the truck now was hers. It looked even worse in morning sun than it had when she first got it under the spaceport floods.

"Well, there's a farm north of town proper and half a klick off the main road," Wetsam said. "We're there to snipe at the Bessies if they barrel straight up the road to Mormont. If they decide to use the farm for their own outpost, though, I'll be bloody glad to have you and anybody else you can scrape up besides."

The snow on the road was unmarked, so Wetsam took

the squad well to the right through the straggling woods. If the wind kept up, the snow swirled from the pavement by the skimmers' air cushions would be wiped out in a few hours anyway. Wetsam was right not to give the Bessies a chance that they didn't need to have, though.

Wetsam was number two in the line and Raney brought up the rear. She had her skimmer punched out to hold the moderate pace. Winter had frozen the undergrowth down to bare canes.

The clean-up slot was proper for Raney's rank—she might even be senior to Wetsam, though she had no intention of pushing the point—but she hoped that her skimmer didn't crap out while the others drove on without her. She would call on the helmet if necessary, but they wanted to hold electronic silence. The Bessies couldn't listen in on the frequency-hopping communications, but helmet commo might alert them to the Slammers' presence.

The farm that was to be the squad outpost was a one-and-a-half-story fieldstone building in a large yard. There was a shed, a chicken coop, and a shoulder-high woodpile ten meters long.

The fence was probably more of a way to dispose of stones plowed up from the field than a barrier. It was waist-high on three sides, but on the back toward the woods it was low enough for a healthy skimmer to hop. Raney and another member of the squad stopped just short of it. Each in turn then lifted the front of the other's machine while its rider gunned the fans. They parked against the rear of the building with the other skimmers.

Wetsam had opened the slanting door in the ground

against the rear wall. Beneath was a root cellar which reached some distance back under the house proper.

"Okay, here's our hide," Wetsam said. "Blessing, you take Sparky and Carl to tear apart them sheds. The rest of us'll use the timbers to brace the cellar roof in case the house gets shelled. Raney, there's a window in the roof peak. Central hasn't warned us yet, so I'm not expecting anybody down the road till we're set up here. Just in case, though, you keep an eye out. All right?"

"Roger," Raney said. Her sub-machine gun didn't have the punch to be effective on targets five hundred meters away, but the other squad members were used to working together. Besides, shooting at scouts would just warn the Bessies that the farm was a target worth dealing with.

The only door to the house was in the front. It was ajar; a trickle of snow had blown over the board floor. The fireplace—Raney checked it with thermal imaging on her face-shield—was cold.

The stairs to the loft were almost steep enough to be called a ladder. When Raney started up, a dog began yapping above her. She paused, then lunged up two steps and raised her head above floor level behind the holographic sights of her sub-machine gun.

A little girl stared big-eyed from the side of a bed. She held a puppy in one arm and was trying to clamp its muzzle shut with the other hand. She shrieked and dropped the dog when Raney appeared. The yapping continued, punctuated by slobbering as the puppy tried to lick tears from the girl's face.

Raney stepped onto the loft floor. She could stand

upright if she stayed under the ridgepole. There weren't supposed to be any civilians left in the district, but besides the kid—she looked about eight—there was an old man lying in bed. The quilt over his chest rose and fell slightly, but his face was as still as wax.

"What are you doing here, kid?" Raney said. "You'll get blown to Hell! You were supposed to evacuate."

"Grampa can't go!" the girl said. "The Da Costas said they wouldn't carry him, he'd just die anyway, but I won't leave him!"

"Look, sometimes you gotta cut your losses, kid," Raney said. She squatted to bring her head more on a level with that of the kneeling girl. "You know, save what you can. I'm sorry, but your grandfather isn't going to make it much longer even without a shell landing on top of him."

Which was what was going to happen a couple minutes after the squad started shooting.

"I won't!"

Raney sighed. "What's your name, kid?" she said, trying to sound calm and friendly. This was just one more screw-up. That's what a war was: one bloody screw-up after another.

"Celie," said the girl. She hugged the dog close again. "And this is Bubbles."

Instead of keying her helmet, Raney bent over the ladder and shouted, "Sarge! Wetsam! I need you soonest!"

Glass splintered. Instead of coming around to the door, Wetsam had knocked out a back window. Through it he called, "What the hell is it, Raney?"

"We got civilians! Get up here!"

"Bloody hell," the squad leader snarled. More glass broke, but it was some moments before Wetsam appeared through the doorway from the back room. He'd have used the butt of his weapon to clear glass from the casement, but that left sharp edges. Nicking an artery by accident could let your life out as sure as a powergun would.

"Celie, come stick your head over," Raney said. Obediently the girl came and looked down the stairs beside Raney. Bubbles waddled over also, whining.

"Bloody *hell*," Wetsam said.

"There's an old guy in the bed, too," Raney said. "He's on his last legs, but she won't leave him."

"The bloody National Guard swore they'd cleared all the bloody civilians from the bloody area!" Wetsam said as he started up the stairs.

"Hey, you don't suppose the locals might be bloody useless, do you?" Raney said. She stood and eased Celie back from the stairhead with her. "We've never run into that on other deployments, have we?"

"Joke," Wetsam said as he joined them in the loft. He stared at Grampa and made a sour expression with his lips. "But we're still stuck with them."

"Do we get the Guard in Mormont to pick 'em up?" Raney asked. "We can't carry the old guy on our skimmers."

"They didn't take him before, so why're they going to now?" Wetsam said. The puppy was sniffing his boots. "Besides, I don't want a bunch of Guards tramping around here. If the Bessies ignore us till we decide to get noticed, we got a lot better chance of retiring."

"Well, then we got to bring them down into the cellar

with us," Raney said. She thought about retirement, but it was just a gray blur. She knew she wasn't going back to Hagel's World—ever; but there wasn't any other planet that she *wanted* to be. The Slammers were the only place she'd been that seemed like home.

"Hell, it's cramped already," Wetsam said, but he wasn't really arguing. "Bloody hell."

"You know what's going to happen to the upper floors," said Raney. "Want me to go down and you reach him down to me on the floor?"

"Yeah, I don't have a better idea," Wetsam said. He bent over the bed and gripped the old man around the shoulders.

"What are you *doing*?" Celie said, and her puppy started to yap again.

"We're going to get your grampa some place safer," Raney said, going down the stairs backward. It wasn't going to be *very* safe, but it was the best they could do for now. It was all they had themselves, but the Slammers got paid for it.

The dog suddenly squatted and peed on Wetsam's boots. Wetsam didn't react, maybe didn't even notice. Raney wouldn't have blamed him if he'd kicked Bubbles downstairs, but then the kid would make even more noise than the dog had.

Wetsam bent, lowering the old man. Raney stood with one boot on the floor and the other on the first step. She surged up, then eased back when she had a hand on each side of grampa's ribs.

He weighed next to nothing, but she felt his breath on her cheek as she stepped back. It smelled sour.

Bubbles bounced down the stairs front-first, circling and yapping as Raney walked to the door. She wasn't going to try fitting Grampa through the jagged casement.

The girl scooted down ahead of Wetsam. Just as well that Raney didn't need help carrying the old man.

Celie walked beside her, holding one of Grampa's dangling hands. "Are you going to save us from the Filth?" she asked.

"Huh?" said Raney, then realized that "Filth" must be the local name for citizens of the Republic of Bessarabia. "Well, we're going to try to give the Bessies a bloody nose if they come this way, but maybe they won't."

"You'll save us," the little girl said firmly. "I *know* you will."

"If Central was right about what's coming down the road tonight . . . ," Wetsam said from behind them. He was carrying the bedding and even the thin mattress. "I figure we'll be lucky to save our own asses."

Raney didn't respond, but she sure didn't disagree.

Grampa was still alive, though the only evidence of that was the occasional wheeze of breath through his open mouth. The girl huddled against him; the puppy varied between sniffing at the crouching Slammers and trying to wriggle between the two civilians.

The heaters in Raney's helmet, boots and gloves kept her functional, but the bare skin of her face prickled beneath the face-shield. They'd created the hide by slanting the beams of the outbuildings from the back wall of the cellar to the floor. The kitchen table, the front door and the cellar door lay on the supports to catch debris and slide it away if the building above them collapsed.

It would have been reasonably warm with nine people and a dog crammed in, if they hadn't had to remove the cellar door. It wasn't a real bunker, but as a hide where they could keep out of the sight of Bessies heading for Mormont, it'd do. It had to.

The sun was low beyond the woods behind them, and the blurred gray of the sky was shading deeper. It wasn't the sort of night that ever became pitch black, though; the bare branches would still be faintly silhouetted against the overcast at midnight. A mist was rising.

Celie hadn't spoken for half an hour, and her eyes were closed. Wetsam was letting the squad sleep three at a time, but Raney had stayed awake. Dozing on the truck, followed by the surprise of finding the civilians, seemed to have cured the normal loginess of Transit.

They were watching the road through tiny sensors placed on the stone fence. "Visitors!" Raney said in a harsh whisper when her face-shield careted movement. All the troopers had probably seen the vehicle, but it was a lot easier to call the alert than learn that you were the only one after all.

Troopers shifted, ready to rush up the stairs. "Stay where you are!" Wetsam snapped.

Raney checked the indicator lights on her submachine gun, green/green/red: loaded, sights on, safety on. The other troopers were going over their weapons also.

A pair of four-wheeled vehicles with sloping bodies came down the road from the direction of the Bessarabian frontier. One head stuck over the top of each compartment.

The scout cars probably had armor, but it couldn't be very heavy. Snow swirled from beneath the wheels. They were moving at about 40kph; Raney's display would calculate the exact speed if she thought there was any reason to. She didn't.

Wetsam reported to the command in Mormont. Then he said, "Nothing for us, troopers. But I don't guess it'll be much longer."

The second scout car halted near the trackway to the farm where the Slammers waited. The leader continued toward Mormont, but the driver slowed to half his previous speed.

The scout car was within a hundred meters of the town when light flickered from the upper stories of buildings on the edge of town. Moments later Raney heard the crackle of coil-guns and the distant *whang*-eeeee of ricochets.

The scout car halted. Instead of turning, it accelerated straight back in the direction from which it had come: the vehicle had reversible steering.

A much louder *crash!* sounded from somewhere within Mormont. The car at the farm junction exploded, gutted by a heavy slug which had pierced it the long way. Parts of the engine blew out through the plating and diesel fuel erupted over the road.

The surviving vehicle fanned the deep red flames when it drove through them, still accelerating. It was going over 60kph as it vanished around a curve. That was probably its top speed.

Wetsam took his hand from the shoulder of the trooper who had started to get up. "Not your business, Kenner," the sergeant said. "Not till I tell you it is."

The anti-tank slug hitting the scout car had been louder than a high-speed collision, and the *whump!* of the fuel igniting had rattled windows in the house. The old man didn't move, but the puppy ran out into the yard yapping. Celie sat up straight.

"Did you kill the Filth?" she demanded. "Are we safe?"

"Stay where you are, darling!" Raney said, because the girl looked as though she might try to run up into the yard. "No, it's not over. Besides, that was your own people, not us."

Taggert must be hiding the Slammers' presence for as long as possible. If they'd asked Raney, she would've told them to fool the Bessies into thinking that there were already too many Slammers in Mormont to dare attacking. The Bessies probably knew that only one transport had landed, though.

Anyway, Taggert was the CO. It didn't matter what a sergeant-gunner thought.

"What kinda army do the locals have, anyway?" asked Kenner. He looked at the squad leader, but Wetsam just shrugged.

"Small arms, pretty much," said Raney, who always studied the briefing cubes on a deployment. "All but the cadre's militia, though every male adult has some training. Those half-kilo slug guns are about all the heavy weapons they've got. The Bessies are mechanized, which is why the Commonwealth hired us."

"Who do the Bessies have working for them?" another trooper asked.

"Nobody," Raney said. "They figured it was a better use of their money to build hardware and use it themselves. They can't afford mercs."

"We'll ram their hardware straight up their asses!" Wetsam spat. Most of his troopers grunted agreement.

In the long run that was probably true, Raney thought—if the Bessies didn't capture the spaceport tonight. The trick was holding Mormont and whatever other roads led into the Commonwealth until the rest of the Regiment landed.

Green fireballs sailed across the sky, heading south: the tail flares of Bessie bombardment rockets. The sharp ripping sound of the rockets' passage was a half-second delayed from the lights' passage overhead, but the second and third salvoes were so close behind the first that it all blurred into vicious chaos.

Celie began to cry; the dog outside stood at the mouth of the cellar and yapped. The sound of both was lost in the roar of the bombardment.

Warheads began to detonate. Only an experienced ear would have recognized that most of them were going off in the air instead of among the buildings of Mormont. Cyan light flickered across the rockets, setting them off. The high airbursts weren't exactly harmless—fragments would be falling like steel hail across Mormont—but they wouldn't damage the Slammers' vehicles or infantry which had overhead cover.

The tribarrels of the two combat cars were on air defense, slapping down incoming shells. The 2cm bolts—

the same as the shoulder weapons of Wetsam's troopers—packed enough energy to detonate the bursting charge of any shell, even armor-piercing rounds if for some reason the Bessies were using those.

The sensors picked up movement on the road again. "All right, my children," Wetsam said. "Time to take your places. Keep bloody below the wall till I tell you, or I'll blow your bloody heads off myself."

Raney led the way up the stairs because Wetsam had assigned her to the northwestern corner of the farmyard. He was on the southwestern corner himself, with his five troopers spaced out the north-south length between the sergeants, parallel to the road.

Raney low-crawled briskly toward her slot. The shallow furrows of the garden were frozen, turning the ground into a sheet of corrugated metal. At least there was no undergrowth. Humans had carried bamboo with them to more planets than they hadn't; Raney would rather squirm through razor ribbon than a well-grown stand of the stuff.

She wished that she'd thought to tell the little girl to stick by the old man, but the Commonwealth hadn't hired the Slammers to babysit. They were well and truly about to earn their pay now.

The fog was getting thick. Raney switched her helmet visuals to thermal imaging. The feeds from the sensors shifted automatically. She viewed the yard—mostly the stone wall—on the top half of the face-shield, and the view through the northernmost sensor on the bottom.

You never wanted to watch *only* remote feeds and just assume everything in your immediate surroundings was fine. Raney had once had the hell bitten out of her by the local equivalent of ants, but that had been a cheap lesson. She'd known a guy on Warwick who'd been knifed by a local who moved *very* quietly.

Bessie vehicles were coming down the road in column three abreast. The leading rank had eight wheels and turrets mounting big coil-guns. Those would throw projectiles at least as heavy as slugs from the anti-tank guns the National Guard had waiting for them in Mormont. Two pairs of wheels were well forward on the chassis, which meant that the frontal armor was thick enough for hard use.

The second rank was of six-wheeled armored personnel carriers with automatic coil-guns in small turrets. The gun of the outer vehicle slewed toward the farm half a klick away. As the column rumbled forward, the APC fired short bursts toward the wall. The whole eastern file followed suit as each vehicle came far enough around the curve for their guns to bear on the farm.

Raney squeezed as low as she could in the hard ground. If she could have fit in a furrow, she would have. Most of the bursts were high, but some projectiles ricocheted wildly from the stone.

A few slugs were made from noble metals. They bounced off in vivid neon colors along with the usual orange-red sparks of steel.

Bits shattered from the hard stone. Concentrated fire could knock holes in the wall as sure as a wrecking ball, but that wasn't what was going on now. The Bessies weren't firing at *something*, they were firing because they were nervous. Shooting made them feel that they were taking action.

Raney knew that and knew that the sprayed projectiles weren't a danger to the thick wall. She still didn't like it.

There were ten ranks of Bessie vehicles, maybe eleven—Raney was counting to take her mind off the situation, not because there was any real need. The third and last ranks were of the large gun vehicles. Besides the APCs, there were several APC chassis which mounted a short, 10cm barrel or thereabouts, in a turret in the middle of the hull.

When the head of the column was within a kilometer of Mormont, the leaders stopped. The following vehicles spread to either side. The ground was lightly wooded, but even the APCs could bull their way through the brush.

Unexpectedly, the final rank of APCs pulled left when they reached the farm track. They started toward the house in line. The rear guard of gun vehicles waddled on toward Mormont.

The light was gone by now, and the mist was heavy enough to swirl in vortices above the APC guns as they probed the wall and house beyond. Driving bands vaporized in the jolts of electricity that sent projectiles through the coil guns. Gaseous metal spurted skyward like smoke signals.

The kid'll be fine if she just stays in the cellar. If she can't do that, she's too dumb to live. Too bloody dumb!

"On my word," Wetsam said calmly on the squad frequency. He was a good sergeant; Raney wished she'd had more like him in her days as a trooper. "Turrets first, then tires. Squad . . . *light 'em up!*"

The approaching vehicles had moved slightly out of line. The leader was within a hundred meters of the fence, the other two were only twenty meters behind. Raney rose with the others, but she didn't have a useful target for her sub-machine gun yet.

The coil gun of the second APC was firing, but that stopped when three cyan bolts hit the turret simultaneously. The copper plasma from a 2cm weapon had an enormous wallop. An orange fireball bloomed above the white droplets of molten armor. That must have been hydraulic fluid from the traversing mechanism, since the coil-gun didn't have combustible ammunition.

Two bolts hit the leader's turret and one the turret of the last vehicle. Raney's face-shield blacked out the plasma track; without filtering they would have been as dazzling in thermal imaging as they would to the unaided eye.

The leading APC's coil-gun fired another burst. Four plasma bolts, then a fifth, hit the turret, finishing what the first two bolts had failed to do. The vehicle stopped; the second APC collided with it while trying to turn right.

The final APC turned left, presenting its broadside to Raney. She walked short bursts down the tires, one and the next and then the third.

The tires had run-while-flat cores, but Raney's bolts ignited the rubber casings. Foul blackness billowed from sullen flames. After a few moments the casings exploded, spewing doughnuts of smoke sideways.

Bessie infantry in the body of the APC threw open the back hatch. Three soldiers stumbled out, unharmed but panicked by the ambush and the *Whump! Whump!*

Whump! of their own tires. Raney began to shoot, aiming for the center of mass.

Her second target vanished in a white flash and a bang so loud that it threw down part of the stone wall. The fellow must have been carrying a satchel of buzzbombs; a single warhead wouldn't have caused such a blast.

Raney rolled into a kneeling position again. As she did, something went off inside the leading APC. An orange flash ruptured the hull seams and lifted the turret from its ring. It hung skew for an instant, then slipped down inside the vehicle's body.

All three wrecks were burning. Figures, probably infantry from the second APC, moved blindly in the thick smoke. They were bright targets on Raney's infrared display. She dropped one and saw the chest of another disintegrate at the impact of a 2cm bolt.

Raney changed magazines. Her sub-machine gun's iridium muzzle glowed white. She'd kept her bursts short, but a firefight like this was hard on guns and shooters both. She gulped air through her mouth despite the toxic foulness—smoke, ozone, and Lord knew what from the burning vehicles. She simply needed more air than her nose filters allowed her.

Raney couldn't see Mormont from her position, but she switched the bottom of her display to a sensor on the opposite corner of the farmyard while she scanned the road north to the border directly. The Bessie gun vehicles were moving into the town, wreathed in iridescence as their heavy coil-guns fired.

Buildings collapsed, and a slug ricocheted a thousand meters in the air in an arc which wavered between magenta and violet. The sounds of the shots and the impacts was like the rush of a distant thunderstorm.

The nearby APCs continued to burn, but the only movement around them was occasional debris wobbling in the air currents. Raney wondered how many personnel the vehicles held.

However many there'd been, they were all dead now.

The APCs which had gone down the road with the main attack were disgorging their infantry. The troops spread out, following the heavy armor in. The APCs fired their automatic weapons, aiming high to clear the dismounted infantry. Explosive shells from the support vehicles bloomed red on the distant roofs, but the sound of the bursting charges was lost in the sharp electrical cascade of the coil guns.

Wetsam and two of his troopers had an angle on the force attacking Mormont. The nearest of the Bessies was over a kilometer away, but powergun bolts were line-straight. The 2cm weapons were heavy enough to be lethal to humans at any range. The sniping wouldn't decide the battle, but bolts striking from behind would unsettle better soldiers than the Bessies who'd attacked the farm had seemed.

Raney tried to link to the sensors in one of Taggert's combat cars, but her helmet didn't have the power to lock the signal. The amount of electronic hash from coil-guns and plasma would make commo difficult even for the Slammers within Mormont.

Raney had been in a street battle like Mormont on her second—or was it the third?—deployment with the Slammers, on Puerto Miro, back before she'd transferred to combat cars. She remembered aiming up through a street-level window in the cellar and firing 2cm bolts into the overhang of a Central Government tank.

She'd been trying to jam the turret. Instead she had set off stored ammunition in a blast that had brought the building down on top of her. Her back and breast armor had saved her life, but the six hours before her squadmates dug her out had been the longest of her life.

The crew of that tank had had an even worse day, though; briefly, of course. The Bessies in Mormont tonight weren't doing much better.

Buzzbombs detonating in the town made the air flicker white. The Bessies and the National Guard used similar weapons, so the explosions could be from either party. The three orange gouts of ignited diesel fuel were Bessie casualties, though: probably the funeral pyres of heavy gun vehicles which had led the attack.

Mormont's streets weren't wide to begin with, and buildings brought down by the Bessies' own bombardment would have narrowed them even more. In a point-blank fight, the advantage was all with the defenders crouching in alleys with buzzbombs.

"*All Taggert elements,*" said the commo helmet. "*Bessie Command has ordered his forces to withdraw. Out!*"

"Whee-ha!" said one of Wetsam's troopers. He must be the man nearest to Raney, because he hadn't used helmet commo.

"*Wetsam, this is Command,*" said Taggert's voice. Because Raney was on the command net, she got the call also, though she doubted that the El-Tee meant to inform her directly. *"Bring your squad back into town and report to me in the plaza. Move well to the east so you won't meet the Bessies running the other way. Over."*

"Sir, we're in a good place to hammer 'em when they pass by on the road," Wetsam said in an urgent tone. *"We've taken out three APCs and their smoke covers us, over."*

"Negative, Sergeant," said Taggert. *"They've got plenty left to roll over an outpost. If they start taking fire from the flank they'll do just that. Get your asses back here soonest. Command out."*

"Roger," said Wetsam. *"Out."*

Apart from the signal from Central—which was obviously netted in to Bessie communications—Raney wouldn't have been sure that the attackers were pulling back, but the fighting in Mormont had certainly quieted down. For an instant she regretted losing the chance to hit the Bessies from the flank, but the El-Tee was probably right to recall them. They were facing at least a full armored battalion, and Wetsam's squad had lost the advantage of surprise.

"Squad, we're heading back," Wetsam ordered. *"We'll swing a little wider out from the road this time and reenter town from the east. Watch the trooper in front of you, and if we run across any Bessie stragglers, waste them before they know who we are. Out."*

Raney expected somebody to argue, but the only responses were grunts and muttered Rogers. She was glad to get out. She'd agreed with the idea when Wetsam first suggested that they stay, but a moment for thought had showed her that the farm would be a deathtrap.

Her opinion of Taggert went up a little. He was green, but he'd stayed cool after a nasty battle at knife range.

Raney straightened—there was no reason to keep low now—and gasped with pain. Her left hip felt like she'd been bumped by a tank. When the satchel of buzzbombs went off, she must've hit the ground harder than she'd realized. She ought to replace the sub-machine gun barrel while she was at it.

"*Sarge,*" called Blessing, bending over a trooper lying on the ground. "*I got Sparky's weapon and ammo. What do we do with the body?*"

"*Leave him,*" said Wetsam through helmet commo. "*We'll police him up after things quiet down, or anyway somebody will. How about his helmet, over?*"

"*He took a round front to back through the forehead,*" Blessing said, switching to commo. Though Raney was part of the squad's net, her helmet wasn't synched with medical readouts like those of the rest of the squad. "*It's no more use now than Sparky is. Out.*"

"*Roger,*" said Wetsam. He started for the farmhouse and the parked skimmers.

If I'd taken one through the head, none of them might have noticed. Not that I'd be caring then either.

A Bessie APC raced up the road. A tire was rubbing; it sounded like a long wail of terror. Raney wondered if the driver had bothered to reboard his troops before driving away and whether any of the troops from that vehicle had survived.

She thought of what she could do if she'd had her gun jeep. And she thought about the chance that had fired a slug through Sparky's skull and not her own . . . because that's all it was, chance, when the Bessies had replied to the ambush with a blind fusillade.

The puppy was running around, barking in terror. Raney hadn't thought about the civilians since the shooting started. She felt a stab of guilt for forgetting the little girl, but what the hell was she supposed to have done?

The glass was gone from the two front windows. A few holes scarred the panel of the open door, but it was still on its hinges. The blast that knocked down Raney and part of the farmyard wall had probably cleared the window casements.

Slugs had chewed the roof, leaving a score of gaps where broken slates had fallen in bits. The ground beneath the eaves was a ridge of rubble, and more must have dropped inside.

They'll be all right if they stayed low. The cursed dog is all right.

"Hell, we're screwed!" Blessing snarled from around the back corner of the house.

"No, it'll be all right," Wetsam said. "We may have to double up, that's all."

Raney said nothing as she walked forward. Her face was blank. She gripped her sub-machine gun firmly, but that was a reflexive response to tension.

Slugs had passed through the front and hit the back of the roof from below. The whole back half had lost integrity and slid down in a slate avalanche, covering the ground behind the house. Wetsam and his troopers were scrambling to clear the skimmers from a pile of broken rock.

The dog got out. Then, *the dog had been out.*

The pile of slate dipped in the center where much of it had poured into the open cellar. If the Slammers hadn't removed the door, Celie and her grandfather would've been trapped inside, beyond saving in the time the squad had available. Instead, the wave of slate might have crushed—

Raney looked down. The child was still huddling against the old man. They were wedged into the back edge of the hide, where they'd been when the troopers ran out to their fighting positions. The cascade had stopped just short of the girl's feet.

"Celie, get up here *now!*" Raney said. If she went down to fetch the girl, her weight would trigger a further rush of stone. Celie might be able to scramble high enough to grab the sling of Raney's weapon, though.

Celie looked up, then began blubbering. She buried her face in the old man's chest again.

"Raney!" Wetsam called in much the same tone that Raney had used to the girl. "Give us a hand here! We've gotta get out. You want to get us all killed?"

He was right. Bringing more fire down on the farmhouse from the withdrawing Bessies wasn't going to help the civilians. Raney slung her sub-machine gun and began tossing broken slates out into the yard.

Her crappy skimmer had been on the end of the line where it wasn't hit by the falling slates. That was pretty typical of the way things had been going on this deployment.

The steering yoke of Wetsam's skimmer was badly

bent, and the left side of Kenner's plenum chamber had been bashed in badly enough to prevent the rear fan from swiveling properly. Nonetheless with a second trooper riding pillion behind Blessing, the squad made it back into Mormont without further drama.

Raney didn't worry about her skimmer the way she had on the way out. She had a splitting headache and the inside of her throat felt as though somebody had scoured it with barbed wire. The chance of having to walk back to Mormont had dropped well down on her list of concerns.

Now and again she thought about the kid as she guided her skimmer through the woods, but even those feelings were grayed out by the battle at the farmhouse. Serious emotions would've taken more energy than she had left.

Wetsam had to detour twice after they got into Mormont proper. The fieldstone buildings were solid, but a heavy enough shock turned their walls into loads of riprap.

Direct fire from the gun vehicles had brought down a number of buildings, and a few Bessie rockets had gotten through. The spilled rocks were barriers that most of the squad's skimmers couldn't climb in their present state.

They were in the central plaza before Raney was aware of it; she had been following Blessing's skimmer instead of noting what was around her. Part of her knew that she'd taken more of a knock from the explosion than she'd thought at the time, but even the aware part didn't care very much.

Both combat cars had survived, but the fighting compartment of Taggert's had been penetrated just behind the right wing gun. The tribarrel hadn't been damaged—it was back in air defense mode now—but Raney didn't suppose the gunner had been so lucky.

One of the Bessie gun vehicles had made it to the edge of the plaza. An arm protruded from a turret hatch.

The vehicle's tires were still burning, but a light breeze from the south carried most of the smoke away. There were several other fires in the northern part of the town. Guardsmen in gray uniforms had gathered upwind, peering at the wreck.

Taggert stood with Krotcha beside *Camptown*. He raised his face-shield as Wetsam pulled up beside him. The lieutenant had aged twenty years since Raney last saw him. The lower edge of his face-shield had the mirror-bright sheen of iridium, vaporized from tribarrel bores and redeposited on the synthetic crystal.

"Sarge," Taggert said, "the Bessies are going to hit us again in three hours. They've got reinforcements, infantry and armor. The infantry's conscript and they don't have APCs, but the armor's heavies that'd been hung up behind the artillery train."

"Hell," said Wetsam. There was no emotion in the word. "Can we hold 'em?"

"Not if we wait for them to hit us," Taggert said. "The Guards lost most of their anti-tank guns and they're low on buzzbombs. I'm going to take the cars and a squad of infantry in a sweep around the east and then hit 'em while they're still forming up. Krotcha—"

He nodded to the infantry platoon leader. Krotcha hadn't spoken since the outpost returned.

"—says you're the right man to lead the infantry since

he'll be in charge of the defense back here. You in shape for it?"

"I guess," Wetsam said. "Beats getting it in the neck. We'll need skimmers, though. We had damage, and Raney's here was crap from the start."

"You can pick your skimmers," Taggert said. "Raney's with me, though."

The El-Tee glanced at her. His eye sockets looked like pits, partly because he'd rubbed them with hands covered in redeposited metal.

"Sergeant, can you handle that tribarrel?" Taggert said, thumbing toward the wing gun above him.

"Sure," Raney said. She knew she didn't sound enthusiastic. She wondered if she had a concussion.

She focused on the weapon, tilted northward against the sky. "Do we have time to change barrels? Those look shot out."

"Get at it," Taggert said. "We're moving out in ten minutes."

The combat car had a ladder at the back, but Raney boarded in the usual fashion for veterans: onto the step in the plenum chamber, to the top of the plenum chamber, to the cab slope while grasping the fighting compartment bulkhead, and then swinging her legs into the fighting compartment. She'd never been assigned as crew to a combat car before, but anybody who'd been in the field for a few deployments had ridden them.

The interior was cramped as usual, packed with coolers, ammo crates, and personal gear. Raney hadn't expected to find a trooper on his hands and knees,

mopping at the bloodstains with what seemed to be a
tunic.

The fellow looked up when Raney's boots banged
down. He was young and bumped sideways in surprise at
her presence.

The uniform fabric wasn't absorbing much blood, but
it was obviously important to the trooper to do *something*.
Blood had painted his own back and side, but it didn't
seem the time to mention that.

She said, "I'm Raney," and gave him as broad a smile
as she could manage. She probably looked like death
warmed over herself. "I guess I'm your new right gunner."
The trooper looked horrified. *Does he think I'm a newbie?*

"I usually crew a jeep, but it's deadlined for now,"
Raney added, just in case. She took the gun out of air-
defense mode and swung the rack with spare barrels out
from the bulkhead. There were three, so she could change
the whole set. "Ah, that looks to be like a job for a steam
hose."

The trooper stood up. "I'm Meese," he said. Raney
was deliberately bending over the gun so that Meese
didn't have to decide whether or not to offer his bloody
hand. "Ah, yeah, but the hose went west when the bustle
rack caught it. I thought I ought to do, you know, what I
could."

"I know what you mean," Raney said. She hit the barrel
wrench with the heel of her hand to break the threads
loose. "I never got used to it either, and I've been out on a
lot of deployments. As soon as we're back from this run,
we'll borrow a hose or cobble something together, right?"

That was more of a lie than not; even as a newbie,

Raney's emotions had shut down at things like the way the gunner died. She drank more than she maybe ought to between deployments, but that was nobody's business but her own.

They needed a left gunner, though. Meese was better than an infantryman who hadn't been trained on tribarrels, so it was worth coddling him a little.

Raney traded the worn barrel for a glistening new one from the rack, then replaced the second and third as well. They were in better shape than she'd thought from the ground, but a mission like the one Taggert had outlined deserved the best preparation she could give it.

She took the handgrips of the tribarrel and swung it lock to lock. It gimbaled smoothly. It felt good to be back behind the big weapon; she seemed to have lost the headache, and her vision was sharper again too.

Taggert climbed aboard, his face-shield still up. He looked alert but worn. He nodded to Raney and Meese, then switched the bow-gun back on manual.

Something flopped to the deck of the fighting compartment. It was a hand, still wearing a Slammer's issue glove. It had been caught in the elevation mechanism.

The lieutenant didn't seem to know what the object was. Meese stared transfixed.

Raney took the last reload drum out of an ammo canister and hooked it on the end of the barrel rack the way she usually did. She picked up the hand and dropped it into the canister, then locked the lid down again.

"We'll bury it with the rest of the body when we get back," she said.

Taggert blinked. "Right," he said and dropped his face-shield. Over the general push he said, *"All right, Taggert Force, saddle up. Wetsam, send the scouts out. Troops, follow in plotted order. Out."*

Two skimmers moved south, deeper into the town. Taggert's combat car lifted from the cobblestones, rotated in its length, and followed at a fast walk. The El-Tee wasn't heading east by the route the outpost had come home by, probably because of the collapsed houses.

The two scouts were out of sight before *Camptown* began to move. The combat car's sensors were very good, but even the best electronics wouldn't spot a Bessie crouching in a spider hole with a buzzbomb.

The scouts' eyesight wouldn't spot that either, but the chances were good that the sound of the skimmers would bring the hostile out early. It was better to lose a single trooper than the lead car.

That was a logic Raney had understood since her first deployment. She grinned slightly. This was the first time she remembered finding it comforting, though.

The other three infantry followed *Camptown*, closely for the moment; they would space out beyond town. The second car, *Cormorant*, was the rear guard.

It had begun to snow again, a scattering of big flakes at first. Gusts of small flakes arrived on a cold wind before the task force turned northwest again on a narrow lane. The drifts were already high enough to hide landmarks, but the region had been mapped in detail before the satellites had gone down.

Raney could have followed Taggert Force's progress on her face-shield, but instead she surveyed her half of the immediate terrain. That took concentration, because in a gun jeep she was usually responsible only to the front. The wing gun pivoted one hundred eighty degrees, though she would have to push the El-Tee out of the way if she needed to light up a target who'd waited till the car had passed.

Raney grinned again. She'd had officers she would willingly have knocked down, given half an excuse, but she didn't have any complaint about Taggert thus far.

Her face-shield was on thermal imaging again. The terrain was a blur of vague shapes, as though she was viewing a reef from under water. A human, even insulated by thick clothing, would show up like a flare on a clear night, however.

"*El-Tee, we've got a problem,*" Wetsam said. He was using the command net rather than the general push. "*Amorato's batteries are losing power. I can replace him at scout, but what about him? Because we can't leave him here alone. Over.*"

Taggert swore. "*A skimmer carrying double can't hold forty-plus kph we need for the timing,*" he said, "*and the cars don't have room for four.*"

Raney smiled at that. Cramming a fourth trooper in body armor into the fighting compartment—certainly into *Camptown* now, but realistically with any car in the field—would crowd it dangerously when the shooting started. On route marches, it was just miserably uncomfortable.

"*All right, Wetsam,*" Taggert said after a pause. "*Tell Amorato to come alongside. I'll stop and take him aboard. We'll dump the skimmer, over.*"

"Sir, this is Raney," she said. She was on the command net by sufferance, but she was here regardless and she had something to say. "We can couple the skimmer's charging cable and keep on moving. Over."

"That's against regs, Sergeant," Taggert said. *"Besides, this is broken country and we're going into action. It's not safe. We'll take him aboard, over."*

"El-Tee, she's right," said Wetsam. *"Sir, we do it all the time in the field. Somebody's batteries always crap out. Over."*

And if you're worried about being safe . . . Raney thought, but the words didn't reach her lips. *Then you're in the wrong line of work.*

"And I'm a newbie on my first deployment and don't know squat, eh?" Taggert said.

Neither sergeant spoke. Raney kept her eyes on the brush outside the car.

Taggert unexpectedly laughed. *"Well, that's true enough. Wetsam, bring your man alongside and show me the way to couple him and still move, so that I'll know how to do it myself next time. Taggert out."*

Cormorant had an overlength—three-meter—cable in its equipment locker, so they used that rather than the two-meter cables aboard *Camptown*. Amorato would be able to slip behind the combat car in tight terrain but move to the left out of the worst of the big vehicle's wash most of the time. The coupled trooper would have to mind his driving so that he didn't wind up with the car for a hood ornament, but he didn't complain.

Raney checked the skimmer's diagnostics through her helmet. It was charging, rather than running directly off *Camptown*. She'd been afraid the skimmer might have a dead short, which would make Amorato a pedestrian as soon as he uncoupled. There was obviously a problem, but it wouldn't become acute until after the battle that was certainly coming in the near future.

"*Taggert Force, hold at the marked locations, over*," the El-Tee ordered. It didn't affect Raney and the other gunners, but a map appeared on the displays of the infantry and the drivers of the combat cars.

Camptown slowed, then wallowed to a halt. The fans idled, spinning just fast enough to keep positive pressure in the plenum chamber. They were still loud.

They had reached a streambed, visible only as a clear track—snow-covered ice—lined by frozen reeds. It meandered through brush. Ahead was a heavily forested slope which made Raney frown.

Woods like that would be a bitch to squeeze through in a gun jeep, and a combat car was *much* wider. The car had the power to bull through all but well-grown trees with boles of fifteen or twenty centimeters, but that would make as much racket as road construction. They had to hope that the Bessies weren't keeping a good watch to their flanks and rear.

That was likely enough: the Bessies were convinced that they were the attackers and that all they had to worry about were the Mormont defenses. The Slammers had to take a chance if they were going to save the route to the spaceport.

This was a *hell* of a chance, granted; but if the port was

captured, Taggert Force didn't have anywhere to run to anyway.

Camptown's sensors had been gathering information from the other side of the ridge ahead of the task force. Injector pumps, spark plugs, magnetic suspension dampers, vehicle diagnostic computers—anything electrical gave off a signal. The combat car's AI ran them through identification algorithms and plotted them onto a terrain map. Taggert forwarded the map to every helmet.

"*Force,*" Taggert said on the general frequency. "*The Bessies are rearming and fueling along the main road down the next valley. They're clumped up, and many of them are coupled to fuel trucks. Infantry, move up to the edge of the trees where you've got a sight line, then reverse your skimmers and dismount. When I give the signal, take out fuel and ammunition vehicles, and then the civilian trucks that have brought the Bessie conscripts.*"

Taggert coughed to clear his throat. He couldn't have sounded more assured if he'd been Colonel Hammer and he had the three tank companies in line beside him. He went up another notch in Raney's estimation.

"*When the infantry is in position,*" he said, "*the cars will drive through the Bessie line, then drive back. We'll be behind most of the fighting vehicles—*"

Arrows on the display showed the two blue arrows careening past a muddle of red dots, then reversing. Raney wished she thought it was going to be that simple.

"*—so we'll be hitting them from the back. The four heavies—*"

A line of four red dots pulsed. The were the

southernmost Bessie elements and would be leading the thrust into Mormont.

"—have axial weapons that're pointing south, so don't worry about them until we've got all the turreted gun vehicles out of the way. They're the danger to us. Any questions, over?"

"Sir, Cormorant Six," said the other car's commander. "The Bessie artillery's only a kay north of here. If we withdraw north, we can get them too, over."

"Negative, Cormorant," Taggert said. "We're not getting greedy. We'll recover the infantry and head back to Mormont after we've had a little target practice. Now, further questions? Over."

Nobody spoke.

"Good," said Taggert. "Taggert Force, take your positions. Taggert out."

The five infantry moved ahead, into the woods. A moment later, Camptown started forward at a fast walk.

The creek broke open under the downdraft supporting their thirty tonnes. Water sprayed to the side in crystal droplets.

Raney scanned the terrain. She thought, I still haven't rebarrelled my sub-machine gun.

Bessie artillery began firing again while Taggert Force was sliding and crunching through the forest. Raney barely noticed the rockets. The intake roar of Camptown's fans dimmed all other noise, and the green/white tracers in her peripheral vision didn't interfere with her focus on the red beads of predicted targets plotted on her face-shield.

When they came over the hill, *Cormorant* closed up so tightly that when it knocked down a sapling which *Camptown* had missed—no driver could track perfectly in terrain so broken—hard-shelled fruit showered onto Raney from the treetop. It was as much luck as training that she didn't trigger a wild burst into the woods.

It had been a *lot* like the patter of bark and clipped branches when ambushers sprayed their first shots high in a forest. The best way to handle an ambush was to charge through behind overwhelming gunfire . . .

Raney's grin was humorless. She'd screwed up in the past, but never that bad. Well, it hadn't happened this time either.

A whine filled the valley before them. It was so loud that Raney could feel it over the intake howl. She recognized it from a deployment five years before on Princip, where Government tanks used railguns which stored their power in great uranium flywheels. When they were at full spin, they made just that sort of sound.

Wetsam broke squelch twice, indicating all his troopers were in position. They'd been loose with commo on the march, but the infantry sergeant wasn't taking chances now that they were in the same valley as the Bessies.

Camptown twitched left, around a sandstone outcrop swathed in the roots of the bush growing over it. "*Hit it, Bolan!*" Taggert said on the vehicle channel.

The combat car lurched, bouncing upward as the driver coarsened his blade pitch. The fans were already running at full output.

Camptown thundered through the last ten meters of

woods. The trees were scattered, but the car hit one that Bolan would surely have driven around if they'd had the leisure. They had thirty tonnes and the help of gravity behind their rush. The bulging plenum chamber butted the tree out by the roots and sent it cartwheeling down the slope like a drum major's baton.

Snow was still falling, and the fans kicked more up from the ground. Raney walked a burst across a group of humans, probably dismounted infantry.

She lifted her muzzles, shifting fire onto trucks moving south on the road. The troops on the ground were more dangerous—any one of them could fire the lucky shot that blew Raney's brains out—but the Slammers couldn't kill all the Bessies. The purpose of this attack was disruption, not annihilation, and exploding vehicles were about as disruptive as you could hope for.

Thermal imaging didn't allow ranging: a child with a stick three meters away looks the same as a gunman at six—but that didn't matter now. Everything within the valley was hostile, and to anything but serious armor a 2cm bolt was lethal at line of sight.

Raney hit the cab of the first truck. It slewed off the road as she put another short burst into the truck body. The blindingly vivid bolts were stenciled black across her face-shield, but the fires they lit were white blossoms in the thermal display. Fabric and plastics burned at the plasma's touch; some metals ignited also, and flesh too fed the flames.

Camptown continued to accelerate now that they didn't have to hold their speed down to that of the skimmers. They careened through the last of the trees and bumped over the floor of the valley. This was the first time Raney had crewed a combat car, but she found aiming to be surprisingly easy. She was experienced in shooting on the move, and the car was a more stable gun platform than her familiar jeep was.

Fireballs erupted to the left and ahead, fuel bowsers hit while coupled to Bessie armored vehicles. Fires bathed Raney in radiance and fogged the side of her face-shield.

She hit the cab of the second truck, which stopped; then the third, whose fuel tank ruptured. That vehicle was already a bubble of fire when it crashed into the one ahead.

Raney ignored the figures running away from the trucks, some of them on fire. She was slewing her gun toward a line of vehicles parked off the road—they were probably empty, but they'd burn just the same—when something clanged through the combat car.

Camptown spun end for end in a vicious whipcrack. Raney slammed into the rear bulkhead, caromed against the left wing gun—Meese had just crashed into Lieutenant Taggert—and finally hit the deck splay-legged beneath her own tribarrel.

The fans stalled—the jolt had tripped circuit breakers. The car skidded stern first, plowing a broad furrow across the ground. A rooster-tail of ice and frozen turf rained down, some of it falling into the fighting compartment.

There was a round hole the size of a commo helmet in the left rear of the compartment and a larger hole in the right side, slightly forward of the first. The exit hole was noticeably oval: the slug had started wobbling when it punched its way through the side armor the first time.

Raney wasn't sure where she was or what had happened. She got to her feet. Nothing looked familiar. The spade grips of a tribarrel were in front of her and she grabbed them from reflex. Memory flooded back with the familiar contact.

Camptown was pointing in the opposite direction from what Raney last remembered. Fire and wreckage scarred the ranks of Bessie vehicles which had been preparing to attack Mormont. Taggert, Meese, and the guns of the following combat car had raked them, turning fuel trucks into fireballs and smashing the combat vehicles' light rear armor.

The four newly arrived Bessie heavies were side by side a half-kilometer away. Following Taggert's orders the Slammers hadn't shot at them, but a ghostly plume of ionized metal hung over the vehicle on the near end of the line. That banner was the driving band of a slug weighing a full kilogram, vaporized when a jolt of electricity flung the projectile down the gun bore.

The big vehicle had six wheels on a side, all of them steerable. The Bessie commander had used the enormous centrifugal force of the flywheel to rotate his vehicle in place, facing around more quickly than a jeep could have done. He then used the rest of the flywheel's inertia to power the round he fired at *Camptown*.

Every once in a while a mercenary met someone who was very, very good. More often than not, that was the mercenary's last experience. The saving grace here was that shifting the vehicle and firing the shot had slowed the flywheel to a crawl. It would take minutes to spin it up to the point that the gun could fire again.

"Bolan, go!" Raney shouted. "Go go go!"

She felt *Camptown* shiver as the driver brought his fans back on line. With luck either the orders or common sense would get them going, but that was out of her hands. She held the tribarrel's muzzles low and ripped a long burst across the six left-side tires of the heavy which had nailed them.

The tires burst in quick succession, throwing gobbets of flaming rubber in all directions. That wouldn't disable the big gun; it ran the length of the hull's axis with only a stub of the barrel projecting from the heavy bow armor. It made it next to impossible for the vehicle to move, however, even if the crew was willing to fight from a hull which was wrapped in the filthy red flames of its own tires.

Bolan got *Camptown* moving forward—that is, back toward the slope the Slammers had attacked from. They seemed to be crawling, but that might just be because everything had speeded up in Raney's mind.

She sprayed the other three heavies, cyan flashes lighting the flanks and louvered rear panels as well as hitting some of the tires. Her face-shield was on direct visuals now. She didn't remember changing mode, but it was all right. Fuel fires threw up great torches which reflected from the snow.

"Taggert Force, withdraw!" said the El-Tee's voice. *"Withdraw at once, out!"*

Raney kept firing at the heavies until her gun shut off when it ran out of ammunition. The iridium barrels blazed like incandescent lights. She ejected the empty ammo drum and locked a fresh one in place.

As *Camptown* wove through the straggling limit of the

trees, Raney opened fire again. She had the tribarrel pivoted to its lock and had to lean over the edge of the compartment to see her sights. She was trying to hit the heavies again, but a pair of APCs were in the way. They were already burning, but she raked them anyway. The barrels were already shot out, so why not?

"*El-Tee?*" Wetsam said. "*Can you take Talbert aboard? I've got him double with me, but he's gorked out from painkillers and can't hold on so good. Over.*"

"*Roger,*" Taggert said. "*Force, we'll hold up on top of the ridge. Over.*"

He turned and said, "*Raney?*"

She was watching the dots on her readout. Both cars had come through—*Cormorant* was close behind them—but there were only four skimmers. That was okay; skimmers were even easier to replace than troopers were, and there was a galaxyful of eighteen-year-olds just as desperate to get off-planet as Raney had been.

The El-Tee tapped her on the shoulder. "*Raney?*" he said. Repeated, she realized; thinking back, she remembered the sound of him speaking a moment before.

"*Sorry sir,*" she said. "*Over.*"

"*I just wanted to say 'Good job,' Sergeant,*" Taggert said. "*You may have saved our asses back there.*"

"*That was Bolan, I'd say,*" said Raney. "*But thanks. Over.*"

"*If you ever want to transfer to cars, there's a platoon sergeant's slot open for you here.*"

"Umm," said Raney. Her mind was drifting. She went back to watching beads of light on her face-shield.

Taggert and Meese hoisted Talbert into the fighting

compartment with wounds in both legs and a silly grin on his face. His eyes were closed and he was snoring softly.

Taggert Force paralleled the main road for the last three kays into Mormont. They passed close enough to the outlying farm to see that several heavy shells had landed on the house since the squad left it.

Raney didn't say anything. There was nothing to say.

Raney had heard the vehicle purring up the road from Mormont, but it wasn't until it pulled into the track to the farm that she paid attention. There was nothing to worry about: G Troop and a platoon of tanks from H Company had passed six hours before, heading north.

She tossed another piece of meat—it was labeled meat in the ration pack; it was pink but had no grain—to the puppy. Only then did she turn on the stump of gatepost where she was sitting.

Baur wove the gun jeep past the burned-out Bessie APCs and pulled up. He looked startlingly clean in ordinary battledress, which reminded Raney to check that her field roll—fatigues in a ground sheet—was in the side rack along with the driver's own. Apart from the rips and ordinary grime, Raney's sleeves were stiff with redeposited iridium which had sublimed off the bores of her tribarrel.

Her long bursts into the Bessie heavies had been a brutal misuse of the weapon. Her lips smiled. They'd done the job, though; and she'd been being misused pretty badly herself at the time.

"Hey, Sarge," Baur said. "They said I'd find you here. We're supposed to join Third Platoon in Servadac. I don't guess it's that big a rush with the Bessies asking for peace, though. The rest of the team in Mormont was stood down, so if you want to wait . . . ?"

"Naw, nothing here for me," Raney said. She started to get up, then thumped back heavily when her legs twinged. "Give me a moment, is all."

"I'm in no hurry," said Baur. He got out of the jeep and stretched, looking around. "Blood and Martyrs. You were part of this?"

"Yeah, they drove right up to us in the fog instead of dismounting," Raney said. The puppy had finished sniffing Baur's boots. She threw the last of the meat to her. "It was hairy for seven of us even with the Bessies making it easy. I think we were supposed to be hitting the column from behind when the last of them passed. There wasn't much of that, but I guess it worked out okay."

She tried again to get up, this time putting her hand on the stone for a little extra boost. She made it, wobbling for a moment.

Baur looked at the long grave bordered with small rubble from the house. There were three larger headstones, though Raney hadn't had anything to mark them with.

"Bloody hell," Baur said, not loudly. "You lost three outa seven, Sarge?"

"Just one," said Raney. "They called him Sparky."

"Sparkman?" said Baur. "Red hair and bad acne scars?"

Raney shrugged. "I never saw him by daylight," she said. "The other two were civilians, but I had the engineers make room here instead of dumping them in the trench with the Bessies."

The mass grave was closer to the road, covered with a tumulus shoveled up from the wall around the field. There was a layer stones over Sparky and the locals too, but Raney had told the guy with the backhoe to cover them with dirt in case somebody wanted to plant flowers there sometime.

"Come on, Bubbles," Raney said, squatting down with her hands out. "We're going home to Third Platoon."

"Hey?" said the driver.

"We've got a mascot, Baur," Raney said. Holding the dog, she walked to her seat behind the tribarrel. "Her name's Bubbles."

Dave supplied this afterword, "The Slammers and Me," for the story.

1

I started to title this essay *Colonel Hammer and Me*, but that would be wrong. Only one story in the series is primarily about the regimental commander, and that one—"But Loyal to His Own"—was written at Jim Baen's request (made in the hall of a convention hotel at the 1974 Worldcon where we first met).

I spent most of 1970 in Viet Nam and Cambodia with the 11th ACR, the Blackhorse Regiment. I was a draftee with the rank of Spec4 and later Spec5. In WWII or today, those ranks would have been corporal and buck sergeant. I wasn't concerned with grand strategy or the Big Picture.

I was just trying to stay alive and to carry out whatever duties an officer, generally a low-ranking officer, gave me. In the field those duties included shit-burning.

Very few of the Hammer stories involve anything even vaguely on a strategic level. Nobody asked *me* what we should do in Viet Nam.

Maybe they should have, though. In Interrogation School my class (all college graduates) had a map exercise to determine how to drive the North Vietnamese Army from a section of War Zone C. We determined that it was impossible: the enemy could only be defeated in large numbers if they chose to attack us. If they just hid in the bamboo, we couldn't reach them. According to the instructors, this was the wrong answer.

When I got to War Zone C myself, I found that my classmates and I had been right. (It was still the wrong answer so far as the strategic thinkers in Washington were concerned, which strengthened my contempt for those strategic thinkers.)

2

I began writing seriously after I got back to the World and civilian life. Though I wasn't aware of it at the time, the Hammer stories became my way of sorting through my memories and trying to make sense of my experiences in the army.

Recently I've come to the realization that those experiences don't make sense: they were a waste, a tragedy, and they shattered to rubble the guy I'd been in 1968. Writing the Hammer stories *did* give me an outlet for that anger, though; an outlet which didn't involve me

382 *David Drake*

winding up dead or in jail, likely results of some of the other options.

When I say that writing helped me keep it between the ditches, I don't mean that the problems disappeared: writing helped me control my feelings, but the worldview, the mindset, that I . . . hmm, I was about to say "gained," but I'm not sure that's the right word. The mindset which I developed in Southeast Asia, I'll say, is still the bedrock of my personality.

A number of people have asked me whether I've lost my feel for the Hammer series in the eight or nine years since I most recently wrote a story in it. Judge for yourselves, of course, but I personally think it's obvious that the damage is still there. The ordinary civilian I was in 1968 was ground to pebbles. In the past forty years I've glued enough of the pebbles together to pass for normal under most circumstances; but trust me, I'll never be a civilian again, much as I would like to be.

3

But that brings me to a final point, something I didn't realize myself until shortly before I started to write this story. A friend asked me whether I would rather be a Nam vet with my present writing career or a lawyer who hadn't been drafted.

I started to say that I would much rather not be so screwed up, and that being a writer has never been that big a deal to me. Both those things are true, but I realized that they didn't completely answer her question.

I know a lot of writers whom I don't respect. Likewise, I know a lot of lawyers and *really* a lot of people with

Duke diplomas whom I don't respect. Therefore I don't see why anybody should respect me because I'm a writer, a lawyer, or a Dukie.

The thing is, I *do* respect anybody who served with me in the Blackhorse or in a comparable unit, in Nam or elsewhere. They may be drunks or druggies, they may have screwed up their lives beyond belief or redemption, but they once put it on the line in a way that very few people do.

Unless you've been a part of an elite combat unit in a war zone, you can't really understand what it feels like. There's Us and there's Them, and Them is everybody else: the fat cats and politicians, the actors and sports stars. They all count for less than we do, because *we* are the Blackhorse.

Purely because of luck—you'll note that I don't say "good luck"—I became part of one of those elite combat units. The status comes with a price, which "Save What You Can" makes pretty clear to readers; but I honor the status in others, and I would be unwilling to give it up in myself.

As messed up as I am, I'm proud to be able to say, "*I* rode with the Blackhorse."

THE END

THE MANY WORLDS OF DAVID DRAKE

IF YOU LIKE...
YOU SHOULD TRY...

DAVID DRAKE
David Weber

DAVID WEBER
John Ringo

JOHN RINGO
Michael Z. Williamson
Tom Kratman

ANNE MCCAFFREY
Mercedes Lackey
Liaden Universe® by Sharon Lee & Steve Miller

MERCEDES LACKEY
Wen Spencer, Andre Norton
Andre Norton
James H. Schmitz

LARRY NIVEN
Tony Daniel
James P. Hogan
Travis S. Taylor

ROBERT A. HEINLEIN
Jerry Pournelle
Lois McMaster Bujold
Michael Z. Williamson

HEINLEIN'S "JUVENILES"
Rats, Bats & Vats series by Eric Flint & Dave Freer

HORATIO HORNBLOWER OR PATRICK O'BRIAN
David Weber's Honor Harrington series
David Drake's RCN series

HARRY POTTER
Mercedes Lackey's Urban Fantasy series

THE LORD OF THE RINGS
Elizabeth Moon's *The Deed of Paksenarrion*

H.P. LOVECRAFT
Larry Correia's Monster Hunter series
P.C. Hodgell's Kencyrath series
Princess of Wands by John Ringo

GEORGETTE HEYER
Lois McMaster Bujold
Catherine Asaro
Liaden Universe® by Sharon Lee & Steve Miller

GREEK MYTHOLOGY
Pyramid Scheme by Eric Flint & Dave Freer
Forge of the Titans by Steve White
Blood of the Heroes by Steve White

NORSE MYTHOLOGY
Northworld Trilogy by David Drake

URBAN FANTASY
Darkship Thieves by Sarah A. Hoyt
Gentleman Takes a Chance by Sarah A. Hoyt
Carousel Tides by Sharon Lee
The Wild Side ed. by Mark L. Van Name

SCA/HISTORICAL REENACTMENT
John Ringo's "After the Fall" series

FILM NOIR
Larry Correia's The Grimnoir Chronicles

CATS
Sarah A. Hoyt's Darkship Thieves series
Larry Niven's Man-Kzin Wars series

PUNS
Rick Cook
Spider Robinson
Wm. Mark Simmons

VAMPIRES & WEREWOLVES
Larry Correia
Wm. Mark Simmons

NONFICTION
Hank Reinhardt
Tax Payer's Tea Party
by Sharon Cooper & Chuck Asay
The Science Behind The Secret by Travis Taylor
Alien Invasion by Travis Taylor & Bob Boan